Shortlisted for the
for Best Thriller

'It's been obvious
operations are bei
The reason for that is quite simple – villains, the good ones, can always spot a police officer, no matter how good their cover. Police officers all undergo the same training, and pretty much have the same experiences on the job. It's that shared experience that binds them together, but it also shapes them, it gives them a standard way of behaving, common mannerisms. They become a type.'

Tina nodded. 'We could always spot Vice on the streets,' she said. 'Stuck out like sore thumbs.' She grinned. 'Thumbs weren't the only things sticking out.'

For a moment Tina thought that the Assistant Commissioner was going to accuse her of flippancy again, but he smiled and nodded. 'Exactly,' he said. 'So what we want to do is to set up a unit of police officers who haven't been through the standard Hendon training. We need a special sort of undercover officer,' said Latham. 'We need people who have enough strength of character to work virtually alone, people who have enough, how shall I describe it . . . life experience . . . to cope with whatever gets thrown at them, and we need them with a background that isn't manufactured. A background that will stand up to any scrutiny.'

Also by Stephen Leather

Pay Off
The Fireman
Hungry Ghost
The Chinaman
The Vets
The Long Shot
The Birthday Girl
The Double Tap
The Solitary Man
The Tunnel Rats
The Bombmaker
The Stretch
The Eyewitness

Spider Shepherd thrillers

Hard Landing
Soft Target
Cold Kill
Hot Blood
Dead Men
Live Fire
Rough Justice (July 2010)

Jack Nightingale supernatural thrillers

Nightfall

Stephen Leather was a journalist for more than ten years on newspapers such as *The Times*, the *Daily Mail* and the *South China Morning Post* in Hong Kong. He began writing full time in 1992. His bestsellers have been translated into more than ten languages. He has also written for television shows such as *London's Burning*, *The Knock* and the BBC's *Murder in Mind* series. You can find out more from his website, www.stephenleather.com.

STEPHEN LEATHER

Tango One

HODDER

First published in Great Britain in 2002 by Hodder and Stoughton
A division of Hodder Headline

A Hodder paperback

17

A CIP catalogue record for this title
is available from the British Library

ISBN 978 0 340 77035 1

Typeset in Plantin by Hewer Text UK Ltd, Edinburgh
Printed and bound in the UK by
CPI Mackays, Chatham ME5 8TD

Hodder and Stoughton
A division of Hodder Headline
338 Euston Road
London NW1 3BH

For Jenny

Acknowledgements

I am indebted to John C. Cummings, retired USAF Combat Controller, and James Clanton, USAF Major (Retired), for their help on aviation matters, and to Sam Jenner for the inside track on the Caribbean drugs trade.

Denis O'Donoghue was once again invaluable when casting his professional eye over the manuscript, and I'm especially grateful to my fellow Dublin-based thriller-writer Glenn Meade for getting me through a particularly nerve-wracking case of writer's block.

Sarah Binnersley has line-edited many of my books over the years and as always my work is the better for her keen eye for detail and her no-punches-pulled opinions. And I'm especially grateful to Carolyn Mays at Hodder & Stoughton for overseeing *Tango One* from beginning to end.

The Home Office Consolidated Circular to the Police on Crime and Kindred Matters (Home Office Circular 35/1986, Paragraph 1.92).

a. No member of a police force, and no public informant, should counsel, incite or procure the commission of a crime.
b. Where an informant gives the police information about the intention of others to commit a crime in which they intend that he shall play a part, his participation should be allowed to continue only where

    i. he does not actively engage in planning and committing the crime;
    ii. he is intended to play only a minor role; and
    iii. his participation is essential to enable the police to frustrate the principal criminals and to arrest them (albeit for lesser offences such as attempt or conspiracy to commit the crime, or carrying offensive weapons) before injury is donc to any person or serious damage to property.

The informant should always be instructed that he must on no account act as *agent provocateur*, whether by suggesting to others that they should commit offences or encouraging them to do so.

The man had been tied to the chair for so long that he'd lost all feeling in his hands and feet. His captors had used thick strips of insulation tape to bind him to the wooden chair and slapped another piece across his mouth, even though he was in a basement and there was no one within earshot who cared whether he lived or died.

The three men who'd brought him to the villa hadn't said a word as they'd dragged him out of the back of the Mercedes and hustled him across the flagstones into the pink-walled villa. He'd lost a shoe somewhere and his big toe poked through a hole in his blue woollen sock.

The tape across his mouth pulsed in and out with each ragged breath as he looked around the room where he was being kept prisoner. No windows. A single door that had been bolted when the three men left. Bare walls, stone with a thick covering of yellowing plaster. A concrete floor. A single fluorescent striplight above his head. One wall had been shelved with slabs of rough local timber and there was a scattering of tinned goods at eye level – Heinz baked beans, Batchelor's peas, bottles of HP sauce and boxes of Kellogg's cornflakes and PG Tips. The cravings of an Englishman abroad.

The man fought to steady his breathing. Panic wasn't going to get him anywhere. He had to stay calm. He had to think.

In front of him a Sony digital video camera stood on a tripod, its single lens staring at him full on. The man stared back. He had a bad feeling about the camera. A very bad feeling.

He strained to hear where the three men were, but no sound penetrated the depths of the basement. He hadn't heard them leave the villa or the Mercedes being driven away, but that meant nothing. The soundproofing of the basement worked both ways.

The man tested his bonds. The tape was grey and metallic looking, the type used by plumbers, and while it was only an inch wide, it had been wound around his limbs so many times that they might as well have been made of steel. He tried to rock the chair backwards and forwards, but it was big and heavy and he could barely move it.

He swallowed. His throat felt raw and every breath was painful, but at least the pain proved that he was alive.

He racked his brains, trying to think where he'd gone wrong. He must have made a mistake somewhere along the line, and if he could just work out what it was, maybe he'd be able to put it right. Had someone recognised him, had he said something to give himself away, some stupid slip that he hadn't noticed but which they'd picked up on? He replayed all the recent conversations he'd had but nothing came to mind. He was too professional to make mistakes. Too careful. Too scared.

He knew two of the men who'd brought him down to the basement. One was Scottish, the other Brazilian. He'd known them both for almost two years. He'd drunk with them, whored with them, on occasions almost felt that they were friends. However, when they'd picked him up on the pavement outside the hotel their eyes had been hard and their faces set like stone, and he'd known even before they'd grabbed him that he was in trouble.

The third man, the one who'd driven, was a stranger. Hispanic, jet-black hair that had been swept back, and high cheekbones pockmarked with old acne scars. The driver had kept turning around and grinning at him, but like the other two hadn't said a word during the drive to the villa.

Initially the man had tried to bluff it out, to make a joke of it, then he'd faked anger, saying that they had no right to treat him that way, then he'd threatened them. They'd said nothing. The Scotsman had jabbed the barrel of a large automatic into the man's ribs and kept his finger tight on the trigger. Eventually the man had fallen silent and just sat between his captors, his hands in his lap.

He heard footsteps on the stone steps that led down to the basement and he tensed. The door opened. He recognised the man who stood in the doorway. He was a shade over six feet tall with chestnut-brown hair that was unfashionably long, pale green eyes and a sprinkling of freckles over a nose that had been broken at least twice. Dennis Donovan.

'Don't get up, Andy,' said Donovan, and laughed harshly.

The Brazilian appeared at Donovan's shoulder and grinned, showing yellowish, smoker's teeth.

Donovan and the Brazilian walked into the basement and closed the door. Donovan was wearing a red short-sleeved polo shirt and khaki chinos, a Rolex Submariner on his left wrist. In his hand was a long kitchen knife. The Brazilian was holding a large plastic bag.

The man said nothing. There was nothing he could say.

Donovan had used his real name, which meant that Donovan knew everything.

'You've been a naughty boy, Andy,' said Donovan, stretching out the man's name as if relishing the sound of it. 'A very naughty boy.' From the back pocket of his chinos he took a black ski mask and slipped it on his head. He walked past the man, so close that he could smell Donovan's aftershave, and bent over the video camera. He pressed a button and then cursed.

'Fucking new technology,' he said. 'Ever tried programming a video recorder, Andy? Bloody nightmare. You need a PhD in astrophysics just to set the timer. Ah, there we go.'

Donovan straightened up. A small red light glowed at the top of the video recorder as the glass lens glared balefully at the man in the chair.

Donovan nodded at the Brazilian, who had also put on a black ski mask. Donovan tossed the knife to him in a gentle arc and the Brazilian caught it deftly with his free hand.

The Brazilian advanced towards the man in the chair, flicking the knife from side to side, humming quietly. The man struggled, even though he knew there was no point in struggling. His conscious brain knew that his life was forfeit, but his animal instincts refused to accept the inevitable and he strained against his bonds and tried to scream through the tape gag as the Brazilian went to work with the knife.

Peter Latham stabbed at the lift button and glared at the floor indicator as if he could speed up its progress by sheer willpower. He shrugged his shoulders inside his grey suit jacket and adjusted his blue and yellow striped tie. It had been a long time since Latham had worn plainclothes during the day and he was surprised at how much he missed his uniform.

The briefcase he carried was the same one he carried into work every day at New Scotland Yard, a present from his wife of going on twenty-five years. Black leather, scuffed at the edges, the gilt weathered on the two combination locks, the handle virtually moulded to the shape of his hand, it was something of a lucky talisman and he planned to keep it until the day he retired.

The lift doors opened and Latham stepped inside. He pressed the button for the fifth floor but the doors remained resolutely open. The hotel was advertised as four-star, but the carpets were stained and threadbare and there was a tired look to the place, like a faded actress who'd long given up on her agent ringing with an offer of work. It was in an area that Latham rarely frequented, just east of the City, London's sprawling financial district, and he'd travelled by black cab instead of using his regular driver. Strictly speaking, as an Assistant Commissioner with the Metropolitan Police, Latham was higher in rank than the man he was coming to see, but the man was an old friend and the manner and urgency of the request for the meeting was such that Latham was prepared to put rank aside.

The doors closed and there was a sharp jolt as the lift started its upward journey. Latham could hear gears grinding somewhere above his head and he resolved to take the stairs on the way down.

The room was at the end of a long corridor punctuated with cheap watercolours of seascapes in fake antique frames. Latham knocked and the door was opened by a man in his early fifties, a few inches shorter than Latham's six feet and several stone heavier.

‘Peter, thanks for coming,’ said the man, offering his hand.

They shook. Both men had strong, firm grips. A handshake between equals.

‘We’re getting a bit old for cloak and dagger, aren’t we, Ray?’ said Latham. Raymond Mackie pulled an apologetic face and stepped aside to allow Latham into the room. Two single beds, a pine-laminated dressing table and wardrobe, and a small circular table with two grey armchairs. There was a bottle of Johnnie Walker Black Label, two glasses and an ice bucket on the table. Mackie waddled over to it, poured two large measures and handed one to Latham. They clinked glasses and drank. Mackie’s official title was Head of Drugs Operations, HODO, generally referred to as Ho Dough, although because of Mackie’s expansive waistline, this was frequently corrupted behind his back to the Doughboy.

A combined television and video recorder stood on the dressing table. Mackie saw Latham looking at the television and he picked up a video cassette. ‘This arrived at Custom House yesterday,’ he said.

‘I hope you haven’t brought me all this way to watch a blue movie,’ said Latham. He dropped down into one of the armchairs and put his briefcase on the floor.

‘I warn you, it’s not pretty,’ said Mackie, slotting the cassette into the recorder and pressing the ‘play’ button. He shuffled over to a sofa and eased himself down on to it as if he feared it might break, then took a long slug of his whisky as the screen flickered into life.

Latham steepled his fingers under his chin. It took several seconds before he realised that what he was seeing wasn’t a movie, but the brutal torture of a fellow human being. ‘Sweet Jesus,’ he whispered.

'Andy Middleton,' said Mackie. 'One of our best undercover agents.'

On the screen, the man in the ski mask was slicing deep cuts across the chest of the bound man, who was rocking back and forth in agony.

'He went missing on Anguilla two weeks ago. This came via Miami.'

Latham tried not to look at the man being tortured and instead forced himself to look for details that might help identify the assailant or the location. The torturer had no watch or jewellery, and was wearing surgical gloves. There was no way of knowing if he was black or white, or even if he was male or female, though Latham doubted that a woman would be capable of such savagery. The walls were bare except for a few shelves to the left. A fluorescent light fitting. Concrete floor. It could have been anywhere.

'Middleton was trying to get close to Dennis Donovan,' said Mackie. 'Donovan's been active in the Caribbean for the past six months, meeting with Colombians and a Dutch shipper by the name of Akveld. Middleton's in was through one of Akveld's associates. He's gone missing, too.'

A second masked figure stepped into the frame holding a plastic bag. He stood for a second or two looking directly at the camera.

'We think this is Donovan,' said Mackie. 'Same build. There's no way of knowing for sure, though.'

The man walked behind Middleton and pulled the plastic bag down over his head, twisting it around his neck. The undercover Customs agent shuddered in the chair, his eyes wide and staring. It was more than a minute before his head slumped down against his chest, but the man behind him kept the bag tight around his neck for a further minute to make sure that he was dead.

The recording ended and Mackie switched off the television. 'Middleton is the third agent we've lost in the Caribbean. Like Middleton, the bodies of the first two haven't been found. They were hoping to bring Donovan down as part of Operation Liberator, but it didn't work out that way.'

Latham nodded. Operation Liberator had been trumpeted as a major victory in the war against drugs – almost three thousand drugs traffickers arrested, twenty tons of cocaine and almost thirty tons of marijuana seized along with thirty million dollars of assets confiscated as part of a massive operation conducted by the United States Drug Enforcement Administration and British Customs. Latham knew that most of the arrests were low-level dealers and traffickers, however, men and women who would have been replaced before they'd even been strip-searched. And thirty million dollars was a drop in the ocean of a business estimated to be worth more than five hundred billion dollars a year.

'Were they killed on tape?' asked Latham.

Mackie shook his head.

'So why this time? What was special about Middleton?'

'It's a warning,' said Mackie, sitting down in the armchair opposite Latham and refilling their glasses. 'He's telling us what he'll do to anyone we send against him.'

Latham sipped his whisky. 'It's unusual, isn't it, killing a Customs officer?'

'Not in the league Donovan's in. If it was just a case of a couple of kilos, maybe, but the last consignment of Donovan's that went belly up had a street value of thirty million dollars. If the DEA catch him with the goods, he'll go down for life without parole.'

'Even so, he could just give them a kicking and send them packing, couldn't he?'

'I guess we've become a thorn in his side and this is his way of saying enough is enough.'

'And is it? From your perspective?'

Mackie looked at the Assistant Commissioner with unblinking grey eyes. 'I knew all three of them, Peter. I worked with Andy way back when. Checking cars at Dover, believe it or not. I'm not going to send any more men into the lion's den.'

'So he's won?'

'Not exactly.' Mackie fell silent and stared at a painting of a vase of flowers above one of the beds.

'Spit it out, Ray,' said Latham eventually.

'We've had an idea,' said Mackie, still studying the painting.

'Well, I guessed that much.'

'The problem is, no matter how good our agents are, and Andy Middleton was one of the best, an operator like Donovan can still spot them. They don't have his background, his instincts. No matter how good they are, they're still playing a role. One slip, one wrong move, and their cover's blown.'

Latham nodded but didn't say anything.

Mackie put his glass on the table and stood up, his knees cracking like snapping twigs. He walked around the room, his left shoe squeaking each time it touched the floor. 'We put our guys through the most intense training imaginable, same as you do with your SO10 people. We teach them about surveillance and counter-surveillance, we teach them how to act, how to think like a criminal. And up against low-level operators they pass muster. You see, if it walks like a duck and talks like a duck, then the bad guys assume that it's probably a duck. But probably isn't good enough for a man like Donovan. First, he only does business with people he's known personally for a long time. He treats all strangers with suspicion. And he has an instinct for undercover agents. It's as if he can smell them. Apart from the three who've died, I've had half a dozen bail out of their own accord, convinced that Donovan was on to them.'

'I get the picture, Ray. I even get the duck analogy. But what do you want from me? From the Met?'

Mackie took a deep breath and turned to look at the Assistant Commissioner. 'Virgins,' he said, quietly. 'We need virgins.'

Jamie Fullerton gritted his teeth as he pounded along the pavement on the last leg of his two-mile run. He was barely sweating and knew that he had the stamina to run for at least another hour, but he had nothing to prove. If it had been the weekend he might have pushed himself harder, but it was Monday, the start of a new week. The start of a new life. He looked left and right and dashed across the King's Road, heading for his basement flat in Oakley Street. London wasn't the most convenient place in the world for an early-morning run, but Fullerton couldn't abide the clinical efficiency and mechanical contraptions of a health club. Fitness was a way of life to him; it had nothing to do with spending an hour on an exercise bike reading the *FT* and listening to the latest Simply Red CD.

He increased the pace as he turned into Oakley Street and sprinted the last hundred yards, then stood stretching as he held on to the black railings at the top of the stairs that led down to his flat. A blonde in a smart pale green suit carrying a Louis Vuitton briefcase flashed him a dazzlingly white smile and he grinned back.

'Looking good,' she said, then she was gone, heading for South Kensington Tube station.

Fullerton had seen her three times during the past week and had the feeling that she was deliberately timing her journey to coincide with his return from his run. He'd noticed the wedding ring on her finger the first time he'd seen her, but her smiles were getting wider and there was a definite swing to her hips as she walked away. She was pretty enough, but she was in her early thirties, probably a decade his senior, and Fullerton had long since passed through the stage of being attracted to older women.

He went down the metal steps to his front door and let himself in. The flat had a minimum of furniture: two simple grey sofas facing each other either side of a coal-effect gas fire, a low coffee table made from some dark veneer that hadn't been within a mile of a genuine tree, and a sideboard which was bare except for an inoffensive African wood carving that he would have thrown out if it hadn't been high up on the list of the landlord's inventory that he'd had to sign when he'd taken on the lease.

Fullerton stripped off his tracksuit top and tossed it on to the sofa by the window before dropping on to the beige carpet and doing his daily one hundred and twenty sit-ups. He was sweating by the time he finished, but his breathing was still regular and though his abdominal muscles ached he knew that he was nowhere near his limit.

He walked through to the bathroom, which was as

utilitarian as the sitting room, and showered before going into the bedroom with a towel wrapped around his waist. On the back of the bedroom door a dark blue uniform with silver buttons hung on a wooden hanger. He picked up the hanger and grinned at the uniform.

'A fucking cop,' he chuckled to himself. 'Who'd've believed it?'

He tossed the uniform on to the bed. The helmet with its gleaming silver emblem of the Metropolitan Police was on the dressing table and Fullerton picked it up. He placed it on his head and adjusted the chin strap. It was heavy but it sat firmly on his head. He turned to look at his reflection in the mirrored door of the wardrobe. He stopped grinning and snapped to attention, then slowly saluted. 'Evening all,' he said. He flexed his biceps, then stepped into a bodybuilder's pose. His towel slid to the floor and he grinned at his naked reflection.

He jumped as his doorbell rang, and his face flushed involuntarily as he realised how ridiculous he looked, naked except for a policeman's helmet.

He put the helmet on the bed next to the uniform, wrapped the towel around his waist and rushed down the hallway to the front door. He opened it, expecting to see the postman, but instead was faced with a man in his thirties wearing a dark blue blazer and grey slacks, like a holiday rep preparing to greet a planeload of holiday-makers.

'James Fullerton?' asked the man, his face a blank mask as if he didn't care either way whether or not he was.

'Yes?' said Fullerton hesitantly.

'There's been a change of venue,' said the man.

'And you are?'

'The man who's been sent to take you to the new venue,' he said without a trace of humour. He was holding a set of car keys in his right hand. His shoes were as highly polished as the pair that Fullerton kept in the bottom of his wardrobe. Policeman's shoes.

'Look, I'm supposed to be at Hendon at eight thirty,' said Fullerton. 'The police college.'

'I know what Hendon is, sir,' said the man in the blazer. 'You're to come with me instead.'

'Do you have a letter or something?'

'No,' said the man coldly. 'No letter.'

Fullerton looked at the man. The man returned his look with total impassivity as he clasped his hands together over his groin and waited patiently. It was clear that he wasn't going to divulge any further information. 'Right,' said Fullerton. 'Let me get dressed.' He started to close the door.

'The uniform won't be necessary, sir.'

Fullerton stopped closing the door. 'Excuse me?'

'The uniform. It won't be necessary.'

Fullerton frowned. 'What do I wear, then?'

The man in the blazer leaned forward as if about to whisper conspiratorially. 'Frankly, sir,' he said, 'I couldn't give a fuck.'

Fullerton closed the door and stood in the hallway with his head in his hands wondering what the hell was going on. His application to join the Metropolitan Police had been accepted three months earlier, and the letter telling him when to report to Hendon had arrived shortly afterwards. The sudden change of plan could only be bad news.

Cliff 'Bunny' Warren poured a slug of milk over his Shredded Wheat, dumped on two heaped spoonfuls of brown sugar and carried the bowl over to the Formica table in the corner of his kitchen. He wrapped his dressing gown around himself, propped up a textbook against the wall and read as he ate. *Reforming Social Services*. The content of the book was as dry as the cereal straight from the packet, but Warren knew that it was required reading. He was already behind in his Open University reading and had a stack of videos next to the television that he still had to watch.

The doorbell rang, three sharp blasts as if whoever was ringing was in a hurry. Warren put down his spoon and walked slowly down the hallway. He put the chain on the door before opening it. The part of Harlesden he lived in was home to an assortment of drug addicts and petty thieves who wouldn't think twice about kicking down a door, beating him senseless and taking what few possessions he had. His upstairs neighbour, a widower in his seventies, had been broken into six times in the past two years.

A white man in a dark blue blazer smiled through the gap. 'Clifford Warren?'

'Who wants to know?'

'I've a car waiting for you, sir.'

Warren's brow furrowed as he opened the door further. Parked in the street a few doors away was a brand new Vauxhall Vectra that was already attracting the attention of two West Indian teenagers.

'You don't want to leave it there,' warned Warren. 'Not if you want to see your radio again.'

The man took a quick look over his shoulder. 'Thanks for the tip, sir,' he said. 'I'll wait with the vehicle.'

'Does every new recruit get this treatment?' asked Warren.

'You're a bit of a special case, I'm told, sir,' said the man, adjusting his red and blue tie. 'I've been told to tell you that the uniform won't be necessary.'

'Am I in some sort of trouble?' asked Warren, suddenly concerned.

The man shrugged. 'Not that I'm aware of, sir, but then they don't tell me much, me being a driver and all.' He looked at his watch. 'Best not to be late, sir.'

Warren nodded. 'Okay, okay,' he said and closed the door as the man went back to guard his car.

He walked slowly into his bedroom and took off his dressing gown. His police uniform was hanging from the key that locked the wardrobe door. He reached out and stroked the blue serge. Warren had thought long and hard before applying to join the Metropolitan Police. He'd had a few minor convictions when he was a teenager, mainly joyriding and stealing from cars, and he'd been up front about his past during the many interviews they'd put him through. However, in the wake of a slump in recruitment, the Met had been forced to drop its requirement that applicants had a completely trouble-free past. They were especially keen on Warren as he was West Indian, and were currently bending over backwards to increase their intake of ethnic minorities. It was racism, albeit acting in reverse, and Warren figured that he might as well take advantage of it. However, the presence of the man in the blazer waiting in the car outside suggested that his entry into the ranks of the Metropolitan Police wasn't going to go as smoothly as he'd hoped.

Christina Leigh lit her first cigarette of the morning, inhaled deeply, then spent a good thirty seconds coughing as she walked slowly towards the kitchen, wrapping her robe around her. 'Tomorrow I'm giving up,' she promised herself for the thousandth time.

She switched on the kettle and heaped two spoonfuls of Nescafé Gold Blend into a white mug. As she took a second pull on her Silk Cut she frowned at the clock above the ten-year-old refrigerator. 'Eight o'clock?' she muttered. 'How the hell can it be eight o'clock already?' She hurried back into the bedroom and took her blue uniform out of the wardrobe and laid it carefully on the bed. Her regulation shoes sat on her dressing table, gleaming under the fluorescent striplight above her mirror, and her hat hung on a hook on the back of the door. She picked up the hat and sat it carefully on her head, then adjusted the angle. Try as she might, it didn't look right and she wondered whether day one at Hendon would involve teaching recruits how to wear the bloody things. At least she didn't have to wear the same silly pointed helmets as the men. The doorbell rang and she jumped.

She rushed to the door of her flat and flung it open. A grey-haired man in his early fifties smiled down at her. He was wearing a dark blue blazer and grey trousers and must have been almost seven feet tall, because Tina had to crane her neck to look at his face.

'Whatever you're selling, I really don't have the time,' she said. She took a quick pull on her cigarette. 'Or the money. And how did you get in? The front door's supposed to be locked.'

'Didn't anyone tell you that smoking in uniform is grounds for dismissal?' said the man in a soft Northumbrian accent.

'What?' said Tina, but as soon as the word had left her mouth she realised that she was still wearing the police hat. She grabbed it and held it behind her back.

'I'm not a cop,' she said. 'Not yet. A police officer, I mean. I'm not actually a police officer.' She leaned over and stabbed the cigarette into an ashtray on the hall table. 'What do you want?'

The man smiled at her, the skin at the side of his eyes creasing into deep crow's feet. 'Christina Leigh?'

'Yes?' said Tina hesitantly.

'Your chariot awaits.'

'My what?'

'Your car.'

'I don't have a bleedin' car. I barely have enough for a bus ticket.'

'I'm here to drive you, Miss Leigh.'

'To Hendon?'

'To an alternative venue.'

'I'm supposed to report to Hendon half past eight.' She took a quick look at the Swatch on her wrist. 'And I'm running late.'

'Your itinerary has been changed, Miss Leigh, and I'm here to drive you. You won't be needing the uniform, either. Plainclothes.'

'Plainclothes?'

'The sort of thing you'd wear to the shops.' He smiled. 'I wouldn't recommend anything outrageous.'

Tina narrowed her eyes. 'Am I in trouble?' she asked, suddenly serious.

The man shrugged. 'They treat me like a mushroom, miss. Keep me in the dark and—'

'I know, I know,' Tina interrupted. 'It's just that I had the course work, I've read all the stuff, and I was up all night polishing those bloody shoes. Now you're telling me it's off.'

'Just a change in your itinerary, miss. That's all. If

you were in any sort of trouble, I doubt that they'd send me.'

Tina pounced. 'They?'

'The powers that be, miss. The people who pay my wages.'

'And they would be who?'

'I guess the taxpayer at the end of the day.' He looked at his watch. 'We'd best be going, miss.'

Tina stared at the man for a few seconds, then nodded slowly. 'Okay. Give me a minute.' She smiled mischievously. 'Make-up?'

'A touch of mascara wouldn't hurt, miss,' said the man, straight faced. 'Perhaps a hint of lipstick. Nothing too pink. I'll be waiting in the car.'

Tina bit down on her lower lip, suppressing the urge to laugh out loud. She waited until she'd closed the door before chuckling to herself.

By the time she was opening the wardrobe door she'd stopped laughing. The arrival of the grey-haired stranger on her doorstep could only be bad news. The day she'd learned that the Metropolitan Police had accepted her as a probationary constable had been one of the happiest in her life. Now she had a horrible feeling that her dreams of a new life were all going to come crashing down around her.

The driver said not one word during the forty-minute drive from Chelsea to the Isle of Dogs. Jamie Fullerton knew that there was no point in asking any of the dozen or so questions that were buzzing around his brain like angry wasps. He'd find out soon enough, of that much he was sure. He stared out of the window of the Vectra and took long, slow breaths, trying to calm his thumping heart.

When he saw the towering edifice of Canary Wharf in the distance, Fullerton frowned. So far as he knew, none of the Metropolitan Police bureaucracy was based out there – it was a financial centre, pure and simple. Big American banks and Japanese broking houses and what was left of the British financial services sector.

The Vectra slowed in front of a nondescript glass and steel block, then turned into an underground car park, bucking over a yellow and black striped hump in the tarmac. The driver showed a laminated ID card to a uniformed security guard and whistled softly through his teeth as the barrier was slowly raised. They parked close to a lift, and Fullerton waited for the driver to walk around and open the door for him. It was a silly, pointless victory, but the man's sullen insolence had annoyed Fullerton.

The driver slammed Fullerton's door shut and walked stiffly over to the lift. To the right of the grey metal door was a keypad and he tapped out a four-digit code. A digital read-out showed that the lift was coming down from the tenth floor.

The driver studiously ignored Fullerton until the lift reached the car park and the door rattled open.

'Tenth floor, sir,' said the driver, almost spitting out the honorific. 'You'll be met.' He turned and headed back to the car.

Fullerton walked into the lift and stabbed at the button for the tenth floor. 'You drive carefully, yeah?' Fullerton shouted as the door clattered shut. It was another pointless victory, but Fullerton had a feeling that he was going to have to take his victories where he could.

He watched as the floor indicator lights flicked slowly to ten. The lift whispered to a halt and the door opened.

There was nobody waiting for him. Fullerton hesitated, then stepped out of the lift and stood in the grey-carpeted lobby, looking left and right. At one end of the corridor was a pair of frosted glass doors. Fullerton frowned. The lift door closed behind him. He adjusted the cuffs of his white shirt and shrugged the shoulders of his dark blue silk and wool Lanvin suit. Fullerton had decided that if his uniform had been declared surplus to requirements, he might as well go into battle dressed stylishly. Plus it had been another way of annoying the tight-lipped driver – the suit probably cost as much as the man earned in a month.

Fullerton took a deep breath and headed towards the glass doors. He had just raised his right hand to push his way through when a blurry figure on the other side beat him to it and pulled the door open.

Fullerton flinched and almost took a step back, but he recovered quickly when he saw that the man holding the door open was wearing the uniform and peaked cap of a senior officer of the Metropolitan Police.

'Didn't mean to startle you, Fullerton,' said the man.

'I wasn't startled, sir,' said Fullerton, recognising the man from his frequent television appearances. Assistant Commissioner Peter Latham. The articulate face of British policing – university educated, quick witted and about the only senior police officer able to hold his own against the aggressive interrogators of *Newsnight*. Latham was the officer most likely to be wheeled out to defend the policies and actions of the Metropolitan Police, while the Commissioner stayed in his spacious wood-panelled office on the eighth floor of New Scotland Yard, drinking Earl Grey tea from a delicate porcelain cup and planning his retirement, only two years and a knighthood away.

'This way,' said Latham, letting the door swing back. Fullerton caught it and followed the Assistant Commissioner through a lobby area and down a white-walled corridor bare of any decoration to a teak veneer door where four screwholes marked where a plaque had once been.

Latham pushed the door open. The office was about the size of a badminton court, with floor-to-ceiling windows at one end. Like the corridor outside, the walls were completely bare, except for a large clock with big roman numerals and a red second hand. There were brighter patches of clean paint where paintings or pictures had once hung, and screwholes where things had been removed. The only furnishings were a cheap pine desk and two plastic chairs. Latham sat down on one of the chairs so that his back was to the window. There were no blinds or curtains, and through the glass Fullerton could see hundreds of office workers slaving away like worker ants in the tower opposite.

Latham took off his peaked cap and placed it carefully on the table in front of him. His hair seemed unnaturally black, though the grey areas around his temples suggested he wasn't dyeing it. He motioned for Fullerton to sit down. Fullerton did so, adjusting the creases of his trousers.

'You know who I am, Fullerton?' said the Assistant Commissioner.

Fullerton nodded. 'Sir,' he said.

'No need for introductions, then,' said the senior police officer. He tapped the fingers of his right hand on the desktop. The fingernails were immaculately groomed, Fullerton noticed, the nails neatly clipped, the cuticles trimmed back. 'Tell me why you wanted to join the force, Fullerton.'

Fullerton's brow creased into a frown. His application to join the Metropolitan Police had been accepted after more than twenty hours of interviews, a battery of psychological and physical tests, and a thorough background check. He'd been asked his reasons for wanting to join more than a dozen times and he doubted that Latham expected to hear anything new or original. So why ask the question, unless he was being set up for something? Fullerton's initial reaction was to go on the offensive, to ask the Assistant Commissioner why he was being asked the question at such a late stage and by such a senior officer, but he knew that there'd be nothing to be gained. He forced himself to smile. 'It's the career I've always wanted, sir,' he said. 'A chance to do something for the community. To help. To make a difference.'

Latham studied Fullerton with unsmiling brown eyes, his face giving nothing away. Fullerton found the face impossible to read. He widened his smile a little and sat back in his chair, trying to look as relaxed as possible.

'I'm not totally altruistic, obviously,' said Fullerton, lifting his hands and showing his palms, doing everything he could to show the body language of someone who was open and honest, with nothing to hide. 'I don't want an office job, I don't want to sell people life insurance they don't want or spend my life with a phone stuck to my ear. I want to be out and about, dealing with people, solving problems.'

Still no reaction from Latham. No understanding nods, no smiles of acceptance. Just a blank stare that seemed to look right through Fullerton.

'Frankly, sir, I'm not sure what else I can say. Everyone knows what a police officer does. And it's a job that I want to do.'

Fullerton smiled and nodded, but there was no reciprocal gesture from Latham. His neatly manicured fingers continued to drum softly on the desktop. 'How did you feel when you weren't accepted on to the accelerated promotion scheme?'

'A little disappointed, but I figured that if I joined as an ordinary entrant, my talents would soon be realised. It might take me a year or so longer to reach the top, but I'll still get there.' Fullerton deliberately tried to sound as optimistic as possible, but he was already beginning to accept that something had gone wrong and that Latham had no intention of allowing him to join the Metropolitan Police. Why the clandestine meeting, though, why hadn't they just written to him with the bad news? None of this was making any sense at all, and until it did, Fullerton had no choice but to go along for the ride.

'Those talents being?'

Fullerton was starting to tire of Latham's game-playing. He leaned forward and looked Latham in the eyes, meeting his cold stare and not flinching from it. 'The talents that were recognised by the interview board, for one,' he said. 'The talents that got me in the top five per cent of my university year. At Oxford.' He used the name like a lance, prodding it at Latham, knowing that the Assistant Commissioner had only managed a second-class degree from Leeds.

For the first time Latham allowed a smile to flicker across his face. He stopped tapping his fingers and gently smoothed the peak of his cap. 'What about your other talents?' said Latham quietly, his voice hardly more than a whisper. 'Lying? Cheating? Blackmail?'

The three words hit Fullerton like short, sharp punches

to his solar plexus. He sat back in his chair, stunned. 'What?' he gasped.

Latham stared at Fullerton for several seconds before he spoke again. 'Did you think we wouldn't find out about your drug use, Fullerton? Do you think we're stupid? Was that your intention, to join the Met and show us all how much smarter you are? To rub our noses in our own stupidity?'

Fullerton put his hands on his knees, forcing himself to keep them from clenching. 'I don't know what it is you think that I've done, sir, but I can assure you . . .' He tailed off, lost for words.

'You can assure me of what?' asked Latham.

'Someone has been lying to you, sir.'

'Oh, I'm quite sure of that, Fullerton,' said Latham.

'Whatever they've told you, it's lies. Someone is trying to set me up.'

'Why would anyone do that?' asked Latham.

Fullerton shook his head. His mind whirled. What the hell had happened? What did Latham know? And what did he want?

'Are you denying that you are a regular user of cocaine?' asked Latham.

'Emphatically,' said Fullerton.

'And that you smoke cannabis?'

'I don't even smoke cigarettes, sir. Look, I gave a urine sample as part of the medical, didn't I? Presumably that was tested for drugs use.'

'Indeed it was.'

'And?'

'And the sample you gave was as pure as the driven snow.'

'So there you are. That proves something, doesn't it?'

Latham smiled thinly. 'All it proves is how smart you are, Fullerton. Or how smart you'd like to think you are.'

Fullerton leaned forward again, trying to seize back the initiative. 'My background was checked, sir. No criminal record, not even a speeding ticket.'

'Are you denying that you take drugs on a regular basis?'

'Yes.'

'And that you were caught dealing cannabis while at university?'

Fullerton's eyes widened and his mouth went dry.

'Caught with three ounces of cannabis resin in the toilets at an end-of-term concert?' Latham continued, his eyes boring into Fullerton's.

Fullerton fought to stop his hands from shaking. 'If that had been the case, sir, I'd have been sent down.'

'Unless your tutor also happened to be a customer. Unless you threatened to expose him if he didn't pull strings to get the matter swept under the metaphorical carpet. Might also explain how you managed to graduate with a first.'

'I got my degree on merit,' said Fullerton, quickly. Too quickly, he realised. 'There's no proof of any of this,' he said. 'It's all hearsay.'

'Hearsay's all we need,' said Latham. 'This isn't a court, there's no jury to convince.'

'Is that what this is all about? A conviction for possession that wouldn't even merit a caution?'

'Do you think I'd be here if that was all that was involved, Fullerton? Don't you think I'd have better things to do than interview someone who thinks it's clever to get high now and again?'

Fullerton swallowed. His nose was itching and he badly

wanted to scratch it, but he knew that if he took his hands off his knees they'd start trembling.

'I'm not interested in slapping the wrist of a recreational drug-user, Fullerton, but I am very interested in knowing if you're serious about wanting to be a police officer. A real police officer.'

'Yes, sir. I am.'

Latham looked at Fullerton, his mouth a tight line. He nodded slowly. 'Very well. From this moment on I want absolute truth from you. Do you understand?'

Fullerton licked his lips. His mouth was bone dry. 'Agreed, sir.'

'Thank you,' said Latham. 'Exactly what drugs do you use?'

'Cocaine, sir. Occasionally. Cannabis. Ecstasy on occasions.'

'Heroin?'

'In the past, sir. Only inhaling. Never injecting.'

'LSD?'

'Not since university, sir. I didn't like the loss of control.'

'Would you consider yourself an addict?'

Fullerton shook his head emphatically. 'I don't have an addictive personality, sir. I use because I enjoy it, not because I need it.'

'That's what all addicts say.'

'I've gone without for weeks at a time, sir. It's not a problem.'

'And you switched urine samples?'

'I gave a friend fifty quid for a bottle of his piss.'

'And your tutor at Oxford? You pressurised him?'

Fullerton nodded. 'But only for the cannabis thing, I swear. I got the first on merit.'

'Do you still deal?'

Fullerton grimaced. 'That depends, sir.'

'On what?'

'On your definition of dealing.'

'Selling for profit.'

Fullerton grimaced again. 'I sell to friends, and it'd be stupid to make a loss on the deal, wouldn't it? I mean, you wouldn't expect me to sell at a loss.'

'That would make you a dealer,' said Latham.

Fullerton could feel sweat beading on his forehead, but he didn't want to wipe it away, didn't want Latham to see his discomfort. 'What's this about, sir?' he asked. 'I assume there's no way I'm going to be allowed to join the force. Not in view of . . . this.'

For the first time, Latham smiled with something approaching warmth. 'Actually, Fullerton, you'd be surprised.'

'Don't you think it's going to be tough for you in the Met, being a nigger?' said Assistant Commissioner Latham.

At first Cliff Warren thought he'd misheard, and he sat with a blank look on his face.

Latham folded his arms across his chest, tilted his head back slightly and looked down his nose at Warren. 'What's wrong, Warren? Cat got your tongue?'

Still Warren thought he'd misunderstood the senior police officer. 'I'm not sure I understand the question, sir.'

'The question, Warren, is don't you think that being black is going to hold you back? The Met doesn't like spooks. Spades. Sooties. Whatever the latest generic is. Haven't you heard? We're institutionally racist. We don't like niggers.'

Warren frowned. He looked away from Latham's piercing gaze and stared out of the window at the tower block opposite. It was like a bad dream and he half expected to wake up at any moment and find himself looking at his brand new uniform hanging from the wardrobe door. This didn't make any sense. The drive to the Isle of Dogs. The lift with a security code. The empty office, empty except for a desk and two chairs and a senior police officer whom Warren recognised from his many television appearances, who was using racist language which could lose him his job if it was ever made public.

'I'm not sure of your point, sir,' said Warren.

'My point is that it's not going to be much fun for you, is it? Pictures of monkeys pinned up on your locker. Bananas on the backseat of your patrol car. Memos asking you to call Mr K.K. Clan.'

'I thought the Met wanted to widen its minority base,' said Warren.

Latham raised an eyebrow. 'Did you now?' he said. 'And you were eager to take up the challenge, were you?'

'I wanted the job, yes.'

Latham steepled his fingers under his chin like a child saying his prayers and studied Warren with unblinking eyes. 'You're not angered by what I've just said?' he said eventually.

'I've heard worse, sir.'

'And you're always so relaxed about it?'

'What makes you think I'm relaxed, sir?'

Latham nodded slowly, accepting Warren's point.

'That was a test, was it, sir?'

'In a way, Warren.'

Warren smiled without warmth. 'Because it wasn't really a fair test, not if you think about it. You're in uniform, I'm hoping to become an officer in the force that you command, I'm hardly likely to lose control, am I?'

'I suppose not.'

'See, if you weren't an Assistant Commissioner, and you'd said what you'd said outside, in a pub or on the street, my reaction might have been a little less . . . reticent.' Warren leaned forward, his eyes never leaving Latham's face. 'In fact,' he said in a low whisper, 'I'd be kicking your lily-white arse to within an inch of your lily-white life. Sir.' Warren smiled showing perfect slab-like white teeth. 'No offence intended.'

Latham smiled back. This time there was an amused glint in his eyes and Warren knew that he'd passed the test. Maybe not with flying colours, but he'd passed. 'None taken,' said the Assistant Commissioner. 'Tell me about your criminal record.'

'Minor offences,' said Warren without hesitation. 'Taking and driving away when I was fourteen. Driving without due care and attention. Driving without insurance. Without a licence. Criminal damage.' Warren's criminal past had been discussed at length prior to his being accepted as a probationary constable.

'And there's nothing else that we should know about you, nothing that might have influenced our decision to allow you to join the force?'

'The interviews and tests were wide-ranging, sir,' said Warren.

'You didn't reveal your homosexuality,' said Latham.

'I wasn't asked,' said Warren without hesitation.

'You didn't think it relevant?'

'Clearly the interviewers didn't.'

'Your home situation would have been enquired about. Your domestic arrangements.'

'I live alone.'

'So you have random sexual partners?'

Warren's lips tightened. It appeared that Latham was determined to keep testing him, but Warren couldn't fathom what was going on. The time for such questions had long passed: all the Met had to do was to say that his services weren't required. There was no need for such taunting, especially from a senior officer like Latham.

'I'm not sure that my sexual history is relevant, sir,' said Warren. 'With respect.'

'It might be if it left you open to blackmail,' said Latham.

'Homosexuality isn't illegal, sir.'

'I'm aware of that, Warren, but any deviation from the norm makes an officer vulnerable.'

'Again, sir, I don't think that homosexuality is regarded as a deviation any more. These days it's seen as a lifestyle choice.'

Latham nodded slowly. 'One that you're not ashamed of?'

'I'm not ashamed of being black and I'm not ashamed of being gay, sir. So far as revealing my sexuality, I wasn't asked and I didn't tell. I certainly didn't lie.'

'And your criminal record? How do you feel about that?'

'Do you mean am I ashamed of what I did?'

Latham didn't react to the question, clearly regarding it as rhetorical, and continued looking at Warren.

Warren shrugged. 'Of course I'm ashamed. I was stupid. I was undisciplined, I was running wild, I was just an angry teenager out looking for kicks who didn't know how close he was coming to ruining his whole life. I was lucky not to be sent down, and if it wasn't for the fact that I was assigned one of the few social workers who actually appeared to care about her work, I'd probably be behind bars right now and not sitting here in your office.' Warren looked around the bare office. 'This office,' he corrected himself. 'Wherever we are, I assume this isn't where you normally conduct your business. What's this about, sir? My criminal record's an open book, and I don't see that my being gay is a bar to me joining the Met.'

Latham tapped his manicured nails silently on the desktop. The windows were double-glazed and sealed so no sound penetrated from the outside. It was so quiet that Warren could hear his own breathing, slow and regular.

'What sort of criminal do you think you would have made, Warren?' Latham said eventually.

'Back then? A very bad one. If I'd been any good at it, I wouldn't have been caught so often.'

'And now?'

Warren raised his eyebrows in surprise. 'Now?' he repeated.

'Suppose you hadn't been turned around by the altruistic social worker assigned to you. Suppose you'd continued along the road you'd started on. Petty crime. Stealing. Where do you think it would have led to?'

'Difficult to say, sir.'

'Try.'

Warren shrugged. 'Drugs, I guess. Dealing. That's what most crime comes down to these days. Everything from car break-ins to guns to prostitution, it's all drugs.'

'And what sort of drug dealer do you think you'd make?'

Warren frowned. It wasn't a question he'd ever considered. 'Probably quite a good one.'

'Because?'

'Because I'm not stupid any more. Because now I'm better educated than the average villain. I've a knowledge of criminal law and police procedure that most villains don't have. And to be quite honest, I consider I'm a hell of a lot smarter than most of the police officers I've come across.'

'I don't suppose you were that blunt at your interviews,' said Latham.

'I think we've moved beyond my being interviewed, sir. Whatever it is you want from me, it's not dependent on my being politically correct. I'm not going to Hendon, am I?'

'Not today, no,' said Latham, 'but this isn't about stopping you becoming a police officer, Warren, I can promise you that. You scored highly on all counts during the selection procedure, you're exactly the sort of material we want.' Latham pulled on his right ear, then scratched the lobe. 'The question is, exactly how would you be able to serve us best?'

Warren's forehead creased into a frown, but he didn't say anything.

'You see, Warren, putting you in a uniform and having you walk a beat might make for good public relations, but realistically it's going to make precious little difference to the crime figures.' Latham took a deep breath, held it, then exhaled slowly. 'What we'd like, Warren, is for you to consider becoming an undercover agent for us. Deep undercover. So deep, in fact, that hardly anyone will know that you work for the Met.'

Warren's eyes narrowed. 'You're asking me to pretend to be a criminal?'

Latham shook his head. 'No, I'm asking you to become a criminal. To cross the line.'

'To be a grass?'

'No, you'll still be a police officer. A grass is a criminal who provides information on other criminals. You'll be a fully functioning police officer who will be keeping us informed of the activities of the criminals you come across.'

'But I won't wear a uniform, I won't go to Hendon? No probationary period?'

'You'll never pound a beat. And the only time you'll go anywhere near a police station is if you get arrested. The number of people who'll know that you are a serving police officer will be counted on the fingers of one hand.'

'For how long?'

'For as long as you can take it. Hopefully years. Ideally, you'll spend your whole career undercover.'

Warren ran his hand over his black hair, closely cropped only two days earlier in anticipation of his new career. 'So I'd be a police officer, but undercover? I'd never be in uniform?'

'That would be the intention, yes.'

'If I'm not going to Hendon, how would I be trained?'

'You wouldn't,' said Latham. 'That's the whole point. We don't want you tainted.'

'Tainted?'

'At present undercover operatives are drawn from the ranks,' said Latham. 'We spend years training them to be policemen, then we send them undercover and expect them to act like criminals. It's no wonder it doesn't work. Doesn't matter how long they grow their hair or how they try to blend, they're still policemen acting as criminals. We don't want you to put on an act, Warren. We want you to become a criminal. You already have the perfect cover – you have a criminal record. We want you to build on that.'

'I can break the law? Is that what you're saying?'

For the first time Latham looked uncomfortable. 'That's not a conversation we should be having,' he said, adjusting his cuffs. 'That'll come later with your handler. I'm here to ask you to take on this assignment. I have a high profile: you know that if you have my word that the Met is behind you one hundred per cent, then you're not going to be left hanging in the wind down the line, if that's not mixing too many metaphors.'

'And if I refuse?'

Latham grimaced. 'As I've already said, you'll be an asset to the force. You can start at Hendon tomorrow, just one day late. I'm sure you'll have an exemplary career, but what I'm offering you is a chance to make a real difference.'

Warren nodded. 'How much time do I have to think about it?'

Latham looked at the large clock on the wall. 'I'd like your decision now,' said the Assistant Commissioner. 'If you have to talk yourself into the job, you're not the person that we're looking for.'

'Can I just get one thing straight?' asked Tina, fidgeting with the small gold stud earring in her left ear. 'Am I joining the Met or not?'

'Not as a uniformed constable, no,' said Assistant Commissioner Latham softly.

Tears pricked Tina's eyes, but she refused to allow herself to cry. 'It's not fair,' she said, her lower lip trembling.

'You shouldn't have lied, Tina. Did you seriously believe we wouldn't find out?'

'It was a long time ago,' said Tina, looking over the

senior policeman's shoulder at the tower block opposite. 'A lifetime ago.'

'And you didn't think that being a prostitute would preclude you from becoming a police officer?'

'I was fifteen!' she protested.

Latham sat back in his chair. 'Which doesn't actually make it any better, Tina. Does it?'

A lone tear trickled down Tina's cheek. She shook her head, angry with herself for the way she was behaving, but she'd been so looking forward to joining the Met. It was going to be a new start. A new life. Now it had been snatched away from her at the last minute. She groped for her handbag on the floor and fumbled for her cigarettes and disposable lighter.

'I think this is a non-smoking office,' said Latham as she tapped out a cigarette and slipped it between her lips.

'Fuck you,' she hissed, clicking the lighter. 'I need a fag.' She lit the cigarette and inhaled deeply, then blew a plume of smoke at the ceiling.

'You knew that if your criminal record came to light, you'd be in trouble,' said Latham quietly.

Tina glared at him. 'I don't have a criminal record,' she spat. 'I was cautioned for soliciting. Twice. Under a different name. I wasn't even charged.'

'You were a prostitute for more than a year, Tina,' said Latham. 'You were known to Vice. You were known on the streets.'

'I did what I did to survive. I did what I had to do.'

'I understand that.'

'Do you?' said Tina. 'I doubt it. Do you know what it's like to have to fend for yourself when you're still a kid? To have to leave home because your stepfather spends all his time trying to get into your knickers and your mum's so drunk she can't stop him even if she wants to? Do you know what's it like to arrive in London with nowhere to stay and a couple of quid in your pocket? Do you? I don't fucking think so. So don't sit there in your made-to-measure uniform with your shiny silver buttons and your pimp's fingernails and your pension and your little wife with her Volvo and her flower-arranging classes and tell me that you understand, because you don't.'

Tina leaned forward. 'Don't think I haven't met your sort before, because I have. Squeaky clean on the outside, pillar of the fucking community, but what you really want is a blow job from an underage girl in the front seat of your car because your little wife hasn't had her mouth near your dick since England won the World Cup.'

She took another long pull on her cigarette. Her hand was shaking and she blew smoke straight at Latham. He didn't react, just kept looking at her through the cloud of smoke.

Tina closed her eyes. 'I'm sorry,' she whispered.

'I'd expect you to lash out, Tina,' said Latham.

Tina opened her eyes again. She took another drag on her cigarette, this time taking care to blow the smoke away from the Assistant Commissioner. 'If I could turn the clock back, I would. But back then, I didn't have a choice,' she said. Tina looked around the office, her eyes settling on the large clock on the wall, the red hand ticking away the seconds of her life. 'You had to bring me here to tell me this, yeah?' she said. 'You couldn't have written? Or phoned?'

'I wanted to talk to you.'

She turned to look at him and fixed him with her dark green eyes. 'You wanted to see me squirm?'

Latham shook his head. 'It's not that, Tina.'

'So what is it, then?'

'I've a proposition for you.'

'I knew it!' Tina hissed. 'You're all the bloody same. I do it for you, you turn a blind eye to my past. *Quid pro* fucking *quo*.'

Latham smiled sadly and shook his head. 'I'm sorry to disappoint you, but I'm probably the most happily married man you've ever met. Just listen to what I have to say. Okay?'

Tina nodded. She looked around for an ashtray, but there wasn't one so she stubbed the cigarette out on the underside of the desk, grimacing apologetically. 'Okay,' she said.

'Your past precludes you from joining the Metropolitan Police as a normal entrant,' Latham continued. 'You can understand why. Suppose you had to arrest someone who knew you from your previous life? Suppose your past became public knowledge? Every case you'd ever worked on would be compromised. It wouldn't matter how good a police officer you were. All that would matter is that you used to be a prostitute. It would also leave you open to blackmail.'

'I know,' sighed Tina. 'I just hoped . . .' She left the sentence hanging.

'That it would remain a secret for ever?'

Tina nodded. 'Pretty naïve, yeah?'

Latham smiled thinly. 'Why did you apply to join the police, Tina? Of all the jobs that you could have done.'

'Like what? Serving in a shop? Waitressing?'

'There's nothing wrong with either of those jobs. You can't be afraid of hard work or you wouldn't have applied to join the Met. I've seen your CV, Tina. I've seen the jobs you've done to make a living and the courses you've taken to get the qualifications you never got at school.'

Tina shrugged.

'Why the police?' Latham asked again. 'Why not the army? The civil service? Nursing?'

'Because I want to help people like me. People who were shat on when they were kids.'

'So why didn't you become a social worker?'

'I want to make a difference. I want to help put away the bastards who break the rules. Who think it's okay to molest kids or steal from old ladies.' Tina rubbed the back of her neck with both hands. 'Why all these questions? You've already said that I can't join the police.'

'That's not what I said,' said Latham. 'I said you couldn't join as a uniformed constable, but there are other opportunities available to you within the force.'

'Washing up in the staff canteen?'

Latham gave her a frosty look. 'It's been obvious to us for some time that our undercover operations are being compromised more often than not. The reason for that is quite simple – villains, the good ones, can always spot a police officer, no matter how good their cover. Police officers all undergo the same training, and pretty much have the same experiences on the job. It's that shared experience that binds them together, but it also shapes them, it gives them a standard way of behaving, common mannerisms. They become a type.'

Tina nodded. 'We could always spot Vice on the streets,' she said. 'Stuck out like sore thumbs.' She grinned. 'Thumbs weren't the only things sticking out.'

For a moment Tina thought that the Assistant Commissioner was going to accuse her of flippancy again, but he smiled and nodded. 'Exactly,' he said. 'So what we want to do is to set up a unit of police officers who haven't been through the standard Hendon training. We need a special sort of undercover officer,' said Latham. 'We need people who have enough strength of character to work virtually alone, people who have enough, how shall I describe it . . . life experience . . . to cope with whatever gets thrown at them, and we need them with a background that isn't manufactured. A background that will stand up to any scrutiny.'

'Like a former prostitute?'

'While your background precludes you from serving as a regular officer, it's perfect for an undercover operative,' said Latham. 'The very same contacts that would damage you as a regular officer will be a major advantage in your role undercover.'

'Because no one would ever believe that the Met would hire a former prostitute?'

Latham nodded. 'I have to tell you, Tina, it won't be easy. Hardly anyone will know what you're doing; you won't be able to tell anyone, family or friends. So far as anyone will know, you'll be on the wrong side of the tracks.'

'What if anything went wrong?'

'You'd have back-up,' said Latham, 'but that's down the line. What I need now is your commitment to join the unit. Then your handler will take over.'

'Handler? You make me sound like a dog.' Tina grinned. 'How much does the job pay?'

'You'll be on the same rate of pay as an ordinary entrant. There'll be regular increases based on length of service and promotion, and overtime. But again, these are details to be worked out with your handler. My role is to demonstrate that your recruitment is desired at a very high level. The highest.'

'Does the Commissioner know?'

Latham frowned slightly. 'If you're asking officially, I'd have to say that you'd need to put a question of that nature to the Commissioner's office. Unofficially, I'd say that I wouldn't be here if I didn't have his approval. I'm certainly not a maverick.'

Tina reached over and picked up her pack of cigarettes. She toyed with it, running her fingers down the pack, standing it on each side in turn. She took a deep breath. 'Okay,' she said. 'I'm in.'

Latham beamed. 'Good. That's very good, Tina.'

'What happens now?' she asked.

'You go home. Someone will be in touch.' He pushed back his chair and held out his hand. 'I doubt that we'll meet again, but I will be watching your progress with great interest, Tina.'

Tina shook his hand. It was smooth and dry with an inner strength that suggested he could crush her if he wanted.

It was a familiar sensation, and Tina struggled to remember what it reminded her of.

It was only when she was in the lift heading back to the car park that she remembered. One of her first customers had been an obese man with horn-rimmed spectacles with thick lenses who wheezed at the slightest exertion. He'd wanted to take her home, and at first Tina had refused because all the girls on the street where she worked had told her that she was safer staying in the punter's car, but he'd offered her more money and eventually she'd given up and gone with him, only after insisting that he paid up front.

Home was a two-up, two-down house in East London with stained carpets and bare light bulbs in the light fittings. He'd shown Tina into his front room and stood at the doorway, wheezing as he watched her reaction to the dozens of glass tanks that lined the walls. In the tanks were snakes. All sorts of snakes. Big ones coiled up like lengths of hosepipe, small ones that dangled from bare twigs, some asleep, others watching her intently with cold black unfeeling eyes, their tongues flicking in and out.

The man made Tina give him a blow job in the middle of the room, and he stood there wheezing as she went down on her knees in front of him, her eyes shut tight as she tried to blot out the image of the watching snakes.

Afterwards, after she'd wrapped the used condom in a tissue and tossed it under one of the tanks, he'd taken out a large python and made her stroke it. At first she'd refused, but then he promised to give her an extra twenty quid so she touched it, gingerly at first. When she realised it wasn't going to hurt her she became more confident and ran her hands down its back. She'd thought it might be wet and slimy but it was cool and dry and she could feel how strong it was, how easily it could crush the life out of her if it should ever coil itself around her. The punter had got all excited at the sight of Tina caressing the snake and had offered her money for some really weird stuff, stuff that Tina didn't like to think about, and she'd rushed out of the house without the twenty pounds he'd promised. Tina shivered at the memory and groped for her cigarettes.

Assistant Commissioner Latham paced up and down in front of the window. 'I'm still not convinced that we're doing the right thing here,' he said.

Gregg Hathaway unhooked the clock from the wall and

placed it on the table. 'Morally, you mean?' Hathaway was wearing a dark brown leather jacket, blue jeans and scuffed brown Timberland boots. He had a slight limp, favouring his left leg when he walked.

Latham gave Hathaway a cold look. 'I was referring to their training and handling,' he said.

Hathaway shrugged carelessly. 'It's not really my place to query operational decisions,' he said. 'I leave that up to my masters.' He was a short man, thought Latham: even if he didn't have the limp, he wouldn't have been allowed to join the Met. He was well below the Met's height requirements, even though they'd been drastically lowered so as not to exclude Asians. The intelligence services clearly had different criteria when it came to recruiting, and there was no doubting Hathaway's intelligence.

'They applied to join the police, not MI6,' said Latham.

Hathaway went back to the wall and pulled out a length of wire that had been connected to the small camera in the centre of the clock. The wire led through the wall and up into the ceiling to the video monitor on the floor above, from where Hathaway had watched all three interviews. Latham had been upstairs to check that there was no video recording equipment. Under no circumstances was there to be any record of what had gone on in the office, either on tape or on paper. Officially, the three interviews hadn't taken place. Latham's diary would show that he was in a private meeting with the Commissioner.

'I suppose you do get a different sort of applicant than we do at Six,' said Hathaway, coiling up the wire and placing it on top of the clock. 'They've been trying to widen the intake, but it's still mainly Oxbridge graduates that get in. Wouldn't get the likes of Cliff Warren applying. Fullerton maybe.'

'I suppose so. How do you think they'll do?'

Hathaway ran a hand through his thinning sandy hair. 'You can never tell. Not until they go undercover. Fullerton's a bit cocky, but that's no bad thing. Warren's probably the most stable of the three, but he's not been put under pressure yet. The girl's interesting.'

'Interesting?'

'She worked hard to get away from the life she had. Now we're going to send her back. I'm not sure how she'll cope with that. I was surprised that she agreed.'

'I'm not sure that she had much choice.' Latham looked at his watch. His driver was already waiting in the car park downstairs and there was no reason for the Assistant Commissioner still to be in the office. No reason other than the fact that he still had misgivings about what he was doing.

Hathaway put the clock and the wire into an aluminium briefcase and snapped shut the lid. 'Right, that's me, then.' He swung the briefcase off the table.

'Take care of them,' said Latham.

'I haven't lost an agent yet,' said Hathaway.

'I mean it,' said Latham. 'I know they're not my responsibility, but that doesn't mean I'm washing my hands of them.'

Hathaway looked as if he might say something, but then he nodded curtly and limped out of the room.

Latham turned and looked out of the window. He had a nagging feeling that he'd done something wrong, that in some way he'd betrayed the three individuals who'd been brought to see him. He'd lied to them, there was no doubt about that, but had he betrayed them? And if he had, did it matter in the grand scheme of things? Or did the ends justify the means? He looked at his watch again. It was time to go.

Tina wound down the window and flicked ash out. Some of it blew back into the car and she brushed it off the seat. 'Sorry,' she said to the driver.

He flashed her a grin in the rear-view mirror. 'Doesn't matter to me, miss,' he said. 'First of all, I'm a forty-a-day man myself. Second of all, it's not my car.'

'You work for the police, right?'

'Contract,' said the driver. 'Former army, me. Did my twenty years and then they said my services were no longer required.'

Tina took another long pull on her cigarette. 'Do you want one?' she asked, proffering the pack.

The driver shook his head. 'Not while I'm driving, miss. You know what the cops are like. They did that sales rep a while back for driving with a sandwich on his seat.'

'Yeah. It was in all the papers, wasn't it? You'd think they'd have better things to do with their time, right?'

The driver nodded. 'You'd think so. Mind you, army's pretty much the same. It'd all go a lot more smoothly if there was no bloody officers, pardon my language.'

Tina smiled and settled back in the seat. 'You know what that was about, back there?' she asked.

'No, miss. We're mushrooms. Keep us in the dark . . .'

'And feed you bullshit. Yeah, you said.'

'It's got to be important if they're using us, that much I can tell you. Our company isn't cheap.'

Tina closed her eyes and let the breeze from the open window play over her face. She wondered who would contact her. Her handler, Assistant Commissioner Latham had said. No name. No description. Her handler. It had the same echoes as pimp, and Tina had always refused to have anything to do with pimps. When she'd worked the streets, she'd worked them alone, even though a pimp offered protection. So far as Tina was concerned, pimps were leeches, and she'd despised the girls she'd seen handing over their hard-earned money to smooth black guys in big cars with deafening stereo systems. Now Tina was getting her own handler. The more she thought about it, the less comfortable she was with the idea, but when doubts did threaten to overwhelm her, she thought back to Assistant Commissioner Latham, with his ramrod straight back and his firm handshake and his immaculate uniform. He was a man she could trust, of that much she was sure. And he was right: there was no way she could have expected to serve as a regular police officer, not with her past. Try as she might to conceal what she'd once been, it was bound to come back to haunt her one day. At least this way she was being up front about her past, using it as an asset rather than fearing it as the dirty secret that would one day destroy her career. But could she really do what Latham had asked? Go back into the world she'd escaped from and work against it? She shivered and opened her eyes. Maybe that was exactly what she had been working towards her whole life. Maybe that was the way of vindicating herself. If she could use her past, use it constructively, then maybe it had all been worth it. Her cigarette had burned down to the filter and she flicked it out of the open window.

The Vectra turned into the road where Tina lived and the driver pulled up in front of the three-storey terraced house. 'Here we are, miss,' he said, twisting around in his seat.

Tina jerked out of her reverie. 'Oh, right. Cheers, thanks.' She put her hand into her handbag. 'I suppose I should . . .'

He waved her offer of a tip away with a shovel-sized hand. 'It's all taken care of, miss. You take care, hear?'

Tina nodded and got out of the car. She stared up at the house as the Vectra drove away. The paint on the door and windows was weathered and peeling and the roof was missing several slates. One of the windows on the top floor was covered with yellowing newspapers. An old woman lived there, so Tina had been told, but she'd never seen anyone going in or out.

She unlocked the front door and pushed it closed behind her. The door was warped and the lock didn't click shut unless it was given a hard push. The area had more than its fair share of opportunistic thieves wandering around looking for an opportunity to pay for their next fix. The hallway smelt of damp and the flowery wallpaper was peeling away from the corner over the door. Tina's flat was on the ground floor, tucked away at the back. It had originally been the kitchen and scullery of the house, but the developer had managed to cram a small bedroom, a poky sitting room and a kitchenette and bathroom into the space. There was barely enough room to swing a cat, but as Tina would joke with the few friends she'd had around, she was allergic to cats anyway.

She let herself into her flat and kicked off her clunky black shoes, tossing her handbag on to the sagging sofa by the window. Latham hadn't told her when her handler would get in touch, or how. Did that mean she was to wait in until he called? They had her mobile number so maybe he'd phone. Tina realised that she was already thinking of her handler as a 'he', but it could just as easily be a woman.

She went through to her cramped bathroom and ran herself a bath as she wiped off her make-up. She poured in a good slug of bath salts, lit a perfumed candle, and soaked for the best part of half an hour. After she'd towelled herself dry she dressed carelessly, throwing on an old pair of jeans and a baggy sweater, and tied her hair back with an elastic band.

She padded into the kitchenette and switched on the electric kettle, then swore out loud as she remembered that she'd intended to buy milk on the way home. She opened the fridge in the vain hope that there might be a splash of milk left in the carton, then jumped as her doorbell rang.

She rushed out into the hallway and opened the front door. A short man in a brown leather jacket was standing on the doorstep. He ran a hand across his thinning hair. In his other hand was a black laptop computer case. 'Christina Leigh,' he said, a statement of fact rather than a question.

'Yes?' she said, frowning.

'Gregg Hathaway. You're expecting me, right?' he asked.

Warren heard the wail of an ambulance siren as he got out of the Vectra and headed down Craven Park Road towards his house. He didn't want his neighbours to see the car or the driver. The noise barely registered with Warren as he walked through the crowds of shoppers. Sirens – be they police, ambulance or fire engines – were an all too regular occurrence in Harlesden. He turned left and saw that his street had been closed off midway with lines of blue and white tape. Three police cars had been parked haphazardly, their doors open and blue lights flashing.

In the middle of the road a man and a woman dressed in white overalls were studying a red smear and what looked like a pool of vomit, and a man in a sheepskin jacket was drawing chalk circles around several cartridge cases.

There was a gap in the police tape along the pavement, so Warren went over to the overweight uniformed constable who was guarding it. He nodded down the road. 'Okay if I go on through?' he asked. 'I live in number sixty-eight.'

'Sorry, sir, this is a crime scene. You'll have to go back to the main road and cut through Charlton Road.' The officer was in his forties with chubby face and a drinker's nose.

Warren pointed down the road. 'But that's my house there.'

'Nothing I can do, sir. This is a crime scene.'

Warren nodded at the two SOCO officers. 'No, that's the crime scene over there. This is the pavement, and that's my house. All I'm asking is that you let me walk along the pavement to my house.'

The constable folded his arms across his chest and tilted his head back. 'I'm not arguing with you, sir,' he said, stretching out the 'sir' to leave Warren in no doubt that civility was the last thing on the officer's mind. 'You'll have to go back the way you came. You must be used to shootings by now, living here. You should know the procedure.'

Warren stared at the officer, who slowly reached for the radio receiver that was clipped to his jacket.

'Not going to give me a problem are you, sir?' he said, his eyes hardening. 'Obstructing a police officer, disorderly conduct, threatening behaviour, there's a million and one reasons why I could have you taken back to the station right now. So why don't you be a good lad and head off back to the main road like I said.'

Warren exhaled slowly. Two uniformed officers were walking towards one of the cars, deep in conversation. One was an inspector. Warren looked at the inspector and then back to the constable. He considered registering a complaint but dismissed the idea. There was no point. The constable continued to stare at Warren contemptuously. Warren forced a grin and winked. 'You have a nice day, yeah?' he said and walked away.

Warren's heart was pounding, but the only visible sign of his anger was the clenching and unclenching of his hands. He would have liked to have confronted the officer, at the very least to have hit back verbally, but he'd long ago learned that such confrontations with authority were pointless. There was nothing he could say or do that would change the way the man behaved. It was best just to smile and walk away, although knowing that didn't make it any easier to swallow.

Three Jamaican teenagers were huddled outside a newsagent's, wrapped up in gunmetal-grey Puffa jackets with gleaming new Nikes on their feet. Warren nodded at the tallest of the youths. 'What's the story, PM?'

PM shrugged carelessly and scratched the end of his nose. His real name was Tony Blair and he'd been given the nickname the day that his namesake was elected to Number 10. A scar stretched from his left ear to halfway across his cheek, a souvenir of a run-in with a group of white football supporters a few years earlier. 'Jimmy T. took a couple of slugs in the back. Should have seen him run, Bunny. Like the fucking wind. Almost made it.'

Warren shook his head sadly. Jimmy T. was a fifteen-year-old runner for one of the area's crack cocaine gangs.

'He okay?'

'He look dead as dead can be.'

'Shit.'

'Shit happens,' said PM. 'Specially to short-changers.'

'That what he did?'

'Word is.'

Warren gestured with his chin over at the police investigators. 'You told the Feds?'

PM guffawed and slapped his thigh. 'Sure, man. Told 'em who killed Stephen Lawrence while I was at it.'

All three youths laughed and Warren nodded glumly. Shootings were a regular occurrence in Harlesden, but witnesses were rarer than Conservative Party canvassers at election time.

'You saw who did it?'

'Got eyes.'

Warren looked expectantly at PM. The teenager laughed out loud but his eyes were unsmiling.

'Shit, man, I could tell you but then I'd have to kill you.'

Warren smiled despite himself. He wondered how much PM would have told him if he'd been standing there in a police constable's uniform.

'You look wound up, Bunny-man. You want some puff?'

'Nah, I'm sorted. Gotta get back to the house.'

'You got a chauffeur, Bunny?'

Warren kept smiling but he could feel his heart start to race. PM couldn't have seen him getting out of the Vectra, so someone must have seen the car picking him up from his house that morning. 'Minicab,' he said.

'Anywhere interesting?'

Warren chuckled at the question. 'Yeah, PM. I could tell you . . .' He left the sentence unfinished.

PM guffawed. 'Yeah, but you'd have to kill me,' he said, nodding his head as if to emphasise each word.

Warren made a gun from his right hand and mimed shooting PM in the chest. 'You take care, PM.'

'Back at you, Bunny-man,' laughed PM.

Warren headed back to the main road, his head down, deep in thought. He was still annoyed at the attitude of the uniformed constable, and he wondered if the man would have treated him any differently if he knew that Warren was also a policeman. Maybe he would have been more civil, thought Warren, cracked a joke perhaps, but it wouldn't have changed the way the man thought about him. The constable's contempt might have been hidden but it would have still been there. He would see the uniform, but it was Warren's colour that would determine the way he behaved.

PM would react to the uniform, not to Warren's race. If he'd known that Warren was a police officer, there would have been no chat, no banter, just hostile stares and a tight face. His type closed ranks against authority, the authority of the white man.

Warren lost out either way.

Warren sighed. He'd wanted to join the Met because he believed that he could make a difference, but Latham had been right: he'd do more good by playing to his strengths, rather than trying to fit into the established system. On the street, undercover, his colour would be a strength. Trapped inside the uniform, it would be a weakness. Could he spend his career hanging around the likes of PM and his posse, though, pretending to be one of them so that he could betray them?

Warren felt confused, and the more he tried to work out how he felt, the more confused he became. While he'd been sitting opposite Latham in the office, it had all seemed so simple; but on the streets of Harlesden, what the senior police officer had proposed looked less attractive. It meant living a lie. It meant betrayal. Being a police officer was about being a part of a team; working with colleagues you could rely on, working towards a common aim, Us against Them. Latham wanted Warren to be one of Them.

Warren shook his head as he walked. No, Latham didn't want him to be one of Them. He wanted Warren to be in a no-man's land; part of the police force but separate from it, part of the criminal community but there to betray it. A lone wolf.

Jamie Fullerton tossed his suit on to the bed, ripped off his shirt and tie and started doing vigorous press-ups. He breathed deeply and evenly as he pumped up and down, pausing every tenth dip and holding himself an inch above the bedroom carpet before resuming his rhythm.

The doorbell rang and Fullerton froze, his torso parallel to the floor, his arms trembling under the strain. Fullerton frowned. He wasn't expecting anyone. He pushed himself to his feet and pulled on his trousers and buckled the belt. He hurriedly put on his shirt and fastened the buttons as he walked to the front door.

The man who'd rung his bell was almost a head shorter than Fullerton with thinning brown hair, a squarish chin and thin, unsmiling lips. He was carrying a laptop computer in a black shoulder bag. 'Jamie Fullerton?' he said.

'Maybe,' said Fullerton.

The man extended his right hand. 'Gregg Hathaway. You're expecting me.'

Fullerton shook Hathaway's hand. The man had a weak handshake and his fingers barely touched Fullerton's skin, as if he were uneasy with physical contact. Fullerton squeezed the hand hard and felt a tingle of satisfaction when he felt Hathaway try to pull away. He gave the hand a final squeeze before releasing his grip. 'Come on in,' said Fullerton.

He stepped to the side and smiled as Hathaway walked by, rubbing his right hand against his jeans. There was something awkward about his right leg, as if it were an effort for Hathaway to move it.

'You don't mind showing me some form of ID, do you?' asked Fullerton as he closed the front door and followed Hathaway into the sitting room.

Hathaway had put his laptop case on the coffee table and was examining the books that filled the shelves on one wall of the room. He turned to look at Fullerton. 'Your name is James Robert Fullerton, you were born on April fifteenth twenty-six years ago, your parents are Eric and Sylvia, your father committed suicide after he lost the bulk of your family's assets in a series of badly advised stock market investments and your mother is confined to a mental hospital outside Edinburgh.'

Fullerton swallowed but his throat had gone so dry that his tongue felt twice its normal size and he started to cough.

'Is that enough, or shall I go on?'

Fullerton nodded. 'You don't look like you're in the job.'

'Neither do you. That's the point. Black with two sugars.'

Fullerton frowned. 'Sorry?'

'You were going to offer me a coffee, right? Black with two sugars.'

'Right. Okay,' said Fullerton. It was only when he was in the kitchen filling the kettle that he realised how quickly Hathaway had taken control of the situation. The man was physically smaller than Fullerton, maybe a decade older, but with none of the bearing or presence that Latham had shown. Underneath the softer exterior, however, there was a toughness that suggested he was used to being obeyed.

By the time he returned to the sitting room with two mugs of coffee on a tray, Hathaway had powered up his laptop and was sitting on the sofa, tapping on the keyboard. He'd extended his right leg under the coffee table, as if it troubled him less when it was straight. He'd run a phone line from the back of the computer to the phone socket by the window.

'You computer literate, Jamie?' said Hathaway, slipping off his leather jacket and draping it over the back of the sofa.

'I guess so,' said Fullerton. He held the tray out, and Hathaway helped himself to the black coffee. 'You're the handler, right?'

'Handler suggests physical contact,' said Hathaway. 'Ideally we won't ever meet again after today.' He gestured at the laptop. 'This is a safer way of keeping in touch.'

Fullerton sat down in an easy chair and put his coffee on the table by the laptop.

'And you'll be handling the others?'

'The others?' said Hathaway, frowning.

'The other members of the team.'

Hathaway's frown deepened. 'Team? What team?'

'I just thought . . .' Fullerton left the sentence hanging.

Hathaway pushed the computer away and sat back, looking at Fullerton through slightly narrowed eyes. 'You do understand what's being asked of you, Jamie?'

'Undercover work,' said Fullerton. 'Deep undercover. Longterm penetration of criminal gangs.'

Hathaway nodded slowly. 'That's right, but not as part of a team. You'll be working alone. You'll have online access to me, and an emergency number to call if you're in trouble. If necessary we'll send a shedload of people to pull you out, but while you're undercover you're on your own.'

'Okay. Got it.' Fullerton ran his hand through his fringe, brushing his hair out of his eyes. 'But what I don't get is Latham's insistence that we don't get any training. What about firearms? Anti-surveillance techniques? Things like that?'

'You watch gangster movies, Jamie?'

Fullerton was nonplussed by the apparent change of subject, but he nodded.

'See how the bad guys hold their guns? One handed, waving them around, grips parallel to the ground? Half the gang-bangers in Brixton hold them that way now. Couldn't hit a barn door, but they see it in the movies so that's what they do. Okay, so I put you through a police firearms course. We'd teach you to shoot with both hands, feet shoulder width apart, sighting with your stronger eye, exhaling before pulling the trigger, blah, blah, blah. You'd hit the target every time at twenty-five yards, but first time you ever use a weapon in anger you might as well have a flashing neon sign over your head saying "COP". Any techniques we give you will identify you as a police officer.'

'Okay, but what about anti-surveillance? What's the harm in teaching me how to shake a tail?'

Hathaway grinned. 'You've been reading too many cheap spy novels, Jamie.'

Fullerton felt his cheeks flush red and he sat back in his chair, crossing his arms defensively.

'If anyone follows you, it's best you deal with them in whatever way you come up with yourself,' continued Hathaway. 'Use your instincts.'

Fullerton nodded. What Hathaway was saying made sense, but there was an obvious flaw to his argument. 'What if I'm on my way to see you? If I can't shake them, that puts you at risk.'

Hathaway tapped the laptop screen. 'Like I said, that's what this is for,' he said. 'We won't be meeting face to face. All contact will be online.'

'But my cover,' said Fullerton. 'You'll be giving me my cover, right?'

'I'm going to help you with that, of course, but basically we'll be sticking to your true background.'

Fullerton grinned. 'And that includes the drugs, yeah?'

'Sure,' said Hathaway. 'One of the things that trips up a lot of undercover agents is that they can't touch drugs. No court is going to convict if one of the investigating officers turns out to have smoked a joint or snorted a line. You're in a different league. You do whatever comes naturally, and if that involves getting high, then that's up to you.'

'Okay if I do a line now?' Fullerton asked.

Hathaway flashed him a humourless smile. 'I'd rather you didn't.'

'I was joking,' said Fullerton. He could see from the look on Hathaway's face that they didn't share the same sense of humour. 'But won't my drug-taking affect the cases I'll be working on?'

'In what way?'

'Won't my evidence be tainted?'

'No, for a very simple reason. You won't ever be required to give evidence in court. You'll be supplying us with information and leads which will be passed on to the appropriate investigating teams, but it will be up to them to supply the evidence to convict.'

Fullerton picked up his mug of coffee and sipped it slowly. 'So I'm getting official permission to snort coke? Funny old world, isn't it?'

'There's nothing official about this briefing, Jamie,' said Hathaway. 'From the moment you agreed to Assistant Commissioner Latham's proposal, everything has been off the record.'

Fullerton's lips tightened and he put the mug back on the coffee table. 'That's what I figured,' he said. 'Nothing in writing, nothing on file.'

'It's for your own protection, Jamie,' said Hathaway. 'The Met still has more than its fair share of bad apples.'

'Is that going to be part of my brief, too? Corrupt cops?'

'Absolutely,' said Hathaway.

'And will you be giving me specific targets?'

Hathaway smiled. 'You're getting ahead of me, Jamie, but yes, we will be asking for you to look at specific targets. Tangos, as we call them.' There was a document pouch on the side of the laptop case, sealed with Velcro. It made a ripping sound as Hathaway opened it. He took out a large glossy colour photograph and slid it across the coffee table to Fullerton.

'Meet Dennis Donovan. Tango One.'

Cliff Warren picked up the photograph and studied it. It was a man in his mid to late thirties. He had a square face with a strong chin, pale green eyes and a sprinkling of freckles across a broken nose. The man's chestnut-brown hair was windswept, brushed carelessly across his forehead. 'Tango?' he said.

'Tango is how we designate our targets,' explained Hathaway. 'Dennis Donovan is Tango One. Our most wanted target.'

'Drugs?' said Warren.

'One of the country's biggest importers of marijuana and cocaine. Virtually untouchable by conventional methods. He's so big that we can't get near him. Den Donovan never goes near a shipment and never handles the money. He never deals with anyone he doesn't know.'

'And you expect me to get close to him?' said Warren, bemused. He passed the photograph back to Hathaway. 'Unless you haven't noticed, I'm black. Donovan's white. It's not like we went to the same school, is it? Why's he gonna let me get close to him?'

'We don't expect it to happen overnight,' said Hathaway. 'Donovan is a longterm project. He's not even in the country at the moment. Most of the time he's in the Caribbean. I'll supply you with details of his known associates, and as you go deeper all you have to do is keep an eye out for them. It's going to take time, Cliff. Years. You build up contacts with his associates, and use them to put you next to Donovan.'

'You make it sound easy,' said Warren.

A police car sped down the road outside the house, siren wailing.

'Not easy, but possible. Donovan is a major supplier, you'll be a dealer.'

'You said he didn't go near the gear.'

'He doesn't, but if you can get into his inner circle we

can get him on conspiracy. He's also been shipping drugs into the States. If we can tie up to a US delivery, the Americans will put him away for life.'

Warren raised his eyebrows. 'I'm working for the Met, right? How does that involve Yanks?'

'There's no national barriers when it comes to drugs, Cliff. It's way too big a business for that. They reckon that every year some three hundred billion dollars of illegal money gets laundered through the world banking system, and almost all of it is from drugs. Three hundred billion dollars, Warren. Think about that. No one agency can fight that sort of money. In the States the market for illegal drugs is worth sixty billion dollars a year. In the UK about five billion pounds is spent on heroin, cocaine, marijuana, amphetamines and ecstasy. The drug suppliers are working together, so the anti-drug agencies are having to share their resources.'

'So I might end up working for the DEA?'

'With rather than for,' said Hathaway. 'It'll be more a question of sharing intelligence.'

'So they won't know who I am?'

'No one will know you're undercover, except me. And Latham.'

Warren frowned. 'But what if I come across other undercover agents? Won't they report back on me?'

'Sure, but all they'll report on is your criminal activity. That's just going to add to your cover.'

'Do I report on them?'

'You report on everything.' He patted the laptop computer in front of him. 'That's what this is for. Everyone you meet, everything you hear, everything you do, you e-mail to me. You supply the intelligence, I process it and, if necessary, act on it.'

Warren gestured at the photograph. 'This Donovan, why's he so important?'

'Because he's big. Responsible for maybe a third of all the cocaine that comes into this country. If we take him out, we reduce the amount on the streets.'

'You reckon?' said Warren. 'All you'll do is push up the street price for a while. Take out Donovan and someone else will move in to fill the gap. That's how it works. Supply and demand.'

'So we take out Donovan, then there'll be a new Tango One and we'll take him out, too. And we keep on going.'

Warren sighed. 'It's not a war we can win.'

'Putting murderers in prison doesn't mean that murders won't continue to happen,' said Hathaway, 'but murderers still belong behind bars. Same goes for men like Donovan. Not having second thoughts, are you?'

Warren shook his head fiercely. 'I only have to look out of the window to see the damage drugs do. But I know how it works in the real world, Gregg. You put a dealer behind bars, there's half a dozen want to take over his customers. Clamp down on the supply and the price goes up, so there's more crime as the addicts raise the extra cash they need. More break-ins, more muggings.'

'We're not interested in the guys on the street,' said Hathaway. 'We're after the big fish. Guys like Dennis Donovan. Put Donovan behind bars and it will make a difference, I can promise you that.'

Warren reached over and picked up the photograph of Donovan again. He looked more like a footballer reaching the end of his career than a hardened criminal.

'He's thirty-four years old, married with a six-year-old

son. Wife is Vicky. She's twenty-seven. They've got a house in Kensington, but Donovan spends most of his time in the Caribbean.'

'Are they separated?' asked Warren.

'No, it's just easier for him to operate out there. He was under round-the-clock surveillance here – Customs, police, the taxman. Couldn't take a leak without someone recording the fact. His kid's settled in school and his wife likes shopping, so they've resisted moving out there. Donovan's over here every month or so and they spend all their holidays in the sun, so it seems to be working out okay.'

'Is he still under the microscope?'

'Sure, but it's more to keep the pressure on him than it is to catch him in the act.'

Warren wrinkled his nose. 'Why do you think I'm going to do any better than the teams who've already been targeting him?'

'Because you won't be watching him, Cliff. You'll be working for him, ideally.'

'And just how do I get to him?'

'You start dealing.' Hathaway nodded at the window. 'Most of the crack cocaine sold in the streets out there can be traced to Donovan if you go back far enough.'

'If you know that, why don't you arrest him?'

'Knowing and proving are two very different things, Cliff.'

'So the idea is for me to work my way up the supply chain until I get to Donovan?'

'That's the plan.'

'That's not a plan,' said Warren. 'That's a wish. A hope. It's what you do when you get the biggest piece of turkey wishbone, that's what that is.'

Hathaway leaned forward. 'It's what'll happen in an ideal world. But even if you don't get close to Donovan, you'll still be supplying us with useful intelligence. Whatever you do, wherever you end up, you keep your eyes and ears open for news about this man. Tango One.'

Tina Leigh ran both hands through her hair, brushing the strands behind her ears. 'I'm not a criminal. Why's Donovan going to be interested in me?'

Hathaway looked away, awkwardly.

'I'm his type, is that it?'

'You're a very sexy girl, Tina.'

Tina glared at him, 'Go screw yourself.'

'Give me a chance to explain, Tina. Please.'

'You don't need to explain. I used to be a hooker, so now I'll just lie back and spread my legs for a gangster. Well, fuck you, Hathaway. I worked my balls off to put that behind me. I ain't going back for you or anyone.'

She stood up and Hathaway put his hands up in front of his face as if he feared she might attack him. 'That's not what I said. And that's not what I meant.'

'I know exactly what you meant. I can't join the Met because I worked the streets, but I'm being given official approval to sleep with a gangster. How fucking hypocritical is that?'

'I didn't say you had to sleep with him, Tina.' He waved at her chair. 'Please sit down and hear me out.'

Tina raised her right hand to her mouth and bit down on the knuckle of her first finger, hard enough to feel the bone beneath the skin. She wanted to throw Hathaway out of her flat, she wanted to yell and scream and call him every name under the sun, but she brought her anger under control. 'Okay,' she said. She sat down and crossed her legs, lit a cigarette, the third since Hathaway had arrived, and waited for him to continue.

'Donovan's out of the country most of the time, but he comes back regularly on flying visits. When he does come back, we know of several clubs that he frequents. We'd like you to apply for a job, whatever job you think you'd be suitable for. Once you're employed, we'd want you to keep your ears open. You pass on anything you hear. And if you can get near Donovan, that'll be the icing on the cake.'

'These clubs? What sort of clubs are they?'

Hathaway pulled a pained face again. 'They're sort of executive entertainment bars . . .' He tailed off as Tina's face hardened.

'Lap dancing clubs?' she hissed. 'You want me to be a fucking lap dancer?'

'Lap dancing isn't prostitution,' said Hathaway. 'Students do it to work their way through college, single mothers do it, it's totally legal and above board.'

Tina took a long pull on her cigarette and blew smoke at Hathaway. He looked uncomfortable but didn't say anything.

'I don't believe this. I don't fucking believe this.'

Still Hathaway said nothing.

'It's not much of a plan, is it? Putting me undercover in a lap-dancing bar in the hope that Donovan wanders in and spills his guts.'

'Give us some credit, Tina.'

'Why should I give you any credit at all? You say you know who this guy is and what he's doing. Why can't you put him away yourself?'

'Knowing and proving are two different things, Tina.'

'I thought with new technology and stuff there was no way anyone could hide any more.'

Hathaway nodded. 'You're right. We can tap his phones, we can watch him from CCTV, from satellites even. We have his DNA and fingerprints on file, we know almost everything there is to know about Dennis Donovan, but we can't catch him in the act. And if we stick to using traditional methods, we probably won't.'

'See, that doesn't make sense to me. How can he operate if you've got him under surveillance?' She flicked ash into an ashtray shaped like a four-leafed clover.

'Because at the level Donovan operates, it's all about contacts. It's not as if he hands over a briefcase of cash and picks up a bag of drugs. He has a conversation with a Colombian. Face to face. On a beach maybe. Or walking down a street. Somewhere he can't be overheard. Then he talks to a shipping guy. Probably a guy he's used a dozen times before. Then money gets transferred from a bank in the Cayman Islands to a bank in Switzerland and the Colombian puts the drugs on a ship and the ship sets sail. Donovan flies to Amsterdam and has another meeting with a couple of guys from Dublin and money is transferred between two other bank accounts and the drugs are unloaded on the south coast of Ireland and driven up to Belfast and on to a ferry to the UK. We put him under the microscope and what do we have? Donovan chatting to his friends, that's what we have. And even if we could hear what he was saying, he'd be talking in code. It wouldn't mean a thing to a court.'

'So the plan is he's going to open his heart to me when he sees me dancing around a silver pole? Just as a matter of interest, Gregg, is there a Plan B?'

Hathaway chuckled and leaned back, putting his hands behind his neck and stretching out. 'You're right to be suspicious, Tina, but we have thought this through. This is long term. Years rather than months. If we put you undercover now, you might not get to meet Donovan for two years. Three. But the pool he swims in isn't that big and I have no doubt at all that you'll come across his associates if not the man himself. And they're going to open up to you because you're a pretty girl.' He held up a hand heading off her attempt to interrupt him. 'I'm stating that as a fact, Tina, I'm not trying to soft soap you. Put guys together with booze and pretty girls and tongues start to loosen. These guys work under such secrecy that often they're bursting to tell someone. To boast. To show what big men they are.'

Tina had smoked the cigarette down to the filter and she stubbed it out in the ashtray. She took another and lit it. She offered the pack to Hathaway but he shook his head. 'Let's suppose I agree to do this,' she said. 'What happens to the money?'

Hathaway looked confused. 'What money?'

'I'll be a police officer, right? On standard pay and conditions?'

Hathaway nodded.

'But if I'm working in a – what was it you called it – an executive entertainment bar? If I'm working there, I'll get wages. And tips.'

'Yours to keep.'

Tina blew smoke up at the ceiling, a slight smile on her lips. 'Do you know how much those girls earn?' she asked.

'Sixty, seventy grand. Sometimes more.'

'Yeah,' said Tina. 'That sounds about right. And I get to keep it, yeah?'

'Every penny.'

Jamie Fullerton's jaw dropped. 'Let me get this straight,' he said. 'Any money I make from illegal activities is mine to keep?'

'It has to be that way,' said Hathaway. 'Believe me, the powers that be aren't happy with the idea, but we don't have any choice.'

'And I won't ever be asked to pay the money back?'

'I don't see how that could ever happen.'

Fullerton stood up and paced around the sitting room. 'And you're going to set me up in this new life? Make me look like a criminal?'

'Initially. Hopefully you'll become self-funding quite quickly.' Hathaway waved at the section of bookshelves devoted to art. 'You studied art history at university. Got a first, right?'

Fullerton nodded.

'So we'll build on that. Set you up in a gallery. Give you some works of art to get you started. And we'll put some stolen works your way. To add authenticity.'

Fullerton's eyes widened in astonishment. 'You're going to give me stolen paintings? To sell? And I get to keep the money?'

Hathaway wiped his forehead with his hand. He looked uncomfortable and when he spoke he chose his words carefully. 'What we will be doing is establishing your cover, Jamie. This isn't a game. If Donovan, or anyone else for that matter, discovers who you are or what you're doing, your life will be on the line.'

Fullerton nodded. 'I understand, but how does me being an art dealer get me close to Donovan?'

'He's an art freak. A bit of a collector, but he appears to be more interested in visiting galleries. He also uses galleries and museums as meeting points. What we're suggesting is that you establish a small gallery, then start moving into the drugs business. You presumably have your own suppliers?'

'Sure.'

'So start with them. Start increasing the quantities you buy from them, then move up the chain.'

'And then you bust them?'

Hathaway shrugged. 'That depends. We're after the big fish, Jamie, not street dealers. Not everyone you tell us about is going to be brought in, but all the information you give us will go on file. You just keep working towards Donovan.'

Fullerton sat down. 'How do you know this will work?'

'We don't. It's a new strategy.'

'It's a gamble, that's what it is.'

'Maybe,' Hathaway conceded.

'You're gambling with our lives.'

Hathaway frowned. 'Our? What do you mean?'

'I'm assuming I'm not the only agent you're sending undercover. You don't strike me as the type who'd put all his eggs in one basket.'

Eventually Hathaway nodded slowly. 'Don't assume anything, Jamie. Don't go into this thinking that there'll be other undercover agents who'll pull your nuts out of the fire if anything goes wrong. You can't trust anyone. Is it a risk? Of course. But the uniformed bobby walking the beat puts his life at risk every day. He never knows when a drunk's going to try to hit him with a bottle or a drug addict's going to stick him with an HIV-infected needle. In a way, you'll be in a better position, because you'll know the dangers you're facing.'

Fullerton exhaled deeply. 'Have you ever done it?' he asked. 'Gone undercover?'

Hathaway nodded. 'Several times, but never long term. A few months at most.'

'What's it like?'

'It means living a lie. It means developing a second personality that has to become more real than your own. Everything you say and do has to be filtered through the person you're pretending to be. It means never being able to relax, never being able to let your guard down.'

'That's what I thought.'

'But you'll be in a slightly different position. When I was working undercover, I was pretending to be a villain. You'll be the real thing.'

Cliff Warren stood up and walked through to his kitchen. 'Do you want a beer?' he asked over his shoulder.

'Thanks,' said Hathaway.

Warren opened his fridge door and took out two bottles of Sol. They clinked bottles and Warren sat down again. 'What happens if I get arrested?' he asked.

'It's up to you, but once you've revealed to anybody that you're undercover, you're of no further use.'

'But if I get pulled in on drugs charges, I could be facing a long prison sentence.'

Hathaway nodded. 'You could indeed.' He drank from the bottle but his eyes never left Warren's face.

'So what do I do?'

'You could go through the system and serve your time. If that's what you were prepared to do. It would do wonders for your cover, Cliff.'

Warren sat stunned as the ramifications of what Hathaway was proposing sank in. 'You'd expect me to serve time?'

'It'd be your call, Cliff. No one would force you. At any point you can ask to be pulled out.' Hathaway reached over to his jacket and took out a brown leather wallet. From it he removed a pristine white business card which he handed to Warren. Printed in the middle was a single London telephone number. 'You can call this number at any time of the day and night. You'll either speak to me direct, or you'll speak to someone who will immediately transfer you to me, no matter where in the world I am. No matter what trouble you're in, we'll have you out of it within minutes.'

Warren ran the card between his fingers. 'It's a get-out-of-jail-free card,' he said quietly.

'Sort of,' said Hathaway, 'but it can only be used once. The moment you reveal you're undercover, it's over. There's no having a quiet word with the investigating officers, no smoothing things over behind closed doors. You're either in or you're out.' He pointed at the card. 'Memorise the number. Then destroy the card.'

He turned around the laptop so that Warren could see the screen.

'The same goes for what I'm going to show you on the computer. You're going to have to memorise the procedures and passwords. You must never write anything down.'

Tina watched as Hathaway tapped away at the keyboard. 'So I'll be e-mailing you reports, is that it?' she asked.

'It's the safest way,' he said. 'No meeting that can be watched, no phone conversations that can be tapped. You just find yourself an internet café and Robert's your mother's brother.'

'My mother didn't have a brother, but I get your drift.' She pointed at the laptop, a grey Toshiba. 'Do I get to use this?'

Hathaway shook his head. 'Absolutely not,' he said. 'Under no circumstances must you ever use your own machine. Everything you do will be stored somewhere on your hard disk. Someone who knows what they're doing will be able to find it. I'll use this to show you what to do, but once you're up and running you should use public machines. There are internet cafés all over the place these days.'

He sat back from the laptop. On screen was a web page and he tapped it with his forefinger. 'This is SafeWeb,' he said. 'It's a state-of-the-art privacy site. You can use it to move around the web without being traced. No one knows who you are or what you're doing. That goes for sites you visit or any e-mail you send or receive. It's so secure that the CIA use it.'

'Okay,' said Tina hesitantly, 'but does that mean you think someone will be watching me?'

'If you get close to Donovan, or to any of his associates, there'll be all sorts of agencies crawling over you, Tina. The Drugs Squad, Customs and Excise, Europol, the DEA, law enforcement agencies right across the world will put you under the microscope. And every one of them will have the capacity to open your mail, listen in on your phone calls and intercept your e-mail. If any one of them were to discover that you were an undercover agent, your life would be on the line.'

'Even though they're the good guys?'

'Someone at Donovan's level can't operate without help from the inside.'

'Bent cops?'

'Bent cops, bent DEA agents, bent politicians,' said Hathaway. 'There is so much money involved in the drugs trade that they can buy almost anyone. Everyone has their price, Tina. And Donovan has the money to meet it.'

Tina tilted her head on one side. 'What about you, Gregg? What's your price?'

Hathaway flashed her a tight smile. 'I prefer to be on the side of law and order.'

'White hat and sheriff's badge?'

'I don't do this for the money, Tina.'

'You're on some sort of crusade, are you?'

'My motivation isn't the issue.' He turned the laptop towards her. 'Once you've logged on to SafeWeb, type in this URL.' His fingers played across the keyboard. The new web page loaded then the screen turned pale blue.

She looked at the graphics and wording on the screen. It appeared to be an online store selling toiletries. There was a 'Feedback' section where e-mails could be sent to the company.

'That's where I send my stuff?' she asked.

'That's it. But first you have to log on. For that you'll need a password. Something you'll never forget so that you won't have to write it down. It can be a number, or a word. Anything up to eight characters.'

Tina gave him a password and watched as he tapped it in. His fingernails were bitten to the quick and there were nicotine stains on the first and second fingers of his right hand. He was a smoker, yet he'd turned down her offer of a cigarette when he'd first arrived at her flat. She wondered how much she should read into the nicotine stains and the bitten nails.

'Sure you don't want a cigarette?' she asked, offering her pack.

He shook his head, his eyes still on the screen. 'Gave up, six weeks ago.'

'Wish I could.'

'Anyone can. Just a matter of willpower.'

Tina blew smoke but was careful to keep it away from Hathaway. 'Is that when you started biting your nails?'

Hathaway flashed her a sideways look. 'Not much gets by you, does it, Tina?' He gestured at the screen. 'Right, this is you logged on. If there's a message for you, there'll be an envelope signal here. If you want to send me a message, you click here.' Hathaway clicked on a letter icon. 'Then it's just like any word processing or e-mail programme. When you've finished, click on "send" and you're done. If you want to attach any photographs or documents, use the paper-clip icon here.'

'What sort of photographs?'

'Anything you think might be of use to us.'

'And am I supposed to be in contact with you every day?'

Hathaway ran his hand down his face and rubbed his chin. 'I'd advise against that. Once a week would be enough, but you want to avoid making it a routine. If you sit down at a computer every Saturday morning, it's going to be noticed. Vary it.'

'What if you need to get in touch with me? Say there's a problem and you need to warn me.'

'That's not going to happen. We're not going to be watching you, Tina. You will be one hundred per cent on your own. From time to time I might need to brief you on operations, perhaps point you in the direction of possible targets, but I won't be expecting instant results. Weekly contact will be fine.'

Tina stubbed out her cigarette. 'Will you be running other agents, Gregg?'

Hathaway's face hardened. 'Why do you ask?'

'Because you're going to a lot of trouble over little old me,' she said with a smile. She nodded at the laptop. 'The website, you, Latham. I can't believe this is all being done just for my benefit.'

Hathaway nodded slowly, a slight frown on his face as if assessing what she'd said. 'Suppose I was having this conversation with someone else. You wouldn't want me to tell them about you, would you?'

'That sort of answers my question, doesn't it?'

Hathaway smiled thinly and folded his arms. 'There's nothing I can say. Other than lying to you outright, and I'm not prepared to do that.'

'And are they all being sent against Tango One?'

'That I can't tell you, Tina.'

'But suppose one of your people gets close to Donovan and I see them. If I send you details of what they were doing, doesn't that put them in the spotlight?'

'All your reports will come through me and I won't pass on anything that would put another operative in danger.' He smiled again. 'Assuming that there are other operatives.'

Tina walked over and sat on the arm of the sofa. 'The reports I send. What will you do with them?'

'I'll go through them and pass on whatever intelligence there is to the appropriate authorities.'

'But isn't there a danger that it could be traced back to me?'

'I'll make sure that doesn't happen,' he said. 'When you do file, by all means highlight anything you think might be linked to you, but frankly it's the big players I'm interested in. Donovan and the like. I'm not going to risk blowing your cover for anything less.'

'Blowing my cover!'

Hathaway closed his eyes and put his hand to his temple as if he had a headache. 'That came out wrong,' he said. He opened his eyes again. 'What I mean is that the important thing is that you stay in place. That is my primary concern, keeping you undercover as long as possible. The only reason I'd want to pull you out is if it meant putting Donovan behind bars.'

Tina stared at Hathaway. She knew next to nothing about the man who was about to become her handler, who would have her life in his hands.

'You realise that you can't ever tell anyone what you're doing?' said Hathaway. 'No matter how much you want to. No matter how much you think you can trust the person. There'll be times when you'll want to talk to someone. To confide.'

'I don't think so.'

'What about your family?'

'I haven't seen them for six years. Don't want to see them again. Ever.'

'Friends?'

'Not the sort I'd confide in. About anything.'

'It's going to be lonely, Tina.'

'I'm used to being on my own.'

'And how do you feel about betraying people who might well become your friends? Your only friends?'

Cliff Warren took a long pull on his bottle of Sol while he considered Hathaway's question. He wiped his mouth with the back of his hand. 'Thing is, they won't really be friends, will they? They'll be criminals and I'll be a cop.'

'Easy to say now, Cliff, but you might feel differently three years down the line.'

'If they're criminals, they deserve to go down. Are you playing devil's advocate, is that what's going on here?'

'I just want you to face the reality of your situation, that's all.'

Warren pursed his lips and tapped his bottle against his knee. 'I know what I'm letting myself in for.' He leaned back in his chair, looked at the ceiling and sighed mournfully. 'Funny how things work out, innit?'

'In what way?'

'By rights I should be square bashing at Hendon. Left, right, left, right, back straight, arms out. And instead I'm gearing up to hit the streets as a drug dealer.' He lowered his chin and looked over at Hathaway. 'That's a point, where do I get my cash from?'

'I'll be supplying funds. At least in the early stages. And drugs.'

At first Warren thought he'd misheard, then the implications of what Hathaway had said sank in and he sat upright. 'Say what? You'll be giving me drugs?'

'You'll be operating as a dealer. You can't be out there selling caster sugar.'

'The police are going to be giving me heroin?'

Hathaway winced. 'I was thinking cannabis,' he said. 'Just to get you started. You ever taken drugs, Cliff?'

Warren shook his head. 'Never. Saw what they did to my folks.' Warren's mother had died of a heroin overdose when he was twelve. His father was also an addict and had ended up in prison for killing a dealer in North London. Warren had been passed from relative to relative until he'd been old enough to take care of himself, and it seemed that every household he stayed in was tainted in some way by drugs. He had steadfastly refused to touch so much as a joint. 'I don't see that's a problem, though. Plenty of dealers don't use.'

'Absolutely, but you're going to have to know good gear when you see it.'

'I've got people can show me. The stuff you're going to give me. Where's it coming from?'

'Drugs we've seized in previous operations,' said Hathaway. 'They're destroyed if they're no longer needed as evidence. We'll just divert some of it your way.'

Warren took another drink. His heart was pounding and he felt a little light headed. It wasn't the alcohol – he'd barely drunk half of his beer – it was an adrenalin rush, his body gearing for fight, fright or flight in anticipation of what lay ahead. He felt his hand begin to shake and he pressed the bottle against his knee to steady it. This was no time to have the shakes. 'There's one word I haven't heard you mention,' he said.

Hathaway raised an eyebrow. 'What's that?'

'Entrapment.'

'It's no defence in an English court,' said Hathaway. 'Cases have gone as high as the House of Lords and the end result has always been the same – entrapment evidence can't be excluded from a trial, because there is no substantive defence of entrapment in English law.'

'I thought there'd been cases where undercover officers had obtained confessions and the confessions weren't admissible because they hadn't administered the caution?'

Hathaway smiled. 'It's a grey area,' he said. 'You're right, a confession without a caution required under the Police and Criminal Evidence Act of 1984 would be technically inadmissible. But that wouldn't apply if you weren't questioning them as a police officer. Anything they tell you would be admissible if it was a conversation between equals. Or at least as if they perceived it as a conversation between equals.'

'But if I'm encouraging the commission of a crime, doesn't that give them a way out?' asked Warren. 'They could say that I was leading them on, that I was waving money around saying that I want to buy drugs. They could claim that if I hadn't approached them they wouldn't have committed the crime in the first place. How are you going to get a conviction on that?'

'We won't. We'll note the transaction and the people involved, but we won't be moving in to arrest them. A couple of busts like that and your cover would be well and truly blown. It's information we want, Cliff. Good quality intelligence that will help us mount effective operations. The last thing we're going to do is to put you in court holding a Bible and swearing to tell the truth.' Hathaway drank from his bottle of Sol, then leaned back and studied Warren for almost a minute. 'Entrapment isn't covered by PACE or by the codes of practice issued under PACE,' he said, eventually. And it is one hundred per cent true that claiming entrapment isn't a defence under English law. But there were Home Office guidelines issued in 1986 which do refer to entrapment. Basically the Home Office said that no informant must act as an *agent provocateur*, that is he or she mustn't suggest to others that they commit an offence or encourage them to do so.'

'But that means . . .' Warren began.

Hathaway held up a hand to silence him. 'That's what the Home Office says, but between you, me and that cheese plant in the corner, the likes of Dennis Donovan don't pay a blind bit of notice to the Home Office, so why should we?'

'That's a dangerous route to start along,' said Warren. 'You're saying the rules aren't fair so you're going to break them?'

'What I'm saying is that established procedures aren't going to catch Dennis Donovan. We're going to have to be more . . .' He searched for the word. 'Creative,' he said eventually.

'But if it ever gets out that I've been acting as an *agent provocateur*, all bets are off,' said Warren. 'He'd be able to take you to the European Court of Human Rights, any conviction would be quashed, and he'd sue you for millions.'

'But he won't ever find out,' said Hathaway. 'No one will. You are going to be so far undercover they'll need a submarine to find you. That's why we've gone to all this trouble, Cliff. Only a handful of people will know what you are doing, and they'll never tell. From now on your only contact with the police will be me, and we'll only be communicating via a secure website.'

'So I really will be on my own?'

'It's the only way, Cliff. Are you up for it?'

'I guess so.' He saw from the look on Hathaway's face that the answer wasn't emphatic enough. 'Yes,' he said, more determinedly. 'Yes, I am.'

'Good man,' said Hathaway. His fingers started to play across the keyboard. Warren moved over to sit next to him.

Tina rolled over and hugged her pillow. She'd been in bed for almost three hours and was no closer to getting to sleep. Her mind was in a whirl. Her meeting with Latham. Her briefing from Hathaway. It had all been such a shock. One minute she'd been all geared up for joining the Metropolitan Police, wearing a uniform and pounding a beat. The next, she was preparing to become a lap dancer, which, no matter how Hathaway had portrayed it, was in her eyes only one step up from being a street-walking prostitute. She'd worked hard for her qualifications. Bloody hard. She'd set her heart on a career, a real career, and that had been taken away from her. By men.

She felt tears well up, but screwed her eyes tightly closed, refusing to cry. It always seemed to be men who were screwing up her life. Her stepfather, crawling into her bed late at night, whispering drunkenly and licking her ear. The punters, always trying to get her to do it for free or without a condom. Her neighbours, sneering and leering as she left to walk the streets in short skirt, low-cut top and knee-length boots. The police, patronising and condescending. And now Latham and Hathaway. They were worse than pimps. Worse than her punters.

She opened her eyes and sat up, still clutching the pillow to her stomach. A sudden wave of nausea swept over her and she rushed to the bathroom. She barely managed to get her head above the toilet bowl before throwing up. She flushed the toilet and drank from the cold tap, then wiped her mouth with a towel. She stared at her reflection in the mirror above the sink. 'Bastards,' she said. 'Bastards, bastards, bastards.'

She went back into the sitting room and dropped down on to the sofa. Could she trust them? And was she even capable of doing what they wanted? She felt nauseous again and took deep breaths to steady herself. What if it went wrong? What if she wasn't up to the job, what if she slipped up and someone found out that she was an undercover cop? Hathaway had given her a phone number to memorise. Her way out. Her once in a lifetime 'get out of jail free' card. Two years down the line, three years, would there still be someone at the end of the lifeline? She stared at the phone on the coffee table. A voice on the end of the phone and a website were to be her only points of contact, Hathaway had said. She drew her legs up underneath her and rested her head on the pillow. One of the reasons she'd been so keen to join the Met was because she wanted to be a member of a team, to be surrounded by colleagues who could support her if she was in trouble, to be part of a group. The police she'd come across when she'd worked the streets had always been the enemy, but she'd envied them their camaraderie. She knew the girls on the streets with her, but they were the competition. They might help each other out with loans or cigarettes and even offer advice on which punters to avoid, but there was never the familiarity and intimacy that the police had. Tina wasn't sure if she had what it took to work on her own. Undercover. Living a lie.

Tina reached over and picked up the phone. She placed it on the pillow and ran her fingers along the smooth, white plastic.

Twenty-four seven, Hathaway had said. Twenty-four hours a day, seven days a week, there'd be a voice at the end of the phone. One call and she'd be pulled out.

She picked up the receiver and listened to the dialling tone, then put it back. She ran her hands through her hair and then rubbed the knotted muscles at the back of her neck. She stared at the phone. What if he'd been lying? What if there was no lifeline? She snatched at the receiver and tapped out the number on the keypad as quickly as she could, not wanting to give herself time to change her mind. It started to ring. Tina closed her eyes. It was answered on the third ring. 'Yes?' It was a man's voice. It might have been Hathaway, but Tina couldn't tell, not from the single word.

There was a faint buzzing on the line, like static.

'What do you need?' said the voice after a long pause. It was flat and emotionless, almost mechanical, but Tina was sure now it was Hathaway.

'Nothing. Wrong number,' she said and replaced the receiver.

She replaced the phone on the coffee table and carried the pillow back to her bed. She lay down and curled up into a foetal ball and within five minutes she was fast asleep.

Three Years Later

Marty Clare took a long draw on his joint and held the smoke deep in his lungs as he watched the two girls on the bed. The blonde was on top, the redhead underneath, their legs and arms entwined as they kissed. Clare scratched his backside, then exhaled slowly, blowing blue smoke over the two girls.

'Come on, girls, let the dog see the rabbit,' said Clare in his gravelly Irish accent. The two girls moved apart. The redhead reached up for the joint and Clare handed it to her as he slid down next to the blonde. Sylvia, her name was. Or Sandra. Clare hadn't been paying attention to their names. All he'd been interested in was how much they'd charge for a threesome, and the price had been reasonable considering their pneumatic breasts and model-pretty faces. They were Slovakians, the blonde twenty-one and the redhead barely out of her teens. From the way they were going at each other on the bed, Clare figured they were probably genuinely bisexual. Not that he cared over-much either way: the evening was about satisfying Clare's urges, not theirs.

Clare kissed the blonde and she moaned softly and opened her mouth, allowing his exploring tongue deep inside. She reached down between his legs and stroked him. Clare felt the redhead's tongue on his back, gently licking between his shoulder blades.

The redhead reached and gave the joint to the blonde, then pressed her lips against Clare's mouth, practically sucking the breath from him. She rolled on top of him and began to move downwards, kissing and gently nipping at his flesh with her teeth. Clare ran his fingers through her hair and groaned in anticipation of the pleasures to come. The blonde sat up with her back against the headboard and blew smoke up at the ceiling. Clare held out his hand for the joint. As she passed it to him there was the sound of cracking wood and shouts from the room next door, then booted footsteps and shouts. The bedroom door crashed open and half a dozen uniformed policemen burst into the room with a series of rapid flashes that temporarily blinded Clare.

Clare dropped the joint on to the redhead's back and she screamed. The blonde made a run for it and Clare grinned despite himself: she was totally naked and the apartment was on the top floor of a sixteen-storey building. The only way out was blocked by two very large men in black raincoats. They were grinning, too, because the redhead was screaming and cursing and trying to get off the bed. The glowing joint had rolled against her leg and burned her thigh. She fell to the floor and then scrabbled on her hands and knees towards the bathroom door. The blonde had changed direction and decided that she was going to make a run for the bathroom, too, but she collided with the redhead and they both fell to the ground in a tangle of limbs. There were more flashes as a man in a grey anorak and jeans photographed the two women.

Clare burst out laughing and so did the uniformed policemen. They grabbed the girls and a female officer picked up their clothes. The two men in raincoats moved to the side and the girls were hustled down the hallway. The redhead started to cry but the blonde was more vociferous, screaming that she wanted to call her lawyer. The man with the camera followed them out of the room.

Clare picked up the still-burning joint and took a long pull on it. He held it up and offered it to the two detectives. They shook their heads.

'So what's the charge, guys?' asked Clare nonchalantly. 'Is it the sex, the drugs or the rock and roll?'

The taller of the two detectives picked up an ashtray and carried it over to the bed.

Clare was naked but he made no move to cover himself up. His well-muscled torso was still glistening with sweat. He stubbed out the joint.

'Martin Clare, you are under arrest for conspiring to export four tons of cannabis resin,' said the detective.

Clare's face tightened but he continued to smile brightly.

'Cannabis that we currently have in our possession at Rotterdam docks,' the detective continued. 'What is it they say in your country, Mr Clare? You are nicked?'

'That'll do it,' said Clare. 'What the fuck. Let me get my pants on, yeah?'

Robbie picked up his sports bag as soon as the bell started to ring, but dropped it by the side of his desk after Mr Inverdale gave him a baleful look. Mr Inverdale finished outlining the essay he wanted writing for homework, then turned his back on the class. There was a mad scramble for the door. Robbie pulled his Nokia mobile from his sports bag and switched it on. He'd sent Elaine Meade a text message before the start of class and was keen to see if she'd replied.

'Outside with that, Donovan,' said Mr Inverdale, without turning around. 'You know the rules.'

Robbie hurried out into the corridor. He had one text message waiting. Robbie's heart began to pound. Elaine was the prettiest girl in his year, bar none. Blonde with big blue eyes like the pretty one in Steps and a really cute way of wrinkling up her nose when she laughed. He pressed the button to collect the message and tried to ignore the growing tightness in his stomach. The text message flashed up. 'I'M BACK. COME HOME NOW – DAD.'

Robbie grinned and pumped his fist in the air. 'Yes!' he said. It had been more than two months since Robbie had seen his father.

He stuffed the phone back into the sports bag and headed for the school gates. He looked around nervously but there were no teachers in the playground. It was lunch break and everyone was rushing towards the refectory. Robbie walked purposefully through the gates and broke into a run, his sports bag banging against his leg.

He was sweating and out of breath by the time he reached his house. His mother's silver-grey Range Rover was parked in front of the house. Next to it was a dark green Jaguar, its engine still clicking under the bonnet. Robbie ran his finger along the paintwork. His dad didn't like British cars: he said they were always breaking down and that you couldn't beat the Germans for quality engineering. Robbie walked down the side of the house and through the kitchen door. There were two bulging Marks and Spencer carrier bags on the counter top next to the sink and two mugs by the kettle.

'Dad!' There was no answer.

Robbie put his sports bag on the kitchen table and ran

through to the sitting room. Empty. He went back into the hall. 'Dad?' His voice echoed around the hallway.

Robbie went up the stairs, one hand on the banister. He could hear voices coming from his parents' bedroom. Robbie broke into a run and pushed open the bedroom door, grinning excitedly. He froze when he saw the two figures on the bed. Two naked figures. His mother on top, sitting down, her spine arched and her head back. She turned to look at him, a look of horror on her face.

'Robbie?' she gasped.

Time seemed to stop for Robbie. He could see the beads of sweat on her back, a stray wisp of blonde hair across her face, a smear of lipstick on the side of her mouth.

The man on the bed was lying on his back, trying to sit up. 'Oh shit,' he said. He put a hand up to his forehead. 'Shit a fucking brick.'

Robbie recognised the man. It was Uncle Stewart, but he wasn't really an uncle, he was a friend of his father's. Stewart Sharkey. His father always looked serious when Uncle Stewart came around to the house, and they'd lock themselves in the study while they talked. The only time Dad wasn't serious with him was when it was Christmas and Uncle Stewart came around with presents for Robbie and his parents. He always brought really good presents. Expensive ones.

'That's my mum!' Robbie shouted. 'That's my fucking mum!'

'Robbie . . .' said his mother, pleadingly.

'Shit, shit, shit!' said Sharkey, holding his hands over his eyes and banging the back of his head against the pillow.

Robbie's mother wrapped the duvet around herself and twisted around to face him. 'Robbie, this isn't—'

'It is!' he screamed. 'I know what it is! I can see what you're doing! I'm not stupid.'

Robbie's mother stood up, and the man grabbed a pillow and held it over his groin. 'What are we going to do?' he asked.

Robbie's mother ignored him. She took a step towards Robbie, but he moved backwards, holding his hands up as if trying to ward her off. 'Don't come near me!' he yelled.

'Robbie. I'm sorry.'

'Dad's going to kill you. He's going to kill both of you!'

'Robbie, it was an accident.'

Robbie pointed at her. 'I'm not stupid, Mum. I know what you're doing. I'm going to tell Dad.'

'Vicky, for God's sake, do something!' hissed Sharkey.

Vicky turned to him. 'Stay out of this, Stewart.'

'Just handle it, will you?'

Robbie backed out of the bedroom and rushed down the hallway. His mother hurried after him.

'Robbie! Robbie, come back here!'

Robbie stumbled at the top of the stairs and his hands flailed out for balance. His sports bag swung between his legs and he fell forward, his mouth working soundlessly, panic overwhelming him.

Vicky ran into the hallway just in time to see her son pitch headlong down the stairs. She screamed and let the duvet slip from her fingers.

Robbie banged down the stairs in a series of sickening thumps.

'Robbie, no!' yelled Vicky, as she rushed towards the top of the stairs. Behind her, Sharkey called out, wanting to know what was wrong.

The hallway seemed as if it were telescoping away from Vicky as she ran. She couldn't see Robbie, but she could hear the thuds as he tumbled down. Thump. Thump. Thump. What horrified Vicky was Robbie's silence as he fell. No groans, or shouts or curses. Just the gut-wrenching thumps. Then silence. The silence was a million times worse than the sound of the fall.

Vicky reached the top of the stairs. Robbie was lying at the bottom, face down, his head turned to the side. There was blood on his mouth. Vicky felt as if she'd been punched in the stomach and she put a hand against the wall to steady herself. 'Please, God, don't let this be happening,' she whispered.

She hurried down the stairs two at a time and crouched next to him. She put a hand on his shoulder and squeezed gently. 'Robbie, love? Robbie?' His chest moved as he took a breath, and Vicky said a silent prayer of thanks.

Robbie's eyes flickered open.

'Robbie, love, are you all right?' Vicky asked.

His face screwed up into a snarl. 'Don't touch me!'

'Robbie, love . . .'

'Get off me,' he said. 'I saw you. I saw what you were doing.'

'Robbie . . .'

He pushed her away and got to his feet. He wiped his mouth and stared at the blood on his hand. 'You look ridiculous,' he said.

Vicky realised that she was naked and she moved her hands to cover her crotch.

'I hate you,' said Robbie.

Sharkey appeared at the top of the stairs, buttoning his shirt. 'Has he calmed down?'

Robbie pointed up at Sharkey. 'My dad's going to kill you!' he shouted venomously.

'Robbie,' said Vicky, 'please don't say that.'

She reached out to touch him but Robbie hit her hand away. 'And you!' he shouted.

Sharkey started downstairs. 'There's no need to be stupid, Robbie,' he said.

Robbie backed away.

Vicky looked over her shoulder. 'Stewart, leave this to me. Please.'

'If he says anything to Den . . .'

'Shut the hell up!' she shouted.

'I'm just saying . . .'

'Don't say,' she yelled. 'Don't say anything. You've caused enough . . .' Before she finished the sentence she heard Robbie fumbling with the lock on the front door. 'Robbie!' she shouted. 'Robbie, come back.'

She dashed towards the door but Robbie was too quick for her. He pulled the door open, slipped out and slammed it behind him. Vicky scrabbled at the lock, but by the time she got the door open Robbie was already sprinting along the pavement. The strength drained from Vicky's legs and she slumped to the floor, tears streaming down her cheeks.

Sharkey walked slowly down the stairs, buttoning the cuffs of his shirt. 'Shit,' he said quietly. 'What are we going to do now?'

The wind blowing off the Caribbean Sea tugged at Den Donovan's hair and flicked it across his eyes. He brushed it away and shaded his eyes with the flat of his hand. The waves of the turquoise sea were flecked with white and Donovan could taste the salt on his lips. 'Thought I might get a boat, Carlos,' he mused, staring out across the water. 'What do you think?'

Carlos Rodriguez shrugged. 'I always get seasick,' he said.

'I was thinking a big boat. Stabilisers and that. Save me flying between the islands. I could travel with style.'

'I still get sick,' said Rodriguez.

Donovan started walking down the beach, his sandals digging into the sand. In the distance a line of loungers were shaded by pink and green striped umbrellas. Rodriguez hurried after him.

Donovan looked across at the road to his right. Barry Doyle was leaning against Donovan's silver-grey Mercedes, his arms folded across his massive chest. Doyle gave Donovan the merest hint of a nod, letting him know that everything was clear on the road. Donovan looked over his shoulder. The nearest person was a hundred yards away, and that was an obese woman in a too-small bikini, who was paddling with her toddler son and yelling at him in German every time he went out too far into the sea.

A small jet banked overhead and turned towards Bradshaw Airport. More well-heeled tourists, thought Donovan, probably booked into a suite at the Jack Tar Village Beach Resort or the Four Seasons Resort on the neighbouring island of Nevis, where a quarter of the island's workforce slaved away to make sure that the everyday inconveniences of life on a Third World island didn't intrude into their five-star compound. St Kitts wasn't one of Donovan's favourite places, but it was an ideal setting for a meeting with one of Colombia's biggest cocaine suppliers.

'How's everything?' Donovan said, keeping his voice low.

'The freighter is leaving Mexico this evening,' said Rodriguez.

'And the consignment?'

'The fuel tanks of the yellow ones.'

'The yellow ones?'

'We thought they'd be easier to spot.'

'Every yellow one?' asked Donovan.

Rodriguez nodded. 'Every one.'

'Isn't that a bit . . . predictable?'

Rodriguez grinned. 'Less risk of confusion. You'd prefer we used engine or chassis numbers? You want to go down on your hands and knees with a flashlight?'

Donovan chuckled. The cocaine Rodriguez was supplying had been transported from Colombia into Mexico, where there was a factory manufacturing Volkswagen Beetles, the cult car that was still in demand around the world. Up to four hundred Beetles a day rolled off the production line in Puebla, and many went overseas. Rodriguez had bought up a consignment of sixty of the cars and had arranged to ship them to the United Kingdom.

'Don't worry, Den,' said Rodriguez. 'Palms have been well greased at both ends. Yellow, green or rainbow coloured, no one is going to be going near those cars.'

'Sweet,' said Donovan.

'And my money?'

'I'll put the first tranche in this afternoon.'

'And the rest on arrival?' said Rodriguez.

'Soon as we've got the gear out.' Donovan slapped the Colombian on the back. 'Come on, Carlos, have I ever let you down?'

'Not yet, my friend, but a little bird tells me that you have been talking to Russians.'

'Carlos, I talk to a lot of people.'

'Russian pilots. With transport planes. Staying at a hotel in Anguilla. Not far from your villa, in fact.'

Donovan raised an eyebrow. 'I'm impressed, Carlos.'

'Knowledge is power,' said the Colombian.

'I thought money was power.'

The two men stopped and faced each other, the warm sea breeze rustling their clothes.

'Knowledge. Money. Power. They are all connected,' said the Colombian. 'These Russians, they have been flying Soviet weapons into Colombia for FARC, you know that?'

Donovan nodded. FARC was the initials of the Revolutionary Armed Forces of Colombia, the country's biggest rebel group. 'Not these guys. But they're friends of the guys you're talking about.'

'Guns in, cocaine out. It's a dangerous game, my friend. We wouldn't want the rebels becoming too strong. We have friends in the Government, you know that.'

Donovan nodded. It was one of the reasons that the Rodriguez cartel had been so successful. 'I've no interest in their cocaine, Carlos. You have my word. I'm talking to them about some business on the other side of the world. Poppy business.'

Rodriguez smiled. 'Be careful, Den. The Russians are not to be trusted. They are vicious thugs who will kill you at the drop of a hat.'

Donovan laughed and patted the Colombian's shoulder. 'Carlos, they say exactly the same thing about the Colombians.'

The Colombian laughed along with him. 'And maybe they're right, my friend. Maybe they are right.'

Donovan heard his name being called from the road. It was Doyle, waving Donovan's mobile phone in the air. He never carried it himself, and he never discussed business on it. He was all too well aware of how easily the authorities could listen in to cell phones, which was why he'd arranged to meet Rodriguez on the beach. Anyone trying to eavesdrop would be easy to spot, and the wind and the crashing surf would make long-distance electronic surveillance difficult if not impossible.

'I think your associate is trying to attract your attention,' said Carlos dryly.

Donovan glared over at Doyle who was now walking across the sand in their direction, still waving the mobile phone like a conductor trying to energise an orchestra. 'You'd better push off, Carlos,' said Donovan. 'I'm going to have a quiet word with Mr Doyle.'

'It's always difficult to get good people,' said the Colombian. 'I could tell you stories. Another time, though.' He walked away down the beach, the cream linen trousers of his suit cracking in the wind like the sails of a racing yacht.

Donovan strode towards Doyle. 'What the fuck are you playing at?' he yelled. 'I told you to stay on the road. And if that fucking phone is switched on I'll shove it so far up your arse that your teeth'll vibrate when it rings.'

'It's Robbie,' said Doyle, so quietly that his Scottish burr was almost lost in the wind. 'He sounds hysterical. Something about Vicky.'

'Oh Christ,' said Donovan. He grabbed the phone out of Doyle's hand and slammed it to his ear. 'Robbie, what's wrong?'

As Robbie explained what had happened, the colour drained from Donovan's face. He walked to the water's edge as he listened to his son, occasionally whispering quietly into the phone, barely noticing the waves that lapped over his Bally loafers.

When Robbie had finished, Donovan told him not to worry, that everything would be all right, that he'd take care of it.

'Dad, you have to come home. Now.'

'I will, Robbie. I promise.'

'Now,' Robbie repeated.

'A day or two, Robbie. I've got to get a flight and stuff. Where are you?'

Robbie sniffed. 'I don't know,' he said.

'What do you mean, you don't know?'

'I'm near school. I ran away. But I don't know where to go.'

'Call your Aunty Laura. Right now. She'll pick you up.'

'I don't want to go home, Dad.'

'You don't have to. You can stay with your aunt until I get there.'

Robbie said nothing and for a moment Donovan thought that he'd lost the connection.

'Robbie, are you there?'

'Yeah, I can hear you,' said Robbie. There was another long silence, with Donovan listening to nothing but the crackle of static. 'Dad?' said Robbie eventually.

'Yes?'

'Are you going to kill them?'

'Don't be silly, Robbie,' said Donovan. 'Look, hang up and call Aunty Laura. Tell her what's happened and that I'll call her.'

'Okay, Dad.'

'I love you, Robbie.'

'I love you too, Dad.'

The line went dead. Donovan threw back his head and screamed obscenities into the wind. 'Kill them?' he yelled. 'I'll rip them limb from fucking limb when I get my hands on them!'

* * *

Stewart Sharkey put his hand on Vicky's shoulders. 'It'll be okay,' he said.

Vicky shook her head fiercely. 'How the fuck's it going to be okay?'

Tears trickled down her cheeks. Sharkey tried to brush them away, but Vicky threw up her hands and forced him back.

'Leave me alone!' she shouted. 'This is all your fault.'

Sharkey looked hurt by her outburst. 'That's not fair, Vicky,' he said.

'Fair! Den's not going to care what's fucking fair!' she hissed.

Sharkey reached out a hand to hold her arm but Vicky took a step back. 'Look, maybe Robbie won't say anything,' he said.

'He's got a mobile. He'll call Den.'

'We can say he's confused.'

'Oh, grow up, will you, Stewart? He saw us in bed. Where the fuck's the confusion?' She slammed her hand against the wall. 'You shouldn't have come around. I always said never here, didn't I? Your place or hotels, that's what we agreed. I said never here, didn't I? But you had to do it in the bed. Den's bed. Like a dog pissing on another's territory.'

Sharkey sat down on the stairs. 'It takes two, Vicky,' he said quietly.

She whirled around and raised her hand as if to slap him, but then she shuddered and began to cry, great heaving sobs that wracked her slim body. Sharkey stood up and held her and this time she didn't try to push him away. He stroked her hair. 'I'm sorry, love,' he said.

'He'll kill us,' she sobbed. 'Stewart, you know what he's like. Oh God, how could I have been so stupid?'

'We want to be together, you know we do. He was going to have to know some time.'

'But not like this. Not with Robbie . . .' She started to cry again.

Sharkey rested his cheek against the top of her head and closed his eyes. He knew that she was right. He more than anyone knew what Den Donovan was capable of.

'We've got time,' he said.

'Time?'

'To move. To make plans. For a new life.'

'What about Robbie? We have to take Robbie with us.'

'Later,' said Stewart.

'He's my son,' protested Vicky.

'Of course he is,' said Sharkey. 'But he's Den's son, too. He'll lead Den to us.'

Vicky looked up at him, her cheeks wet with tears. 'I can't leave him,' she said. 'He hurt himself when he fell downstairs.'

'He was fine, Vicky. He ran out of here like a bat out of hell.'

'But I don't even know where he is.'

'He'll go around to a friend's house,' said Sharkey. 'Or he'll call Den's sister. And he'll be on the phone to his father. Don't worry about Robbie, Vicky. Worry about yourself.'

'I want to be sure that he's okay.'

'We don't have time, love,' said Sharkey. 'We're going to have to go now.'

'Go where?'

'I've got an idea,' said Sharkey, smoothing her hair with the flat of his hand. 'Just trust me.'

Vicky began to sob again and Sharkey held her tightly.

* * *

Donovan called his sister from a call box close to a beachfront café. Barry Doyle stood by the car looking uncomfortable. Laura answered on the fifth ring. 'Den, thank God. I can't believe this,' she said.

'Have you got Robbie there?'

'He's watching TV with my kids,' she said. 'He's in a right state, Den.'

'Let me talk to him, yeah?'

Laura called Robbie to the phone and handed the receiver to him.

'You okay, Robbie?'

'When are you coming home, Dad?'

'Soon, Robbie. Don't worry. You can stay with Aunty Laura until I get there, okay?'

'I guess. What about school? Do I still have to go?'

'Of course you do.'

'But it's miles away.'

'Aunty Laura'll drive you. Just be a good boy for her, yeah, until I get things sorted.'

'What are you going to do, Dad?'

'I'm gonna get a ticket and then I'll come and see you.'

'I meant about Mum. And him.'

'I'll get it sorted, Robbie, don't you worry. You can stay with me, I'll take care of you. Chin up, yeah?'

'Okay, Dad.'

'Put your aunty on, will you?'

Robbie handed the phone to Laura. 'Thanks, Laura.'

'Anything I can do, Den, you know that. Can't believe what the stupid cow's gone and done.'

'Yeah, you and me both. I need a favour, Laura.'

'Anything.'

'Can you go around to the house? Robbie's passport's in the safe in the study. You got a pen?' Donovan gave her the combination of the safe. 'Get the passport, and there's cash there, too. And a manila envelope, a biggish one. In fact, clear everything out, will you?'

'What if she's there, Den?'

'It's my house, and Robbie's my son. I don't want her doing a runner with him. I said Robbie could go to school but I'm having second thoughts.'

'You can't keep him off school, Den. There's laws about that.'

Donovan rubbed the bridge of his nose. 'Yeah, you're right. Can you run him there and pick him up? Make sure he gets inside. And have a word with the headmistress. Vicky's not to go near him.'

'She's his mother, Den, they won't . . .'

'Just do as you're fucking told, will you!' Donovan shouted, and immediately regretted the outburst. 'I'm sorry, Laura. I didn't mean that.'

'It's okay, Den. I'll talk to the school, explain the situation to them. But you're going to have to come back and talk to them yourself. You're his dad, I'm just his aunt.'

'I'll be back, don't worry about that. Are you okay looking after him for a while?'

'You don't have to ask, Den. You know that.'

Donovan cut the connection and dialled again. A man answered. Donovan didn't identify himself, but told the man to get to a clean phone and call him back. Donovan gave him the St Kitts number. The man began to complain that he didn't have enough coins to make an international call from a phone box. 'Buy a fucking phone card, you cheap bastard,' said Donovan, and hung up.

Donovan paced up and down as he waited for the man to ring back.

* * *

Laura's husband, Mark, drove her over to Donovan's house. She'd asked a neighbour to sit in with the children, who were so engrossed in the Cartoon Channel that they didn't even ask where Laura and Mark were going.

'We've met this Sharkey guy, haven't we?' asked Mark, accelerating through the evening traffic.

'Yeah. That barbecue last time Den was over. He's an accountant or something.'

'And she was in bed with him?'

'That's what Robbie said.'

'Stupid bitch.'

'Yeah.'

'Fancy doing it in her own bed.'

Laura flashed him a withering look.

He grimaced. 'I meant she was a stupid bitch for doing it in the first place. But if you're going to have an affair, you don't shit on your own doorstep, do you?'

'Well, I'll bear that in mind, honey,' she said, frostily.

'You know what I mean. How did Den sound?'

'Angry.'

'He'll kill her.'

'I hope not.'

'You know what your brother's like. What he's capable of.'

'Yeah. And so does Vicky.'

'Christ, what a mess.'

They drove the rest of the way to Kensington in silence. Mark pulled up outside Donovan's house. Vicky's Range Rover was parked outside.

'Shit,' said Laura. 'She's still home.'

'Maybe not,' said Mark. 'She might have left in his car.'

'Leave behind a Range Rover? Come on. Vicky's not the sort to say goodbye to a thirty-thousand-pound car.'

'She can't take it overseas. And even if she could, it'd make her a sitting duck.'

Laura realised that her husband was probably right and she relaxed a little. Despite her brother's assertion that the house belonged to him, Laura wasn't sure how well she'd be able to cope with a confrontation with Vicky. She took the house keys from her bag and climbed out of the car.

Laura opened the front door. She had the combination of the burglar alarm, but there was no bleeping from the console so she figured that Vicky hadn't set it. She was about to step inside when Mark put a hand on her shoulder. 'Best let me go in first, kid,' he said. 'Just to be on the safe side.'

Laura smiled at him gratefully and moved to let him go inside.

Mark quickly walked down the hall, checked the two reception rooms and the kitchen, then came back into the hallway, shaking his head. 'No one here,' he said. He looked up the stairs. 'Vicky?' he shouted.

'She'll be well gone,' said Laura.

They went upstairs to the master bedroom. The duvet was thrown over a chair by the window and two pillows were on the floor at the foot of the bed. Laura opened the doors to the fitted wardrobes. Among the clothes still hanging there were more than two dozen empty hangers. Laura walked into the ensuite bathroom. She opened the medicine cabinet over the sink and ran a hand over the medicines and toiletries.

'She's left him,' she said.

Mark came up behind her. 'How do you know?'

'No contraceptive pills. No razor. No toothbrush.'

'You should have been a detective,' said her husband. 'She'll have to run a long bloody way to escape from Den.'

'Can you get some clothes from Robbie's room?' asked Laura. 'There's something Den wants me to do.'

As Mark went along the hallway to Robbie's bedroom, Laura headed downstairs. She opened the door to the study and walked over to a large oil painting hanging behind an oak desk. It was of two old-fashioned yachts sailing into the wind, and a similar one hung on the wall opposite. Laura reached for the ornate gilt frame and pulled the right-hand side away from the wall. Behind was a gunmetal-grey safe with a circular numbered dial in the centre. She'd written the combination on the back of a Marks and Spencer receipt, but it took her several goes before she could get the door open. The safe was empty. Laura swore under her breath. She wasn't looking forward to giving her brother the bad news.

Chief Superintendent Richard Underwood buttoned up his coat and pushed open the door. He walked out of Paddington Green police station and nodded at two Vice Squad detectives before walking down Harrow Road. He turned up his collar against the wind that always seemed to whip around the station, no matter what the season.

He walked past the first two phone boxes, the old-fashioned red types, the insides littered with prostitutes' calling cards. The third was about half a mile from the station, on Warwick Avenue, close to the canal. Underwood tapped in the pin number of his phone card, then the number in St Kitts. It rang out for so long that he thought maybe he'd taken down the wrong number, but then Donovan answered.

'You'd better be quick, Den, there's only twenty quid on this card.'

'Yeah, put it on the tab, you tight bastard,' said Donovan. 'Look, I need to know what my position is back in the UK.'

'Fucking precarious, as usual.'

'I'm serious, Dicko. I'm going to have to come back.' He told Underwood what had happened.

'Hell, Den, I'm sorry.' Underwood had known Donovan for almost twenty years and Vicky Donovan was the last person he'd have expected to betray her husband.

'Yeah, well, I need to know where I stand.'

'You're Tango One. So far as I know, that's not changed.'

'It's been four bloody years since I left.'

'Memories like elephants. They'll be all over you like a rash if you come back.'

'Check it out, will you?'

'If that's what you want, Den, sure. I'll call you tomorrow. This number, yeah?'

'Nah. I'm getting a flight back this afternoon.'

'Bloody hell, Den. Don't get manic about this. Softly, softly, yeah?'

'Don't worry, Dicko. I'll stop off in Europe. Germany maybe. I'll call you from there.'

'Just remember Europol, that's all. You're Most Wanted all over Europe.'

'I'll be okay. One more thing. I want you to get Vicky and that bastard Sharkey red-flagged. They leave the country, I want to know.'

'You're not asking much, are you?'

'I'm serious, Dicko. If they run, I want to know where they run to.'

'Don't do anything stupid, Den.'

'You can do it, yeah?'

Underwood sighed. 'Yeah, I can do it.'

'Cheers, mate. Let's talk again tomorrow.'

The line went dead in Underwood's ear. He felt his stomach churn and he popped a Rennie indigestion tablet into his mouth.

Donovan walked over to the convertible Mercedes. Doyle had the door open for him. 'You okay, boss?' he asked.

Donovan didn't reply. He tapped on the dashboard with the palms of his hands as Doyle climbed into the driving seat.

'Where to, boss?' asked Doyle.

Donovan's hands beat even faster on the dashboard as he tried to collect his thoughts. He'd flown to St Kitts purely to meet the Colombian, but his return flight was to Anguilla, and that didn't get him any closer to London. He needed a ticket, he needed to speak to his sister, and he needed to confirm the collection of the several hundred kilos of Colombian heroin that was on its way to Felixstowe.

Doyle watched him nervously. Donovan hadn't explained what the problem was, but he'd overheard enough of the conversation with Robbie to realise that it was personal and that he had better tread carefully. He started the car and blipped the engine.

Donovan stopped beating a tattoo and his forehead creased into a deep frown. 'Oh shit,' he whispered.

'Boss?'

'Shit, shit, shit.' Donovan turned to stare at Doyle, but there was a faraway look in his eyes as if he was having trouble focusing. 'I need a computer. Now.'

'The resort, yeah?'

Donovan nodded. The Jack Tar Resort Hotel was supposedly for movers and shakers who wanted to escape from the trials and tribulations of the world of commerce, but it had a fully equipped business centre that was often better attended than the pool. Donovan leaned back in the cream leather seat and massaged his temples with his fingertips.

The mobile phone rang. Doyle had put it on the console by the gear stick and he grabbed at it with his free hand. 'Yeah?' He handed it to Donovan. 'It's Laura.'

Donovan listened in silence as his sister told him what had happened at the house. And how the safe had been emptied. Donovan cursed. 'Everything, yeah? No passport? No envelope?'

'The cupboard was bare, Den. Sorry.'

'Okay, look, Laura, I think you'd best keep Robbie away from school until I get back. If she's got his passport she might try to get him out of the country. Just tell the school he's sick or something.'

'Will do, Den.'

'And you know what to do if she turns up at your house?'

'She'll get a piece of my mind if she does, I can tell you.'

Donovan smiled to himself. He'd seen his sister in full flow, and it wasn't an experience to be relished. 'Do me another favour, Laura. Call Banhams in Kensington. Get them to change all the locks and reset the alarm with a new code. Any of the paintings missing?'

'Bloody hell, Den, how would I know?'

'Gaps on the wall would probably be a clue, Laura. Hooks with nothing hanging from them.'

'I'm so pleased that you haven't lost your sense of humour, brother-of-mine. I didn't see any missing, no.'

Donovan considered asking his sister to arrange to put the paintings into storage, but figured they'd probably be safe enough once the house was secured. The last time he'd had them valued was five years ago, and they'd been worth close to a million pounds in total. The art market had been buoyant recently and Donovan figured they'd probably doubled in value since then. Vicky didn't share his love of art and he hadn't told her how much the paintings were worth. 'I'll call you later, Laura. And thanks. Tell Robbie I love him, yeah?'

Donovan cut the connection and tapped the phone against his chin. Changing the locks and resetting the alarm was all well and good, but Donovan knew that he was shutting the stable door after the horses had well and truly bolted.

Doyle drove into the hotel resort, giving the uniformed security guard a cheery wave, and pulled up in front of Reception. 'Wait here,' said Donovan. He walked quickly through the huge reception area, his heels clicking on the marble floor. He jogged up a sweeping set of stairs and pushed open the door to the hotel's business centre.

A pretty black girl with waist-length braided hair flashed him a beaming smile and asked him for his room number. Donovan slipped her a hundred-dollar bill without breaking his stride. 'I'll just be a couple of minutes,' he said. He sat down at a computer terminal in the corner of the room and said a silent prayer before launching Internet Explorer and keying in the URL of a small bank in Switzerland. He was asked for an account number and an eight-digit personal identification number.

Donovan took a deep breath and prepared himself for the worst as he waited for his account to be accessed. The screen went blank for a second and then a spreadsheet appeared, listing all transactions for the account over the past quarter. Donovan sagged in the leather armchair. There was just two thousand dollars left in the account.

He left the bank's site and tapped in another URL, this one for a bank in the Cayman Islands. Ten minutes later and Donovan had visited half a dozen financial institutions in areas renowned for their secrecy and security. His total deposits amounted to a little over eighty thousand dollars. In total sixty million dollars was missing.

Mark Gardner flicked through the channels but couldn't find anything to hold his attention. Reruns of old comedy shows that he half-remembered watching, films that he'd already seen on video, and shows about cooking or decorating. He looked up as Laura came into the room holding two mugs of hot chocolate.

'He's asleep,' she said, handing him a mug and sitting down on the sofa next to him. She swung her legs on to his lap and lay back, resting the mug on her stomach.

'What do you think he's going to do?'

'Robbie?'

'Your brother.'

Laura ran a finger around the lip of her mug. 'He'll look after Robbie. You know how much his son means to him.'

'I thought he wasn't allowed in the UK. I thought the cops were after him.'

'He was under surveillance.'

'He was Britain's most wanted,' said Gardner. 'Tango One, they called him.'

'Tango just means target. It means they were looking at him, it doesn't mean he's done anything wrong.'

'There's no smoke without fire.'

'Yeah, and an apple a day keeps the doctor away. Are

we going to swap clichés all night? Den's Den and that's the end of it.'

'I know, love, and I think the world of him. And Robbie. But I don't want us to get caught up in the middle of something.'

Laura took her legs off her husband's lap and sat up. 'Like what?'

'I don't know what. But Vicky's got a temper and you know what Den's like.'

'What, you think they're going to come in here with guns blazing?'

'You know that's not what I mean, but there's going to be one hell of a court battle over Robbie. They'll both want custody.'

'She got caught sleeping around, Mark. It'll be open and shut.'

'It's never open and shut in British courts. It'll be a dirty fight, thousand-pound-an-hour lawyers at thirty paces.'

'That's not our problem.'

There was a scuffling at the doorway and they both jumped. Laura's hot chocolate slopped over her knees.

It was Robbie, rubbing his eyes. 'I can't sleep,' he said.

Laura put her mug on the coffee table, and went over and hugged him. 'What's wrong, Robbie?' she asked.

'I had a bad dream,' he said.

She led him over to the sofa. Mark shuffled over to make room for them. He put a hand around Robbie's shoulder. 'You'll be okay, Robbie.'

'Where's Dad?'

'He's coming,' said Laura.

'I want my dad,' said Robbie, and the tears started to flow again.

'I know you do,' said Laura. She looked across at Mark

and he shrugged. There was nothing either of them could say or do to make things any easier for Robbie. All they could do was to wait for Den Donovan.

Laura put her cheek against the top of Robbie's head and whispered softly to him. After a while the tears stopped and a few minutes later he was snoring softly. Laura smiled at her husband. 'I'll put him in Jenny's room. I don't want him sleeping on his own tonight.'

'Good idea,' said Mark. 'Shall I take him up?'

Laura shook her head. 'He's not heavy.' She carried him upstairs. Seven-year-old Jenny was fast asleep on top of her bunk bed. Jenny had shared a room with her sister until Julie had declared that she was too old to be sharing and had insisted on a room of her own. At the time Julie had been all of four years old and Jenny had been three. Jenny had insisted on her own list of demands – including keeping the bunk bed for herself, and a change of wallpaper.

Laura eased Robbie into the lower bunk and pulled the quilt up around him. She bent down and kissed him on the forehead. 'Sleep well, Robbie,' she whispered.

As she straightened up, the phone rang. There was an extension in the master bedroom, but Laura headed downstairs, knowing that Mark would pick it up. As she walked into the sitting room, he had the receiver to his ear.

'Is it Den?' she mouthed.

Mark shook his head. 'You'd better speak to Laura,' he said into the receiver, then held it out to her. 'It's Vicky,' he said.

Laura took the phone. 'You've got a damn cheek, calling here,' she said coldly.

'Is Robbie there, Laura? I've been trying his mobile but it's switched off.'

'He's asleep.'

'For Christ's sake, Laura, I just want to talk to him.'

'I don't think that's a good idea.'

'I'm his mother, for God's sake!'

'He's had a bad day. He needs to sleep. He's in a state, Victoria. I don't think you talking to him is going to help. Where are you anyway?'

There was a brief pause. 'I can't tell you. I'm sorry.'

'You're in London, right? I went around to the house but you weren't there.'

'What were you doing at my house?' Vicky asked quickly.

'First of all it's Den's house. Second of all, it's none of your business. Whatever rights you had you forfeited when you screwed Sharkey in Den's bed.'

'Will you stop saying that!' shouted Vicky. 'You make it sound so bloody sordid.'

'Victoria, it was sordid. Sordid and stupid.'

'You've spoken to Den, haven't you?'

'What if I have?'

'What did he say?'

'What do you think he said?' asked Laura.

'He's coming back, isn't he?'

'No, Victoria, he's going to stay out in Anguilla for a few months. Of course he's coming back. Like a bat out of hell.'

'What am I going to do? This is a nightmare.'

'Why did you empty the safe?' asked Laura.

'I didn't steal anything. The money was for me, for running the house.'

'And Robbie's passport? Why did you take that?'

'What the hell's going on, Laura?' shouted Vicky. 'Why were you in my house?'

'Den wanted Robbie's passport. And the money. He

knows you cleared the safe, and he told me to change the locks. He doesn't want you back in the house, Victoria.'

'He's planning to take Robbie back with him to Anguilla, isn't he?'

'I'm going to hang up now,' said Laura. Mark stood in front of her, trying to listen in, but Laura twisted away from him. She hated her sister-in-law for what she'd done, but she didn't want Mark to hear how upset she was.

'Please, Laura, let me speak to him. I just want him to know that I love him.'

'No. Not tonight. Call again tomorrow.'

'Laura . . .' sobbed Vicky.

Laura replaced the receiver. Her hand was shaking and her knuckles had gone white. She hadn't realised how tightly she'd been gripping the phone. Mark put a comforting arm around her shoulder.

'I'm sorry, love,' he said.

She rubbed her head against his. 'If I ever catch you in bed with your accountant, I'll disembowel you with my bare hands,' she whispered. 'And that's a promise.'

Donovan chartered a small twin-engined plane to fly him and Doyle back to Anguilla. Donovan went into the charter firm's offices and made arrangements for another flight later that day. He booked a private jet and left a deposit in cash and then walked over to the terminal building where he made three calls from a payphone while Doyle went to pick up the car.

The first call was to a German who had access to passports and travel documents from around the world. Not forgeries or copies, but the genuine article. He wasn't cheap but the goods he supplied were faultless. The German gave Donovan a name and Donovan repeated it to himself several times to make sure he'd memorised it. The second call was to the agent who made most of Donovan's travel arrangements. He was far from the cheapest on Anguilla, but he was the most secure. Donovan explained what he wanted and gave him the name that he'd memorised. The third call was to Spain, but it wasn't answered. An answer machine kicked in and Donovan said just ten words in Spanish and hung up.

Doyle arrived in the Mercedes, and Donovan climbed in the back and sat in silence during the drive to his villa. It wasn't just that he had a lot on his mind. The DEA and British Customs, and whatever other agencies were operating in the millionaires' paradise, weren't above planting any manner of surveillance device in the vehicle while it had been parked at the airport. Until it had been swept, the Mercedes was as insecure as a mobile phone conversation.

Doyle stayed in the car while Donovan went into the villa and packed a Samsonite suitcase and a black leather holdall. He wasn't over-concerned with what went into the luggage: it was merely part of the camouflage. A man in his thirties flying alone into the UK from the Caribbean without any luggage would be guaranteed a pull by Customs. From the wall safe in the study of the villa, Donovan took a bundle of US dollar bills and stuffed them into the holdall. On the way out he picked up a Panama hat and shoved it into the holdall.

He threw the bags into the back of the car, then got into the front with Doyle. 'I'd better see the Russians first,' he said. 'Then we'll go and see the German.'

Doyle drove to a five-star hotel about a mile from

Donovan's villa. They found the Russians sitting by the pool. Gregov was the bigger of the two, broad shouldered and well muscled with a tattoo of a leaping panther on one forearm and the Virgin Mary on the other. His grey hair was close cropped, thick and dry, and his weathered face was flecked with broken blood vessels. He looked in his early fifties, but Donovan knew that he was only thirty-five.

Gregov stood up and pumped Donovan's hand. 'Champagne, huh?' he asked, gesturing at a bottle of Dom Perignon in a chrome ice bucket beaded with droplets of water. The two Russians had been on the island for five days and Donovan had never seen them without an opened bottle of champagne within arm's length.

'No can do,' said Donovan. 'I've got to get back to the UK.'

'Who are we going to party with?' said Gregov's partner, Peter, who stayed sprawled on his lounger. Peter was the younger of the two men, a six-footer with a wiry frame. Like Gregov, his hair was cut close to his skull, but his was a fiery red and there was a sprinkle of freckles across his snub nose. His face was red from sunburn and his legs and arms tanned, but his chest remained a pasty white. Below his left nipple two bullet wounds were visible, star-shaped rips in his chest that had healed badly leaving uneven ridges of scar tissue.

'From what I've seen, you don't need me to help you two party,' laughed Donovan.

'You really have to go?' asked Gregov.

'I'm afraid so.'

'But we can do business, yes?' asked Peter, swinging his legs off the lounger and putting his bare feet on to the tiles.

'Definitely,' said Donovan.

'Because we can go elsewhere,' said Peter.

'Not that we want to,' said Gregov, flashing his partner a warning look. 'Den, we want to do business with you.'

'And I with you, Gregov. I've got a personal matter to take care of back in London, but then I'll get back to you and we'll do a deal.'

'This personal matter. Can we help? We have connections in London.'

Donovan shook his head. 'Nah, that's okay. I'm on top of it.' He clapped Gregov on the back. 'Look, your bill's taken care of. Anything you want, it's on me. I've got your UK office number and the number of your office in Belgrade. They'll be able to get in touch with you?'

Gregov nodded. 'We are backwards and forwards between the UK and Turkey three times a week but we check in every day. The earthquake relief charities are paying us thirty thousand dollars a flight to take in their people and equipment. Good money, huh? Famine and earthquakes are good money makers for us, Den. Not quite as profitable as your business, but a good living, yes.'

'You've done well, you and Peter. The Russian Army's loss, yeah?'

Gregov nodded enthusiastically. 'Yes, their loss, our gain. Fuck Communism, yes?'

'Definitely,' said Donovan. He made a clenched fist and pumped it in the air. 'Capitalism rules.'

The two Russians laughed then took it in turns to hug Donovan and Doyle.

After they'd said their goodbyes to the Russians, Doyle drove Donovan to the far east of the island, where the German lived in a villa three times the size of Donovan's. It was surrounded by a twelve-foot-high wall topped with razor-sharp anti-personnel wire first developed for the Russian gulags. The two men were checked out by closed-circuit television cameras and then the twin metal gates clunked open. Doyle edged the Mercedes slowly up the curving gravelled driveway. They passed two more cameras before pulling up in front of the German's palatial villa. Doyle waited in the car while Donovan got out and went to find the German.

Helmut Zimmerman greeted Donovan at the front door, grasping him in a brutal bear hug and then slapping him on the back. 'Next time I could do with more notice, Dennis,' he said. He was a big man, almost six inches taller than Donovan's six feet, with broad shoulders that strained at his beach shirt and muscular thighs that were almost as wide as Donovan's waist. Everything was in proportion except for Zimmerman's hands, which were as small and delicate as a young girl's, almost as if they'd stopped developing at puberty.

'This isn't by choice, Helmut.'

'You have time for a drink?'

'I haven't even had time to take a piss,' laughed Donovan. 'I've got to be back at the airport by six.'

Zimmerman took Donovan along a marble-floored hallway, either side of which stood alabaster statues of Greek warriors. Above their heads electric candles flickered in a line of ornate crystal chandeliers.

At the far end of the hallway hung a massive gilded mirror, twice the height of a man. Donovan grinned at their reflection. 'Helmut, you live like a Roman fucking emperor,' he said.

'You like it, huh? I'll send my interior designer around to see you. Your place is so . . . stark. Is that the word? Stark?'

'Yeah, stark's how I like it.'

To the left of the mirror was a white door with a gilt handle. Zimmerman opened it with a child-like hand and led them down another corridor to a windowless room with white walls, a huge Louis XIV desk and decorative chairs. A tapestry of a goat herder playing pipes to his flock hung on one of the walls, and a collection of antique urns was displayed on glass shelves on another. Behind the desk a bank of colour monitors was linked to CCTV cameras inside and outside the villa. On one of the monitors Donovan could see Doyle sitting in the Mercedes, tapping his fingers on the steering wheel.

'He is not going with you?' asked Zimmerman, sitting down at the desk. It was at least ten feet wide but the German's bulk dwarfed it.

'Not this trip,' said Donovan.

Zimmerman pulled open one of the desk drawers and took out three passports. All were European Union burgundy. He handed them to Donovan one at a time. 'One United Kingdom, one Irish and one Spanish. As requested.'

Donovan checked all three carefully, even though he knew Zimmerman never made a mistake. Donovan's picture was in all three passports, though each had a different name and date of birth. The passports were genuine and would pass any border checks. Zimmerman had a network of aides across Europe who made a living approaching homeless people and paying for them to apply for passports they'd never use. The passports were then sent to Anguilla, where Zimmerman replaced the photographs with pictures of his paying customers.

'Excellent, Helmut, as always.' Donovan took an envelope from his jacket pocket and slid it across the desk. Thirty-six thousand dollars.

Zimmerman put the envelope, unopened, into the drawer and shut it. Donovan smiled at the open demonstration of trust, well aware, however, that if he ever tried to cheat the German, it would take just one phone call to Europol to render the passports useless.

'So,' said Zimmerman, placing his hands flat on the desk and pushing himself up, 'until next time, Dennis.'

Donovan put the passports into his jacket pocket, and the two men shook hands before Zimmerman showed Donovan out of the villa.

Doyle already had the door of the Mercedes open. They drove in silence to the airport. Doyle parked in the short-term car park and they walked together to the terminal.

'I should come with you, boss.'

'Double the chance of us being flagged, Barry. Better you take care of business here.'

Donovan ran through a mental checklist of everything that needed to be done. He didn't appear to have forgotten anything, but he knew that the devil was always in the details.

'Okay, boss?' asked Doyle.

'Sure,' said Donovan. 'You know how I hate small planes.' It wasn't flying that was worrying Donovan, it was what Carlos Rodriguez would do when he discovered that his money hadn't been paid into his account. Doyle would bear the brunt of Rodriguez's fury, but if Donovan told Doyle to make himself scarce it would be a sure sign of guilt. Doyle would have to stay and face the music.

The pilot and co-pilot were already warming up the engines by the time they reached the sleek white Cessna Citation. Doyle took Donovan's luggage from the boot of the Mercedes and the owner of the charter company came out to help load it into the plane. Donovan shook hands with Doyle, then hugged the man and patted him on the back. 'You take care, you hear,' said Donovan.

'Sure, boss,' said Doyle, momentarily confused by the sudden show of affection.

Donovan shook hands with the owner of the charter company, and then climbed into the back of the plane. The co-pilot closed the door and two minutes later they were in the air, climbing steeply over the beach and banking to the west. Donovan peered out of the window. Far below he could see the Mercedes heading back to the villa. Donovan flashed the car a thumbs-up. 'Be lucky, Barry,' he whispered. He settled back in the plush leather seat. It was a two-hour flight to Jamaica.

Marty Clare strained to lift the bar, breathing through gritted teeth, sweat beading on his brow. A large Nigerian stood behind him, spotting for him, his hands only inches from the bar: this was Clare's third set, and he was lifting his personal best plus a kilo.

'Come on, man, one more,' the Nigerian urged.

Clare roared like an animal in pain, his face contorted into a snarl, his arms shaking, his knuckles white on the bar, then with a final explosion of air from his chest the bar was up and on its rests.

The Nigerian patted Clare on the back as he sat up. 'Good job.'

Clare grinned and took a swig from his water bottle.

A young, blond guard walked over to them. He was barely out of his teens, his pale blue uniform several sizes too big for him. 'Mr Clare? Visitor for you.'

Clare nodded, amused as always at the politeness of the Dutch guards. 'I was going to shower,' he said.

'I was told to bring you now, Mr Clare,' said the guard.

The guard led Clare out of the gym, across a garden being tended by a dozen inmates, and into the main building, where he showed Clare into an interview room. A notice on one wall warned of the dangers of drugs, and offered prisoners free counselling or places in drug-free units. The DFUs were a soft option and Clare had applied to be admitted when he'd first been sent to the detention centre. His application had been refused, however, because prisoners had to be able to speak Dutch, and Clare had never bothered to learn the language. There was no point: every Dutch person he knew spoke perfect English.

Unlike the furniture in the British penal system, the Formica-topped table and four orange plastic chairs weren't bolted to the floor. Clare pulled one of the chairs away from the table and sat on it with his back to the wall. He crossed his legs and waited. He closed his eyes and concentrated on slowing his heart rate. He'd started to study meditation techniques from a couple of books he'd borrowed from the detention centre library.

He heard someone walking down the corridor outside the room and Clare concentrated on the sound. The footfall was uneven, one leg seemed to be dragging slightly. The door opened but Clare kept his eyes closed. The visitor walked into the room and closed the door.

'I could come back later if it's a bad time,' said the man.

Clare opened his eyes. Standing in front of him was a man in his mid thirties wearing a long belted leather jacket with the collar turned up, dark blue jeans and Timberland boots. He was short, probably under five six, thought Clare, and he didn't look as if he worked out. He had thinning, sandy hair and bright inquisitive eyes. His face was weasly, Clare decided. It was the face of an informer. A grass. The face of a man who couldn't be trusted.

'Though frankly, the way your life is turning to shit, I think today is about as good as your life is going to get for the foreseeable future.'

'And you would be?' asked Clare, putting his hands behind his neck and interlocking his fingers.

'I would be the bearer of bad news,' said the man. 'A harbinger of doom.' He walked over to the table and sat down on one of the plastic chairs. His right leg was the one that was causing him trouble. It gave slightly each time he put his weight on it.

'Would it be asking too much for you to show me some identification?' asked Clare.

'Indeed it would, Marty,' said the man, mimicking Clare's soft Irish burr.

Clare unlocked his fingers and leaned forward, his eyes hard. 'Then what the fuck are you doing here?' he asked.

The man returned Clare's stare, unfazed. 'I'm your last chance, Marty. I'm giving you the opportunity to dig yourself out of the pile of shit you've got yourself into.'

Clare grinned and waved his arm dismissively. 'This? This is a holiday camp. I've got a room of my own, a five-star gym, a library, three meals a day, cable TV, including satellite porn shows. I get the *Daily Mail* and the *Telegraph* and I can get CDs and videos sent in. Hell, I might book a place here every summer. Might even bring the family. The kids'll love it.'

'Yes, but you're not going to be here for ever, Marty.'

Clare snorted. 'Do you have any idea how hard it is to get into a Dutch prison? There's only twelve thousand cells in the country, it takes six months to get on the waiting list for a transfer from a detention centre to a real prison. And that's after a guilty verdict. It's easier to get a hip replacement on the NHS in the UK than it is to get a cell in a Dutch prison.'

'Got it all planned, haven't you?'

'A: it was only marijuana. B: I never went near the stuff. C: my lawyers are shit hot. D: I'm as innocent as a newborn babe. E: worst possible scenario, I stay here for a year or two, work out and eat well. Probably add ten years to my life.'

Clare smiled confidently at his visitor, but the man said nothing, and just shook his head sadly at Clare, as if he were a headmaster being lied to by a sulky schoolboy.

Clare stood up. 'So if you're thinking about playing some sort of mind game with me, forget it. I'm a big boy, I can take care of myself.'

'The Americans want you, Marty.' The man said the words slowly as if relishing the sound of each one.

'Like fuck.'

The man smiled, pleased that he'd finally got a reaction from Clare. 'So far as they're concerned, you're a Class 1 DEA violator.'

'Bullshit.'

'Why would I make up something like that, Marty?'

Clare ran a hand through his hair, still damp from his workout. 'Who are you? A spook? MI6? Customs?'

'Sit down, Marty.'

Clare stood where he was.

'Sit the fuck down.'

Clare sat down slowly.

'One of those containers was on its way to the States. New Jersey.'

'Says who?'

'Says the ship's manifest. See, it's all well and good not going near the gear, Marty, but that does mean that sometimes the little details can be overlooked. Like the ultimate destination of the consignment. One container was to be dropped off at Southampton, the other was to stay on board and be taken to New Jersey.'

Clare sat back in his seat and cursed.

The man smiled. 'Someone trying to rip you off, Marty? Whatever happened to honour among thieves?'

'You should know. You had someone undercover, right?'

'Nothing to do with me, Marty. I'm just the bearer of bad news.'

Clare forced himself to smile, even though he had a growing sense of dread. His visitor was too confident, too relaxed. Clare felt as if he were playing chess with someone who could see so far ahead that he already knew how the game would end, no matter what moves Clare came up with. 'The Dutch'll never extradite me to the States.'

'Maybe not, but they'd send you back to the UK. And you know about the special relationship, don't you? Labour, Conservative, doesn't matter who's in power, when the US shouts "jump", we're up in the air with our trousers around our knees.'

'I'm Irish,' said Clare.

'Northern Irish,' said the man quietly. 'Not quite the same.'

'I'm an Irish resident.'

'Some of the time. Your Irish passport won't save you, Marty. The Dutch will send you back to the UK, then you'll be extradited to the US. The DEA will go to town on you. A container full of top-grade marijuana bound for the nation's high-school kids? You'll get life plus plus. And they'll seize every asset you've got in the States. That house in the Florida Keys. What did that set you back? Two million?'

'That's not in my name. It's a company asset.'

'Well, gosh, Marty, I'm sure the DEA'll just let you keep it, then.'

'This isn't fucking fair!' shouted Clare.

The man smiled triumphantly, knowing that he'd won.

Clare felt his cheeks flush and he wiped his mouth with his hand. His throat had gone suddenly dry. 'I want a drink,' he said.

'Don't think even the Dutch'll run to a Guinness,' said the man.

'A drink of water,' said Clare.

The man pushed himself to his feet and walked to the door. He opened it and said something in Dutch to a guard standing in the corridor, then closed the door and went back to his seat.

'Why would you want the Americans to have me?' asked Clare.

'Who said I did?' asked the man.

'You didn't seem too upset at the prospect of me being banged up in a Federal prison.'

'Doesn't affect me one way or the other, Marty.'

'Nah, you've got an agenda,' said Clare. 'You're taking your own sweet time to get to it, but you've got something on your mind.'

'If you're so smart, how come you let an undercover agent get so close that you're facing a life sentence?'

Clare's face tightened. 'So you have got someone on the inside?'

'Oh grow up, Marty. How else do we get you guys these days? Diligent police work? Bloody contradiction in terms, that is, and we both know it. Grasses and undercover agents, that's how we get you. We turn your people or we put our own people in. How we got you doesn't matter – what matters is that we've got you by the short and curlies and the DEA is baying for your blood.'

There was a knock on the door and the young guard appeared carrying two paper cups of water on a cardboard tray. He gave a cup to Clare and put the tray and second cup in front of Clare's visitor. The man thanked the guard in Dutch. He waited until the guard had closed the door before speaking again.

'You know what your best option is, don't you, Marty?'

Clare groaned. 'You are so transparent,' he said. 'You want me to grass, right?'

'Want is putting it a bit strong, Marty. Whether or not you decide to co-operate isn't going to affect me one way or the other. My life won't change: I'll still go out, get drunk, get laid, watch TV, one day retire to a cottage in the country and catch trout. Frankly, I couldn't care less. I'd be just as happy thinking of you growing old in a windowless cell wearing a bright orange uniform and eating off a plastic tray. Oh, you'll get TV, but I don't think they'd let you within a mile of a porn channel.'

'I'm not a grass. If you know anything about me at all you'd know I never grass.' Clare sipped his water.

'And I admire that, Marty. Really, I do.'

'I'll get so lawyered up that they'll never get me out of here. There's the European Court of Human Rights. I'll take it to them. I'll fight it, every step.'

'That's the spirit, Marty. Exactly how were you planning on paying for this expert legal representation?'

Clare frowned. 'What do you mean?'

'Lawyers. Money. Sort of go together like . . . well, like drug dealers and prison.'

Clare sniggered contemptuously at his visitor. 'What do you make in a year?' he asked.

'I get by.'

'You get by? You don't know what getting by is. Whatever you earn in a year, multiply it by a thousand and I've got more than that tucked away. Think about that, you sad fuck. You'd have to work for a thousand years to get the sort of money I've got.'

The man took a slow drink from his paper cup, then placed it carefully on the table. 'And that, Marty, brings me to my second order of business, as it were.'

Clare felt a chill in his stomach, suspecting that things were about to take a turn for the worse. He tried to keep smiling, but his mind was racing frantically, trying to work out what was coming next.

'Your money situation might not be quite as clear cut as you seem to think,' said the man.

'What the fuck do you know about my money situation?'

'More than you'd think, Marty.'

'Who the hell are you? And don't give me that bringer of bad news crap. You're a Brit, so you've no jurisdiction here. I don't have to talk to you.'

'Do you want me to go, Marty? Just say the word and I'll leave you to your weights and your porn channel until the men from the CAB pay you a visit. But by then it'll be too late.'

'What the hell would the CAB be wanting with me?'

'Take a wild guess.'

Clare took another drink from the paper cup. His hand

was shaking and water slopped over his arm. He saw his visitor smirk at the show of emotion and Clare hurriedly put the cup down on the floor. The Criminal Assets Board was an Irish organisation, set up to track down the assets of criminals living in Ireland. Their initial brief had been to run drug dealers and other criminal undesirables out of the Irish Republic, and they had been so successful that their remit had been expanded to cover tax evaders and white-collar criminals. Their technique was simple – they tracked down assets and put the onus on the owner of the assets to prove that they were acquired by legitimate means. Homes, land, money, bonds. And if the owner couldn't prove that the assets weren't connected to criminal activities, the CAB had the right to confiscate them.

'All my stuff in Ireland's legit,' Clare said.

'It's in your wife's name, if that's what you mean. But that's not quite the same as legit, is it? And what about the property development in Spain? And the villas in Portugal? You probably thought you were being really clever putting ownership in an Isle of Man exempt company, but CAB are wise to that.'

Clare swallowed. His mouth had gone dry again but he didn't want to pick up the paper cup. He folded his arms and waited for the man to continue.

'They found your accounts in St Vincent and they're homing in on your accounts in Luxembourg. Then there's your Sparbuch account. Do you know where the name comes from, by the way?'

Clare shook his head. He was finding it difficult to concentrate. The man's voice seemed to echo in Clare's ears, as if he were talking at the end of a very long tunnel.

'From the German, *Sparen*, which means save, and

Buch, which means book. Brilliant concept, isn't it, for guys in your line of work? An anonymous account operated under a password. No signature, no identification, completely transferable. He who has the passbook and codeword has the money. Got yours just before the deadline, didn't you? Smart boy, Marty. Austria stopped issuing Sparbuch accounts in November 2000. You had the inside track on that, I bet. You can still get them in the Czech Republic, but Austrian schillings are so much more confidence-inspiring than Czech crowns, aren't they?'

Clare slumped in his chair. He felt as if a strap had been tightened across his chest and every breath was an effort of will.

'Are you okay, Marty? Not having a heart attack, are you? Though I have to say, the Dutch do have an excellent health care system.'

'Who grassed me up?' gasped Clare, his hand on his chest.

'Who do you think?'

Clare frowned. Sweat was pouring down his face. He rubbed his hand across his forehead and it came away dripping wet.

'By the way, I think you were being a tad optimistic on your figure of a thousand times my annual salary. I reckon at best you've got five million quid salted away and CAB know where pretty much all of it is.'

Clare's mind was in a whirl. The only person who knew about the Sparbuch account was his wife Mary, and he trusted her with his life. The realisation hit him like a punch to the solar plexus. 'Mary.'

The man grinned. 'Ah, the penny has finally dropped, has it? She was none too happy with your arrest situation – the two Slovakian girls . . .'

Clare closed his eyes and swore. The man with the camera. 'You bastard,' he whispered.

'The women, plus the fact that CAB were prepared to cut her a deal on the house and the Irish accounts pretty much puts your balls on the fire, Marty.'

Clare opened his eyes. 'What the fuck do you want?' he asked.

'A chat, Marty.'

'About what?'

'Den Donovan.'

Donovan spent the night at the Hilton Hotel in Kingston. He checked in wearing a Lacoste polo shirt and slacks, but when he checked out of the hotel in the morning he was wearing baggy denim jeans, a T-shirt that he'd bought in a gift shop in Rasta colours with 'I Love Jamaica' spelled out in spliffs, and a woollen Rasta hat. If the receptionist thought his attire incongruous for a business hotel, she was professional enough to hide her opinion behind a bright smile of perfect teeth.

Donovan knew that he looked ridiculous, but then so did most of the Brits returning home after two weeks of sun, sand and sex in Jamaica. The worst that would happen was that he'd get a pull by Customs at Stansted, but they'd be looking for ganja, not an international drugs baron.

He settled his account with American dollars and tipped the doorman ten dollars for opening the back door of a taxi and putting his suitcase and holdall in the boot. It was a thirty-minute ride to the Norman Manley International Airport. Donovan had no idea who Norman Manley was, or why the Jamaicans had named their airport after him, and he didn't care. The only thing he cared about was that it was a relatively easy place to fly to the UK from.

He put on a pair of impenetrable sunglasses and joined the hundred-yard-long check-in queue for the charter flight. Honeymooning couples who were just starting to think about what married life meant back in dreary, drizzly England; middle-aged holidaymakers with sunburned necks, keen to get back to good old fish and chips; and spaced-out funseekers who were biting their nails and wondering if it really had been a good idea to tuck away their last few ounces of Jamaican gold into their washbags. There was a sprinkling of Rasta hats, several with fake dreadlocks, and lots of T-shirts with drugs references, so Donovan blended right in.

It took almost an hour to reach the front of the queue. He handed over the passport and ticket and flashed the Jamaican girl a lopsided grin. 'Wish I could stay longer,' he said.

'Honey, you can move in with me any time,' laughed the girl, 'but you'd have to lose the hat.'

'I love my hat,' he said.

'Then it's over, honey. Sorry.' She checked the passport against the name on the ticket. Donovan's travel agent had worked wonders to get him a seat on the charter flight. A scheduled flight would have been easier, but there'd be more scrutiny if he arrived at Heathrow. Holidaymakers returning to Stansted would barely merit a second look. The agent must have had a pre-dated return ticket issued in the UK and then FedExed it out to Kingston. It had arrived first thing that morning as Donovan had been eating his room service breakfast. The unused Stansted–Jamaica leg section of the ticket had already been discarded. It was that sort of creativity that merited the high prices the agent charged. Donovan was paying more for the cramped economy seat to

Stansted than it would have cost to fly first class with British Airways.

The check-in girl ran him off a boarding card and handed it back to him with the passport. 'I'd wish you a good flight but it looks like you're flying already,' she laughed.

Donovan bought a pre-paid international calling card and phoned the number in Spain. The answer machine kicked in again and Donovan left another message. The Spaniard could be difficult to get hold of at times, but that was because his services were so much in demand.

Vicky Donovan put her hands up to her face and shook her head. 'I can't do this, Stewart. I can't.'

Sharkey reached over and massaged the back of her neck. 'We don't have any choice, Vicky. You know what he's capable of.'

'But running isn't going to solve anything, is it? He'll come after us.' A car horn sounded behind them and Vicky flinched.

'Relax,' said Sharkey. 'He's miles away.'

'He'll be on his way. And if he isn't, he'll send someone.' She looked across at Sharkey, her lower lip trembling. 'Maybe if I talk to him. Try to explain.'

'He was going to find out some time, Vicky,' said Sharkey. 'We couldn't carry on behind his back for ever.'

'We were going to wait until Robbie was older, remember?' Tears welled up in her eyes. 'I can't leave Robbie. I can't go without him.'

'It's temporary.'

'Den won't let us take him, Stewart. You know how much he loves him.'

Sharkey shook his head. 'He left him, didn't he? He left both of you.'

'He didn't have a choice.'

'We all have choices.' Sharkey took her hand. He rubbed her wedding ring and engagement ring with his thumb. The wedding ring was a simple gold band, but the engagement ring was a diamond and sapphire monstrosity that had cost six figures. Sharkey knew its exact value because he'd been with Donovan when he'd bought it from Mappin and Webb with a briefcase full of cash. Vicky had shrieked with joy when Donovan had presented it to her, down on one knee in a French restaurant in Sloane Square. Now Sharkey hated the ring, hated the reminder that she was Donovan's woman. 'He'll calm down eventually,' he said soothingly, even though he knew that it would be a cold day in hell before Den Donovan would forgive or forget. 'I'll get a lawyer to talk to him. We'll come to an arrangement, don't worry. Divorce. Custody of Robbie. It'll be okay, I promise.'

Sharkey stroked Vicky's soft blonde hair and kissed her on the forehead. She wasn't wearing make-up and her eyes were red from crying, but she was still model pretty. High cheekbones, almond-shaped eyes with irises so blue that people often thought she was wearing tinted contact lenses, and flawless skin that took a good five years off her real age. She would be thirty on her next birthday, a fact that she was constantly bringing up. Would Sharkey still love her when she was thirty? she kept asking. Would he still find her attractive?

'We shouldn't have taken the money, Stewart. That was a mistake.'

'We needed a bargaining chip. Plus, if we're going to hide, that's going to cost.'

'You'll give it him back, won't you?'

'Once we've sorted it out, of course I will.' He smiled and corrected himself. 'We will, Vicky. We're in this together, you and me. I couldn't have moved the money without your authorisation. And I'm the one who knew where it was. And where to put it.'

Sharkey pulled her towards him and kissed her on the mouth. She opened her lips wide for him and moaned softly as his tongue probed deep inside. He kissed her harder and she tried to pull away but Sharkey kept a hand on the back of her neck and kept her lips pressed against his until she stopped pulling away and surrendered to the kiss. Only then did Sharkey release her and she sat back, breathing heavily.

'Christ, I want you,' said Sharkey, placing his hand on her thigh. 'We've time. We don't have to check in for our flight for three hours.'

'Stewart . . .' said Vicky, but he could hear the uncertainty in her voice and knew that he'd won. He pulled her close and kissed her again and this time she made no attempt to pull away.

Donovan stayed airside when he arrived at Stansted. It had been the flight from hell. The teenager occupying the seat in front of him had crashed it back as soon as the wheels left the runway and didn't put it upright until they were on final approach to land in the UK. Donovan had downed several Jack Daniel's with ice, but the seat was so small and uncomfortable that there was no chance of sleeping. Plus, there was the small matter of the four-year-old sitting behind him who thought it was fun to kick the seat in time with badly hummed nursery rhymes.

He collected his luggage and went through Customs

without incident, still wearing his sunglasses and Rasta hat. Like most UK airports, Stansted had installed a video recognition system during the late nineties. Closed-circuit television cameras scanned passengers departing and arriving, cross-checking faces against a massive database. The system, known as Mandrake, was still in the test phase, but Donovan knew that his photograph, along with all other top players in the international drugs business, was in the database. The technology was almost ninety-five per cent accurate, final checking always had to be done by a human operator, but it could still be fooled by dark glasses and hats. Donovan had been told by one of the high-ranking Customs officers on his payroll that once the system had been debugged and was running smoothly, the airport authorities would insist that all head coverings and sunglasses be removed in the arrival and departure areas. They were already working out how to avoid the expected flurry of lawsuits from Sikhs and others for whom a covered head was an act of religious expression.

There were only two uniformed Customs officers in the 'Nothing To Declare' channel and they were deep in conversation and didn't seem in the least bit interested in the charter flight passengers. Donovan knew that the lack of interest was deceptive – the area was monitored by several hidden CCTV cameras, and Customs officers behind the scenes would be looking for passengers who fitted the profile of drugs traffickers. Donovan's Rasta hat and druggie T-shirt would actually work in his favour – it would mark him out as a user, but no major drug smuggler would be wearing such outlandish garb.

Donovan passed through without incident. He shaved and washed in the airport toilets and changed into a grey polo neck sweater and black jeans. He kept his sunglasses on and carried a black linen jacket. He dumped the Rasta hat and T-shirt in a rubbish bin.

He had two hours to kill before his Ryanair flight to Dublin, so he stopped off at a cafeteria for a plate of pasta and a glass of wine that came out of a screw-top bottle, and read through *The Times*, the *Daily Telegraph* and the *Daily Mail*.

His seat on the Ryanair jet was if anything smaller than his charter seat, but the flight took just under an hour. There were no immigration controls between the UK and Ireland, so there was no need for Donovan to show his passport.

He collected his Samsonite suitcase, walked through the unmanned blue Customs channel and caught a taxi to the city centre. Donovan was a frequent visitor to the Irish capital. It was the perfect transit point for flights to Europe or the United States. From here he had the option of travelling to and from the UK by ferry, or of simply driving up to Belfast and flying to London on what was considered a UK internal flight.

The taxi dropped Donovan at the top of Grafton Street, the capital's main shopping street. It was pedestrianised and packed with afternoon shoppers: well-heeled tourists in expensive designer clothes rubbing shoulders with teenagers up from the country, marked out as the Celtic Tiger's poor relations by their bad skin, cheap haircuts and supermarket brand training shoe. Careworn housewives pushing crying children, groups of language students with matching backpacks planning their next shoplifting expedition, all remained under the watchful eyes of security guards at every shopfront, whispering to each other in clunky black transceivers.

Donovan carried his suitcase and holdall into the Allied

Irish Bank, showed an identification card to a uniformed guard and went down a spiral staircase to the safety deposit box vault.

'Mr Wilson, haven't seen you for some time,' said a young man in a grey suit and a floral tie. He handed a clipboard to Donovan, who put down his suitcase and holdall and signed in as Jeremy Wilson.

'Overseas,' said Donovan. 'The States.'

'Welcome back to the land of the living,' said the young man. He went over to one of the larger safety deposit boxes and inserted his master key into one of its two locks, giving it a deft twist. 'I'll leave you alone, Mr Wilson. Give me a call when you're done.'

Donovan waited until he was alone in the room before putting his personal key into the second lock and turning it. He opened the steel door and slid out his box. It was about two feet long, a foot wide and a foot deep and heavy enough to make him grunt as he hefted it up on to a teak veneer desk with partitions either side to give him a modicum of privacy.

The single CCTV camera in the vault was positioned behind Donovan, so no one could see what was in the box. He lifted the lid and smiled at the contents. More than a dozen brick-sized bundles of British fifty-pound notes were stacked neatly on the bottom of the box. On top of the banknotes lay four gold Rolex watches, four passports and two burgundy-coloured hard-back account books. They were Czechoslovakian Sparbuch accounts, one with a million dollars, and the other containing half a million. With the appropriate passwords, they were as good as cash.

Donovan placed his holdall next to the metal box and packed the money into it, then put the passbooks and passports into his jacket pocket. He put the UK passport that he'd used to fly from Jamaica into the box, then replaced the box in its slot and locked the metal door.

He pressed a small white buzzer on the desk and the young man came back and turned the second lock with his master key. Donovan thanked him and carried his suitcase and holdall upstairs.

Donovan walked to St Stephen's Green and along to the taxi rank in front of the grand Shelbourne Hotel. A rotund grey-haired porter in a black uniform with purple trim took the suitcase from him and loaded it into the boot of the lead taxi. Donovan gave him a ten-pound note and kept the holdall with him as he slid into the rear seat.

'Airport?' asked the driver hopefully.

'I want to go to Belfast,' said Donovan. 'You up for it?'

The driver grimaced. 'That's a long drive and my wife'll have the dinner on at six.'

'Use the meter and I'll treble it.'

The driver's eyebrows shot skywards. He nodded at the holdall. 'Not got drugs in there, have you?'

Donovan grinned. 'Chance'd be a fine thing. No. But I've got a plane to catch. Do you wanna go or shall I give the guy behind the biggest fare he'll have this year?'

'I'll do it,' said the driver, 'but the wife'll have my balls on toast.'

'Buy her something nice,' said Donovan, settling back into the seat. 'Usually works for me.'

The driver laughed. 'Yeah, wives, huh? What can you do with them? Can't live with them, can't put a bullet in their heads.' He laughed uproariously at his own bad joke and started the car.

Donovan looked out of the window, tight lipped. Flecks of rain spattered across the glass. It always seemed to be raining when he visited Dublin, and he couldn't remember ever seeing blue skies over the Irish capital.

The taxi pulled into the afternoon traffic and Donovan closed his eyes. He'd forgotten to call the Spaniard, but he could do that when he reached Belfast.

Stewart Sharkey nodded towards the bar. 'Do you want a drink?' he asked Vicky. Their flight hadn't been called and the boarding gate was only a short walk away.

Vicky shook her head. 'It's a bit early for me. You go ahead, though. I'm going to use the bathroom.'

'Are you all right?' asked Sharkey, putting his hand on her shoulder.

Tears welled up in her eyes. 'I don't know, Stewart. I don't know how I feel. I'm sort of numb, it's like I'm going to faint or something. Like I keep stepping outside my own body.'

'Good sex will do that every time,' joked Sharkey, but she pushed his hand away.

'This isn't funny,' she hissed. They'd checked into one of the airport hotels, and the sex had been quick and urgent, almost frantic. Sharkey hadn't even given her a chance to get undressed and there had been no soft words, no caresses. Just sex. It was as if he'd wanted to show that she was his. That he could take her whenever he wanted. She'd wanted him, too, but not like that. She'd wanted to be held, to be comforted, to be told that it was all right, that he'd protect her.

'I know it isn't,' soothed Sharkey, 'but there isn't much else I can do just now except try to lighten the moment, right? We've got a plane to catch, then we can plan what we do next.'

Vicky forced herself to smile. 'Okay,' she said.

Sharkey hugged her and she rested her head against his chest. He nuzzled his face into her. He could smell the cheap shampoo from the hotel room. 'You know I love you,' he whispered.

'You bloody well better,' she said, slipping her arms around his waist and squeezing him. 'I wouldn't want to go through all this for the sake of a quick shag.'

'It's going to work out, trust me.'

She squeezed him again, then released her grip on him and wiped her eyes. 'I look a mess,' she said. 'Go get your drink. I'll see you in a couple of minutes.'

She walked away quickly, her skirt flicking from side to side. It was one hell of a sexy walk, thought Sharkey. Vicky Donovan was a head-turner, and that might turn out to be a problem down the line. Men looked at stunning blondes with impressive cleavages and shapely legs, and the more men who looked at her, the more chance there was of someone recognising her.

Donovan thrust a handful of fifty-pound notes at the driver, making sure that he couldn't see inside the holdall. 'Sterling okay?' he asked. 'I don't have any Euros.'

'I suppose so,' said the driver, carefully counting the notes. His face broke into a smile when he realised how much money he was holding. He reached into the taxi's glove compartment and handed a dog-eared business card to Donovan. 'You need a lift again, you call me, yeah? The mobile's always on.'

'Sure,' said Donovan. 'Pop the boot, yeah?'

The driver unlocked the boot and Donovan pulled out his suitcase. He walked into the terminal building and bought a business class ticket to Heathrow at the British Airways desk.

Before checking in he took his holdall and suitcase into the toilets and pulled them into a large cubicle designed for wheelchair access. He put most of the money into the suitcase, since it was less likely to be noticed there than in the holdall. He wasn't committing an offence by flying from Belfast to London with bundles of fifty-pound notes, but he didn't want to attract attention to himself. He kept one passport, one of the UK ones, in his jacket pocket and hid the rest in a secret compartment in his wash bag.

He washed his hands and face, checked his reflection in the mirror, and put his dark glasses back on. Belfast Airport was saturated with CCTV cameras, and like all British airports was equipped with the face-recognition system that he had successfully evaded at Stansted. He took the Panama hat from his holdall and put it on his head at a jaunty angle.

He checked in for the flight and winked at his suitcase as it headed off on its lonely journey down the conveyor belt.

He bought a UK telephone card and called the Spaniard from a payphone. This time the Spaniard answered.

'Fuck me, Juan, where the hell have you been?'

'*Hola, Den. ¿Qué pasa?*'

'I'll give you *qué pasa*, you dago bastard. My world's going down the toilet tit first and you're sunning yourself on some bloody beach.'

'I wish that were true, *amigo*. I have only just got back from . . .' the Spaniard chuckled to himself . . . 'wherever I was,' he finished. Like Donovan, Juan Rojas had a serious distrust of the telephone system. 'You will no doubt read about it in the papers, *mañana*. So what can I do for you, my old friend?'

'Same old, same old,' said Donovan. 'I'd like a face to face.'

'*Amigo*, I am only just off a plane,' said Rojas.

'Don't fucking give me *amigo*, you garlic-guzzling piece of shit, are you gonna help me or do I have to call the Pole? The way the currency is, he's a lot cheaper than you are.'

'If this is your idea of romancing me, I have to tell you, old friend, it's not making me wet between the legs.' He paused, but Donovan knew that he'd got the Spaniard's attention so he said nothing. Eventually Rojas broke the silence. 'Where?' he asked.

'Remember the last time we met in the UK?'

'Vaguely. My memory isn't what it was.'

'The park.'

'Ah. Where the animals were.'

Donovan frowned. The animals? They hadn't met at the zoo. It had been on Hampstead Heath. Then he smiled. It was the Spaniard's idea of a joke. They'd seen several cruising homosexuals, and when they'd walked past one, Rojas had pulled Donovan close and planted a noisy wet kiss on his cheek. 'Yeah, Juan. The animals. Tomorrow, okay? Same time as before, plus two, okay?' Nine o'clock at night. Dark.

'I will be there, *amigo*, with a huge hard-on for you.'

Donovan laughed out loud and hung up.

He sat in the business class lounge sipping a Jack Daniels and soda until his flight was called.

Vicky splashed water over her face and then stared at her reflection in the mirror above the washbasins. She looked terrible. Her eyes were red from crying and her skin was blotchy around her nose. She put her hands on her cheeks and pulled the skin back. The wrinkles vanished as the skin tightened across her cheekbones. Twenty-nine going on fifty is how she felt. She hated what she saw in the mirror. She looked tired and scared and hunted.

She took a lipstick from her handbag and carefully applied it, then brushed mascara on to her lashes. She put her face close to the mirror and admired her handiwork. Even if she looked like shit, she might as well look like shit in full warpaint. She stood up straight and pulled her shoulders back, then turned her head right and left. Twenty-nine. Thirty next birthday. God, how could she be thirty? Thirty was halfway to sixty. She shuddered at the thought of grey hair and mottled, wrinkled skin and receding gums and brittle bones. Or maybe not. Maybe with a good plastic surgeon and if she ate right and gave up smoking and drinking she could put off the decay for a further decade.

She walked out of the ladies'. To her left was a rank of public phones. She stopped and stared at them. No calls, Stewart had said. Calls could be traced, and he'd insisted that they both throw away their mobiles before leaving for the airport. She fumbled in her handbag and pulled out her purse. She had a British Telecom card that still had several pounds on it. She picked up the receiver of the phone in the middle of the row and slotted in the card, then tapped out the number of Robbie's mobile. It rang through immediately to his message bank and she cursed.

It was three o'clock, so he was probably still at school, and the teachers insisted on penalty of detention that all phones were switched off in class. They were the new must-have accessory and had long passed the stage of being a status symbol. Virtually every pupil now had a phone, so status came from having the latest model, and Robbie's was state of the art, a present from Den.

She was about to hang up, but then she changed her

mind. 'Robbie, it's Mum. I just called to say hello. You know I love you, don't you?' She paused, as if expecting an answer. 'I am so sorry about what happened, love, I really am. If I could turn back the clock . . .' She felt tears well up in her eyes and she blinked them back. A family of Indians walked by, chattering loudly: an old man in a grubby turban and a bushy beard, a young married couple with three young children and a grandmother bringing up the rear, all dressed in traditional Indian garb. She turned away from them, not wanting them to see her pain. 'I'm going away for a few days, Robbie. Not far, I promise. But I'm going to see you again soon, I miss you so much . . .' The answering service buzzed and the line went dead. Vicky put a hand up to her eyes and cursed quietly. She replaced the receiver and pulled out the phone card.

'What are you doing, Vicky?'

Vicky jumped and almost screamed. She whirled around to find Sharkey standing behind her. 'What the hell are you doing creeping up on me like that?' she hissed.

'Who were you phoning?'

'It's none of your business who I was phoning,' she said, trying to push past him. 'You shouldn't be spying on me.'

He put a hand on each shoulder and lowered his head so that his eyes were level with hers. 'I wasn't spying, I just came to see where you were,' he said quietly. 'I didn't creep up on you, you had your back to me. And in view of our situation, I think I do have a right to know who you were phoning. You know as well as I do how easy it is to trace calls.'

'We're at the fucking airport, Stewart. We've left the car outside. He's going to know we were here, so one call isn't going to make a difference.'

'That depends on who you called.'

'I didn't call Den, if that's what you're worried about.'

'I'm not worried, I just want to know, that's all.'

She glared at him for several seconds. 'I was calling Robbie.'

'I told you, no calls. No fucking calls!'

'I wasn't going to tell him where we were going!' she protested.

'Vicky, you can't tell him anything. Period. Okay?'

'I just want to talk to him.' Her voice was a tired croak, almost a death rattle. She sounded at the end of her tether.

Sharkey kissed the top of her head. 'And you will do, Vicky. I promise, but let's get ourselves sorted first. Let's make sure we're not vulnerable. Then we can approach Den from a position of strength.'

He straightened up and put an arm around her shoulder.

'Come on, you need a stiff drink.'

He half pushed, half led her towards the bar. All the fight seemed to have gone out of her, and once she stumbled and Sharkey had to grab her to stop her falling. He guided her to the bar and helped her on to a stool before ordering her a double vodka and tonic. She drank it with shaking hands, almost in one gulp, and he ordered another for her.

As Vicky Donovan was downing her third vodka and tonic and Stewart Sharkey was anxiously looking at his watch, Den Donovan was less than a hundred yards away, collecting his suitcase from the carousel in Terminal One. Even though he was wearing his Panama hat and sunglasses, he kept his head down until he was out of the terminal building. The sky was a leaden grey, threatening drizzle if not an outright shower. Donovan joined the queue for a black cab, and forty-five minutes later he was being driven down the Edgware Road. He told the taxi driver to drop him in front of a small rundown hotel in Sussex Gardens. The reception desk was manned by a bottle-blonde East European girl with badly permed hair and a large mole on the left side of her nose. She had a pretty smile and spoke reasonable English. She told Donovan that they had a double room available and that she'd need to see a credit card.

Donovan told her that his credit cards had been stolen while he was on holiday, but he had a passport and was happy to leave a large cash deposit. She seemed confused by his request, but after she'd spoken to her manager on the phone she nodded eagerly. 'He say okay. Three hundred okay for you?' Three hundred pounds was just fine. Donovan never used credit cards if he could possibly help it – they left a clear trail that could be followed. He gave her six fifty-pound notes and she held up each one to the light above her head as if she knew what she was looking for. He checked in under the name of Nigel Parkes, which was the name on one of the UK passports he was carrying.

Once in his room, Donovan opened his suitcase and took out a reefer jacket and an old New York Yankees baseball cap and put them on. He peeled off several hundred pounds in fifties from one of the bricks of banknotes in his suitcase and shoved them into his wallet. Then he put his sunglasses on, locked his door and went out with the door key in his pocket.

He walked down Edgware Road past the packed Arab coffee houses and the banks with camels and squiggly writing on the front. Little Arabia, they called it, and Donovan could see why. Three quarters of the people on the streets were from the Middle East: fat women covered from head to foot in black, grizzled Arabs in full desert gear, teenagers dripping with gold wearing designer gear and shark-like smiles. Not a pleasant place, thought Donovan. You never knew where you were with Arabs. He'd almost lost an eye in a shoot-out with three Lebanese dealers in Liverpool when he was in his late teens, and he'd refused to do business with Arabs ever again. Arabs and Russians. You couldn't trust either.

He walked into an electrical retailer's and bought eight different pay-as-you-go mobile phones and two dozen Sim cards. A CCTV camera covered the cash register, but Donovan kept his head down and the peak of the baseball cap hid virtually all his face as he handed over the cash.

'You gotta lot of girlfriends?' asked the gangly Arab behind the counter.

'Boyfriends,' said Donovan. He leered at the shop assistant. 'What time do you finish, huh?'

The shop assistant took a step back, then looked at Donovan quizzically, trying to work out if he was serious. 'You make joke, yes?'

'Yeah, I make joke,' said Donovan.

The shop assistant laughed uneasily, put the phones and Sim cards in two plastic carrier bags, and gave them to Donovan. Donovan walked back to the hotel. He stopped off at a newsagent on the way and bought five twenty-pound phone cards.

There were four power points in the room, and Donovan put four of the mobile phones on charge before heading for the shower.

Barry Doyle stretched out his hand for his beer and took a sip from the bottle, keeping his towel over his eyes. He was lying by the side of Donovan's pool, recovering from a two-hour work-out in his boss's gym. The staff of three – a maid, a handyman and a cook – stayed in a small house on the edge of the compound and were available around-the-clock even when Donovan was away, so Doyle figured he might as well take advantage of the amenities on offer. The cook was superb, a rotund Puerto Rican woman in her late fifties who knew her way around a dozen or more cuisines and who could whip up poached eggs and beans on toast just the way Doyle liked them. Just the way his mother used to make them.

He heard footsteps and Doyle smiled under the towel. It would be Maria, the maid. Twenty-two years old, an hour-glass figure and a Catherine Zeta-Jones smile. Doyle had been lusting after Maria ever since she started working for Donovan, and he'd told her to bring him a fresh iced beer every half an hour.

'Thanks, Maria,' he said, spreading his legs apart to give her a good look at the bulge in the front of his swimming trunks.

Rough hands grabbed both arms and yanked him up off the sun-lounger. The towel fell to the floor and Doyle blinked in the sudden sunlight. A squat man stood in front of him, brown skinned with a thick moustache and heavy eyebrows. Doyle squinted and his eyes slowly focused. Carlos Rodriguez.

'Where is he?' asked Rodriguez.

'He's not here,' said Doyle.

Rodriguez slapped him, hard. 'Where is he?'

'What the fuck is your problem?' spat Doyle. Blood trickled from the side of his mouth and he winced as he ran his tongue over a deep cut inside his cheek.

Rodriguez slapped him again and the men on either side of Doyle tightened their grip on his arms.

'He flew to Jamaica yesterday,' hissed Rodriguez. 'Why?'

'Look, Carlos, what's going on? There's no need for this. If you've got a problem with Den, you'll have to talk to him. I'm not his fucking keeper.'

Rodriguez stepped forward and grabbed Doyle's throat. He had long fingernails and they dug into Doyle's flesh as he squeezed. 'I *want* to talk to him, you piece of shit. That's why I need to know where he went.' Doyle tried to speak, but Rodriguez's grip was too tight and he couldn't draw breath. He started to choke and Rodriguez took his hand away. Doyle coughed and blood splattered over Rodriguez's cream linen suit. Rodriguez looked down at the spots of blood disdainfully. 'Do you have any idea how much this suit cost?' he said quietly. 'Any idea at all?'

'I'm sorry,' gasped Doyle.

Rodriguez dabbed at the blood spots with a white handkerchief. 'He flew to Jamaica and then he disappeared. I'm assuming he's not lying on the beach smoking ganja, so where the fuck is he?'

Doyle heard a scraping noise behind him and he twisted his head around. A fourth man in his twenties, thickset with a neatly trimmed goatee beard and weightlifter's forearms, had pulled the large umbrella from its concrete base. He grinned at Doyle and tossed the umbrella on to the tiled floor. He knelt down next to the umbrella base and took a length of chain from the pocket of his chinos.

Rodriguez grabbed Doyle by the hair. 'Don't look at him, look at me. He's not your problem, I am.'

Doyle's eyes watered from the pain and he glared at the Colombian.

'Good,' said Rodriguez soothingly. 'Anger is good. So much more productive than fear. Anger makes the body and the mind work more efficiently, but fear shuts everything down. So how is your mind working now? Your memory returning, is it? Where is he?'

Doyle felt hands running around his waist but when he tried to look down Rodriguez jerked his head up.

'How deep do you think the pool is at this end?' asked Rodriguez.

'What?'

'The pool? Twelve feet, do you think?'

Doyle swallowed nervously. 'This is stupid.'

Rodriguez let go of Doyle's hair and slapped him twice, forehand and backhand. He had a chunky diamond ring on the little finger of his right hand and on the second blow it sliced through Doyle's cheek. Doyle felt the flesh part and the blood flow but he wasn't aware of any pain. It was as if his whole body had gone numb. Rodriguez was right. Fear was totally unproductive. His body was shutting down. Preparing for death.

'Are you calling me stupid?' hissed Rodriguez.

'No.' Doyle tried to touch his injured cheek but the man on his right twisted his arm up behind his back.

'There must be something wrong with my ears, then, because I thought I heard you say I was stupid.'

'I said *it* was stupid. The situation.'

Rodriguez smiled without warmth. 'The situation? That's what this is, a situation?'

The man with the weightlifter's forearms knelt down in front of Doyle, his face level with Doyle's crotch. He had the chain in his hands and he passed it around Doyle's waist and fastened it with a small padlock. The man leered at Doyle as he stood up.

'I meant that it's pointless getting heavy with me. Den's the one you want.'

'Which is why I'm asking you for the last time. Where is he?'

'London.'

Rodriguez frowned. 'London? He said he was wanted in England. He said he couldn't go back.'

'His wife's been screwing around. He's gone back to sort it out.'

Rodriguez started to chuckle. So did the man with the weightlifter's forearms. 'Sauce for the goose, that's what you English say, right? Donovan's dick is hardly ever inside his pants.'

Doyle said nothing. The man with weightlifter's forearms walked behind him and Doyle heard the umbrella base being pushed along the floor towards the pool. The chain tightened around Doyle's waist, and his heart began to pound.

'Carlos, don't do this,' Doyle said, his voice a dry croak.

'Where is my money?'

'What money?'

'The ten million dollars that Donovan was supposed to pay into my account yesterday.'

'He didn't say anything to me about money. I swear.'

The umbrella base received another push and it grated across the tiles. It was only a foot away from the edge of the swimming pool, and the chain was now taut. The two men either side of Doyle shoved him closer to the pool.

'I swear!' Doyle screamed. 'Help me! Somebody help me!' His voice echoed around the pool area.

'Scream all you want,' said Rodriguez. 'The hired help want to live as much as you do, my friend. They won't interfere. And they will have a sudden lapse of memory when the police arrive.' He sniggered. 'They might even say you were acting suicidal.' Rodriguez dangled the padlock key in front of Doyle's face, then tossed it into the far end of the pool. The shallow end.

'How do I get in touch with him?' Rodriguez asked.

'He said he'd call.'

'He has no cell phone in London?'

'He doesn't trust them.'

'His house in London. You have the number?'

Doyle nodded at his mobile phone, next to his beer on the white cast-iron table by the sun-lounger. 'It's in my phone. Look, if he calls I'll tell him you want to talk to him. I'll tell him how pissed off you are.'

'You will?' said Rodriguez, smiling affably. 'That's so good of you.'

'Oh Jesus, please don't do this to me.'

Rodriguez grinned at the man with the weightlifter's arms. 'Now he's asking for your help, Jesus.' He pronounced it the Spanish way. Hey-zeus. 'Maybe he thinks you've a softer heart than me.'

Jesus grinned and said something to Rodriguez in rapid Spanish. All four men laughed.

'Please don't . . .' begged Doyle.

Rodriguez nodded at Jesus, and Jesus put his foot on the umbrella base and shoved it into the pool. At the same time, the two men holding Doyle pitched him into the water. There was a loud splash and all four men scattered to avoid the water as the concrete block and Doyle disappeared under the surface.

Chlorinated water lapped over the edge of the pool a few times, then the surface went still. The four Colombians peered into the water, shading their eyes against the burning afternoon sun. Doyle was waving his arms and legs around like a crab stranded on its back and a stream of bubbles burst from his mouth and rippled to the surface.

Jesus looked at his watch. 'What do you think?' he asked. 'Ninety seconds?'

'Nah,' said Rodriguez. 'Less. He didn't catch his breath when he went in.'

The Colombians laughed and watched as Doyle died.

The dyed-blonde receptionist looked up as Donovan walked down the stairs. She smiled. 'You go out?' she asked.

'Just for a couple of hours.'

'You leave key?'

Donovan shook his head. 'Nah, I'll keep it with me.' He walked up to the counter. She was holding a book. 'What are you reading?'

'I learn English.' She held up the book and showed it to him. 'I go school every morning.'

Donovan took the book, flicked through it and handed it back. 'Your English is great,' he said. 'Where are you from?' He looked into her eyes as he talked. They were a deep blue with flecks of grey.

'Poland. Warsaw.'

'Great country. Beautiful city. Amazing art galleries.'

She raised her eyebrows in surprise. 'You have been to Warsaw?'

'I've been pretty much everywhere.' He winked at her and put on his baseball cap. 'Catch you later.'

Donovan walked down Sussex Gardens towards Edgware Road, confident that the hotel was still a safe area. The receptionist had shown no signs of tension, no fear, no look in the eyes that suggested that someone had told her that she was to report his movements, that he was anything other than a tourist passing through. Now he knew what her regular reactions were, he'd easily spot any changes.

Donovan walked along Edgware Road, stopping to look in several shop windows. Each time he stopped he checked reflections to see if anyone was following him. That was the beauty of Edgware Road: white faces stuck out.

At the corner of Edgware Road and Harrow Road was a pedestrian underpass. Most people used the pedestrian crossings at the traffic lights above ground, but Donovan walked slowly down the sloping walkway whistling softly to himself.

Underground there were public toilets, a newsagent's and a shoe repair shop, but more importantly there were half a dozen exits. Donovan loitered for a while until he was satisfied that no one had followed him down, and then he walked quickly up the stairs that led to the Harrow Road exit, close to Paddington Green police station. Donovan kept his head down – Paddington Green was where the Metropolitan Police's Anti-Terrorist Squad was based, and the area was saturated with CCTV cameras.

Donovan knew that there were more than a million CCTV cameras scattered across the United Kingdom, giving it the dubious distinction of having more of the prying electronic eyes per head of population than anywhere in the world. More than two hundred thousand new cameras were added every year. On average, a UK citizen going about his lawful business in the capital would be captured on three hundred cameras on at least thirty different systems every day. They were in shops, office buildings, in ATMs, on buses, there was almost nowhere that wasn't covered. The police already had access to all the networks, but their ultimate aim was to have them all linked and tied to the Mandrake face-recognition system. While the ordinary citizen probably wasn't over-concerned about the lack of privacy, believing the police line that no one but criminals had anything to fear from saturation CCTV coverage, Donovan was far from being an ordinary citizen.

He headed towards Maida Vale, and stopped at the Church of St Mary, a red brick building long-ago blackened by exhaust fumes from the stream of traffic that pelted along the nearby A40. Just along from the tumbledown churchyard was a small park with two old-fashioned red phone boxes at its entrance. Donovan sat on a bench in the graveyard and took out a mobile phone. He'd only been able to charge it for half an hour, but that would be long enough for what he wanted. He tapped out the number of Richard Underwood's direct line, dialling 141 first so that his number wouldn't show up on Underwood's phone.

The chief superintendent answered with a long groan before saying, 'Yes?'

'What's up, Dicko? Piles giving you jip?'

'The perfect end to the perfect day. Where are you?'

Donovan smiled to himself. 'A shithole, that's where I am,' he said. 'You know the churchyard on the Harrow Road?'

'Yes,' said Underwood, suspiciously.

'Fifteen minutes. I'll call the one on the right.'

'Why don't I call you?'

'Because I don't want this phone ringing, that's why. Fifteen minutes, yeah?'

Donovan cut the connection before the policeman could argue. He walked around the churchyard a couple of times, then went and stood behind a clump of trees. A few minutes later, Underwood came walking briskly from the direction of the police station, his raincoat flapping behind him, a look of intense discomfort on his jowly face. He was a large man, overweight rather than big boned, with a large gut that strained over the top of his trouser belt. He reached the two red phone boxes and stamped his feet impatiently, his hands thrust deep into the pockets of his raincoat.

Donovan took out his mobile phone and dialled the number of the phone box. A second or two later and the phone in the box on the left started to ring. Donovan grinned as he watched Underwood jump, then stand and stare at the phone box. He put his head on one side, then looked at the phone box on the right, as if to reassure himself that it wasn't the one that was ringing. He looked around, then pulled open the door to the box on the left and picked up the phone.

'You said the one on the right,' the policeman said.

Donovan chuckled. 'Right, left, what's the odds? You're breathing heavily, Dicko, you out of condition?'

'It's a long bloody walk and you know it. With cameras all the way.'

'Not by the church. Besides, who'd be watching you? You're a watcher, not a watchee.' He started walking towards the phone boxes.

'Whereabouts are you?'

'Not far, Dicko. Not far.'

'Don't piss me around, Den. This isn't a sodding game.'

'Behind you.'

Underwood turned around and his jaw dropped as he saw Donovan striding across the grass towards him. 'What the fuck are you doing here?' he exploded.

Donovan laughed and put his mobile phone away. Underwood stood in the callbox, the phone still pressed against his ear, his mouth open in surprise. Donovan pulled the door open for him. 'Breathe, Dicko. Breathe!'

Underwood's cheeks had flared red and his eyes were wide and staring.

'Bloody hell, I'm not going to have to give you the kiss of life, am I?' said Donovan.

'What the fuck's going on?'

'Put the phone down and let's have a chat, yeah?'

Underwood stood staring at Donovan for several seconds, then he slowly replaced the receiver. 'You said you were somewhere in Europe.'

'Well, strictly speaking, I am. Last I looked, Britain was still in the EC and you reported to Europol.'

'It's an information- and resource-sharing organisation. We don't report to them,' said Underwood stiffly. 'But that's not the point.'

'I know it's not the point, I was just making conversation. Come on, you soft bugger.'

Underwood squeezed out of the phone box and the two men walked down the Harrow Road, towards the canal that meandered through Little Venice before winding its way to Regent's Park and Camden.

'You shouldn't be here, Den.'

'You can say that again. But that bitch'll get my boy if I don't do something.' Donovan had already decided not to mention the missing sixty million dollars. The fewer people who knew about that, the better.

'You think you'll get custody?'

'I'm his bloody father.'

'Yeah, but . . .'

'There's no buts, Dicko. I'm his dad, and his mum was caught stark bollock naked doing the dirty with my accountant. No judge in the land is going to give him to a woman like that.'

'You and judges aren't on the best of terms, truth be told.'

'Fuck you.'

'You know what I mean.'

They walked down Warwick Avenue and turned left on Blomfield Road, parallel to the canal. On one side, the side along which the two men were walking, stood beautiful stucco houses with carefully tended gardens costing millions of pounds. The other side of the water was lined with utilitarian council flats with featureless walls and blank windows. A narrowboat packed with tourists put-putted towards Camden. A group of Japanese tourists were photographing as if their lives depended on it, and both Donovan and Underwood automatically turned their faces away.

'How did you get into the country?' asked Underwood.

'Need to know,' said Donovan. 'What's my situation?'

'Same as it's always been.'

'Shit.'

'They've got long memories, Den. You can't just run off and expect to come back to a clean slate. Life's not like that.'

'So I'm still Tango One?'

'Strictly speaking you've dropped down the ranks a bit, but as soon as it's known you're back, you'll be up there in pole position.'

'Hopefully I'll get Robbie and be out of here before anyone knows where I am.'

'Well, I'll keep my fingers crossed.'

'What have they got on me that's current?'

'That's the good news,' said Underwood. 'So far, nothing.'

'That's something.'

'Yeah, but you haven't heard the bad news yet.'

Donovan said nothing. Ahead of them was a pub. The

Paddington Stop. It sounded as if it belonged to an age when passing bargees would stop off for a refreshing pint, but it was as ugly as the council flats opposite and had been built decades after the last working barge had travelled the canal. The two men looked at each other. They both nodded at the same time and headed towards the pub.

Underwood waited until he had a pint of lager in front of him and there was no one within earshot before continuing. 'Marty Clare,' he said, and sipped his lager.

Donovan toyed with his Jack Daniels and soda, a slight frown on his face. 'He's in Amsterdam, right?'

'He's in Noordsingel Detention Centre in Rotterdam is where he is,' said Underwood. 'And he's preparing to sing like the proverbial.'

Donovan shook his head. 'No way. Not Marty.'

'His lawyer is dotting the "t"s and crossing the "i"s as we speak.'

'You know this for a fact?'

Underwood gave him a disdainful look but didn't say anything. Donovan cursed.

'What've they got on him? He could do Dutch porridge standing on his head.'

'The Yanks want him. One of the consignments was earmarked for New Jersey. That's all the DEA need. Assets, money, the works. And if they can get him extradited, they'll throw away the key.'

'Stupid bastard. How'd they get him in the first place?'

Donovan shrugged.

'Come on, Dicko, don't give me that Gallic shoulder thing. Someone grassed?'

'More than that, I think.'

'You think, or you know?'

'Bloody hell, Den, you don't give up, do you?'

Donovan leaned across the table so that his mouth was just inches away from the policeman's ear. 'My fucking life's on the line here, Dicko, now stop pissing around. I need to know where I stand.'

Underwood nodded slowly and put his glass down. 'Undercover Cussie.'

'Dutch or Brit customs?'

'Dutch.'

'Do you have a name?'

'No, Den, I don't have a name. Why the hell would the cloggies tell me who their secret weapons are?'

'Information and resource sharing, you said.'

'Superficial at best. We've linked databases but we all protect our assets. What are you going to do, Den?'

Donovan looked at Underwood, his eyes cold and hard. 'Do you really want to know, Dicko?'

Dicko sucked air in through clenched jaws, then took a long drink of lager.

'How close did they get to me?' asked Donovan.

'Strictly surveillance.'

'No one up close and personal?'

An elderly man in paint-spattered overalls and a shapeless hat walked over to the jukebox, slotted in a coin and jabbed at the selection buttons. Underwood waited until the man had walked back to his space at the bar before speaking again.

'Give me a break, Den. What do you think, I can just wander along to SO10 and ask them what undercover agents they've got in play?'

'You're NCS liaison, aren't you? National Crime Squad would have a vested interest.'

'Which would have been sparked off by what? Do you want me to tell them you're back? Because if you're out in the sunny Caribbean, why would the Met or the NCS give a rat's arse what you're up to?'

'If they've sent anyone against me, I need to know.'

'And I've got another ten years of a career ahead of me.'

'You could retire tomorrow.'

Underwood grinned. 'Not officially.' He had a little under a million pounds secreted away in various offshore accounts, but the money was untouchable until after he'd left the force. Even then he'd have to be careful. A villa in Spain. A decent-sized boat. Maybe a small bar overlooking the sea. But that was a decade away. Until then he had to be careful. He and Donovan went back a long way, longer than he cared to remember at times, and the friendship was something he treasured. However, friendship alone didn't warrant risking spending ten years behind bars on Rule 42 with the nonces and rapists.

'Just find out what you can, Dicko, yeah?'

'Sure.'

'You know I'll see you right.'

'Yeah, I know,' said Underwood. Virtually every penny of the million pounds that Underwood had salted away had come from Donovan. And at least two of the promotions that Underwood had received had been a direct result of spectacular arrests following up on information provided by Donovan. Sure, Donovan always had an agenda of his own, either settling a score or putting a competitor out of business, but Underwood had reaped the benefits, career-wise and financially. He drained his glass. 'I better be going.'

Donovan handed him a folded piece of paper. 'Call me on this number. What about the bitch?'

'Vicky?'

'She is the bitch of the day, yes.'

Underwood looked uncomfortable. 'It's bad news, Den. Guess I'm a bit worried about being the bearer. They left yesterday.'

'To where?'

'Spain. Malaga.'

'No way.'

'Booked on a British Airways flight out of Heathrow. Sharkey left his car in the longterm car park. Left a deposit on his credit card.'

'No way they'd go to Spain. I know too many faces out there. And the car is too obvious. He wanted it found.'

'I'm just telling you what I was told.'

Donovan sat shaking his head. 'It'd make my life easier if they were there.' He made a gun with his hand and mimed firing two shots, then blew away imaginary gun-smoke. 'But they're too smart for that.' He grinned. 'At least Sharkey is.' He frowned, then leaned forward, his eyes narrowed. 'Luggage? They check in any luggage?'

'Hell, Den, how would I know that?'

'You ask. You say, did they check in, and if they did, did they have any luggage? How exactly did you get to be a detective, Dicko?'

'Funny handshake and a rolled-up trouser leg,' said Underwood.

Donovan didn't react to the joke. He spoke quickly, hunched forward, his eyes burning with a fierce intensity. 'It's the oldest trick in the book. Done it myself with Vicky a couple of times. You check in for an international flight. Tickets, passports and all. But you have another ticket for somewhere where they don't check passports. Dublin. Glasgow. The Channel Islands. You pass through Immigration, then you go and check in for your real flight. Tell them you were late so didn't have time to check in at the other side. No passports, ticket can be in any name. Providing you haven't checked in any luggage, the flight you didn't get on will depart on time, give or take, and they won't even take you off the manifest. They'll just reckon you're pissed in the bar or lost in Duty Free. Once you're in Jersey you get the Hovercraft to France. Or from Dublin you fly anywhere.'

'Yeah, maybe.'

'No maybe about it. They've flown the coop.' His upper lip curled back in a snarl. 'They think they're smart,' he whispered, almost to himself, 'but I'm smarter.'

Underwood stood up. He smiled thinly. 'I am sorry about you and Vicky. Really.'

'I'll have the bitch, don't you worry.'

'Don't do anything . . . you know.' He shrugged, not wanting to say the words.

'She screwed him in my bed.'

'She's the mother of your child, Den. Any vengeance you wreak on her is going to affect Robbie.'

'You think he's not been affected already by what she's done?'

'Sure. He'll hate her for it, but at the end of the day she's still his mother. And you're still his dad. I know this isn't easy . . .'

'You know fuck all!' hissed Donovan, banging the flat of his hand down on the table, hard. Several heads turned in their direction, but shouted threats weren't an unusual occurrence in the pub and when it became clear that no one was about to be hit, the heads turned back.

'Just take it easy, that's all I'm saying. I know you, Den. Red rag to a bull, this'll be. Like the Italians say. Best eaten cold, yeah?'

Donovan nodded. He knew that Underwood had his

best interests at heart. 'Just watch my back, Dicko,' he said. 'I'll cover the rest of the bases.'

Donovan went back to the hotel and showered and changed. He ate a steak and salad and drank a glass of white wine at an Italian restaurant on the Edgware Road, reading a copy of the *Guardian* but keeping a close eye on people walking by outside. He paid the bill and then spent five minutes walking around the underpass before rushing above ground and hailing a black cab. He got to Hampstead a full hour before he was due to meet the Spaniard. He walked through the village, doubling back several times and keeping an eye on reflections in the windows of the neat cottages until he was absolutely sure he hadn't been followed.

He walked out on to the Heath, his hands deep in the pockets of his leather bomber jacket. He wore black jeans and white Nikes and his New York Yankees baseball cap, and he looked like any other hopeful homosexual trawling for company.

Donovan went the long way around to the place where he'd arranged to meet Rojas, and lingered in a copse of beech trees until he saw the Spaniard walking purposefully along one of the many paths that criss-crossed the Heath. A middle-aged man in a fawn raincoat raised his eyebrows hopefully but Rojas just shook his head and walked on by.

Donovan smiled to himself. Rojas was a good-looking guy, and he was sure that half the trade on the Heath would get a hard-on at the mere sight of the man. He looked like a young Sacha Distel: soft brown eyes, glossy black hair and a perfect suntan. His looks were actually an acute disadvantage in his line of work – he could never get too close to his quarry because heads, male and female, always turned when he was around. Donovan could imagine the eyewitness reports the police would get: 'Yeah, he was the spitting image of Sacha Distel. In his prime.' That was why Rojas always killed at a distance. A rifle. A bomb. Poison. A third party.

Donovan waited until he was sure that Rojas was alone before whistling softly to attract his attention. Rojas waved and walked over the grass to the copse. He gave Donovan a bearhug and Donovan smelled garlic on his breath. 'Dennis, good to see you again.'

'Don't get over-emotional, Juan. I know you're going to be billing me for your time. Plus expenses. Plus plus.'

Rojas laughed heartily and put an arm around Donovan's shoulders. 'You still have your sense of humour, Dennis. I like that.'

Donovan narrowed his eyes. 'What have you heard?'

Rojas shrugged carelessly. 'I have heard that Marty Clare is in Noordsingel Detention Centre. And that the DEA want to put him in a cell with Noriega.'

'Bloody hell, Juan. I'm impressed.'

'It's a small world, my friend. So is it Marty you want taking care of?'

Donovan nodded.

'I hope you never get angry with *me*, Dennis.'

'But who would I hire to kill you, Juan? You're the best.'

'Bar none,' agreed the Spaniard. 'Bar none.'

'Soon as possible, yeah?'

'I took that for granted. My usual terms.'

'No discount?'

'Not even for you.'

They walked around the copse, their feet crunching in the undergrowth. 'There's something else.' Donovan told Rojas about his wife and his accountant and their departure through Heathrow. The Spaniard listened in silence, nodding thoughtfully from time to time.

'I want them found, Juan.' Donovan handed Rojas an envelope. 'There's their passport details, credit cards, phone numbers. They know I'll be looking for them and they'll be hiding.'

'I understand.'

'When you've found them, I need to talk to them.'

'You mean you want to be there when I . . .' Rojas left the sentence unfinished.

'I need some time alone with them. That's all.' Donovan wasn't prepared to tell the Spaniard about the missing sixty million dollars. 'You can finish up after I've gone.'

'Both of them?' asked Rojas, his face creased into a frown.

'Both of them,' repeated Donovan.

'*Amigo*, are you sure this is a wise course of action?' said Rojas. 'She is your wife. Business is business but your wife is personal. You punish her of course, but . . .' He shrugged and sighed.

'She fucked my accountant. In my house. In front of my kid.'

'And he should die. No question. But your wife . . .'

'She's not my wife any more, Juan.'

'The police will know.'

'They'll suspect.'

The Spaniard shrugged again, less expressively this time, more a gesture of acceptance. He could see that there was no point in arguing with Donovan. His mind was made up.

'Very well. You are the customer and the customer is always right.'

'Thank you.'

'Even when he is wrong.'

They shook hands, then Rojas reached around Donovan and gave him a second bone-crushing bearhug.

'Be careful, Dennis. And I say that from a business perspective, not from personal concern, you understand?'

Donovan grinned. He understood exactly.

The Spaniard winked and walked away across the grass and back to the path. Donovan watched him go until he was lost in the night then he turned and went in search of a taxi.

It was just after eleven o'clock when Mark Gardner got home. He dropped his bulging briefcase by the front door and tossed his coat on to a rack by the hall table. 'Don't ask!' he said, holding up a hand to silence her. 'But if Julie or Jenny ever express any interest in entering the advertising industry, take them out and shoot them, will you?'

Laura handed him a gin and tonic and went into the kitchen. Mark stood and walked through the archway that led through to a small conservatory. He flopped down on one of the rattan sofas and swung his feet carefully up on to the glass-topped coffee table. He sighed and sipped his gin and tonic as he looked out of the french windows. Scattered around the garden were knee-high mushroom-shaped concrete structures in which were embedded small lights. They'd been installed by the previous owner of the house, along with more than two dozen garden gnomes. The gnomes had moved out with the owner, but the mushroom lights had stayed, and while their friends constantly teased them for their lack of taste, Mark and Laura had grown to like the effect at night – small pools of light that looked like miniature galaxies lost in the blackness of an ever-expanding universe.

Mark sank deep into the sofa and sniffed his gin and tonic. Bubbles were still bursting to the surface and he could feel the cold pinpricks on his nose. He knew that he was drinking more than normal, but his agency had recently acquired a batch of new clients and he was keen to make a good impression. A good impression meant longer hours, and longer hours meant he was finding it harder to wind down after work. Without a few strong gin and tonics, his mind would continue to race and he'd find it impossible to sleep. Too many and he'd wake up with a headache, but so far he'd been able to maintain a happy medium. He took another sip and sighed.

Something moved in the garden, something dark, something that was striding towards the french windows. A man. Mark jumped and his drink spilled over his chest. He cursed and scrambled to his feet, the glass shattering on the tiled floor of the conservatory.

'Are you okay?' Laura shouted from the kitchen.

Mark took a step back, away from the french windows. His feet crunched on broken glass. He put his hands up defensively even though the man was a good twenty feet away and on the other side of sheets of security glass. 'Stay where you are, Laura – there's someone in the garden.'

As usual, his wife did the exact opposite of what he asked and came running from the kitchen. 'Who is it?'

'Stay where you are!' he yelled.

Laura appeared in the archway, a tea towel in her hands. Mark looked around for something to use as a weapon and grabbed at a heavy brass vase that they'd bought while on holiday in Tunisia. He hefted it by the neck, swinging it like a club.

The man walked up to the window, his hand raised. He was wearing a leather bomber jacket and had a baseball cap pulled low over his eyes. Mark flinched, fearing that he was going to be shot, but the man's gesture turned into a wave, and when he pressed his face against the glass, Mark sighed with relief.

'It's Den!' said Laura.

'Yes, darling, I can see that now,' said Mark, sarcastically.

Donovan took off his baseball cap and gave Mark a thumbs-up. 'Surprise!' he mouthed.

Mark realised he was still swinging the brass vase and he grinned sheepishly. He put it back on its table and went to unlock the french windows.

Donovan stepped into the conservatory and shook Mark's hand. 'That was some welcome,' he said, nodding at the vase.

'Most people use the front door,' said Mark. 'In fact, our real friends usually phone first.'

Donovan slapped Mark on the back and then rushed over to hug his sister. 'He's still a moaning bugger, then?' he said.

'Like a broken record,' she said, hugging him tight.

'I did warn you about him before you got married.'

'Yes, you did,' laughed Laura.

'I am still here, you know,' said Mark. He knelt down and started picking up the pieces of broken glass.

Donovan moved to help him put the glass splinters on a copy of *The Economist*. 'Didn't mean to spook you, Mark. Sorry.'

'I wasn't spooked,' said Mark. 'You caught me by surprise, that's all.'

'I didn't want to come up the front path, just in case.'

'In case we're being watched?' asked Laura, sitting down. 'Who'd be watching us, Den?'

'I dunno, Sis. I don't know who knows I'm here. Better safe than sorry.'

Mark carefully lifted up the magazine and carried it out to the kitchen. Donovan went to sit next to his sister.

'When did you get back?' she asked.

'Yesterday. How is he?'

'He's okay. Cried his eyes out the first night, now he's sort of numb. Shock.'

Donovan shook his head, his lips tight. 'I'll swing for that bastard Sharkey. And her.'

'That's not going to help Robbie, is it?' She put a hand on his shoulder. 'What are you going to do, Den?'

Donovan shrugged. 'He's going to have to come back with me. I'll get him a new passport and we'll head off.'

'To the Caribbean?' she said, scornfully.

'You say that like it's a bad thing.'

'What about his school? His friends? Us?'

'It won't be for ever, Laura. There are schools there. He'll make friends. You and Mark can come out on holiday.'

Mark appeared at the door. 'What holiday?'

'I'm just saying, if Robbie and I go to Anguilla, you can come and stay.'

Mark and Laura exchanged worried looks.

'What?' said Donovan.

'Nothing,' said Mark.

'Come on, spit it out.'

Mark hesitated, then took a deep breath. 'Look, it's none of my business, Den, but right now Robbie needs stability. Pulling him out of his environment and dumping him on a tropical island is going to be a hell of a shock to his system.'

'It's Anguilla. It's not Robinson Crusoe. We're not

going to be fishing with safety pins and drinking from coconuts. It's more bloody civilised than this shithole called England, I can tell you.'

'Maybe, but this is home. Anyway, I'm not arguing with you. Robbie's your son. End of story. What do you want to drink?'

'JD and soda,' said Donovan.

'You'll be lucky,' said Laura. 'You can have whisky and like it.'

Donovan grinned. 'Okay, but the good stuff, none of that Bell's crap.'

Mark disappeared back into the sitting room. 'He's right, you know,' said Laura.

Donovan nodded. 'Yeah, I know, but the UK's just too hot for me now.' He rubbed his hands over his face. 'Shit.'

'What?'

'I've just remembered. Anguilla's probably not the safest place in the world for me now, either.'

'Why's that?'

Donovan flashed her a rueful smile. 'Small run-in with some Colombians.'

'Hell's bells, Den. And you want Robbie to get involved in that?'

'I'll get it sorted, don't worry.'

'You make sure you do, Den. I'm his godmother, don't forget, and that includes me being responsible for his moral upbringing.' She was only half joking. 'He can stay here, you know. As long as needs be. The kids love him. So do we.'

'I know, Laura, but I'm his father.'

'I know you don't want to hear this, but the fact that you were his father didn't stop you gallivanting off to the Caribbean for months at a time, did it?'

‘Gallivanting?’ grinned Donovan.

‘You know what I mean.’

Mark returned with a tumbler of whisky and soda for Donovan and a fresh gin and tonic for himself. Laura flashed him a warning look. It was his third gin in less than an hour. ‘The last one was spilt,’ he said defensively and sat down on the sofa opposite them.

‘Okay if I see him?’ asked Donovan.

‘Sure,’ said Laura.

They stood up and Laura took Donovan upstairs. She pushed open the bedroom door and stood aside so that Donovan could see inside. Robbie was lying on his front, his head twisted away from the door so that all he could see was a mop of unruly brown hair on the pillow. He tiptoed over to the bunk bed and knelt down, then gently ruffled his son’s hair.

Robbie stirred in his sleep, kicking his feet under the quilt.

‘Don’t worry, Robbie, I’m here now,’ Donovan whispered. He felt a sudden flare of anger at Vicky and what she’d done. Betraying him was bad enough, but to let her son witness her betrayal, that was unforgivable.

He slipped out of the bedroom and Laura closed the door quietly. They went back downstairs and into the conservatory. Donovan picked up his whisky and soda and paced up and down. Laura sat down next to Mark, her hand on his knee.

‘Has she called?’

Laura nodded. ‘Day before yesterday. She said she wanted to speak to him, but I said he was asleep and told her to call back today. She didn’t.’

‘She calls again, just hang up, yeah?’

Laura nodded.

Mark leaned forward, his hands cupping his gin and tonic. 'No offence, Den, but how much trouble are you in?'

Donovan smiled thinly. A very angry Colombian on his trail and sixty million dollars missing from his bank accounts. Quite a lot, really. 'I'll be okay,' he said.

'The police are going to be after you, aren't they?'

Donovan's smile widened. About the only good news he'd had so far had been from Dicko telling him that the police didn't have anything on him – yet. He shook his head. 'They'll be watching me, but there's no warrant. And I'm not planning on being a naughty boy while I'm here, Mark. Cross my heart. I don't intend to be here more than a few days.'

'I wasn't being . . . you know . . .' said Mark. He tailed off, embarrassed.

'I know. It's okay.'

'It's just that we've got a business . . . obligations . . .'

'Mark!' protested Laura. 'Leave him alone!'

Donovan held up his hand to silence her. 'Laura, it's okay. Honest. I understand what he means. Mark, I'll be keeping my nose clean, I promise. And I'm really grateful for what you and Laura are doing for Robbie.'

Mark leaned over and clinked his glass against Donovan's. They toasted each other. 'I'm sorry, Den. Bit stressed, that's all.'

Donovan waved away his apology, then asked Laura if she'd had the locks changed. She went into the sitting room and came back with a set of gleaming new keys and a piece of paper on which she'd written the new code for the burglar alarm system. Donovan took them, drained his glass and then gave his sister a big hug. 'I'm off,' he said. 'I'll drop by and see Robbie tomorrow, yeah? And don't tell him I was here tonight, okay?'

Donovan shook hands with Mark, then left through the french windows, keeping in the shadows as he headed back down the garden.

'Who was that masked man?' whispered Mark.

Laura put her arm around his waist. 'He's really pissed off, isn't he?' she said.

'Understatement of the year.'

'God, I hope he doesn't do anything stupid.'

'I think it's too late for that.' Mark put his arm around her shoulder and pulled her closer to him.

Donovan flagged down a black cab and had it drop him a quarter of a mile away from his house. He put his hands in the pockets of his bomber jacket and kept his head down as he walked along the pavement on the opposite side of the road to his house. He walked slowly but purposefully, his eyes scanning left and right under the peak of the baseball cap. There were no occupied cars, and no vans that could have concealed watchers. A young couple were leaning against a gatepost devouring each other's tongues but they were way too young to be police. An old lady was walking a liver-coloured Cocker spaniel, whispering encouraging noises and holding a plastic bag to clean up after it.

Donovan checked out the houses opposite his own. There was nothing obvious, but if the surveillance was good then there wouldn't be. He walked on. At the end of the road he turned right. Donovan's house was in a block which formed one side of a square. All the houses backed on to a large garden, virtually a small park with trees and a playing field big enough for football, though the garden committee had banned all ball games. Dogs had also been forbidden to use the garden, and there was a string of rules which were rigidly enforced by the committee, including no music, no organised games, no shouting, no drinking, no smoking. Donovan had always wondered why they didn't just ban everyone from the garden and have done with it.

The garden could be entered from the back doors of the houses, but many of them had been converted into apartments, and those on the upper floors, considered as poor relations by the omnipotent garden committee, had to use a side entrance. One of the keys on the ring that Laura had given him opened the black wooden gate that led to the garden. Donovan stopped to tie his shoelaces, taking a quick look over his shoulder. A black cab drove by, its 'For Hire' light on, but other than that the street was deserted. Donovan opened the gate and slipped inside.

He stood for a minute listening to the sound of his own breathing as his eyes became accustomed to the gloom. There were lights on in several of the houses, but most of the large garden area was in darkness. Donovan walked across the grass, looking from side to side to check that no one else was taking a late evening stroll. He was quite alone. For all he knew, the committee had probably issued an edict forbidding residents from using the garden after dark.

He walked quickly to his house. A flagstoned patio area was separated from the garden by a knee-high hedgerow and a small rockery, and as he walked across it a halogen security light came on automatically. There was nothing Donovan could do about the light but he took off his baseball cap. If any of the neighbours did happen to look out of the window, it would be better that they recognised him and didn't think that he was an intruder. As he unlocked the back door, the alarm system began to bleep. He closed the door and walked to the cupboard under the stairs and tapped out the four-digit number that Laura had given him. The alarm stopped bleeping. Donovan left the lights off just in case the house was under surveillance.

Donovan went into the kitchen and took a bottle of San Miguel out of the fridge. He opened it and drank from the bottle. 'Home sweet home,' he muttered to himself. It had never felt like home, not really. During the past three years he doubted if he'd spent more than eight weeks in the house. Vicky had bought all the furniture and furnishings, with the exception of the artwork, assisted by some gay designer she'd found in her health club. Donovan couldn't remember his name, but he could remember a close-cropped head, a gold earring and figure-hugging jeans with zips up either leg. He might have been a freak, but Donovan had to admit he'd done a terrific job with the house. Turns out he'd studied art at some redbrick university and he'd been impressed with Donovan's collection – some of the rooms he'd designed around the paintings, much to Vicky's annoyance.

Donovan went into the study and checked the safe, even though Laura had already told him that it was empty. He stared at the bare metal shelves and cursed. He wondered if Sharkey had been with her when she'd emptied it. Vicky would have thought about the passport, and probably regarded the cash as hers, but would she have realised the significance of the Sparbuch passbooks in the manila envelope? Donovan doubted it, but Sharkey certainly would have known what the passbooks were, and what they were worth. Donovan slammed the safe door shut and put the painting back in place. He ran his fingers along the gilded frame and smiled to himself. Luckily Sharkey was as ignorant of art as Vicky. The oil painting of two yachts was more than a hundred years old, and together with its partner on the opposite wall was worth close to half a million dollars. They were by James Edward Buttersworth, an American painter who loved yachts and sunsets, and both were used to good effect in the two pictures.

Donovan walked around the ground floor and satisfied himself that none of the works of art had been taken. They were all where they should be. Pride of his collection were three Van Dyck pen and brown ink drawings, preparatory sketches the Flemish master had made for a huge canvas that was now hanging in the Louvre. They featured a mother and daughter, and Donovan had bought them shortly after Robbie was born.

Donovan walked slowly upstairs, his hand on the banister. He imagined Robbie doing the same. Hurrying back from school, then rushing upstairs to see his mother. Catching her in the act. Donovan couldn't imagine how Robbie must have felt. Donovan had never seen his mother kiss his father, much less seen them in any sexual situation. Sex wasn't something that parents did. To find his mother in bed with someone else must have ripped the heart out of Robbie's world. Donovan's lips tightened and his free hand clenched into a fist. He'd make sure Vicky paid for what she'd done. Sharkey, too.

He pushed open the door to the master bedroom. The door to Vicky's wardrobe was open. There were lots of empty hangers inside and one of her suitcases was missing. Donovan went over to the bed. He stared at the sheet, picturing the two of them, Sharkey and his wife, screwing their brains out in his bed. Vicky had been a virgin when she'd met Donovan, and clung to her virginity for a full three months before surrendering it to him on her seventeenth birthday. They'd married a year later, and so far as Donovan knew, she'd been faithful to him throughout their marriage. He'd been her first and only lover, that's what she'd said. Usually affectionately, though occasionally, when she suspected that he'd been playing around, she'd thrown it in his face like an accusation. However, he'd never doubted that she'd been true to him, that he was the only man who'd ever taken her. Until Sharkey.

Donovan picked up the quilt and threw it on to the bed. Maybe Sharkey hadn't been her first affair. Maybe there'd been others. Maybe she'd been screwing around behind his back for years. He felt his heart start to pound and he kicked the bed, hard, cursing her for her betrayal. He walked around the upper floor of the house, checking the bedrooms but not really sure what he was looking for. It was more territorial; it was his house and he wanted to pace out every inch of it. He'd sell it, of course. Soon as he could. He wanted nothing more to do with it. It was tainted. He hated the place, he didn't want to spend a minute longer there.

He went back downstairs, reset the alarm and let himself out through the back door. The security light came on, blasting the patio with stark halogen whiteness. Donovan pulled on his baseball cap and hurried off across the grass.

He unlocked the gate leading out of the garden, checked that there was no one around, then slipped through and relocked it. He put his head down and his hands in his pockets and walked briskly along the pavement.

As he walked past a dark saloon he heard a car door open. Donovan tensed. He'd been so deep in his own thoughts that he hadn't noticed anyone sitting in any of the parked cars. He took a quick look over his shoulder. A large man in a heavy overcoat was walking around to the boot of his car, jingling his keys.

Donovan turned away and walked faster. Two men were walking along the pavement purposefully towards him. They were big men, too, as big as the man who was opening the car boot behind him. Donovan stepped off the pavement but they were too quick for him. One grabbed him by the arm with shovel-like hands and the other pulled out something from his coat pocket, raised his arm and brought it crashing down on the side of Donovan's head. Everything went red, then black, and Donovan was unconscious before he hit the ground.

Donovan had bitten the inside of his mouth when he was hit and he could taste blood as he slowly regained consciousness. The left-hand side of his head throbbed and he was having trouble breathing. The room was spinning around him and Donovan blinked several times, trying to clear his vision. It didn't do any good, everything was still revolving. Then he realised it wasn't the room that was spinning. It was him.

He'd been suspended by his feet from a metal girder with rope, and his hands had been tied behind him. His jacket was bunched around his shoulders and he could see his socks and the bare skin of his shins. His nose felt blocked and his eyes were hurting and he had a piercing headache. He'd obviously been hanging upside down for a long time. He coughed and spat out bloody phlegm.

Two pairs of legs span into view. Dark brown shoes. Grey trousers. Black coats. Then they were gone. Machinery. A dark saloon car. Welding cylinders. A jack. A calendar with a naked blonde with impossibly large breasts. A workbench. Then the legs again. Donovan craned his neck but he couldn't see their faces.

One of the men said something in Spanish but Donovan didn't catch what it was. He knew who they were, though. Colombians. He coughed and spat out more blood.

He heard footsteps and a third pair of legs walked up. '*Hola, hombre,*' said a voice. '*¿Qué pasa?*' Donovan twisted around, trying to get a look at the man who'd spoken. It took his confused brain several seconds to process the visual information. A short, thickset man in his mid twenties. Powerful arms from years of lifting weights. A neat goatee beard. It was Jesus Rodriguez, Carlos Rodriguez's nephew and a borderline psychopath. Donovan had seen him several times in Carlos Rodriguez's entourage but had never spoken to the man. He'd heard the rumours, though. Ears cut off. Prostitutes scarred for life. Bodies dumped at sea, still alive and attached to anchors.

'Oh, just hanging around,' said Donovan, trying to sound confident even though he knew that if the Colombian had just wanted a chat he wouldn't have had him picked up and suspended from the ceiling. And the fact that Doyle hadn't called him to warn him about the Colombians meant that he probably wasn't able to. 'You should have let me know you were coming.'

'Where's my uncle's money, Donovan?' said Rodriguez.

Donovan stopped turning. The rope had twisted as far as it would go. He was facing away from the Colombian and all he could see was the black saloon. Its boot was open. That was how they'd got him to the garage. And if things didn't go well, it was probably how he'd leave.

'Somebody borrowed it,' said Donovan.

'Well, *amigo*, I hope they're paying you a good rate of interest, because that loan is going to cost you your life.'

'I didn't steal your money, Jesus,' said Donovan. The rope began to untwist and Donovan revolved slowly.

'So where is our ten million dollars?'

'I'm not sure.'

'That's not the answer I'm looking for, *capullo.*'

Donovan heard metal scraping and a liquid sloshing sound. Something being unscrewed. More sloshing. A strong smell of petrol. Then the three pairs of legs swung into view. One of the men was holding a red petrol can.

Donovan's insides lurched. 'Look, Jesus, I haven't got your money.'

The man with the can started splashing it over Donovan's legs. Donovan began to shiver uncontrollably. His conscious mind, his intelligence, told him that Rodriguez wouldn't kill him while there was a chance that he'd get his money, but he'd heard enough horror stories about the man to know how irrational he could be, especially when he'd taken cocaine. Rodriguez was a user as well as a supplier, and when he was using he was a nasty piece of work.

'If you haven't got my uncle's money, then there's nothing for us to talk about, is there?'

'I've been ripped off. By my accountant.'

'Where is he?'

'I don't know.'

'Wrong answer.'

More petrol was slopped over Donovan's legs. It dripped down his chest and dribbled into his nose, stinging so badly that his eyes watered. He shook his head and blinked his eyes, hoping that the Colombian wouldn't think he was crying.

'I'm looking for him. For God's sake, Jesus, he's ripped off sixty million fucking dollars.'

'Of which ten million is my uncle's.'

'If I had the money, I'd have given it to him. You think I don't know what happens to people who don't pay your uncle?'

'If you didn't, you're about to find out.'

The man with the red can poured the last of the petrol down Donovan's back. It trickled down the back of his neck and dribbled through his hair. The fumes made him gag and he felt as if he would pass out again.

'Why did you run, *capullo*?'

'Because I knew if I didn't pay, this would happen.'

Rodriguez snorted. 'You thought you'd be safe in London, did you?'

'No, but I thought if I could get enough time, I might be able to get the bastard. Get the money back.'

Rodriguez folded his arms and studied Donovan. 'And how were you planning to do that?' he asked.

Donovan forced a smile. 'I thought I might hang him upside down and pour petrol over him. See if that works.'

Rodriguez stared at Donovan with cold eyes, then a smile slowly spread across his face. He threw back his head and laughed. His two companions stood watching Rodriguez laugh as if they didn't understand what was funny. Rodriguez wiped his eyes and shook his head. 'You English, you always keep your sense of humour, no matter what. What's the expression you have? To die laughing?'

'Killing me won't get your uncle's money back, Jesus. That's the one true thing in this situation.'

Rodriguez reached into his coat pocket and took out a gold cigarette lighter. Petrol was pooling on the floor below Donovan's head. Rodriguez crouched down and steadied Donovan with a gloved hand. He looked into his eyes. 'Don't underestimate the fear factor, *amigo*,' he said. 'This will be a lesson to everyone else. Fuck with the Rodriguez family and you'll burn in hell.' He patted Donovan on the face, then straightened up.

Donovan panicked. 'For God's sake, Jesus, I've got money. I can pay you some of it.'

'How much?'

'I don't know.'

'Wrong answer, *capullo*.' Rodriguez raised his hand and clicked the lighter.

Donovan twisted around, thrashing from side to side. 'Jesus, for fuck's sake, stop it.'

'How much?'

'Give me a minute. Let me think. Let me bloody think!'

Rodriguez clicked the top down on the lighter. 'One minute. Then it's barbecue time.' He took a step back and watched as Donovan slowly twisted in the air.

'I've got two Sparbuch passbooks. That's a million and half bucks.'

Rodriguez frowned. 'What's a Sparbuch?'

Donovan cleared his throat and coughed up more bloody phlegm. 'Jesus, I'm choking here. Cut me down, yeah?'

'What is a Sparbuch?' repeated Rodriguez. He clicked the lighter open.

'It's a bank account,' said Donovan hurriedly. 'They're for accounts in Czechoslovakia. The ones I've got are in US dollars.'

'Fine. So give me the money.'

'I don't have the money, I have the passbooks. The money is in Czechoslovakia.'

'So transfer the money.'

'It's not as easy as that. They're bearer passbooks. Whoever has the passbooks and the passwords has the account. You have to show the passbook to get the money. They won't do electronic transfers.'

'That sounds like bullshit,' said Rodriguez. He flicked

the lighter again. '*Me cargo en tus muertos.*' I shit on your dead. As bad a curse as there was in Spanish.

'Look, talk to your uncle!' said Donovan hurriedly. 'I'm offering you money here. Kill me and you get nothing. He's going to be really pissed at you if he finds out afterwards that I was going to pay him, right?'

'My uncle has left this up to me, *capullo*.'

'Right. Fine. So make an executive decision here. Call him and tell him I've got a million and half dollars for him. Use your cell phone, come on.'

Rodriguez studied Donovan with emotionless brown eyes, then nodded slowly. He took a mobile phone from his jacket pocket and dialled a number. He kept staring at Donovan, then said something in Spanish. Donovan kept hearing the word '*capullo*'. Prick. Rodriguez listened, then nodded, then spoke some more. Donovan's Spanish was good but not fluent, and a lot of what Jesus was saying was slang. Gutter Spanish. However, he mentioned the word 'Sparbuch' several times.

Rodriguez walked over to Donovan. 'He wants to talk to you.'

Rodriguez thrust the phone against the side of Donovan's head.

'What's this about Sparbuch accounts?' asked Carlos Rodriguez.

'Everyone uses them in Europe, Carlos. They're better than cash. It's clean money, it's in the fucking bank, for God's sake.'

'But if I want the cash, I have to go to Czechoslovakia?'

'It's a three-hour flight. It's no big deal. But they're better than cash. You owe someone, you give them the passbook and the password.'

There was a long silence and for a moment Donovan

thought the connection had been cut. 'Carlos? Are you there?'

'Where are these passbooks?'

'In my hotel.'

'That still leaves you eight and a half million dollars short.'

'Paintings,' said Donovan. 'I have paintings in the house. Three million dollars' worth.'

'What good are paintings to me?'

'You can sell them. Three million, easy.'

'I'm not an art dealer, *amigo*.'

'Bloody hell, Carlos, work with me on this, will you? With the paintings and the passbooks, I've got almost five million dollars.'

'Which is only half what you owe me. The man who ripped you off. Who is he?'

'My accountant. Sharkey, his name is.'

'And you gave this man access to your accounts.' Rodriguez chuckled. 'I didn't think you were that stupid, *amigo*.'

'He had help,' said Donovan. He was starting to relax a little. At least the Colombian was talking, and so long as he was talking Donovan had a chance.

'Ah yes. Your wife,' said Rodriguez. 'So not only does she fuck your accountant, she helps him steal your money as well. Betrayed twice? You must feel very stupid, no?'

The petrol fumes were making Donovan dizzy and his eyes were watering. Doyle must have told Rodriguez about Vicky and Sharkey. Before he died. 'Yeah, I feel like a right twat, Carlos. Does that make you happy?'

'The only thing that will make me happy is when I have my ten million dollars.'

'Killing me isn't going to get your money back.'

‘So you said. Where is your wife now?’

‘Sitting at home waiting for me. Where the fuck do you think she is, Carlos?’ spat Donovan. ‘She’s on the fucking run, that’s where she is.’

‘You have people looking for her?’

‘The Spaniard.’

‘Rojas is good. Expensive, but good. Does he know your money’s gone?’ Donovan didn’t reply and Rodriguez chuckled. ‘Your situation just gets worse and worse, doesn’t it, *amigo*?’

Jesus Rodriguez was glaring at Donovan, annoyed at having to hold the phone to his mouth.

‘What about when the consignment arrives?’ said Rodriguez. ‘How were you expecting to pay the second tranche?’

‘What can I say, Carlos? I haven’t got the first ten mill, let alone the second.’

‘So even if I take what you’re offering me now, you’re not going to be able to pay for the consignment when it arrives?’

‘If I find that bastard Sharkey, you’ll get your money.’

‘That’s a big “if”, *amigo*. The people who are taking on the cocaine, they have paid you half, yes?’

‘Yes.’

‘Fifteen million?’

‘Eighteen.’

‘I presume they are not yet aware of your financial situation,’ said Rodriguez.

‘God willing.’

Rodriguez chuckled. ‘*Amigo*, you are in so much shit. How can I let you go? If I don’t kill you, they will. And if they kill you, I lose everything.’

‘If I can deliver the gear, they’ll pay me another eighteen

mill,' said Donovan. 'You can have all that. The eighteen plus the passbooks plus the paintings is more than twenty mill. You get your money, they get their gear. Everyone wins.'

'But why do I need you in this equation, *amigo*?' asked Rodriguez. 'Why don't I just tell my nephew to kill you now?'

'It's my deal.'

'It *was* your deal,' he said. 'Who is taking delivery of the cars?' he asked.

Donovan closed his eyes. He could see where Rodriguez was going. 'You can't do this to me, Carlos.'

'*Amigo*, I can tell my nephew to turn you into a flaming kebab and do what the hell I want with the cars, so don't tell me what I can and cannot do.'

Donovan opened his eyes. 'It's being split between Ricky Jordan and Charlie Macfadyen,' he said. 'Fifty–fifty.'

'Jordan I have heard of,' said Rodriguez, 'but who is this Macfadyen?'

'He's a big fish in Edinburgh. They both are. Got the backing of some property guys who were looking to diversify. This is their first big deal but I know them from way back. Solid as they come. Look, let me run with this, Carlos. You'll get your money. All of it.'

'I don't think so, *amigo*. When word gets out how you've been screwed, no one's going to be doing business with you. It'll be open season. I will deal with Jordan and Macfadyen myself.'

'You bastard!'

Jesus Rodriguez took the phone away from Donovan's ear and slapped him across the face. 'Talk to my uncle with respect, *capullo*. With respect.' He slapped Donovan again and then put the phone back to his ear.

'Sorry about that, Carlos,' said Donovan. He spat out more bloody phlegm. 'Your nephew wanted a word.'

'He's a good boy. Very enthusiastic. Now what were you saying? Questioning the marital status of my parents, I seem to remember.'

Jesus started to click his lighter again. 'Okay, okay!' shouted Donovan. 'It's yours! The deal's yours!'

'Good call,' said Carlos Rodriguez. 'Let me talk to my nephew.'

Donovan tried to smile up at Jesus Rodriguez. 'He wants to talk to you.'

Jesus walked up and down as he listened to his uncle, his shoes crunching on the bare concrete. Eventually he put the phone away and walked back to where Donovan was gently swinging.

'You are one lucky *capullo*,' he said. 'I'm staying at the Intercontinental. Tell Jordan and Macfadyen to contact me there. I will explain the new arrangement to them.'

'Okay,' said Donovan wearily.

'How long will it take you to sell your paintings?' asked Rodriguez.

Donovan glared at the Colombian. 'Oh, come on. You'll get your money for the gear, Jesus.'

'My uncle says you owe interest, *capullo*. I will take the passbooks and the money from the paintings.' He held out the lighter. 'Or we end this now.'

The fight went out of Donovan. Suspended from the ceiling and doused with petrol didn't put him in any position to argue with the Colombian. Besides, Carlos Rodriguez did occupy the moral high ground, in as much as there was a moral high ground in the world of drug trafficking. Donovan had promised to pay ten million dollars when the drugs left Mexico. He had failed to come up with the money, and in the circles that Donovan moved in, that was equivalent to signing his own death warrant. Donovan had hoped that he would have been able to find Sharkey before Rodriguez had found him, but his gamble had failed and now he had to pay the price.

'You can have the passbooks tonight,' said Donovan. 'I should be able to sell the pictures within a few days.'

'I will be in London for three days. Bring the money and the passbooks to me at the hotel.' He started to walk away, then hesitated. 'Don't make a fool of me again, *capullo*.'

'I won't.'

'Next time I won't phone my uncle. I don't have to say that I know how to find you, and that I know where your son is, do I?'

'No, you don't,' said Donovan coldly.

Rodriguez nodded. 'Three days,' he repeated, then walked away.

'Jesus!'

Rodriguez turned and raised an eyebrow expectantly.

'Cut me down, yeah?'

Rodriguez nodded at his men. One of them took a penknife from his coat pocket and walked behind Donovan. Donovan felt the rope being cut from around his wrists. His fingers began to tingle as the circulation returned. Rodriguez walked away as the man cut the rope around Donovan's ankles. Donovan hit the ground hard, jarring his shoulder, but he was so numb that he felt hardly any pain. He lay on the concrete floor, gasping for breath.

He heard the doors of the car open and slam shut, then the engine revving. A metal gate rattled up and the car drove out and then he was alone. He sat up, massaging his legs, hardly able to believe that he was still alive. Carlos Rodriguez wasn't the most vicious of the Colombian drug lords, but he was far from being a pushover, and Donovan knew for a fact that he'd killed several times. One simple command from him and Jesus would have happily ended Donovan's life.

Donovan had always got on well with Carlos Rodriguez, which might have explained the Colombian's apparent change of heart. Or maybe Rodriguez had never intended to kill Donovan; maybe it had all been a mind game from the start and Jesus Rodriguez and his two henchmen were pissing themselves laughing as they drove away.

Donovan stood up slowly. He was still drenched in petrol so he took off most of his clothes and draped them on a workbench to dry. He paced up and down as he considered his options, which now appeared to be few and far between.

Marty Clare started his third set of sit-ups. He did three hundred during each early-morning workout, six sets of fifty. His torso glistened and he grunted each time he sat upright, his hands clenched behind his neck, his knees slightly bent.

The man watching Clare was also sweating, but not from exertion. He was a tall, almost gangly, black man in his late twenties with a shaved head and wicked scar on his left forearm. He was wearing a black Adidas tracksuit and his right hand was in his pocket, clenched around an eight-inch-long metal spike that had been carefully sharpened.

The gym was covered by two closed-circuit television cameras that were constantly monitored by prison guards in the control centre. The CCTV cameras were in fixed positions and the man knew that he was standing in a blind spot. The man's hand was sweating but he didn't want to take it out and wipe it because that would mean letting go of the spike. Two men were working with weights, but they had been in the gym for almost an hour and were getting towards the end of their workout.

Clare finished his third set and stood up, wiping his face with his towel. He went over to a press bench and picked up two small free weights, then lay on his back on the bench. The man watched. And waited. He went and sat on an exercise bike and pedalled slowly. The exercise bike was also out of view of the two CCTV cameras.

Clare worked on his arms and pectorals for ten minutes then went back to his sit-ups. The man carried on cycling slowly, his hand still on the spike.

The two men at the weights bench laughed and headed for the door, wiping their faces with their towels.

Clare got to his feet, stretched and groaned, and picked up his towel. He walked past the exercise bikes, humming to himself. The man kept his head down until Clare had gone by, then slid off his saddle and walked up behind Clare, pulling out the spike. Clare turned to look at the man, but before he could react the man sprang forward, grasping for the collar of Clare's T-shirt with his left hand as he thrust the spike forward. Clare twisted and the spike ripped through his shirt. Clare swore and tried to push the man away but the man was too quick and slashed with the spike, cutting Clare's upper arm. Blood spurted across Clare's chest and the man lashed out again, this time with a stabbing movement. Clare fell back, but the man followed through and the spike stabbed into Clare's stomach. He carried on falling back and crashed into an exercise bike, then rolled on to his side. The man raised the spike above his head but then hesitated. Clare was lying in an area covered by the CCTV camera by the door.

The man turned, kept his head down and hurried out of

the gym, thrusting the spike into his pocket as he jogged down the corridor.

Clare put his hands over the wound in his stomach. Blood seeped through his fingers and he screamed up at the CCTV camera. 'You bastards! Get down here!'

The single lens stared down at him dispassionately. Clare groaned and closed his eyes.

Den Donovan woke up with a splitting headache. He wasn't sure if it was the petrol fumes or the clip on the side of the head that had done the damage, but either way his head throbbed every time he moved it. He found a small plastic kettle and sachets of coffee, creamer and sugar on a table next to the wardrobe and made himself a cup of strong coffee. He sat on the bed and sipped it as he considered his options. He didn't appear to have many. He had to give the two Sparbuchs to Rodriguez. He had to sell his paintings and give the proceeds to the Colombian. Then he had to put Jordan and Macfadyen in touch with him and step out of the deal. Which left him with what? Not much, Donovan decided. There was the Russian deal on the backburner, but the Russians would want cash in advance and cash was something that Donovan was fast running out of.

First things first. He picked up one of the unused mobile phones and dialled Macfadyen's mobile number from memory. The answering service kicked in. Donovan didn't identify himself, but just gave the number of the mobile and asked Macfadyen to call him. Charlie Macfadyen was a religious screener of calls, so Donovan wasn't surprised when he called back two minutes later.

'How's it going, you old bastard?' asked Macfadyen.

'I've had better weeks,' said Donovan. 'Where are you?'

'London. There isn't a problem, is there?' asked Macfadyen.

'Not for you, mate,' said Donovan. 'Everything's sweet. But from now on you're dealing with the man direct.'

'Since when?'

'Since today.'

'You okay, mate?' Macfadyen sounded concerned and Donovan was touched.

'Not really. Your man'll explain the situation.'

'I'd rather be dealing with you – better the devil and all that shit.'

'It's not an either or,' said Donovan. 'He wants to deal direct.'

'And you're walking away? Fuck that for a game of soldiers. I don't know him. I do know you.'

Donovan closed his eyes and cursed silently. This wasn't a conversation he wanted to have over the phone.

'We're gonna have to meet,' said Macfadyen. 'Where are you?'

'Can't you just do as you're told?' said Donovan angrily.

'Look, mate, you've got a stack of my bread. How do I know your guy's gonna honour that? *Caveat* fucking *emptor*, right? How do I know it's not gonna be guns blazing when I go to see him?'

'Because he wants to meet at the Intercontinental.'

'Oh, it's in the book of rules now that no one gets shot in a five-star hotel, is it?'

'Your imagination's in overdrive,' said Donovan. 'Take a Prozac, will you?'

'I'm serious, Den,' said Macfadyen. 'I need more than this or you can give me back my bread and we'll call it quits.'

Donovan's head felt like it was splitting in half. He

transferred the phone to his other ear. Giving Macfadyen his money back was an impossibility. And if he refused to go through with the deal, the Colombian would be back with another can of petrol and the lighter, and this time there'd be nothing Donovan could say or do that would stop him going up like a roman candle. 'You know the Paddington Stop, yeah?'

'Little Venice?'

'See you on the terrace in one, yeah?'

'I'm bringing Ricky with me.' It was a statement, not a question.

'Be nice, yeah?' said Donovan. 'We're on the same side here.'

'I bloody hope so, Den. See you in one hour.'

The phone went dead. Donovan pulled the battery off the back of the phone and removed the Sim card. He dropped it into the toilet bowl in the bathroom and flushed, then put a replacement Sim card into the phone. He put on his jacket and headed out. As he was closing the door he hesitated, then went back into the room and got the two Sparbuchs out of his suitcase. The Paddington Stop was less than half an hour's walk if he went the direct route, but that meant walking past Paddington Green police station, and he'd prefer to give it a wide berth. Besides, a long walk might help clear his head.

'So, Mr Clare, how are you feeling?' asked the prison governor. He was a small, portly man in his late thirties with a kindly face and gold-framed glasses.

'How do you think I'm feeling?' said Clare. 'He nearly killed me.'

'Superficial, I'm told,' said the governor.

'If someone stabbed you in the stomach, I doubt you'd

think it superficial,' said Clare bitterly. He was lying in the prison hospital ward. Only three of the eight beds were occupied. The other two patients were prisoners recovering from drug overdoses and were both on the far side of the ward, connected to saline drips. A guard had been standing by the door ever since Clare had been admitted.

'Neither of your wounds were life-threatening, Mr Clare,' said the governor patiently, 'but that's not to say we're not taking the matter seriously. You say you can't identify your assailant?'

'He was black. In his twenties, maybe. I hardly saw him.'

'Many of our inmates are black, Mr Clare. You can appreciate how difficult it is to identify the man from your description.'

'I want out of here,' said Clare. 'Now.'

'The medical facilities here are more than sufficient for your needs, Mr Clare,' said the governor. He looked at a white-coated doctor who nodded on cue.

'I don't give a shit about my medical treatment,' said Clare. 'We all know what this was about. It was Den Donovan. He either wanted to warn me, or he wanted me dead. Either way, I'm out of here. Get me my lawyer, and get me Hathaway. If he wants me to grass on Donovan, he can bloody well make sure I'm taken care of.'

Donovan walked down Sussex Gardens and across Lancaster Gate to Hyde Park. It was a sunny morning but there was a cold breeze blowing across the park so he zipped up his bomber jacket and thrust his hands deep into his pockets. He had his baseball cap and sunglasses on.

Two young women in tight tops, jodhpurs and boots were riding gleaming chestnut horses along the bridle path. Donovan wasn't the only male head to turn and watch them go by. They moved in unison, gripping their mounts with their muscular thighs.

As Donovan watched them ride off, he scanned the park, looking for familiar figures. He'd been checking reflections in windows and car mirrors all the way down Sussex Gardens and had knelt down to tie his shoelaces before entering the park, and he was reasonably sure that he hadn't been followed. He wasn't looking at faces, or even heads, because faces were notoriously hard to recognise, and profiles of heads could easily be changed with wigs or hats or scarves. Donovan checked out bodies. Their shape, their posture, the way they moved. People who were watching or following weren't behaving normally, and no matter how good they were, there'd be signs that could be spotted – a stiffness, a momentary hesitation when they were looked at, an awkwardness about disguising the hands going towards a concealed microphone, a hundred and one things that could give them away. Donovan saw nothing to worry him.

Half an hour later, Donovan was on the towpath opposite the Paddington Stop. He leaned against the railings and waited. There was a terrace between the pub and the canal with half a dozen wooden tables and benches, most of which were occupied by midday drinkers from the nearby council estates.

Donovan saw Jordan and Macfadyen arrive in a bright red Ferrari with the top down. They drove into the car park behind the pub and a couple of minutes later walked out on to the terrace. Donovan stayed where he was and watched with an amused smile as the two men checked out the occupants of all the tables. Jordan shook his head and Macfadyen looked at his watch. Eventually Macfadyen spotted Donovan and said something to Jordan. Both men looked at him across the canal. Donovan pointed to the footbridge and motioned for them to come over.

He walked back along the towpath as Macfadyen and Jordan walked over the bridge.

'What's up, Den?' teased Jordan in his nasal Liverpudlian whine. 'Thought we'd be here mob-handed?' Jordan was average build with a beaked nose and a cleft chin and ears that stuck out like cup handles. He was dressed as usual in black Armani and had a chunky gold ring on his right hand that glinted in the sun. Macfadyen was more casually dressed, sporting a black Valentino leather jacket over a pale green polo-necked pullover, and he had a thick gold bracelet on his right wrist. He was balding and had shaved what hair he had left close to his skull, showing off a curved scar above his left ear that looked like a Nike swoosh. Both men, like Donovan, were wearing sunglasses. Jordan's were Armani.

Den smiled and shrugged. The bridge was an excellent way of making sure he knew exactly who he'd be meeting. If they'd turned up with reinforcements, he'd have been able to beat a hasty retreat back under the A40 and disappear into the Bayswater shopping crowds. 'Just being careful.' He hugged Jordan and patted him on the back. He felt Jordan's hands run down his back, the fingers probing under Donovan's jacket. 'For fuck's sake, Ricky,' he protested. 'What are you looking for?'

Macfadyen was watching, an amused look on his face. 'Yeah, well, you've gotta expect us to be careful, too,' he said. He nodded at the bridge. 'No need for that. You think we'd have come near you if we'd had a sniff that Five-O were on our tail?'

Donovan pushed Jordan away, then took off his jacket and undid his shirt. He pulled his shirt open and showed it to Macfadyen. 'Satisfied?' he sneered.

Macfadyen put his hands up and patted the air. 'Calm down, Den.' He grinned. 'I mean, keep your shirt on, yeah? You've got to admit, this isn't the gospel according to Den, is it?'

'You think I'm setting you up?' asked Donovan, buttoning up his shirt.

'You haven't said what you're doing, have you?' said Jordan.

Donovan turned and started walking across the grassy area towards a children's playground. A few swings, a climbing frame, a rusting roundabout. Every flat surface had been covered in graffiti. Nothing clever or ironic, just names. Tags proclaiming territory like dogs pissing against trees. I wrote this, therefore I exist. Empty cries in an uncaring world.

Jordan and Macfadyen followed Donovan. 'Who is he?' asked Macfadyen in his thick Scottish brogue.

'Carlos Rodriguez. He's Colombian. He's big, Charlie. No way's he going to rip you off.' He stopped to let the two men catch up, then they walked together to the playground.

'He's the supplier?'

Donovan nodded.

'And you're giving him to us?'

'I think Carlos sees it as the other way around,' said Donovan bitterly.

'He's cutting you out?' said Jordan.

'Are you two just gonna keep staring this gift horse down the throat?' said Donovan. 'If I was you I'd be biting my hand off.'

'We don't know him, Den,' said Jordan. 'We do know you.'

'Which is why they want to meet you.'

'He's here?' asked Macfadyen.

'His nephew. Jesus.'

'We meet him, then what?' asked Jordan.

Donovan frowned. 'What do you mean?'

'Future deals. Do we still do business with you?'

Donovan grimaced. It wasn't a question he was able to answer, but he doubted that Rodriguez would ever trust him again.

Macfadyen caught Donovan's look. 'What's happening, Den?'

'Just leave it be, Charlie.'

'Is this to do with Marty Clare being banged up in Holland?' Macfadyen asked.

'No.'

'We heard he's talking.'

Donovan pulled a face. 'He can't hurt me.'

Jordan fiddled with his gold ring. 'This Colombian, he's got our money, right?'

'Sort of.'

'Sort of?' repeated Macfadyen incredulously. 'How can he sort of have eighteen million dollars?'

'He's happy to proceed with the deal. When the consignment arrives you pay him the balance.'

'You sure about that?' asked Jordan.

'Give me a break, Ricky.'

'You can see why we're nervous, Den,' said Macfadyen. 'What happens if we turn up and this Colombian says he never saw our money? They're mad bastards, Colombians. Shoot first and fuck the questions, right?'

'Carlos isn't like that,' said Donovan. He thought that Jesus might well be the sort to shoot before thinking, but he figured it better not to let them know that.

'Even so . . .' said Macfadyen.

'What do you want, Charlie? Spit it out.' Donovan already knew what Macfadyen was going to suggest. It's what he would have insisted on had the roles been reversed.

'You come with us to the meet,' said Macfadyen.

'That's not a good idea and you know it. You, me and the Colombian together in one place. Too many fucking cooks, Charlie.'

Macfadyen looked at Jordan and something unspoken passed between them. Jordan nodded. 'You're there or we walk away here and now,' said Macfadyen quietly.

'That'd be your call, Charlie.'

'We'd be wanting our money back.'

'And I'd be wanting to shag Britney Spears but it ain't gonna happen,' said Donovan.

'Then it'd all get very heavy,' said Macfadyen.

'Britney Spears?' said Jordan. 'You'd shag Britney Spears?'

'I was speaking hypothetically,' said Donovan. 'Look, if it makes you feel any better, I'll introduce you. But once you've shaken hands, I'm outta there. Okay?'

Macfadyen and Jordan exchanged another meaningful look. This time it was Macfadyen who nodded. 'Okay,' said Macfadyen. 'When?'

'Let me make a call.' Donovan took out one of his mobile phones.

Two Dutch plainclothes detectives escorted Marty Clare to the waiting Saab. Clare had insisted through his lawyer that he be taken from the detention centre in a regular car rather than a prison van, and he didn't want any uniforms anywhere near him. Clare's lawyer had spoken to Hathaway at length and had eventually persuaded him to allow

Clare to be interrogated at a hotel on the outskirts of Rotterdam.

As the taller of the two detectives opened the rear door of the Saab, his jacket fell open and Clare caught a glimpse of a holstered automatic. That had been another stipulation of Clare's – he wanted round-the-clock armed protection. The attack in the gym might well have been a warning, but once Donovan found out that Clare was still talking there'd be hell to pay.

The taller detective climbed into the back seat after Clare while the other got into the front and told the driver to head on out.

The car was checked over by two uniformed guards while a third guard examined the ID cards of the two detectives and the paperwork permitting Clare's removal from the centre. There was a photograph of Clare clipped to a letter from the governor's office and the guard carefully checked the likeness against Clare's face. Clare grinned but the guard remained impassive.

The metal gate rattled to the side and the Saab edged forward. A second gate leading to the street didn't start opening until the first gate had closed behind the car.

'This place had better have room service,' said Clare. 'And cable. My lawyer was supposed to have insisted on cable.'

The two detectives said nothing. Clare turned to the policeman next to him and asked if he had a cigarette. The man shook his head. The car edged into the traffic, then accelerated away.

'What is this, the silent treatment?' joked Clare, but the detective just stared out of the window, stony faced.

'Fuck you, then,' said Clare and settled back in the seat, his handcuffed wrists in his lap. The cut on Clare's arm barely bothered him, it had only required three stitches, but the wound in his stomach hurt like hell, especially when he was in a sitting position, so he tried to stretch out his legs to make himself more comfortable. The doctor had given Clare a vial of painkillers but told him to use them sparingly. When the detectives had heard that, they'd taken the tablets off Clare. Clare had laughed in their faces. Suicidal he wasn't.

The driver braked as they approached a set of traffic lights. The lights were green but a white van ahead of them had slowed. The driver muttered under his breath and was about to sound his horn when the lights changed to red. The van pulled up and the Saab stopped behind it.

The detectives spoke to each other in Dutch. The one in the front laughed and Clare had the feeling they were laughing about him. He scowled. He never heard the crack as the window behind him exploded in a shower of glass cubes, and he died instantly as the bullet ripped through the back of his head and spattered brains and blood over the Saab's windscreen.

The driver and the detectives started shouting. Clare's body twitched as a second bullet smacked into the back of his head but he was already dead. The lights changed from red to green and the white van pulled away. Horns began to sound behind the Saab, but they stopped when the detectives piled out of the car, guns raised above their heads.

Juan Rojas unscrewed the silencer from the barrel of his rifle and put it into his briefcase, then swiftly disassembled the weapon and put the pieces away. He closed the briefcase and then examined himself in the mirror above the dressing table. Dark blue pinstripe suit, crisp white shirt, crimson tie. He winked at his reflection. He left the briefcase on the dressing table. It would be collected later by the man who had booked the hotel room.

Rojas had shot Clare from the roof of the hotel. The men in the white van had been working for him, as had the man who had stabbed Clare in the gym. It was an easy shot, just over a hundred metres, but the intersection was overlooked by so many tower blocks that the police would never find out where the bullets had come from. Rojas had wrapped the rifle in a towel and then hurried back through the emergency exit door and into the hotel room.

His mohair coat was hanging on the back of the door and he put it on, then gave his hotel room a once over to make sure that he hadn't left anything behind other than the briefcase. He whistled softly to himself as he waited for the elevator to take him down to the ground floor. Five minutes later he was in a taxi, heading for the airport.

Den Donovan walked along the edge of the Serpentine. Two small children were throwing pieces of bread for a noisy flock of ducks. A large white swan watched disdainfully from a distance. A helicopter clattered high overhead. Donovan kept his head down, more from habit than from any realistic fear that the helicopter was on a surveillance operation.

Macfadyen and Jordan were several hundred yards away, walking together, deep in conversation, though they kept looking across at him. Donovan had insisted on walking to the park, but Macfadyen and Jordan had wanted to drive. They'd parked the Ferrari in the underground car park in Park Lane and were keeping their distance until they'd seen Donovan with the Colombian.

Jesus Rodriguez was standing on the bank of the Serpentine wearing a cream-coloured suit with a white silk shirt buttoned at the neck with no tie.

Donovan hated having to meet Rodriguez out in the open, because it made it harder to spot any surveillance, but Macfadyen and Jordan hadn't wanted a meeting indoors. They hung back as Donovan walked up to Rodriguez.

'Is that them?' asked the Colombian, nodding at Macfadyen and Jordan.

'Yeah. They're jittery. So am I.'

'We're just having a walk in the park, my friend.'

'A Colombian drugs lord, two of the main suppliers of Class A drugs in Scotland, and Tango One. The fact that we're in one place is just about grounds for a conspiracy charge.'

'You worry too much,' said the Colombian. He took a pack of Marlboro from his pocket and slipped a cigarette between his lips. He held his gold lighter up and grinned mischievously at Donovan. 'You changed your clothes, I hope?' Donovan flashed Rodriguez a cold smile and Rodriguez lit his cigarette. He took a long pull on the cigarette and then sighed as he exhaled. He started walking alongside the Serpentine and Donovan went with him. He took the Sparbuchs from his inside pocket and handed them to the Colombian.

Rodriguez flicked through them. 'As good as cash, you say?'

'Better than cash,' said Donovan. 'They're useless without the passwords. And you can fly around the world with them in your pocket and no one's the wiser.'

Rodriguez nodded appreciatively and put the passbooks into his jacket pocket. Donovan handed him a slip of paper with two words written on it. Rodriguez put it in his wallet. 'If it was me, I'd have killed you. You know that?'

'I'd guessed,' said Donovan. He looked around casually. The two men who had been with Rodriguez were some distance away, standing in the shade of a spreading sycamore tree.

'Having said that, my uncle told me to tell you that if you do get your finances sorted out, he would be prepared to resume our business relationship.'

Donovan smiled ruefully. 'I'll bear that in mind, Jesus. Tell him thanks.'

'And you will have the money from the paintings before I leave London?'

'I hope so,' said Donovan.

Rodriguez chuckled dryly. 'Just remember that we have another can of petrol,' he said. 'Now, these two men in black, they know the score?'

Donovan nodded. 'They'll pay you on delivery. Eighteen mill. They have it offshore, so they can transfer to any account you nominate.'

'How much do they know about me?'

'Your name. And that you're the supplier. They're worried it might be a set-up. That's why they want me here.'

Rodriguez grinned. 'So you can protect them?'

'So that if the shit hits the fan, I'll get hit, too.'

'Do you think they're satisfied yet?'

'I'll ask them.' Donovan beckoned at Macfadyen and Jordan. The two men looked at each other, then walked cautiously over the grass towards him. Donovan turned to the Colombian. 'You can trust them, Jesus.'

'My uncle thought he could trust you, *capullo*.'

'This isn't about trust. I was ripped off.'

'The hows and whys don't concern me, all that matters is the money. That's what this business is all about: the movement and acquisition of capital. That's why you must never make it personal. When you make it personal is when you make mistakes.' He patted Donovan on the back again, hard enough to rattle his teeth. 'Remember that.'

'Thanks, Jesus,' said Donovan. 'Did you get that from a Christmas cracker?'

'My father told me that,' said Rodriguez. 'A lifetime ago. Before he was shot in the back of the head by a *capullo* he turned his back on.'

Macfadyen and Jordan joined them. Macfadyen nodded at Rodriguez, then jerked a thumb towards the men under the tree. 'They with you?' he asked.

'They are,' said Rodriguez evenly. 'Do you have a problem with that?'

'Not so long as they stay where they are,' said Macfadyen.

'There are three of you and one of me but you don't see me shitting my pants,' said Rodriguez. He blew a tight plume of smoke that was quickly whisked away by the wind. He nodded at Donovan. 'Perhaps you should do the honours.'

'This is Charlie Macfadyen. Edinburgh's finest. Charlie, this is Jesus Rodriguez.'

The two men shook hands.

'And this is Ricky Jordan.'

'From Liverpool,' said Rodriguez. 'Birthplace of the Beatles.' He shook hands with Jordan. 'I've heard of you, Ricky. You were in Miami two years ago doing business with Roberto Galardo.'

Jordan narrowed his eyes and Rodriguez laughed out loud. 'Don't worry, Ricky, I'm not DEA. Roberto is an old friend. And he quite definitely didn't tell me about you and those three lap dancers.' He winked conspiratorially.

'You do know that the Hispanic one was a transsexual, right?'

Jordan's face flushed and Macfadyen sniggered. 'You never told me about that, Ricky,' he teased.

'She was female,' said Jordan.

'Of course she was,' said Rodriguez. 'By the time you met her.'

Jordan's brow creased into a frown, not sure whether Rodriguez was joking or not.

The Colombian put his arm around Jordan's shoulder and hugged him. 'So, let's talk business, shall we?' He looked across at Donovan. 'Call me at the hotel about the other thing, okay? Two days.'

Donovan nodded. 'You okay now?' he asked Macfadyen.

'Yeah. I guess.'

'I'll leave you to it. Be lucky, yeah?' He flashed Macfadyen a thumbs-up.

'She was definitely a girl,' Jordan continued to protest as Donovan walked away.

Donovan took his time leaving Hyde Park. He had a coffee in the cafeteria overlooking the Serpentine, checking out the faces of the passers-by, then he walked slowly along Rotten Row towards Hyde Park Corner, stopping twice to tie and retie his shoelaces. At one point he looked at his watch and then turned and quickly walked back the way he'd come, looking out for signs of walkers being wrong-footed or watchers whispering into concealed radios.

Once he was satisfied that he wasn't being followed, he walked quickly to the underpass beneath Hyde Park Corner, took the Grosvenor Place exit and flagged down a black cab.

* * *

The glass door to the gallery was locked and a discreet brass plate told visitors that they should ring the bell if they wanted to be admitted. A tall brunette with close-cropped hair and startled fawn eyes studiously ignored Donovan. She was sitting at a white oak reception desk flicking through her Filofax. She'd seen Donovan looking in through the floor-to-ceiling window but had averted her eyes when he'd smiled.

When Donovan finally pressed the bell in three short bursts she slowly looked up, her face impassive. Donovan took off his sunglasses and winked. She gave him a cold look and then went back to examining her Filofax. Donovan pressed the bell again, this time giving it three long bursts.

The brunette stood up and walked over to the glass door on impossibly long legs. She stood on the other side of the glass and put her head on one side, her upper lip curled back in a contemptuous sneer. Donovan figured it was the Yankees baseball cap that marked him out as being unsuitable for admittance, but he was damned if he was going to take it off.

'I'm here to see Maury,' he said.

'Is he expecting you?'

'Just tell him Den Donovan's here, will you?'

She looked at him for several seconds, then pushed a button on her side of the door. The locking mechanism buzzed and Donovan pushed the door open.

'Do you have many customers?' asked Donovan.

The woman didn't reply. She walked away, her high heels clicking on the grey marble floor like knuckles cracking. Donovan watched her buttocks twitch under her short black skirt, then turned his attention to the paintings on the wall opposite the woman's desk. They were modern and mindless, dribbles of paint on over-large canvases, the work of a second-year art student. He took a few steps back, but even distance didn't make the work any more meaningful. There were no price tags on the work, just small pieces of white card with the titles of the pieces. Donovan figured that was always a bad sign, having to give the piece a name. Art should speak for itself.

Scattered around the floor of the gallery were several metal sculptures that looked like the contents of someone's garage welded together haphazardly. Donovan wandered around, shaking his head scornfully.

'Den! Good to see you.'

Maury Goldman strode across the gallery, his hand outstretched. His mane of grey hair was swept back as if he'd been riding a scooter without a helmet. Not that there'd be a scooter on the roads capable of bearing Goldman's weight. He was a fat man, bordering on the obese, and his Savile Row suits demanded at least three times the cloth of a regular fitting. As always, his jowly face was bathed in sweat, but his hand when Donovan shook it was as dry as stone. Goldman appeared only days away from a fatal heart attack, but he'd looked that way for the twelve years that Donovan had known him.

Goldman pumped Donovan's hand, and then hugged him. The brunette gave Donovan a frosty look as she went back to her desk, as if she resented the attention that Goldman was giving him.

'When did you get back?' asked Goldman.

'Day or two. How's business?'

Goldman made a 'so-so' gesture with his hand. 'Can't complain, Den.'

Donovan gestured at the huge canvases. 'Didn't think you went for this, Maury?'

'Favour for a friend,' said Goldman regretfully. 'His son's just graduated . . . what can I say? Maybe Saatchi'll take him under his wing.'

Donovan didn't look convinced and Goldman laughed quietly.

'I need a favour, Maury,' said Donovan quietly.

Goldman took out a large scarlet handkerchief from his top pocket and mopped his brow. 'Come upstairs, we can have a chat there.'

Goldman waddled across the gallery and showed Donovan through a door that led to a stairway. He went up the stairs slowly, with Donovan following.

'You should get a lift installed,' said Donovan.

'I need the exercise,' said Goldman, panting as he reached the top of the stairs and pushed open the door to his private office. He held the door open for Donovan.

The office was a complete contrast to the gallery downstairs, with dark wooden panelling, brass light fittings and a plush royal-blue carpet. The dark oak furniture included a massive desk on which sat an incongruously hi-tech Apple Mac computer. The paintings on the walls were a world apart from the canvases downstairs and Donovan wandered around, relishing the art. Goldman eased himself down on to a massive leather swivel chair behind the desk and watched Donovan with an amused smile on his face.

'This is good,' said Donovan in admiration. 'My god, this is good.' He was looking at a small black chalk and lithographic crayon drawing of an old woman, her face creased into a thousand wrinkles, yet with eyes that sparkled like a teenager's. 'It's a Goya, right?'

'Francisco de Goya y Lucientes, none other,' said Goldman.

'Where the hell did you get it from?'

Goldman tapped the side of his nose conspiratorially. 'Trade secret,' he said.

'Kosher?'

Goldman sighed theatrically. 'Dennis, please . . .'

'It must be worth seven fifty, right?'

'Closer to a mill, but I could do you a deal, Dennis,' said Goldman, taking a large cigar out of a rosewood box and clipping the end off with a gold cutter.

'It's the other way around,' said Donovan, rubbing his chin as he scrutinised the painting. 'I need to sell what I've got.'

Goldman lit his cigar and took a deep pull on it, then blew a cloud of blue-grey smoke towards the ceiling.

'Have you any idea how much damage the smoke does?' asked Donovan.

'I smoke two a day, doctor's orders.'

'I meant to the paintings.'

Goldman flashed Donovan a cold smile. 'Do you want to sell everything?'

'Everything in the house.'

Goldman raised his eyebrows. 'Are you sure you want to do that? Rock solid investments. It's quality you've got there, Den.'

'I'm not doing this by choice, Maury, believe me.'

Donovan walked over to a green leather armchair opposite the desk and sat on one of the arms. He took out an envelope and dropped it on to Goldman's desk. Goldman opened it and took out a sheet of paper on which Donovan had written down an inventory of all the paintings he wanted to sell.

Goldman took out a pair of gold-framed reading glasses and perched them on the end of his bulbous nose. He nodded appreciatively as he ran his eyes down the list. 'We must be talking two mill, Den.'

Donovan nodded. 'Maybe more if they went to auction, but I need this doing quickly.'

'It's never a good idea to rush into a sale, Den.' Goldman leaned forward and tapped ash into a large crystal ashtray. 'You know any bank would lend against those paintings, don't you? Shove them in a vault and take out a loan. You'd pay six per cent, maybe seven.'

'I'd only get half the value. Maybe seventy five per cent if I was lucky. I need all of it, Maury, and I need it now.'

'Now?'

'Tomorrow.'

Goldman's eyes widened. 'Are you in trouble, Den?'

'Not if you sell those paintings PDQ, no. Can you buy them off me?'

Goldman exhaled deeply. 'Two million pounds is out of my league, Den. Give me a week or so and I could maybe fix something up, but you know I could only offer you trade. You need a private buyer.'

'Do you know anyone?'

Goldman shook his head, then took another long pull on the cigar. 'No one who'd buy the lot, Den. It's a great collection you've got, but it's your taste, right. I mean, if they were all Picassos I could shift them within the hour, but you've got a mixed bag. Quality, but mixed. We'd have to split the collection up, find buyers for them individually.'

'Can you do that?' Donovan tried to sound relaxed but he knew that the Colombian's goodwill had been stretched to its limit and there was no way he'd get an extension. It was three million dollars within two days or it was the rest of his life on the run. Or worse.

'I can try, Den.'

Donovan nodded glumly. He could tell from Goldman's voice that the dealer wasn't optimistic.

'I tell you what, I'd be happy to take the Van Dyck sketches off your hands.'

'I'm not giving them away, Maury.'

'What do you think's fair?'

'You should know, Maury, I bought two of them from you.'

'How much did you pay again?'

Donovan grinned. Goldman had a mind like a steel trap and never forgot a trade. 'You sold them to me for twenty grand apiece, Maury, and that was eight years ago. I paid thirty-five grand for the third one, but as they're all preparatory sketches for the same painting, they've got added value as a set.'

Goldman tapped ash into his crystal ashtray. 'A hundred and fifty?' Donovan smiled tightly and Goldman sighed mournfully. 'You're a hard man, Dennis. Two hundred?'

'Two hundred it is, Maury. Cash tomorrow, yeah?'

Goldman nodded. 'I'll get on the phone right away about the rest of your collection. Okay if I come around to the house tomorrow morning?'

'Worried I might not have them?'

Goldman ignored Donovan's sarcasm. 'Ten o'clock all right for you?'

Donovan nodded.

Goldman continued to scrutinise the list. 'I know someone who might help,' he said.

'In what way? A buyer?'

'A dealer. Young guy, he's been making a bit of a name for himself. Bit of a chancer, it has to be said, but he turns over some good stuff. Sails a bit close to the wind when it comes to provenance, but he has cash buyers. Buyers a bit like yourself, if you get my drift.'

'You trust him? This is personal business, Maury. I mean, the paintings are kosher but there's going to be a money trail. I don't have time to do any laundry.'

'He's never let me down, Den. And he knows the faces. God forbid I should put you in touch with my competition, but if you're in a bind, he might be able to help.'

Donovan nodded. 'Okay, then. What's his name?'

Goldman blew a cloud of smoke across the desk, then waved it away with his hand. 'Fullerton. Jamie Fullerton.'

Robbie's thumbs were getting numb, but he didn't want to stop playing with the Gameboy, not while he was so close to beating his personal best. His mobile phone started to ring. He glanced sideways at the phone on the grass beside him. It was a mobile calling him. He put the Gameboy down and picked up his mobile. He didn't recognise the number. He pressed the green button. 'Yes . . .' he said hesitantly.

'Cheer up, you look like you've got the weight of the world on your shoulders.'

'Dad!' Robbie shouted. He grinned and pumped his fist in the air.

'That's better,' said Donovan. 'You haven't forgotten how to smile, then.'

Robbie realised what his father had said. He stood up and looked around the garden, the phone still glued to his ear. 'Where are you?'

'Why? You want to see me?'

'Yes!' Robbie shouted. 'Where are you?'

Donovan stepped out of the kitchen, waving at his son.

'Dad!' Robbie screamed, running towards him. He threw himself at Donovan. Donovan picked him up and swung him around.

'I knew you'd come back,' said Robbie.

'I said I would. You know I always keep my word.'

Robbie put his arms around Donovan's neck and hugged him tight. 'When did you land? You should have called me, I would have come to the airport.'

'I wanted to surprise you,' said Donovan. He didn't want to tell Robbie that he'd been in London for two days, or that he'd been in Mark and Laura's house while he was asleep. 'You want a Big Mac?'

'Burger King's better.'

'Since when?' Last time Donovan had been in London, McDonald's was his son's fast food of choice.

'Burger King's better. Everyone knows that. Are we going home?'

'Home?'

'Our house. You're not going to stay with Aunty Laura, are you?'

Donovan put his son back on the ground and ruffled his hair. 'We can talk about that later,' he said. 'There's something we've got to do first.'

Laura came out of the kitchen. 'Are you staying for dinner, Den?'

'Father and son time,' laughed Donovan. 'Junk food's a-calling.'

They caught a black cab to Queensway and Donovan took his son into Whiteley's shopping centre. Donovan headed towards a photograph machine on the ground floor.

'What are we doing, Dad?' asked Robbie.

'Passport pictures,' said Donovan, helping him into the

booth. He gave him two one-pound coins and showed him how to raise the seat.

'I've already got a passport,' said Robbie.

'Your mum took it,' said Donovan.

'Why?'

'I don't know. You'll have to ask her.'

'Why do I need a passport?'

'For God's sake, Robbie, will you just do as you're told?' Donovan snapped.

Robbie's face fell and he pulled the curtain shut.

Donovan leaned against the machine. 'Robbie, I'm sorry.'

Robbie didn't say anything. There were four flashes and then Robbie got out of the booth. He didn't look at Donovan. Donovan ruffled his son's hair. 'I'm having a bad day, Robbie. I'm sorry.'

'It's all right.' Robbie's voice was flat and emotionless and he still wouldn't look at Donovan.

'We'll go to Burger King, yeah?'

Robbie nodded.

'What are you going to do to mum?'

Donovan's jaw dropped. 'What do you mean?'

'You're not going to let her get away with it, are you?'

'Your mum's made her bed, now she's got to lie in it.'

'Will you get divorced?'

'After what she's done, Robbie, she can't come back.'

'Yeah, I know. I won't have to stay with her, will I?'

Donovan knelt down so that his face was level with Robbie's. 'Of course not.'

'Most of my friends, when their parents split up, they have to live with their mums.'

'Yeah, but this is different.'

'I know, but it's the judge who decides, right?'

Donovan shook his head. 'After what she did, no judge is going to let her take you away from me. That's as long as you want to stay with me. You do want to stay with me, right?'

'Sure!' said Robbie quickly.

'So that's sorted.' Donovan gently banged Robbie's chin with his fist. 'You and me, okay?'

'Okay, Dad.'

The strip of photographs slid out of the machine. Robbie picked it up and studied it. 'I look like a geek.'

Donovan took the photographs off him. 'You look great.' He put the photographs in his pocket. One of the two mobiles he was carrying started to warble. It was the one Rojas was supposed to use. Donovan pressed the phone against his ear. 'How's it going, *capullo*?' he asked, turning away from Robbie.

'The parcel has been dispatched,' said Rojas. 'I'm already working on the second matter.'

'*De puta madre*,' said Donovan.

'You'll send my fee?'

'Absolutely,' said Donovan, though he wished he felt half as confident as he sounded. The line went dead. The Spaniard, like Donovan, always kept calls on mobile phones as short as possible. Even the digitals weren't secure. Virtually no form of communication was these days. Phones, e-mail, letters, all could be intercepted and recorded. Donovan put the phone away and smiled down at Robbie. 'Burger King, yeah?'

Robbie grinned and nodded. 'Great.' They walked together out of the shopping centre. 'Dad, you know I know what *capullo* means, don't you?' asked Robbie.

'I do now,' said Donovan.

Robbie's grin widened. 'You should wash your mouth out with soap.'

'I'll do that, soon as we get home. But burgers first, yeah?'

Stewart Sharkey carried the two glasses of champagne out on to the terrace and handed one to Vicky. She took it but didn't look at Sharkey. She stared out across the azure Mediterranean with unseeing eyes.

'Cheers,' said Sharkey, and touched his glass against hers.

She looked at him slowly, then at the glass in her hand. She frowned, as if seeing it for the first time. 'What have we got to celebrate?' she asked.

'Champagne's not just for celebrating,' said Sharkey. He dropped down on to the lounger next to her.

Vicky stared out over the sea again. The bay was dotted with massive white yachts, each worth millions of dollars, and around them moved smaller boats, like worker ants in attendance to the queen.

'We could get a boat,' said Sharkey. 'Sail away.'

'Den always talked about getting one,' said Vicky, her voice flat and emotionless.

'We can do it, Vicky. Tomorrow.'

'Where would we go?' she said. 'He'll find us eventually.'

'Not here. He's never been to the South of France. Hates the French, you know that. He's no friends here. No contacts.'

Vicky turned to look at him. 'So that's the great plan? We stay in Nice for the rest of our lives.'

'For God's sake, Vicky, snap out of this, will you!'

She sneered at him and looked away.

'I'm sorry,' he said quickly. 'I didn't mean to snap.' Vicky didn't react. Sharkey put down his glass and knelt down by the side of her lounger. He stroked her shoulder. 'This is temporary, Vicky. Just until we get things sorted.'

Vicky shook her head. 'This isn't getting things sorted. This is hiding.'

A red and white helicopter buzzed towards one of the biggest yachts in the bay. Sharkey continued to stroke her shoulder. Her skin was smooth and warm from the sun. He moved his hand up to her neck and ran his fingers through her soft, blonde hair.

'I miss Robbie,' she said quietly.

'I know you do.'

'I don't think you do,' she said. 'You don't have children. You don't know what it's like to have them taken away from you. And that's what Den's going to do. You know that. He'll take Robbie to the Caribbean and I'll never see him again.'

'You took his passport, Den can't take him anywhere.'

Vicky scowled. 'That's not going to stop him. Den's got half a dozen passports. He can just as easily get one for Robbie.'

Sharkey tried to kiss her cheek but she pushed him away. 'Stewart, I don't want to be touched right now. Okay?'

Sharkey put his hands up in surrender. 'Okay. I'm sorry.' He sat down on the edge of her lounger. 'Look, there are things we can do. Things I can do. I'll talk to a lawyer. Get some sort of injunction stopping Den taking Robbie out of the country.'

'You said we couldn't talk to anyone back in the UK?'

'I'll get it done. I'll find a way. And things are going to get hot for Den – he won't be able to hang around London for long.'

Vicky shaded her eyes with the flat of her hand. 'What do you mean?'

'Den's got problems, you know that. Customs and the cops will be waiting for him to put a foot wrong. He can't operate in London. He'll have to go back to the Caribbean. And if I talk to a lawyer, he won't be able to take Robbie with him. Once he's gone, we can go back to the UK.'

'Den won't run away with his tail between his legs.'

'No, but he won't risk twenty years in prison. He's got stuff on the go, and he's going to have to take care of business. He can't do that in London.' Sharkey looked earnestly at Vicky, his eyes burning into hers. 'I know what I'm doing, Vicky. I know this is a mess but you're going to have to trust me. Den's as mad as hell just now, but he'll calm down. He'll negotiate. He'll have to.'

'Because he wants his money back?'

'Exactly.'

'How much did you take, Stewart?'

Sharkey looked away. 'Enough to hurt him. Enough for him to know that he can't push us around.'

'How much?'

Sharkey shrugged. 'A few million. It's not important.'

'How much is a few?'

'Oh, come on, Vicky. This was never about money. You know that.' He took her hand and toyed with her wedding ring. 'I love you. You know I love you. The money's just a way of keeping Den in check. As soon as he's calmed down, we'll give it back. I promise. I've got more than enough to take care of you.'

'You promise?'

'What? That I've got enough money?'

'That you'll pay Den back? Once we've sorted out Robbie and everything.'

Sharkey nodded. 'I promise.'

'I mean it, Stewart. It's one thing to walk out on him. It's another to steal from him.'

'You're not stealing. You're entitled. You had signing rights to all those accounts.'

Vicky shook her head. 'That was just to keep the money safe. He never gave me the money, it was just in my name.'

Sharkey put his hands on her knees. 'Love, we're not stealing from Den. A bit of leverage, that's all I wanted.' Vicky bit down on her lower lip. She looked as if she was about to cry again. Sharkey pinched her chin gently. 'Come on, we've got champagne, we've got the sun, we've got a million-dollar view. Let's at least try to enjoy it.'

Vicky nodded and forced a smile. Sharkey stood up and kissed the top of her head. She reached up for him and her lips moved to find his. He kissed her and slipped his hand down her bikini top, cupping her breast and feeling her nipple stiffen. She moaned and lay back and Sharkey rolled over on top of her, pushing her bikini bottoms down. She opened her legs wide for him and he entered her quickly, covering her mouth with his to stifle her moans.

She scratched her nails down his shirt and clasped her ankles behind his waist as he pounded into her. Vicky's eyes were closed, but Sharkey stared down at her as he thrust back and forth, his face a tight mask even when he came inside her. His mind wasn't on what he was doing. He was thinking about what he was going to do next. Considering his options. It was starting to look as if he was going to have to choose between Den Donovan's millions and Den Donovan's wife. He'd always planned to have both, and the way things stood at the moment, he wasn't sure which he wanted most.

Vicky opened her eyes and Sharkey smiled down at her. 'I love you,' he said, and sounded as if he meant it.

'I love you too,' she said, and closed her eyes again.

The taxi pulled up in front of Laura's house. Robbie gave his father a black look and made no move to get out.

'Look, we can't stay in our house,' said Donovan. 'Not yet.'

'Why not?'

'I told you why not.'

'It's our home, Dad.'

The driver twisted around in his seat and slid back the glass partition. 'Are you getting out here or not?' he asked in a voice that suggested he couldn't care less either way.

'Give us a minute, yeah?' said Donovan.

'I've got a living to earn, you know.'

Donovan's eyes hardened. He stared at the driver. 'The meter's running, so you just turn around and mind your own business, okay?'

The driver hesitated. He tried to meet Donovan's stare but after a few seconds he averted his eyes, mumbled something and then closed the glass partition. Donovan continued to stare at the back of the man's head.

'Dad!' hissed Robbie. 'Stop it.'

Donovan turned to look at him. 'What?'

'Don't do that. He's only doing his job.'

'He's a prick.'

'You always do that.'

'Do what?'

'Lose your temper. It's like you want to start a fight.' Robbie nodded at the house. 'I don't want to stay here.'

'Aunty Laura takes good care of you, doesn't she?'

'That's not the point.'

'What is the point, Robbie?'

Robbie brushed tears from his eyes. He turned his face away so that Donovan couldn't see him cry. Donovan put his arm around his son. Robbie tried to shake him away but Donovan hugged him tightly.

'Just a few days, okay?'

Robbie sniffed. 'Then we can go home?'

'Maybe.'

Robbie turned and looked at Donovan accusingly. 'What do you mean, maybe?'

'Are you sure you want to stay in the house?' asked Donovan. 'Wouldn't you prefer to go to Anguilla?'

'No!' said Robbie quickly. 'No way!'

Donovan was surprised by the vehemence in his son's voice. 'I thought you liked the Caribbean?' he said.

'For holidays, yeah. I don't want to live there.'

'Come on, Robbie. It's got the sun, the beach. You can go swimming every day. You love it there.'

'My friends are here. My school's here.'

'Robbie . . .'

'No!' Robbie shouted. 'I'm staying here! You're not taking me with you!' He fumbled for the door handle and rushed out of the taxi.

Donovan watched him run up to the front door of Laura's house. He started to go after Robbie, but then hesitated and pulled the taxi door shut. He told the driver to go to Sussex Gardens and settled back in the seat.

He closed his eyes and rubbed them with the palms of his hands. Assuming he could sell his paintings and sell them quickly, he'd be able to pay off Carlos Rodriguez, but with the Colombian dealing direct with Macfadyen and Jordan, Donovan had no imminent source of income. And until he tracked down Sharkey and Vicky, he had virtually no assets, either.

Losing the cocaine deal was a major blow, but Donovan had been planning to end his relationship with Macfadyen and Jordan for some time. The money had started to go to their heads in recent months, and the fact that they'd turned up to a meet in a brand new Ferrari and wearing designer gear suggested that they were losing their grip.

The only good news was that Juan Rojas had taken care of Marty Clare. With Clare out of the equation, the authorities had no evidence against him.

Donovan had known Clare for almost fifteen years, and for the past ten he'd considered him a close friend. They'd been drunk together, they'd partied together, and they'd done business together. Clare had concentrated on cannabis and had refused whenever Donovan had offered to cut him in on cocaine or heroin deals. He'd always protested that the risk–reward ratio made hard drugs a dangerous proposition, even though the profits were that much higher. Donovan had always insisted that the risk–reward ratio only mattered if you got caught, and Donovan had never come close to being caught.

The fact that Clare had agreed to co-operate with the DEA came as no surprise to Donovan. The DEA were masters at the art of turning players around. They'd spend years gathering evidence and putting together a watertight case, then they'd move in. More often than not, however, they would offer a deal, smaller fishes giving up bigger fishes until they got to the men at the top, the men like Donovan, who were untouchable by conventional means. When it came to facing a twenty-year sentence in a Federal prison, honour among thieves went out of the window pretty damn quickly. Donovan liked to think that he was made of sterner stuff, but he'd never know for certain how he'd react until it happened to him.

Donovan had had no hesitation in ordering Marty Clare's death. He knew that if their positions were reversed, Clare would have done the same. That was how the game was played. You stood by your friends until they betrayed you, then you made sure that retribution was decisive and swift. Clare knew the rules, and he would have known that the minute he started to talk his life would be on the line. He'd have taken that into consideration, factored it into the equation, risk and reward. The reward – a life in a witness protection programme, but at least there'd be no bars on the windows and no tattooed men wanting to play pick-up-the-soap in the showers. The risk – retribution from Den Donovan. Donovan smiled to himself. He wondered if Sharkey had run the risk–reward calculation for his own situation. He must have done, he must have known how he'd react. Perhaps he'd assumed that his Tango One status would keep him confined to the Caribbean; perhaps he'd assumed that Carlos Rodriguez would do his dirty work for him. Whatever, he'd got the calculation wrong. Retribution would be decisive and swift. And highly personal.

Donovan arrived at the house just after nine thirty the next morning. He let himself in through the back door and tapped in the burglar alarm code. He went to the kitchen to make himself a coffee. The milk in the fridge was well past its sell-by date, so he poured it down the sink and sipped his coffee black.

He walked through to his study and stood looking at the painting that concealed the safe. The yachts were turning into the wind, the sky smeared redly behind them. On the left was the skyline of nineteenth-century New York. Donovan never tired of looking at the picture.

He sat down at his desk and took out one of the mobiles that he hadn't used. He dialled the UK number that Gregov had given him. It was answered by a woman with a Russian accent who said that Gregov was helping to load one of the planes, but that if Donovan didn't mind waiting she'd go and get him.

Donovan swung his feet up on to the desk and whistled softly to himself until Gregov came on the line. 'Den, good to hear from you.'

'Hiya, Gregov. Wasn't sure if I'd catch you.'

'We're flying out tomorrow. Loading up the last of the supplies now. Forty thousand kilos of food and medicine. I love earthquakes, Den. My bread and butter.'

'When are you flying back?' asked Donovan.

'Next week. Are we in business, then?'

'Maybe. I'll try to get the finances sorted then I'll get back to you. Eight thousand kilos, right? At three thousand a key?'

'That's right. Twenty-four total, call it twenty-five with expenses.'

Donovan raised his eyebrows. Twenty-five million US dollars. He wondered how enthusiastic Gregov would be if he knew the true state of Donovan's finances, but the deal Gregov was offering was so sweet that it could be the answer to all his prayers. 'That seems cheap, Gregov.'

'Sure, they're friends of mine. Army buddies. I got them out of a few scrapes in Afghanistan, they sort of owe me. But that's the regular price. Their processing plant is in the middle of nowhere – once it gets anywhere near a big city the price doubles. Out of Turkey it goes up tenfold. It's cheap because I get it at the source. You're not having second thoughts, are you?'

'No, of course not,' said Donovan, trying to sound a lot more confident than he felt.

'Good man,' said Gregov. 'You have the bank account number?'

Donovan said he had.

'When you're ready to move, call Maya at the number you have. She'll get through to me, even if I'm in the air. This is going to be great, Den. Capitalism rules, yeah?'

'Sure,' said Donovan.

The doorbell rang as Donovan cut the connection, and he went through to the hall and opened the front door. Maury Goldman stood there with a tall, blond-haired man in his late twenties, smartly dressed in a dark blue suit and grey shirt. The man looked fit, as if he worked out, and he flexed his shoulders under his jacket as Donovan looked him up and down.

'Den, this is Jamie Fullerton,' said Goldman.

Fullerton stuck out his hand and Donovan shook it. It was a firm, strong grip, and Fullerton held Donovan's look as he squeezed. It wasn't quite a trial of strength, but Donovan felt that Fullerton had something to prove. Donovan continued to apply pressure on the handshake, and Fullerton matched it, then Fullerton nodded almost imperceptibly. 'Good to meet you, Mr Donovan.'

'Mr Donovan was my dear old dad and he's well dead. I'm Den,' said Donovan, waving them into the house. He patted Goldman on the back and closed the door. 'Do you want coffee?' he asked.

'Coffee would be good,' said Fullerton.

Goldman nodded. Donovan took them into the kitchen and made three mugs of coffee, apologising for the lack of milk. Goldman and Fullerton sat down at the pine kitchen table.

'Maury told you what I need?' asked Donovan.

'You want to sell your collection ASAP,' said Fullerton. 'Shouldn't be a problem.'

'I showed Jamie your inventory,' said Goldman. 'He's spoken to several potential buyers already.'

'I hope you don't mind, Mr Donovan,' said Fullerton. 'Den,' he said, correcting himself with an embarrassed smile. 'I thought that with the time pressure, you'd want me to hit the ground running.'

'No sweat,' said Donovan. 'Have you had any feedback?'

'Some of them I can sell for you today, but the others I'm going to have to show. Can I bring people around here to see them?'

'I'd rather not,' said Donovan. 'With respect to your clients, I don't want strangers traipsing around my house. Plus, I'd rather not have people know where they've come from.'

Fullerton smiled easily. 'I understand that, but the alternative is to let me walk out of here with two million quid's worth of fine art. If you're okay with that . . .'

Donovan looked at Fullerton, trying to get the measure of the man. He had an air of confidence that bordered on arrogance and he looked at Donovan with his chin slightly raised, almost as if he were spoiling for a fight. There was also an amused look in his eyes, though, as if he were taking a secret pleasure in suggesting that he bring strangers into Donovan's home. There was something about his smile that reminded Donovan of a shark. He was a good-looking guy and Donovan was sure that Jamie Fullerton had broken his fair share of hearts.

'I'm not sure I'd be keen on that, either,' said Donovan.

'How about we move them to my gallery?' asked Goldman. 'My insurance'll cover them. Anyone interested can come and see them there.'

Donovan nodded. 'That sounds good, Maury. Thanks.' He raised his coffee mug in salute.

'I don't want to talk out of turn, but have you considered the insurance option?' asked Fullerton quietly.

Donovan narrowed his eyes. 'In what way?'

Fullerton grimaced, as if he were having second thoughts about what he was about to suggest.

'Come on, Jamie,' said Donovan. 'Spit it out.'

'It's obvious, isn't it?' said Fullerton. 'They're insured, right? Why put them on the market? You must know people.'

'Must I?' said Donovan coldly.

Fullerton looked uncomfortable. Goldman was pointedly avoiding looking at either of them and was concentrating on a spot somewhere above the wine rack.

'If you don't, I do,' Fullerton said. 'They break in, take the paintings, you claim on the insurance and a few years down the line you get them back, ten pence in the pound.'

Goldman winced but carried on staring at the wall as if his life depended on it.

'You do know who I am, Jamie?'

'Sure.'

'Are you sure you're sure? Because if you know who I am, how do you think the filth would react if they heard that I'd been robbed? First of all, they'd love to get inside my house without a warrant. Second of all, don't you think they'd move heaven and earth to prove that it was an insurance job?'

Fullerton shifted in his seat. 'Stupid idea. Sorry.'

Donovan smiled. 'Nah, at least you're thinking creatively. Under other circumstances it might have been a goer, but the way things are at the moment, I've got to keep the lowest of low profiles. I want them sold legit, and I want cash.'

Goldman tore his attention away from the wall. 'Cash cash?' he asked.

'As good as,' said Donovan. 'Banker's draft. Tomorrow.'

'That's tight,' said Fullerton.

'That's the way it's got to be,' said Donovan.

'Made out to you?'

'Made out to cash.'

'Banks aren't over happy about making drafts out to cash,' said Fullerton.

'Fuck the banks,' said Donovan.

'It's a fair point, Den,' said Goldman. 'It might slow things up.'

Donovan pursed his lips and rubbed the bridge of his nose. He was starting to get a headache again. 'Okay,' he said eventually. 'Get the drafts made out to Carlos Rodriguez.' He spelled out the surname.

'And you want the drafts?' asked Fullerton.

'Yeah. Maybe. Talk to me once you've got them, right?'

'Individual drafts from each sale would be the quickest way,' said Fullerton. 'Is that okay?'

'So long as the total's more than two million quid, Jamie, I'll be a happy bunny.'

Goldman took out a leather cigar case and held it up. 'Okay if I smoke?' he asked.

'Sure,' said Donovan. 'They're your lungs.'

Goldman offered the case to Fullerton, but he shook his head and drank his coffee. Goldman took out a cigar and sniffed it appreciatively.

'One other thing,' said Fullerton, 'and please don't take this the wrong way, Den. Provenance is okay, yeah?'

Donovan smiled tightly. 'Goldman said you weren't over concerned about provenance.'

Fullerton flashed Goldman an annoyed look and Goldman focused all his attention on cutting the end off his cigar and lighting it with a match. 'Well, thanks for the character reference, Maury.'

Goldman pretended not to hear. Fullerton looked back at Donovan and shrugged carelessly. 'Frankly, some of the people I sell to couldn't care less where the paintings come from, so long as the provenance is reflected in the price, that's all. But they might be a bit miffed if they pay top whack for a painting then find out it's got to stay in a locked basement.'

Donovan nodded. 'They're all kosher, Jamie. Maury here can vouch for that.'

Goldman nodded enthusiastically but kept looking at his cigar.

'All the money was well clean by the time it went through Maury's books.' He grinned. 'I had a team of Smurfs working flat out for a month for the Rembrandt in the master bedroom.'

'Smurfs?'

Donovan grinned. 'Another time, Jamie. Just take my word for it, the paintings are clean. Bought and paid for.'

'That's all I need to know, Den. I'm on the case.' He stood up. 'Okay if I start loading the smaller paintings into Maury's car?'

'Sure, I'll give you a hand.'

'We'll send a van for the larger works,' said Goldman. He waved his cigar at Fullerton. 'Take extra care with the Van Dycks, they're spoken for.'

‘Can you get the van here this morning?’ asked Donovan. ‘I’m up to my eyes this afternoon.’

Goldman winked and pulled a tiny Nokia mobile from his jacket pocket. It looked minuscule as he held it against his jowly face. ‘Office,’ he shouted. He smiled at Donovan. ‘Voice-activated dialling. New technology, huh?’ He frowned and said ‘Office’ again, louder this time. His frown deepened and then he cursed and tapped in the number.

Donovan jerked his thumb towards the stairs. ‘Come and look at the Rembrandt,’ he said to Fullerton. ‘It’s not my favourite piece, but it should fetch the most. Maury talked me into it, said it’d be a great investment. He’s a Philistine, but you can’t fault his business sense.’

Fullerton followed Donovan upstairs. The Rembrandt drawing was in an ornate gilt frame to the left of the door, positioned so that Donovan could see it while he was lying in bed. Fullerton whistled softly. ‘Nice,’ he said. He stood back from the picture and stared at it in silence for almost a full minute. It was of a small child reaching for an apple. A boy, but with long hair and an angelic, almost feminine face. The boy was looking around as if he feared being caught taking the fruit, but he was too well dressed to be a beggar or a thief. He was the son of nobility, so maybe the theft was greed. Or a lark. ‘Just look at the hand,’ said Fullerton. ‘You can see the corrections, he must have worked on it for hours.’ He moved to the side to get a slightly different view. ‘Quill and reed pen with a brown ink,’ he said. ‘A very similar drawing went for almost three hundred grand at Sotheby’s in New York a couple of years ago. That was an old man – kids always fetch higher prices.’

'You're as much a Philistine as Maury,' laughed Donovan.

'I'm not saying it's not a great work, I'm just saying it's a very saleable piece. Which is why you bought it, yeah?'

'Can't argue with that, Jamie.'

'I don't think I'll have a problem placing it,' said Fullerton. 'I know a couple of guys with cash that want to put it into art.'

'Clean money?'

Fullerton flashed his shark-like smile again. 'It will be by the time you get it, Den.'

Donovan took the Rembrandt drawing down off the wall and placed it on the bed. He went into the bathroom and pulled a pale blue hand towel off the heated rail and tossed it to Fullerton.

Fullerton carefully wrapped the drawing in the towel. 'Can I ask you something, Den?'

'Anything so long as it's not geography,' said Donovan. 'I hate geography.'

'You've got a decent security system, but weren't you taking a risk, having them on show?'

'It's not like I advertised them,' said Donovan. 'And most opportunistic break-ins are druggies looking for a video or a CD player. They wouldn't recognise a Rembrandt if it bit them on the arse.' He nodded at the drawing that Fullerton was wrapping. 'Even my wife didn't know what that was worth. A scribble, she called it.'

'You didn't tell her what it was?'

Donovan shrugged. 'Vicky had a stack of interests, but art was never one of them. I tried to take her to galleries and stuff but it bored her rigid. More interested in Gucci than Goya.'

Fullerton picked up the Rembrandt. 'Can I see the Buttersworths?'

'Sure.' Donovan took Fullerton down to the study.

Fullerton put the Rembrandt on the desk and studied the painting that covered the wall safe. 'Brilliant,' he said.

'You know about Buttersworth?' said Donovan.

'Did a thesis on nineteenth-century American painters, believe it or not, and I always had a penchant for maritime artists. Look at that sunset, would you? More than a hundred and thirty years ago he painted that. We're getting the same view today that he had then. It's like we're seeing something through his eyes, isn't it, something that's been gone for more than a century. Awesome. Look at the skyline there, New York as it was back then. And just look at the detail in the clouds.' He turned to look at Donovan. 'And you use it to hide a safe. Who's the Philistine now?'

Donovan's jaw dropped. 'How the hell did you know that?'

Fullerton grinned and walked over to the frame. He pointed to the wall to the left of the gilded frame. 'See the indentations there?'

Donovan moved closer and peered at where Fullerton was pointing. He was right, there was a line of small marks where the frame had been pressing against the wall when it was swung away from the safe. 'You've got a good eye,' said Donovan.

'A thief's eye,' laughed Fullerton. 'But don't worry, Den, your secret's safe with me.'

'Bloody thing's empty anyway,' said Donovan.

Fullerton went over to look at the second Buttersworth. 'I think I know just the man to buy these,' he said. 'A corporate finance chap over at Citibank. He's got a bonus cheque eating a hole in his pocket and he's mad about boats. I'm sure he'll jump at them.' He turned and grinned confidently. 'This is going to be a piece of cake, Den. Take my word for it.'

Jamie Fullerton opened the metal gates with his remote control and drove his black Porsche into the underground car park. He was grinning as he stepped into the lift and pressed the button for the penthouse. Three years he'd been waiting to meet Den Donovan, and he'd finally been handed the man on a plate. He couldn't believe his luck. He shook his head. No, it hadn't been luck. He'd been in the right place at the right time, and that had been down to planning, not chance. He'd put a lot of time and effort into cultivating Maury Goldman, once he'd found out that Goldman had been Donovan's art dealer of choice. There'd been other dealers, too. And other contacts. All friends and acquaintances of Donovan, all possible leads to the man himself. And it had worked. He'd been in the man's house. Shaken hands with him. Hell, Den Donovan had actually made him coffee.

Fullerton unlocked his front door and walked through to the kitchen, all polished stainless steel and gleaming white tiles. He opened the fridge and took out a chilled bottle of Bollinger champagne. He picked up a fluted glass and went out on to his terrace which overlooked the fast-flowing Thames. He popped the cork, filled the glass, then toasted himself. His grin widened. 'Onwards and upwards, Fullerton,' he said, then drank deeply. He felt elated, almost light headed. He was in. He was part of Den Donovan's circle. He'd met the man, talked to the man, joked with him. He was in close, and already Donovan was trusting him.

Fullerton went back inside his apartment. He walked along a white-painted corridor to his study with its floor-to-ceiling windows and sat down in front of his computer. He switched on the machine and flexed his fingers like a concert pianist preparing to perform. While the machine booted up he sipped at his champagne.

He logged on to the SafeWeb site and then switched through to the website that Hathaway had assigned to him three years earlier. Hathaway had warned Fullerton about using his own computer, but Fullerton had grown tired of using internet cafés to file his reports. He'd made the decision to use his own machine, though he religiously deleted all incriminating files after each session. Fullerton grinned and started typing.

Gregg Hathaway's office was just five miles away from Jamie Fullerton's penthouse apartment, in the hi-tech cream and green headquarters of MI6, the Secret Intelligence Service, at Vauxhall Bridge on the south bank of the Thames. Unlike Fullerton, Hathaway didn't have a river view – his office was four floors underground. Hathaway preferred to be underground. A view was a distraction that he could do without.

Hathaway sat back in his chair as he scrolled through Fullerton's report with a growing feeling of excitement. Over the years Fullerton had supplied him with increasingly useful intelligence which had helped put more than a dozen top London criminals behind bars, and Hathaway had recommended that Fullerton be promoted to sergeant. What Hathaway read on his screen now was pure gold, though, and it made his pulse race. Dennis Donovan was back in the UK. And was involved with Carlos Rodriguez. Rodriguez was a name that Hathaway was familiar with, a major Colombian player who was high up on the DEA's most wanted list. If they could tie Donovan and Rodriguez together, Donovan could be sent down for a long, long time.

Donovan had to wait almost two hours in the Passport Office before his number flashed up on the overhead digital read-out. He went to the booth indicated, where a bored Asian woman in her late forties flashed him a cold smile.

'I need a replacement passport for my son,' said Donovan. He slipped a completed application form through the metal slot under the armoured glass window.

The woman picked up the application form and flicked through it. 'You say replacement? What happened to the original?'

'He lost it,' said Donovan.

'Did you report the loss?'

'I thought that's what I was doing now.'

The woman gave him another cold smile, then went back to reading the form. 'Was it stolen?'

'I really don't know.'

'Because if it was stolen, you have to report the loss to the police.'

'I'm pretty sure it wasn't stolen,' said Donovan.

The woman looked at the two photographs that Donovan had clipped to the application form. 'We have to be sure,' said the woman.

'I'm sure it's missing,' said Donovan, struggling to stay calm. He was beginning to understand why they needed the armoured glass.

'If it's missing, you'll have to supply your son's birth certificate. And have the photographs signed by his doctor. Or your minister.'

'I just want a replacement,' said Donovan. 'You have his details on file already, don't you?'

The woman pushed the form back through the metal slot. 'Those are the rules,' she said. 'If you're not able to supply the passport, we'll need a birth certificate and signed photographs.'

Donovan glared at the woman. He opened his mouth to speak, but then he saw the CCTV camera staring down at him. The silent witness. He smiled at the woman and picked up the form. 'You have a nice day,' he said, and walked away. Over his head, the digital read-out clicked over to a new number.

Gregg Hathaway walked slowly along Victoria Embankment. His right knee was hurting, had been since he woke up. On the far side of the Thames, the Millennium Eye slowly turned, every capsule on the giant Ferris wheel packed with tourists. Hathaway stood and watched the wheel for a while and wondered what it must be like to see London as a tourist. The buildings, the history, the exhibitions. The Houses of Parliament, Trafalgar Square, Madame Tussaud's.

Hathaway's London was different. Darker. More threatening. Hathaway's London was a city of criminals, of terrorists and drug dealers, of subversives, of men and women who scorned society's laws and instead played by their own rules. Den Donovan was such a man, and the only way he was ever going to be brought down was if Hathaway played Donovan at his own game. Hathaway knew that he was taking a huge risk. Even MI6 had its own rules and regulations, and what Hathaway was doing went well beyond his remit. In Hathaway's mind the end most definitely justified the means, but he doubted that his masters would see it that way.

He turned away from the wheel and sat down on a wooden bench. The river flowed by, grey and forbidding. A sightseeing boat chugged eastwards. More tourists. Cameras clicking, children eating ice cream, pensioners in floppy hats and shorts.

'Nice day for it,' said a voice behind Hathaway.

Hathaway didn't turn around. He'd been expecting the man. A detective inspector working out of Bow Street Police Station whom Hathaway used from time to time. It was a symbiotic relationship that served both men well. Hathaway had an undetectable conduit into the Met; the inspector received information that made him look good. Plus occasional cash payments from the MI6 informers' fund.

The detective sat down next to Hathaway and crossed his legs at the ankles. He wore a charcoal-grey suit and scuffed Hush Puppies. His tie had been loosened and the top button of his shirt was undone. He was in his late thirties but looked older, with frown lines etched in his forehead and deep crow's feet around his eyes. 'So how's life?' he asked Hathaway jovially.

'Same old,' said Hathaway.

The detective took a pack of cigarettes out of his pocket and offered one to Hathaway. Hathaway shook his head. The detective knew that Hathaway had given up smoking, but every time they met, he'd offer him a cigarette none the less.

The detective lit one with a disposable lighter and blew smoke towards the river, waiting for Hathaway to speak.

'Den Donovan is back,' he said.

The detective raised one eyebrow. 'Bloody hell.'

'He's in London. I've checked with Immigration and

there's no record of him coming in, but he's got more identities than Rory Bremner.'

'Your source?'

Hathaway tutted in disgust.

'Worth a try,' grinned the detective. 'Where is he?'

'Not sure, lying low at the moment. He's going to have to pop his head above the parapet fairly soon, though. Money problems.'

'Den Donovan? He's worth millions.'

'Take it from me, he's got cashflow problems. He's selling his art collection. He's already cleared his paintings out of his Kensington house.'

'I know it,' said the detective. 'Is Six going to be looking at him?'

'Not yet.'

'Customs?'

'You've got this to yourself, but I wouldn't expect the Cussies or Six to stand by once they know he's back.'

'And it's because of his money problems that he's here?'

'So far as I know. He was in to see Maury Goldman, the dodgy art dealer in Mayfair. If I get more, I'll give you a call.' Hathaway stood up and winced as he put his weight on his painful leg. The detective didn't notice: he was too preoccupied with how he was going to break the news to his boss.

Hathaway walked away, back towards Vauxhall Bridge. He had no qualms about setting the police on Donovan. He must have known that the moment he set foot back on UK territory he'd be a marked man, and if there'd been no surveillance he'd have been suspicious. This way at least Hathaway would be able to exert some control on the operation.

* * *

Donovan lay on his bed, staring up at the ceiling. He'd tried to get a new birth certificate for Robbie but had been told that it would be at least seventy-two hours. Donovan had phoned the German in Anguilla but the German had said that passports for children weren't something he had in stock and that it would take at least a week to get the necessary documentation together. He could make up a counterfeit within a day but warned that even though his counterfeits were good, he couldn't be held responsible if something went wrong. It wasn't a risk that Donovan was prepared to take. Donovan's plan had been to get a replacement passport for Robbie and take him to Anguilla while he worked out what he was going to do next. There was no way he was going to leave without his son, so he had no choice other than to wait it out in London. With Marty Clare out of the picture, Donovan was in the clear investigation-wise, so there was nothing to stop him moving back into the house with Robbie. The police and Customs would put him under the microscope as soon as they discovered he was back, but Donovan wasn't planning on doing anything in the least bit criminal. He could check out of the hotel, get Robbie back from Laura, and start playing the father.

One of his mobiles rang and Donovan rolled over on to his stomach. It was the mobile that Fullerton and Goldman were to use once they had news of the paintings. Donovan pressed the phone to his ear and lay on his back. It was Fullerton.

'Good news, Den,' said Fullerton.

'I could do with some,' said Donovan.

'That Citibank guy creamed himself over the Buttersworths. I got him to go to seven hundred and fifty. He practically forced the banker's draft on me.'

Donovan sat up. 'That's good going, Jamie.' Donovan had only been expecting half a million dollars for the two paintings.

'That's just the start,' said Fullerton excitedly. 'The Rembrandt. Guess what I got for the Rembrandt?'

'Jamie, I don't want to start playing games here. Just tell me.'

'Eight hundred grand.'

'Dollars?'

'Pounds, Den. Fucking pounds.'

'Bloody hell.' That was well above what Donovan had been hoping for.

'Yeah, tell me about it. The guy's a bit shady, I have to say, but his money's good.'

'You're sure?'

'Sure I'm sure. Besides, he's going to make his draft out to me and I'll get a draft drawn off my account. We'll have it sorted by tomorrow.'

Donovan ran through the numbers. Eight hundred thousand for the Rembrandt drawing. Seven hundred and fifty thousand dollars was about half a million quid. Plus Goldman had promised two hundred thousand pounds for the Van Dycks. So far he had one and a half million pounds. He sighed with relief. At least he was close to getting the Colombian off his back. 'That's brilliant work, Jamie. Thanks.'

'I'm pretty close to selling a couple of others, too. I'm seeing a guy this evening who's looking to invest in stuff and doesn't care over much what he buys so long as it goes up in price.'

'An art-lover, huh?' said Donovan.

'Don't knock it. It's the investors who keep the market rising. If we had to depend on people who actually liked art, you'd still be able to pick up a Picasso for five grand.'

Donovan sighed. He knew that Fullerton was right, but even so, his heart sank at the thought of his lovingly acquired collection being split up and stored away in vaults as an investment.

'Shall I bring you the drafts tomorrow?'

Donovan hesitated. He didn't want to see Rodriguez again, not in the UK, but the drafts had to be hand delivered.

'Den? You there?'

Donovan reached a decision. Fullerton had done a great job in selling the paintings so quickly, and Goldman had said that he had known Fullerton for three years and that he could be trusted. 'Can you do me a favour, Jamie?' he asked.

'Sure,' said Fullerton. 'Anything.'

He sounded eager to please and Donovan wondered how much Goldman had told Fullerton. 'This guy the drafts are made out to. Carlos Rodriguez. I need them delivered. Can you handle that for me?'

'No problem, Den.'

'There's a guy called Jesus Rodriguez staying at the Intercontinental near Hyde Park. He's the nephew of the guy the money's to go to. Can you give them to him in person? Don't just leave them at Reception, yeah? In his hand.'

Fullerton laughed. 'Shall I ask him for a receipt?'

'Yeah, and count your fingers after you shake hands with him,' said Donovan. 'Seriously, Jamie. Jesus Rodriguez is a tough son of a bitch. Don't take any liberties with him.'

'Understood.'

'Second thing. He's expecting two million quid. There's the two hundred grand that Goldman's paying me for the sketches, so I need one point eight mill from you. Anything above that, keep for me, okay? Minus your usual fee, of course.'

'No problem. Pleasure doing business with you, Den. I mean that. If there's anything else you need, don't hesitate, okay?'

Donovan thanked him and cut the connection. He tossed the phone on to the bed and went into the bathroom to splash water on to his face. Jamie Fullerton was proving to be a godsend. At least something was starting to go right.

Gregg Hathaway leaned back in his seat and stared at the message on his VDU. It was from Jamie Fullerton. Hathaway would have preferred Donovan to have taken the money to the hotel, but the fact that Donovan had trusted Fullerton with it was a major breakthrough. It was a direct link between Donovan and one of South America's biggest drug dealers. There was a second terminal to Hathaway's left and he twisted around and tapped on the keyboard. The terminal gave Hathaway direct access to the DEA's database.

He tapped in Rodriguez's name and after a few seconds the Colombian's face appeared. Rodriguez was forty-seven. He'd been born to a wealthy farming family, one of six brothers. Well educated, he spoke five languages and was close to many politicians and businessmen in Colombia, many of whom the DEA suspected of being involved in the drugs trade. Rodriguez had started out working for the Mendoza syndicate but had soon struck out on his own. According to the DEA, Rodriguez was responsible for smuggling cocaine worth more than four hundred million dollars a year into the United States, primarily via Mexico, and was also a major cannabis exporter.

Jesus Rodriguez was the son of Carlos Rodriguez's younger brother and was one of the organisation's hard men, responsible for at least a dozen brutal murders in the Caribbean. According to the DEA report, Jesus Rodriguez was borderline psychopathic and an habitual cocaine user. Hathaway scrolled down through the report. There was no mention of Rodriguez sending drugs to Europe. He smiled to himself. It would do him no harm at all to bring the DEA up to speed. But not just yet. More than a dozen DEA agents worked out of the American Embassy in Grosvenor Square and he didn't want them getting all hot and bothered about the Colombian before Fullerton had delivered the money.

Hathaway picked up a plastic cup of strong black coffee and sipped it. It was all starting to come together. It had been a year in the planning and three years in the execution, but there were just a few more pieces that had to be put into position before he was ready for the end game.

Jamie Fullerton pounded down the pavement towards his apartment block. He'd run a seven-mile circuit, much of it alongside the Thames, but he had barely worked up a sweat. He was so pumped up with adrenalin he felt as if he could run another circuit, but he had work to do.

He jogged into the reception area of the block and winked at the uniformed security guard who sat in front of a bank of CCTV screens. 'Hiya, George.'

'Morning, Mr Fullerton. Great day.'

'And getting better by the minute,' said Fullerton. He jogged into the lift and ran on the spot as it climbed up to the top floor.

The message light on his answering machine was winking and he hit the 'play' button. He dropped down and did fast-paced press-ups as he listened to the message. It was a property developer in Hampstead who had seen four of Donovan's paintings the previous evening and had wanted to sleep on it. Fullerton had sold the man more than a dozen works of art in the past, so had been happy to leave the paintings with him while he made up his mind. It had been a wise decision – the property developer had decided to go ahead and buy them and wanted Fullerton to call around to his home to pick up a bank draft for half a million pounds. Fullerton punched the air in triumph.

He went over to his dining table, a glass and chrome oval that could seat a dozen people. Three bank drafts were lined up next to a modern silver candelabra. The top draft was drawn on Fullerton's own bank. Eight hundred thousand pounds. The buyer of Donovan's Rembrandt had given Fullerton a cheque for the full amount and Fullerton had had it express cleared. Fullerton hadn't told Donovan the identity of the buyer of the Rembrandt, because it might have made him nervous. Like Donovan, the buyer was a major drug dealer, bringing in tens of thousands of ecstasy tablets from Holland every month. He had stacks of cash that he needed laundering, and art was an easy way of cleaning dirty money. Fullerton picked up the draft and held it to his nose, wondering what eight hundred thousand pounds smelt like. It smelt like paper.

The two other drafts were from Goldman and the buyer of the Buttersworth yacht paintings. In the space of eighteen hours Donovan had raised two million pounds, a reflection of the quality of the collection.

Donovan was clearly attached to his art and Fullerton couldn't work out why he was so desperate to sell. According to Goldman, Donovan was worth tens of millions of dollars. Then there was the fact that the drafts had to be made out to the mysterious Mr Rodriguez. Fullerton had asked Hathaway for information on Carlos Rodriguez and his nephew, but so far none had been forthcoming.

Fullerton called the Intercontinental and asked to be put through to Jesus Rodriguez's room. A man with a rough South American accent answered. He said that Mr Rodriguez was busy, but when Fullerton explained why he was calling, a hand was put over the mouthpiece and Fullerton heard muffled Spanish. Then Rodriguez was on the line, oily smooth and saying that he'd see Fullerton in his suite at one o'clock.

He went through to his bathroom and showered, then dressed in a Lanvin suit and Gucci shoes, figuring that if he was hand delivering two million, he might as well look the part. He drove his Porsche to Hampstead and picked up the fourth draft. The drive from Hampstead to the Intercontinental took almost an hour, but he was still ten minutes early, so he sat in Reception until exactly one o'clock before phoning up to Rodriguez's suite.

Two large men in black suits were waiting for him on the seventh floor. They patted him down professionally without speaking, then one of them motioned for him to follow him.

Rodriguez was standing in front of a window offering a panoramic view of Hyde Park. He turned and smiled as Fullerton walked into the room. He was a short man but very muscular as if he spent a lot of time in the gym, dressed in a cream suit and a chocolate-brown shirt. His hair was gelled back and his goatee beard was carefully trimmed. As he held out his hand to shake, Fullerton saw that the nails were carefully manicured and glistened as if they'd been polished. A thick-ridged scar ran along the back of his right hand.

'So you are Donovan's money man?' he asked, gripping Fullerton's hand and squeezing hard.

Fullerton got a whiff of a sickly-sweet cologne. 'He apologises for not coming in person,' he said. He took his hand away and resisted the urge to massage his aching fingers.

Rodriguez laughed harshly. 'I quite understand why he wouldn't want to be seen with me again,' he said.

Fullerton took the drafts from the inside pocket of his jacket and handed them to Rodriguez.

Rodriguez looked through them, nodding his approval. 'Good,' he said. 'At least on this occasion he has kept his word.'

'Was there a problem before?' asked Fullerton. Rodriguez stiffened and Fullerton realised that he'd made a mistake. 'I know Den was very keen that this transaction went ahead smoothly, he was very insistent that you get those today.'

Rodriguez stared at Fullerton. He was still smiling but his eyes were as cold and hard as pebbles. 'How long have you worked for him?' he asked.

Fullerton shrugged and tried to smile confidently. 'I'm not really an employee, as such,' he said quickly. 'I'm an art dealer. Paintings. He needed some works of art placing and I was able to help.'

Rodriguez visibly relaxed. He put the drafts on a coffee table. 'So you know about paintings?'

'Some.'

'You should come and see me some time in Bogotá,' said Rodriguez. 'I too have an interest in art. I would value your opinion.'

'Do you have a card?'

Rodriguez chuckled. 'A card?' He looked across at his two bodyguards and said something to them in Spanish. They started laughing and Rodriguez slapped Fullerton on the back. 'Just ask anyone in Bogotá. They'll tell you where to find me.'

'I will do, Mr Rodriguez.'

Rodriguez nodded at his bodyguards and they steered Fullerton out of the door and into the corridor. Fullerton could hear Rodriguez still chuckling as the door was closed in his face.

Fullerton rubbed his forehead and his hand came away wet. He hadn't realised how much he'd been sweating.

Gregg Hathaway scrolled through Fullerton's report. Jesus Rodriguez had given nothing away, but Hathaway hadn't expected that he would. The Rodriguez cartel were big players, and even the two million pounds Fullerton had delivered was small change to them, so there had to be something else going on.

Donovan had been in a rush to sell his paintings, and he could have got a better price if he'd put them off for auction. That meant he was under pressure. He was paying off Rodriguez, but why? According to Donovan's file, he had access to tens of millions of pounds, much of it in overseas banks. So why bank drafts? Something had clearly gone wrong with Donovan's finances. And if Donovan was short of money, he might be pressurised into making mistakes.

Hathaway sent Fullerton a congratulatory e-mail, and suggested that he try to get closer to Donovan. Not that Fullerton would need much encouragement: it was clear from the reports he was filing that he was champing at the bit.

Hathaway picked up his telephone and called his contact at Bow Street police station. The detective inspector answered on the first ring as if he'd had his hand poised over the receiver.

'Can you talk?' asked Hathaway.

'No problem,' said the detective.

'Have you heard of a Colombian called Carlos Rodriguez?'

'No, I don't think so.'

'A big fish,' said Hathaway. 'A very big fish. Run it by NCS and put in a request for MI6 intelligence. He's Government and judiciary connected, high up on the DEA's most wanted list and has been for a decade or more. He uses his nephew as an enforcer. Jesus Rodriguez. He's got a suite at the Intercontinental.'

'Right . . .' said the detective hesitantly.

'He's getting busy with Den Donovan,' said Hathaway.

'Bloody hell,' said the detective more enthusiastically. 'How long's this been going on?'

'I've only just found out,' said Hathaway. 'Carlos Rodriguez is big in cocaine, mainly through Mexico into the States, but the DEA reckon he's behind several heroin and cannabis cartels too. We haven't had him marked down as bringing stuff into Europe, but if he's linked up with Donovan, that could be about to change.'

'Are Six involved?'

'Not yet. Officially, we'll probably wait until we get an approach from the Americans, and so far that's not been forthcoming.'

'This is big.'

'Huge,' agreed Hathaway. 'God forbid I should try to teach anyone how to suck eggs, but a phone tap would be a good idea, and if I were you I'd be trying to get someone in the hotel.'

'Has Rodriguez met Donovan?'

'I'm not sure if they've met here in London, but I've seen a report from the Customs Drugs Liaison Officer in Miami who says they've been seen together in the Caribbean a couple of times, latterly in St Kitts.'

'What's your take on it?' asked the detective.

'There's something in the wind, I don't think the nephew's here shopping, but they're both old hands at this. I doubt they'll do anything stupid. Whatever they're up to, it must be major to get one of the Rodriguez family out of South America. Stay in touch, yeah?'

'Will do. And thanks for the tip. This is going to do me no harm at all.'

Hathaway replaced the receiver. He began to bite his nails as he reread Fullerton's report.

Donovan was in a black cab on the way to his sister's house when one of his phones rang. It was Underwood, whispering as if he feared he might be overheard. 'They're on to you,' said the chief superintendent.

Donovan gritted his teeth. He knew that it was always going to be a matter of time before the authorities knew that he was back in the UK, but he had hoped he could have remained incognito for a few more days, at least until he'd got things sorted with Robbie. 'Who's they?' he asked.

'Drugs. National Crime Squad. Customs. Uncle Tom Cobbly and all. Congratulations, you're Tango One again.'

'No need for you to sound so bloody pleased about it.'

'What are you going to do?'

'I've got to get a passport for Robbie. I'm not leaving him here on his own.'

'Has your missus been in touch?'

'No,' said Donovan. 'Any joy finding them?'

'I wouldn't hold your breath. They're going to be well hidden if they know what's good for them. I've got them flagged at points of entry, but you know as well as I do how porous our borders are. That's if they even decide to come back.'

'Keep looking, yeah? Any idea who fingered me?'

'Came through Drugs, that's all I know. Anyone on your case?'

'I've not seen anyone.'

'Yeah, well, keep your eyes peeled because it's all hands to the pumps. They're going to be crawling over you.'

'I'm clean, though, right? Nothing current?'

'Not now you-know-who's no longer in the picture. You don't fuck about, do you?'

'He knew what he was getting into. No use crying over spilt milk.'

'Just hope you don't ever get pissed off at me,' said the detective.

'Yeah,' said Donovan. 'Me too.'

Donovan cut the connection. If he was once again Tango One, there was no point in hiding any more. Everything he did would have to be in plain sight.

The taxi pulled up in front of Laura's house. Donovan paid the driver and walked up to the front door. He rang the doorbell and heard Robbie shouting excitedly from inside.

Robbie flung the door open. 'Dad!'

Donovan picked him up and hugged him. 'Hiya, Robbie, been good, have you?'

'Of course. Where were you last night?'

'I got tied up. Business.'

'Can we go home?'

Donovan put his son down and took him inside. Laura was at the kitchen door, wiping her hands on a tea towel. 'You eaten, Den?' she asked.

'Starving, Sis,' said Donovan.

'It's only spag bol and salad.'

'Bring it on,' said Donovan and followed her through to the kitchen. Laura's daughters Jenny and Julie were sitting at a long table with glasses of orange juice in front of them.

'Mark not back?'

'No,' said Laura, busying herself over the oven. 'Working late.'

Donovan sat down at the table and Robbie rushed to sit next to him. 'How was your day?' asked Donovan.

Robbie pulled a face. 'Boring. Aunty Laura said I have to go to school soon.'

'That's right, as soon as I've sorted things out with your headmistress.' Donovan ruffled his hair. 'Only another seven years.' He laughed. 'That's about what you'd get for armed robbery, you know.'

'Den!' admonished his sister.

'And no time off for good behaviour.'

Laura put down plates of spaghetti bolognaise and salad in front of them. The children devoured their pasta while Donovan raised his wine glass to toast his sister. 'Great grub, Sis. Thanks. And thanks for taking care of Robbie.'

Laura winked at Donovan and clinked her glass against his.

'Are we going home tonight, Dad?' asked Robbie.

'Not tonight, kid.'

Robbie put down his fork. 'Why not? Why can't we go home?'

'Because I've got things to do at night, that's why.'

'That's not fair!'

'Who said life was fair?'

'You always say that.'

'Because it's true.'

'I want to go home,' said Robbie petulantly.

'That's a nice thing to say in front of your Aunty Laura,' said Donovan.

'It's okay, Den,' said Laura. 'I know what he means.'

'I know exactly what he means,' snapped Donovan, 'and he's going to have to learn to do what he's told. He doesn't know how lucky he is.'

'You always say that too,' said Robbie, close to tears.

'Yeah, well, according to you I spend my whole fucking life repeating myself, but that doesn't mean that what I say isn't right. Your Aunty Laura and me never had a house like this when we were kids. Never had food like you get. And our stepdad used to kick the shit out of us if we answered back to him. Am I right, Laura?'

Laura looked away, not wanting to get drawn into the argument.

'Dad, I just want to be in my own house, that's all.'

Donovan took a deep breath, trying to calm himself down. 'I know you do, Robbie, but it's difficult just now. Can't you stay here for a few days? Please.'

'And then we can go home?'

'We'll see.'

Robbie wiped his eyes. He pushed his plate away, most of the food untouched.

'Eat your dinner,' said Donovan.

'I'm not hungry,' sniffed Robbie.

Donovan pushed the plate back towards Robbie. 'Eat it.'

'He doesn't have to, Den. Not if he's not hungry.'

Donovan ignored his sister. He tapped the table in front of Robbie. 'You are not leaving here until that's eaten.'

'I'm not hungry,' said Robbie.

'I don't give a fuck if you're hungry or not hungry, you're going to do as you're told,' shouted Donovan, waving his fork in Robbie's face.

Robbie glared defiantly at his father. A tear rolled down his left cheek.

'Den!' hissed Laura.

Donovan turned to look at his sister. She narrowed her eyes and jerked her head at her two daughters, who were staring at Donovan with looks of horror on their faces.

'I'm sorry,' said Donovan. He smiled at the girls. 'Bet you've heard worse from your dad, haven't you, girls?'

They shook their heads in silence. Robbie seized the opportunity and ran out of the kitchen. Donovan stood up to go after him but Laura put a hand on his arm. 'Leave him be, Den.'

'He's got to learn to do as he's told,' said Donovan.

'He's been through a lot,' said Laura.

'We went through a fucking lot,' said Donovan. 'Didn't stop us doing what we were fucking told.' He stopped himself and smiled apologetically at Jenny and Julie. 'Sorry, girls. I know I shouldn't be swearing like this but I've had a hell of a day.' He smiled again. 'A heck of a day,' he corrected himself.

'You're going to have to calm down, Den,' said Laura. 'He's nine years old and you're treating him as if he works for you.'

'I'm under pressure here, Laura. I need to get out of the country and Robbie's going to have to come with me.'

'He can stay here, with us.'

'He's my son. He needs his father.'

'Then it's time you started acting like one, Den.'

Donovan opened his mouth to argue, but he could tell from the look on his sister's face that she was in no mood to back down. He put down his fork.

'You're not leaving the table until you've eaten that,' said Laura.

'Ha, ha,' said Donovan.

'I mean it,' said Laura.

Donovan sighed and picked up his fork. He stabbed a chunk of cucumber and slotted it into his mouth.

'That's better,' said Laura. She smiled brightly at her daughters, who were still nervously watching Donovan. 'So, girls, how was your day?' she asked.

Donovan left Laura's house just before ten o'clock. Mark had returned home an hour earlier and they'd all sat in the kitchen and drunk a second bottle of wine after the two girls had gone to bed.

Before Donovan had left, he'd gone up to say goodnight to Robbie, but Robbie had locked the bedroom door and refused to say anything.

Laura pecked Donovan on the cheek on the doorstep. 'You be careful, Den,' she said. 'And go easy on Robbie.'

'Tell him I'll see him tomorrow. We'll go and have ice cream or something.'

'This isn't about ice cream, Den,' said Laura. 'It's about being a father.'

'I am his father.'

'That's right. And being a father means facing up to your responsibilities.'

'I don't remember our father being especially responsible.' Laura flashed him a tight smile but didn't say anything. Donovan closed his eyes and swore silently as he realised what he'd said. 'Christ, I'm turning into him, aren't I?'

Laura hugged him, pressing her head against his chest. 'No, you're not him. You're not going to run away.'

Donovan put his arms around her and held her close. 'I'm being a right bastard to him, aren't I?'

'No, you're not, but he needs your love and your support, Den. He doesn't need to be bossed around.'

Donovan nodded. 'I'll talk to him tomorrow. I'll get it sorted, I promise.'

They hugged again, then Laura closed the door. Donovan walked along the path to the pavement, then turned and looked back at the house. The bedroom where Robbie was sleeping was on the first floor, the furthest room to the right. Donovan looked up at the window. The curtain twitched. Donovan raised his hand and gave a small wave. The curtain moved to the side and Robbie appeared. He waved down at Donovan, his face close to tears. Donovan smiled and blew his son a kiss. Robbie moved away from the window and the curtain fell back into place.

'Dennis Donovan?'

Donovan whirled around. A small, balding man was walking towards him, his right hand moving inside his fawn raincoat. Donovan reacted immediately, stepping forward to meet the man, his left hand pushing him in the chest, unbalancing him so that he couldn't pull out whatever was concealed underneath the coat. The man started to protest but Donovan carried on moving forward. He grabbed the man's wrist and twisted it hard, then stamped down against the man's shin.

The man yelped and fell back. Donovan kicked the man's feet from underneath him and he slammed into the pavement. Donovan followed the man down, dropping on top of him, his knees pinning the man's arms to the ground. Donovan pulled back his right fist, ready to smash it into the man's face.

'Who the fuck are you?' asked Donovan.

The man was confused, shaking his head, his eyes glazed.

'Who sent you!' shouted Donovan.

'Your wife . . .' spluttered the man. He'd bitten his lip as he fell and a trickle of blood dribbled down his chin.

'Bitch!' shouted Donovan. He lowered his fist. 'How much did she pay you?' he asked.

'Our standard fee. One hundred and twenty pounds plus expenses.'

'What?' Donovan was confused. The going rate for a hit in London was fifteen thousand, minimum.

The front door opened. Mark and Laura were there. 'Den? What's happening?' shouted Mark, rushing down the path to the street.

'Who the fuck are you?' asked Donovan.

'I'm a solicitor's clerk,' said the man, gasping for breath. 'I serve writs in the evenings, for the overtime.'

'You're what?'

Mark rushed up behind Donovan. 'What's going on?' he asked.

Donovan ignored him. 'You've got a writ for me?'

The man nodded, then coughed violently. He tried to nod towards his chest. 'Inside pocket,' he said, then coughed again.

Donovan shoved his hand inside the man's coat and groped around. His fingers found an envelope and he pulled it out. He stared at it. His name was typed on it in capital letters. In the top left-hand corner was the name and address of a firm of City solicitors.

'How did you know where to find me?' Donovan asked.

'I had a list of addresses. This was the third I tried. Can I get up now? My back's killing me.'

'Den, what the hell's going on?' asked Mark.

Donovan helped the solicitor's clerk to his feet and brushed down his raincoat. 'Nothing,' he said. 'It was a misunderstanding, that's all.'

The solicitor's clerk was shaking like a sick dog, and he couldn't look Donovan in the eyes.

Donovan took out his wallet and thrust a handful of fifty-pound notes into the man's hands, then pushed him away. The man walked unsteadily down the street, one hand against the side of his head.

Mark put his hand on Donovan's shoulder. 'Den, would you just tell me what the hell that was all about?' he asked.

Donovan held up the manila envelope. 'Special delivery. Vicky.'

Mark frowned. 'What is it?'

'An injunction,' said Donovan. He ripped open the envelope and scanned the legal papers. 'Shit,' he said.

Laura hurried down the path. 'What's going on?' she asked.

'It's about Robbie,' said Donovan. 'It says I can't take him out of the country. Bitch!' He screwed up the papers and threw them into the gutter. 'I'll kill her!'

'Den, calm down,' urged Laura. She picked up the papers and straightened them out.

Donovan shook his head, refusing to be mollified. 'Who does the bitch think she is? She fucks around behind my back and then she sets the law on me!'

Laura held out the papers to him. 'You're going to have to show these to a lawyer, Den.'

Donovan snatched them from her.

'There's no point in getting upset, Den,' said Mark. 'Just calm down.'

'Calm down? You fucking calm down. He's my son and she's trying to tell me what I can and can't do? Fuck her! She's dead! Dead meat!' Donovan stormed off down the street, the legal documents flapping in his hand.

Mark and Laura hugged each other as they watched him go. Upstairs, the curtain twitched at Robbie's bedroom window.

It was hot and airless in the van, and Detective Constable Ashleigh Vincent was all too well aware that her male partner had been on a curry binge the previous night, but what had happened on the street outside had taken her mind off the pungent odours of chicken vindaloo and Cobra lager. The motordrive clicked away as she took picture after picture of the retreating man in the fawn raincoat.

'Get his car number plate,' said Vincent's partner as she focused on the man's vehicle.

'Gosh, I wish I'd thought of that, Connor,' said Vincent. Her partner had only been in plainclothes for the best part of a month, but he seemed to be under the impression that he was the senior member of the surveillance team.

They'd been sitting in the van outside Mark and Laura Gardner's house for almost twelve hours and had been about to call it a night when Den Donovan had arrived. There was no doubting it was Tango One: they had a dozen surveillance photographs of him Sellotaped up around the darkened window that they were looking through. They'd photographed him arriving in the black cab and going into the house, and waited patiently for him to come out.

The man in the fawn raincoat had caught Vincent by surprise. She hadn't noticed him pull up in his Ford Fiesta and she had no idea how long he had been sitting there waiting for Donovan. The first she'd seen of him was when he walked up behind Donovan, his hand moving inside his raincoat.

Vincent's partner had sworn out loud. 'Fuck, he's got a gun!'

'Bollocks,' Vincent had said, clicking away on the camera. 'If this was a hit, he'd have the gun out.' As the words left her mouth she'd had a sudden feeling of doubt, that maybe she'd called it wrong, but she kept on taking photographs. She'd known she was right as soon as the man called out Donovan's name. If it had been a professional hit, the man would have shot Donovan in the head from behind, there'd have been no warning.

Vincent had been impressed by the speed with which Donovan had moved once he'd been aware of the man. There didn't appear to have been any fear on Donovan's part: he'd moved instinctively, putting the man down and then throwing himself on top. Vincent had kept on taking pictures while her partner continued to curse. 'Fuck me, look at that!'

They'd both watched as Donovan took the envelope from the man's pocket.

'What the hell's that?' Vincent's partner had asked.

'His lottery numbers,' Vincent had said scathingly.

The man in the raincoat drove off in his Ford Fiesta. 'Fill in the log, Connor,' said Vincent, still clicking away on the camera. She couldn't wait until her bosses at the Drugs

Squad saw the pictures. She'd have to find a way to make sure that Connor was otherwise engaged – that way she could claim more of the credit for herself.

Laurence Patterson kept Donovan waiting in Reception for fifteen minutes, but had the good grace to hurry out of his office apologising profusely. He pumped Donovan's hand and ushered him into his office.

'Got a client just been pulled in on a robbery charge, he's screaming blue murder. Sorry.'

'Business is good, yeah?' asked Donovan, dropping down on to a low black sofa. A huge white oak desk dominated one end of the palatial office, but Patterson always preferred to talk to his clients on the sofas by the window and its expansive view of the City. Patterson's firm hadn't deliberately chosen the location to be close to London's financial powerhouses – the offices were just a short walk from the Old Bailey, where the firm's criminal partners did most of their work.

'Busy, busy, busy,' said Patterson, sitting down on the sofa opposite Donovan. 'Can I get you a drink?'

Donovan shook his head. He handed Patterson the writ that the solicitor's clerk had given him. Patterson read through it quickly, nodding and murmuring to himself. He was barely out of his thirties and Donovan had used him for almost seven years. Patterson had a razor-sharp mind, an almost photographic memory and had the ear of the best barristers in London. His father was a big-time villain, now retired on the Costa Brava, whose coming-of-age present to his son had been the names and private telephone numbers of six of the most corrupt coppers in the UK. Patterson had helped get charges dropped against members of Donovan's team on several occasions. He wasn't cheap, nor were his police contacts, but they guaranteed results.

Patterson shook his head to the side, throwing his fringe away from his eyes. He had a long, thin face and a slightly hooked nose, and with his inquisitive eyes he had the look of a hawk on the hunt for prey. 'Seems pretty straightforward,' he said.

'But you can overturn it, right? I want to take Robbie back to the Caribbean with me.'

Patterson rubbed the bridge of his nose and screwed up his eyes as if he had the beginnings of a headache. 'Cards on the table, Den, it's not really my field. This domestic stuff is a specialised area. Would you mind if I pass you over to one of my colleagues?'

Donovan shifted uncomfortably on the sofa. 'I'd prefer you to handle it, Laurence.'

Patterson grinned. 'Better the devil you know, eh?'

Donovan shrugged. That was part of his desire to have Patterson on the case. He knew he could trust Patterson, and didn't relish the idea of having a stranger rooting through his personal business.

'We can do it that way, Den, but to be honest, all that would happen is that you'd talk to me, I'd run it by her, then I'd tell you what she told me.'

'She?'

'Julia Lau. She's been here for donkey's and there's nothing she doesn't know about family law.'

'Lau? Chinese?'

'That's right. And she's fucking inscrutable, Den.'

Donovan wrinkled his nose. He still didn't like the idea of bringing in a lawyer he didn't know.

'You'd be better off having her arguing your case than me, Den. How's it going to look if you've got a criminal lawyer by your side in a custody fight? I keep people out of prison, Den. I don't discuss the finer points of parental control.'

Donovan nodded. 'And she's dead safe, yeah?'

'Anything you tell her is privileged, Den. Like talking to a priest.'

Donovan grinned. 'It's been almost thirty years since I spoke to a priest, and that was to tell him if he patted me on the backside again I'd set fire to his church. Okay, when do I meet her?'

'I'll get her down now. I'll sit in on the initial briefing, yeah?'

'Cheers, Laurence.'

Patterson went over to his desk and picked up his phone. While he was speaking, Donovan stared at a large canvas on the wall opposite him. It was about five feet wide and four feet high and was nothing more than three red squares on a yellow background. Donovan frowned as he looked at the painting, trying to work out what, if anything, the artist had been trying to say. The colours were vivid and the squares were accurately drawn, but Donovan couldn't see anything in the painting that a reasonably competent six-year-old couldn't have copied.

Patterson replaced the receiver and walked back to the sofas.

'How much did you pay for that?' asked Donovan, gesturing at the canvas.

'Fucked if I know,' said Patterson. 'Purchasing gets them by the yard, I think.'

'But you chose it, right?'

Patterson twisted around to get a better look. 'Nah, my secretary makes those sorts of decisions. They get rotated every few weeks.'

'Yeah, it'd look better turned around,' said Donovan.

'It's just something to look at. Makes the clients feel that we've got a creative side.'

Donovan chuckled. 'You've got that all right,' he said. Patterson's creativity had got him out of more than his fair share of scrapes, especially when he'd been named as Tango One.

There was a double knock on the door. It opened before Patterson had time to react, and Julia Lau walked in. She was one of the most unattractive women that Donovan had ever seen. She was overweight, bordering on obese, and her thighs rubbed together in a dark green trouser suit as she waddled over to the sofas, clutching a stack of files and notebooks to her large chest. Her face was almost circular, with thick-lensed spectacles perched precariously on the end of a bulbous nose. When she smiled she showed a mouthful of grey teeth. 'Mr Donovan, so happy to meet you,' she said, extending a hand. Her accent was faultless, pure English public school.

Donovan shook hands with her. She had pudgy, sausage-like fingers with ornate gold rings on each one and fingernails that were bitten to the quick.

'Laurence has told me so much about you.'

Donovan looked at Patterson and arched an eyebrow. 'Has he now?'

'Just that you were a valued client with a matrimonial problem,' said Patterson.

Lau dropped her files and notebooks on to the coffee table and lowered herself down on the sofa next to Donovan. It creaked under her weight and Donovan found himself sliding along the black leather towards her. He pushed himself away from her to the far end of the sofa.

Patterson handed Lau the injunction and she read

through it quickly, her brow furrowed. Donovan looked across at Patterson, who nodded encouragingly. Donovan shrugged. Lau clearly hadn't been hired for her looks, so he could only assume that she was a first-class lawyer.

'Your wife says she believes that you intend to take your son to Anguilla. Is that true?'

'I have a house there.'

'But your matrimonial home is here in London?'

'If you can call it that,' said Donovan bitterly. 'It didn't stop her screwing my accountant there.'

'Your primary residence is here in the UK, though? Is that the case?'

'It's complicated.'

Lau peered at him over the top of her bottle-bottom lenses. 'Try to enlighten me, Mr Donovan. I'll do my best to keep up.' She flashed him a cold smile.

Donovan nodded, accepting that he had been patronising. 'I'm sorry. Yes, the family home is in London, but for various reasons I don't spend much time in the country. I have a home in Anguilla – Robbie and his mother have stayed with me there for weeks at a time. I don't see why he shouldn't be allowed to go there now.'

Lau nodded thoughtfully. Her lips had almost disappeared, leaving her mouth little more than a fine horizontal slash.

'I think it might be best if you enlighten Julia as to the nature of your problems in the UK,' said Patterson.

Donovan grimaced.

'Den, it stays in this office,' said Patterson.

Donovan sighed. 'Okay.' He turned towards Lau. 'I was top of the police and Customs most wanted list,' he said. 'Tango One. Everywhere I went I was followed. My phones were tapped, my bank accounts were looked at, my friends were put under surveillance. It made it impossible for me to operate.'

'Operate?' said Lau.

'To put deals together. To do what I do. So I left the country. In the Caribbean the authorities are more . . . flexible.'

Lau nodded thoughtfully but didn't say anything.

Donovan pointed at the injunction. 'We can get that overturned, right?'

'We can fight this, of course. If nothing else, forbidding him the freedom to travel with his father is a breach of your son's human rights. I must counsel you, however, that this is probably the first shot in what will almost certainly develop into a salvo. I would expect your wife very shortly to move to get custody of your son.'

'No way!' said Donovan sharply.

Lau held up a hand to quieten him. 'There's no point in your wife simply stopping you from taking him out of the country. If you have sole custody, that injunction cannot stand. If I were advising your wife, I would have told her to rush through this injunction, but then to apply for sole custody on the basis that you are an unsuitable parental figure.'

'Bollocks!'

Lau looked at him steadily, unabashed by his outburst. 'That would be my advice to her, Mr Donovan. Please don't take offence, I am sure you are a commendable father, but your wife is going to portray you in the worst light possible. You have, I understand, no gainful employment.'

'I'm not short of a bob or two,' said Donovan.

'That's as maybe, but you don't have a job. Nor, I understand, do you spend much time in the family home.'

Donovan exchanged a look with Patterson. He wondered how much Julia Lau knew about his dealings. Patterson's face provided no clue.

'I travel a lot,' said Donovan.

'Exactly, but any court is going to want to see your son in a stable environment.'

'So I've got to get a nine-to-five job, is that it?'

'Not necessarily, but you'd have to show some legitimate means of support. Your wife will do all she can to demonstrate that you are not a suitable parent.'

Patterson leaned forward. 'What about Den's other . . . activities? Is she likely to bring them out into the open?'

Lau pushed her glasses a little higher up her bump of a nose. 'I doubt that her counsel would recommend that. If she were to highlight any, shall we say, criminal activities, that would be evidence that she was aware of them, and if she were to have profited from them would thereby identify herself as an accomplice. She'd be risking any assets she had. If I were her counsel, I would be advising her to stick to more parental concerns. Your lack of a regular job, your frequent absences from the family home, personal traits.'

'Personal traits?'

'Abuse, physical, verbal or psychological. Whether you'd shown an interest in raising Robbie prior to the separation. Did you, for instance, attend parent–teacher meetings? Take Robbie to the doctor? The dentist? School sports days?'

Donovan grimaced. He'd fallen down on all counts.

'Now, in view of your wife's infidelity, which under the circumstances I think will be uncontested, we can make a very good case for you being granted custody of Robbie.'

Donovan relaxed a little. Finally, some good news.

'However,' continued Lau, 'even if you were to be

granted sole custody, that doesn't necessarily mean that you will be allowed to take Robbie overseas.'

'Why not?' interrupted Donovan.

'Because even if you are granted sole custody, your wife would still have visitation rights, and those rights would be compromised if your son was living outside the country.'

'But she's the one who left,' protested Donovan. 'She went running off with her tail between her legs.'

Lau scribbled a note on a yellow legal pad. 'Do you know where she is?'

'I've got people looking.'

'If we could show that she is herself resident overseas, I think there might be less of a problem convincing a court that you be allowed to take Robbie abroad.'

'We'll see,' said Donovan. If he did find out where his errant wife was, custody wouldn't be an issue. A sudden thought struck him. He nodded at the injunction. 'Her lawyer did that, right?'

Lau nodded.

'If we get to a custody battle, could she do it all through her lawyer or would she have to appear in court?'

'Oh, she'd have to be there,' said Lau. 'Quite definitely. The judge might well have questions for her, and we'd have to argue against their case. You'd both have to give evidence.'

Donovan smiled and sat back in the sofa. If the mountain couldn't go to Mohammed, maybe he could get Mohammed to come to the mountain. If she wanted Robbie, she'd have to come and get him.

'There is the question of a retainer,' said Lau.

'Julia,' said Patterson, frowning. 'Den is a long-standing and valued client, there's no need . . .'

'That's okay, Laurence,' said Donovan, taking a thick envelope out of his pocket. He handed it to Lau.

Lau opened the flap. If she was surprised by the wad of fifty-pound notes inside, she did a creditable job of concealing it. She ran her thumb along the notes. Ten thousand pounds. 'Cash,' she said thoughtfully. 'That'll do nicely.'

Donovan looked over at Patterson and the two men grinned. Donovan nodded. Julia Lau was okay.

Sitting outside the headmistress's study brought back memories of Donovan's own schooldays. Donovan's *alma mater* was a pre-war soot-stained brick building in Salford, with half a dozen Portakabins at one side of the playground for overspill classes. Most of the school's pupils left at sixteen, and in all the time Donovan was there he didn't recall anyone going on to university. Robbie's school was a world apart, all the children squeaky-clean in uniforms that cost as much as a Savile Row suit and no more than twenty pupils in a class. After-school activities for Donovan had been a quick cigarette behind the bike sheds, but Robbie and his peers could choose from a host of sports and activities, all supervised by teachers who actually seemed to enjoy their work.

One wall of the waiting room was covered with awards and trophies that the school had won, with pride of place given over to a large framed photograph of the Duke of Edinburgh paying a visit in the late 1980s.

The door to the headmistress's study opened and for a crazy moment Donovan felt a surge of irrational guilt as if he were about to be given six whacks of a slipper. That had been the punishment of choice meted out when he was at school – it never left a mark but it hurt like hell.

'Mr Donovan? So nice to see you.' The headmistress

was a tall, thin woman with sharp features and long blonde hair tied back in a ponytail. She offered Donovan an elegant hand with carefully painted nails, and they shook. She led him through to her office. Unlike Patterson's office there were no comfy sofas, just an old-fashioned walnut desk with a dark green leather blotter. A brass nameplate on the desk read 'Andrea Stephenson. Headmistress'. No Mrs or Miss, or even Ms. Just her name and her title. A high-backed dark brown leather executive chair sat on one side of the desk, two simple wooden chairs facing it. Donovan could hear the computer on a side table buzzing quietly to itself.

She walked quickly behind the desk and sat down. 'I'm so glad finally to get to meet you, Mr Donovan,' she said. She ran her fingers along a pale blue file on the blotter. It was probably Robbie's file, thought Donovan, in which case she knew exactly how long it had been since Donovan had sat on the uncomfortable wooden chair. 'We are obviously a little bit concerned about Robbie's recent absence from school,' she said. She put on a pair of wire-framed reading glasses, opened the file and glanced down at it. 'Robbie's aunt has been our point of contact, I gather.'

'My sister. Laura.'

'She telephoned to say that Robbie was unwell.'

'That's right.'

The headmistress looked at Donovan over the top of her spectacles. 'Why didn't Mrs Donovan phone us? Or you?'

'I've been overseas,' said Donovan. 'Robbie's doing okay, is he?'

'Robbie's doing just fine,' said the headmistress. 'A little boisterous, but then what nine-year-old isn't? It's not Robbie's behaviour that concerns me so much as his absence, however, I'm putting two and two together and getting the feeling that perhaps there are problems at home? Would I be right in that assumption?'

Donovan nodded and linked his fingers in his lap, though what he really wanted to do was to wipe the patronising smile off the headmistress's face. 'Robbie's mother has left the matrimonial home,' said Donovan. 'I'll be taking care of him from now on.'

'You and Mrs Donovan are separating?'

'Robbie caught her in bed with my accountant.'

'My God,' said the headmistress, a look of horror on her face.

Donovan felt a surge of satisfaction at her reaction, but kept his feelings hidden. He stared impassively at her. 'Exactly,' said Donovan. 'Now she's gone AWOL and I'm taking care of Robbie.'

'Would you like me to talk to Robbie?' said the headmistress.

'I think he's okay. He's taking it well enough. No, what I'm here for is to make sure that you understand the position. My wife isn't to go near Robbie.'

The headmistress frowned. 'I'm not sure I follow you.'

'She's served me an injunction preventing me from taking him abroad, so until we overturn that, he has to stay put. It looks like she's going to try to get custody, and as part of that I think she might try to snatch him back.'

The headmistress nodded thoughtfully.

'Obviously I want Robbie back at school as soon as possible. So I want it made clear that if she turns up at the school she's not to be allowed to take him.'

'Mr Donovan, I'm not sure if I can give you that guarantee. Mrs Donovan is Robbie's mother.' Donovan opened his mouth to argue but she held up her hand and raised her eyebrows as if she were silencing a noisy classroom. 'Do you have some sort of legal backing for your request?'

'Such as?'

'A court order. Something like that.'

'No, but my lawyer is applying for sole custody and we're confident the court will see it our way.'

The headmistress spread her hands, palms upwards. 'Mr Donovan, unless a court forbids your wife access to your son, I'm not sure that we can—'

'You don't understand,' interrupted Donovan. 'She might snatch him. She could turn up with a couple of heavies and whisk him away.'

The headmistress shook her head sadly. 'Mr Donovan, I know your wife. She was a regular attender at Parent Teacher Association meetings. She donated money to our arts club appeal.'

Donovan stood up. The headmistress jerked back in her seat as if she'd been stung. 'If she comes to the school, she's not to go near Robbie,' he said, pointing an accusing finger at her. 'If she does, I'll hold you responsible. Personally responsible.'

'Are you threatening me, Mr Donovan?' she asked, her voice shaking.

Donovan leaned over her desk, invading her space. 'I'm telling you, Miss, Ms or Mrs Stephenson. You know my wife and maybe you don't know me, but believe me, anything happens to my son and you'll get to know me. Do you understand?'

The headmistress nodded.

'Maybe you don't,' said Donovan. He picked up the brass nameplate and waved it under her nose. 'I know your name, and it would take me two minutes to find out where you live.' He slammed the nameplate down on her desk and she flinched. All the colour had drained from the headmistress's face. Donovan smiled. He straightened up and took a step back. 'Let's not get off on the wrong foot,' he said softly. 'Robbie's a good kid. You've done a great job teaching him and I do appreciate that. If it's donations you want, I'd be happy to help out. I can even come to PTA meetings.' Donovan straightened up. 'Thank you for your time. If my wife should turn up at the school, I'd be grateful if you'd call me. Immediately.' He handed her a card on which he'd written the number of one of his pay-as-you-go mobiles.

The headmistress sat with her head down and her hands in her lap. Donovan kept holding the card out to her. Eventually she reached up hesitantly and took it.

'Thank you,' said Donovan.

Donovan went back to the hotel and told the manager he'd be checking out. He went up to his room and quickly packed his things. He was gathering up his mobile phones when he saw that two of them had received voice messages.

One was the phone that Juan Rojas used. Donovan checked that one first. Rojas said nothing of interest, just that he was on the case but that so far he had nothing to report. The second message was from Jamie Fullerton, saying that he had the rest of the money from the sale of the paintings. Three hundred and fifty thousand pounds.

Donovan phoned Fullerton and arranged to meet him at Donovan's house later that night, then went downstairs and paid his bill in cash.

He caught a black cab back to the house, and looked around before opening the front door. He didn't see any obvious surveillance, but now that he was back to being

Tango One he was sure that there'd be watchers somewhere along the street. They could be in a flat across the road, in an attic somewhere, in the back of a van with darkened windows. They might even have set up a remote-controlled camera in a parked car, monitored some distance away. If they were good, he wouldn't see them.

He let himself into the house and took his suitcase upstairs. He stripped off the bedding in the master bedroom and took it down to the kitchen and put it in the washer-dryer, then had second thoughts and stuffed it into black rubbish bags and put them outside by the bins.

He took more rubbish bags upstairs and methodically went through the rooms, putting everything that belonged to his wife into the bags. Clothes. Cosmetics. Videos. CDs. Tapes. Holiday souvenirs. Everything and anything that was personal to her. He filled six bags and threw them out of the bedroom window so that they landed in the back garden with a satisfying thud.

Donovan showered and changed into clean chinos and a polo shirt, and he was combing his hair when the doorbell rang. It was Jamie Fullerton, grinning widely and carrying two red Manchester United holdalls. 'How's it going, Den?' he asked, shifting his weight from foot to foot.

'Fine, Jamie. Come on in.'

Donovan took him through to the kitchen. Fullerton heaved the bulging holdalls on to the kitchen table.

'Beer?' asked Donovan.

'Sure.'

Donovan took two bottles out of the fridge and uncapped them. He gave one to Fullerton and they clinked bottles.

'To crime,' said Fullerton.

Donovan froze, his bottle halfway towards his mouth. 'Say what?'

Fullerton took a mouthful of beer and wiped his mouth with the back of his hand. 'It was a crime, the way I ramped those paintings. Way over the odds, they paid.' He nodded at the holdalls. 'There's your cash. A cool three hundred and fifty, on top of the money I gave the Colombian. Am I good or am I good?'

Donovan put his bottle on the table and unzipped one of the holdalls. It was full of wads of fifty-pound notes. He took out a thick wad and flicked the notes with his thumb.

'It's spotless, Den. You could put that on a church plate with a clean conscience.'

Donovan put the wad of notes into his jacket pocket and zipped up the holdall. Fullerton raised his bottle in salute and Donovan did the same. 'Good job, Jamie. Thanks.'

'You want a line? To celebrate?'

Donovan's face hardened. 'You brought drugs into my house?'

Fullerton grimaced.

'You know I'm under surveillance, right? Tango One, I am.'

'Tango One?'

'That's what the filth call their most wanted. A Alpha, B Bravo, C Charlie. T stands for target and it's T Tango. Tango One, Target One. And I'm it. They're probably out there now. And you brought drugs into my house? How stupid is that?'

'Shit. I'm sorry. It's only for personal use, though. Couple of grams.' He grinned. 'Good stuff, too.'

'Yeah, I can see that from your face. You look like you're plugged into the mains.'

Fullerton took a small silver phial from his pocket. 'Want some?'

'Are you not listening to me, Jamie?'

'Yeah, but if we get rid of the evidence, what can they do? Unless you want me to flush it, but I have to say, Den, this is primo blow. I get it off a guy in Chelsea Harbour who supplies half the TV executives in London.'

Donovan was about to argue, but the cocaine-induced eager-to-please look on Fullerton's face made him laugh out loud. 'Go on then, you daft bastard,' he said, picking up the two holdalls. 'I suppose you deserve it.'

Donovan took the holdalls through to his study. With the Buttersworth painting now gone, the safe was exposed and Donovan decided against putting the money in it. He went upstairs and pulled down the folding ladder that led up to the loft, and hid the holdalls behind the water tank.

By the time he got back to the kitchen, Fullerton had prepared four lines of cocaine on the kitchen table and was rolling up a fifty-pound note.

'You said a line,' said Donovan. 'One line.'

'I lied,' said Fullerton. He bent down and snorted one of the lines, then held his head back and gasped as the drug kicked in. 'Wow!' he said.

Fullerton held out the rolled-up banknote to Donovan but Donovan shook his head.

Fullerton snorted the three remaining lines.

'Be careful, yeah? Don't carry gear when you're anywhere near me. They're going to be looking for any excuse to put me away.'

'Understood, Den.' He made a Boy Scout salute and grinned. 'Dib, dib, dib,' he said.

'You were never a Scout,' said Donovan.

'Was too.'

Donovan grinned and shook his head.

Fullerton drained his lager. 'You want to go out and celebrate?'

'What did you have in mind?' asked Donovan.

'Bottle of shampoo. Pretty girls. On me.'

Donovan thought about Fullerton's offer. He had things to do if he was going to get the house ready for Robbie, but it had been a while since he'd let his hair down. A few drinks wouldn't do him any harm. 'Okay. But no more drugs.'

Fullerton threw him another salute. 'Scout's honour.'

Fullerton's black Porsche was parked a few doors down from Donovan's house. Fullerton drove quickly, weaving through the evening traffic, his hand light on the gear stick and his foot heavy on the accelerator.

They'd only been driving for five minutes when Donovan pointed at a phone box. 'Pull up here, Jamie. I've got to make a call.'

Fullerton groped into his pocket and held out a mobile. 'Use this.'

Donovan shook his head. 'Nah, it's not the sort of call I want to make from a mobile.'

Fullerton pulled up at the side of the road. He gestured with the mobile. 'It's okay, Den. It's a pay as you go. Not registered or anything.'

Donovan took the mobile off him and weighed it in his hand. It was a small Nokia, the same model he'd bought for Robbie for his last birthday. State of the art. 'Let me tell you about mobiles, Jamie. Everything you say into this, or near this, they can listen in to.'

'They?'

'The Feds. Customs. Spooks. With or without a warrant. They're the perfect bugs because you take them with you everywhere you go, and there's so many of them that no one even notices them any more.'

'Den, no one but me has ever touched that phone. No way have they put a bug in it. On my life.'

Donovan shook his head. 'They don't have to. It's all done with systems these days. Once they know the number, they can listen in to every call you make. Every call you receive. But it's worse than that, Jamie. They can tell where you are to within a few feet. They can look into your Sim card and get all the data off it. Your address book, every call you made and every call you received. They can see it all.'

Fullerton raised his eyebrows. He stared at the mobile in Donovan's hand. 'Shit.'

'It gets worse,' said Donovan. 'They can send a nifty program direct to the handset that turns it into a listening device, even when it's switched off.'

'Oh come on,' said Fullerton.

'I'm serious, Jamie. I got it from the horse's mouth. Customs guy out in Miami who's on my payroll. Anything said in a room, they can tune into from a targeted mobile. Even if it's switched off. Okay, so long as they don't know you, you can carry on in your own sweet way, but I'm Tango One and any mobile I go near is a potential threat.' He tossed the phone back to Fullerton. 'And once they've seen you with me, your phone becomes a threat, too.'

Fullerton put away the mobile.

'Why do you think they're so cheap, Jamie?' asked Donovan.

'Supply and demand. Economies of scale.'

'Bollocks,' Donovan sneered. 'It's because the Government wants everyone to have one. Already three quarters of the population have one, and before long every man, woman and child who can talk will have a mobile. Then they've got us. They'll know where every single person is to within a few feet; they'll know who they're talking to and what they're saying.'

'Big Brother,' said Fullerton quietly.

'It's nearly here,' said Donovan. 'Couple of years at most. Between CCTV cameras and mobiles, there'll be no more privacy. They'll know everything about you.' He gestured at the phone box. 'So that's why anything sensitive, you use a brand new Pay As You Go mobile or public land line.'

Donovan climbed out of the car. He took a twenty-pound phone card from his wallet and used it to call Juan Rojas in Spain. The answer machine kicked in almost immediately. Donovan didn't bother with pleasantries or say who was calling. He simply dictated the name and address of the firm of City solicitors that Vicky was using then went back to the Porsche.

'Okay?' asked Fullerton.

'We'll see,' said Donovan. He knew people in London who'd be capable of getting the information he needed from Vicky's solicitor, but by using Rojas he'd keep himself one step removed.

'Problem?' said Fullerton.

'Nah. Come on, let's get drunk.' He twisted around in his seat.

'We being followed?' asked Fullerton.

'Probably,' said Donovan.

Fullerton stamped on the accelerator and the Porsche roared through a traffic light that was about to turn red. He slowed so that they could see if any other vehicles went through the red light. None did. Fullerton took the next left and then swung the Porsche down a side street on the right.

'That should do it,' he said, pushing the accelerator to the floor again.

Donovan nodded. 'Just don't get done for speeding,' he warned.

Fullerton slowed down. Ten minutes later they pulled up in a car park at the side of what looked like a windowless industrial building. Three men in black suits stood guard at an entrance above which was a red neon sign that spelled out 'Lapland'. 'My local,' said Fullerton.

Donovan looked sideways at Fullerton. 'You know Terry, yeah?'

Terry Greene was the owner of the lap-dancing club. He was an old friend of Donovan's, though it had been more than three years since Donovan had been in the club.

'Terry? Sure. He's in Spain, I think. You know him?'

'Used to be my local, too. Way back when.' They climbed out of the Porsche and Fullerton locked it. 'Small world,' said Donovan.

The three doormen greeted Fullerton by name, clapping him on the back and shaking his hand. They were all in their mid-twenties and selected for their bulk rather than their intelligence. Donovan didn't recognise any of them, and from the blank-faced nods they gave him it was clear they didn't know who he was. Donovan preferred it that way. Black Porsches with personalised number plates and VIP access to nightclubs was a great boost for the ego, but Donovan preferred the lowest of low profiles. The Australians had a term for it – the tall poppy syndrome. The poppy that stood taller than the rest was the one that had its head knocked off.

Donovan followed Fullerton inside. The décor had changed since Donovan had last visited the club. The black walls and ultraviolet lights had been replaced with plush red flock wallpaper and antique brass light fittings, and the black sofas and tables where the lap-dancers had plied their trade had gone. In their place were Louis XIV-style sofas and ornate side tables. They'd been going for an old-fashioned bordello look, but it reminded Donovan more of an Indian curry house. The music didn't appear to have changed, though. Raunchy and loud.

There were two raised dancing areas where semi-naked girls gyrated around chrome poles. Sweating men in suits clustered around the podiums, drinking spirits and shoving ten- and twenty-pound notes into G-strings. A pretty waitress in a micro-skirt and a tight bikini top tottered over on impossibly high heels and kissed Fullerton on the cheek. Fullerton fondled her backside and introduced her to Donovan. Her name was Sabrina and she was barely out of her teens. Close up Donovan could she had spots on her forehead and an almost-healed coldsore on her upper lip.

She took them over to a table in a roped-off section with a clear view of both dancing podiums. Fullerton ordered Dom Perignon and Sabrina swung her hips gamely as she tottered off to get it.

'See anything you like, Den?' Fullerton asked, gesturing at the dancing girls.

Donovan checked out the dancers. Two brunettes, two blondes, an Oriental and a black girl. The blondes could have been sisters: they were both tall with long hair almost down to their waists, full breasts and tiny waists. Real-life Barbie dolls. They had the same vacant eyes and fake smiles as the dolls, though they were both good dancers.

Fullerton grinned. 'You like blondes, huh?'

'I like women, Jamie, but yeah, they're stunning.'

'Been there, have you? I'd hate to have sloppy seconds.'

Fullerton chuckled and nodded at the Oriental girl, who

was on her hands and knees in front of a balding guy in a too-tight suit, taking a twenty-pound note from him with her teeth. 'Mimi's my dish of the day and she's the jealous type,' he said.

'Yeah, looks it,' said Donovan. Mimi took the banknote and tucked it into her G-string, then stood up and started to make love to one of the silver poles. 'Thai, yeah?'

'Vietnamese,' Fullerton said. 'Came over here as a boat person when she was six.'

'Doesn't look much older now, truth be told,' said Donovan.

'Get away, she's twenty-two,' said Fullerton. 'And she knows stuff that'll make your eyes water.'

Mimi caught sight of Fullerton, waved girlishly and then climbed down off the podium and rushed over to him. She knelt on the sofa and hugged him tightly, giggling like a schoolgirl. 'Where've you been, Fullerton?' she asked in an East End accent. 'You said you'd be here last night.'

'Busy, busy, busy,' said Jamie. 'Miss me, did you?'

She kissed him on the cheek, leaving a smear of red as if he'd just been slapped. 'Let me dance, yeah?' she said. 'That twat over there's got more money than sense. He's given me two hundred already, thinks he's on a promise.'

'Wonder how he got that idea,' said Fullerton, leering at her ample cleavage. 'Go on, but you're coming home with me, remember?'

Mimi hurried back to her podium. Sabrina returned with their champagne in an ice bucket. She poured the Dom Perignon, winked at Fullerton, then left them to it.

Fullerton sighed and settled back. He put his feet up on the table in front of them and sipped his champagne. 'What's the story with the Smurfs?' he asked.

Donovan looked at him sideways. 'What do you mean?'

'The Rembrandt. You said you got the money from the Smurfs.'

Donovan laughed. 'Nah, you don't get money from Smurfs. You give them money and they clean it for you.'

'Now I'm confused.'

Donovan leaned over. 'Say you've got five hundred grand and it's iffy. You can't take it into the bank and deposit it. Anything over ten grand and you've got to be able to prove it's not ill-gotten gains, right?'

Fullerton nodded.

'You can take it overseas, but flying out with a case of cash is going to guarantee you a pull. So you call in the Smurfs.'

Fullerton was as confused as ever.

'You get half a dozen Smurfs, and you get them to open five bank and building society accounts each. That's thirty bank accounts. Then every day you give them ten grand each and they put between one and three grand into their accounts. It's well below the ten grand limit so they don't get reported. Every day the Smurfs deposit sixty grand. In two weeks the whole five hundred grand is in the system. Then you can transfer the money to wherever you want.'

'And where do you find the Smurfs?'

'Druggies, mainly,' said Donovan.

'Don't they ever run off with the money?'

'Not if they know what's good for them.'

Fullerton giggled.

'What?'

Fullerton waved him away. 'Just the thought of all the Smurfs traipsing around London with carrier bags full of cash, singing "Hi-ho, hi-ho, it's off to work we go". Sort of puts the whole thing in perspective, you know.'

'That's dwarves, not Smurfs,' said Donovan, refilling

their glasses. 'But, yeah, it's a crazy fucking world all the same.'

Fullerton sipped his champagne. 'Do you want a lap-dance?' he asked.

'You're not really my type, Jamie, but thanks.'

'You know what I mean,' said Fullerton. He waved at the girls on the podiums. 'My treat.'

'Maybe later,' said Donovan. He frowned as he saw someone he recognised walking into the club. Ricky Jordan. Jordan waved and walked over. He was with a short stocky man with close-cropped grey hair.

'Den, didn't know this was one of your haunts,' Jordan said. Donovan stood up and the two men hugged. Donovan introduced him to Fullerton. They shook hands. Jordan introduced the other man as Kim Fletcher. Donovan had met Fletcher before, he was one of Terry Greene's crew.

Fletcher patted Jordan on the back and said that he had business to take care of in the office. Before he left he motioned for Sabrina to bring over another bottle of champagne. 'On the house,' he said.

'How did it go with Jesus?' asked Donovan.

'Sweet,' said Jordan. 'Seems like a sharp guy.'

'Be careful, Ricky. He's a vicious bastard.'

'It's only business, Den. We've got the cash and the gear's on the way. Volkswagen Beetles, huh? Whose idea was that?' He slapped Donovan on the back.

'Jesus's uncle. Carlos.'

'Fucking brilliant. Beetles. This one could run and run, Den.'

'Yeah,' said Donovan.

Sabrina arrived with champagne and a glass for Jordan.

'What was your problem with him, Den?'

'Water under the bridge, Ricky. Forget it.'

'Takes me and Charlie to the next level.'

'Yeah, well, just remember who helped you on the way, yeah?'

Jordan leaned over and clinked his glass against Donovan's. 'Cheers, mate.'

'Yeah,' said Donovan ruefully. 'Cheers.'

Fullerton banged his glass against Donovan's. 'Down the hatch,' he said. 'What's this about VWs? If you want a car, I can get you a deal on a Porsche.'

Jordan threw back his head and laughed. 'Bloody hell, Den. Where did you get him from?'

'We're not buying VWs, Jamie,' said Donovan.

'Bloody right, we're not,' said Jordan.

'I'm confused,' said Fullerton.

'Good, let's keep it that way,' said Donovan. He threw a warning glance at Jordan. Fullerton had done a great job selling Donovan's paintings, but he still wasn't sure how much he could be trusted.

'How's it going, boys?'

The three men looked up. It was one of the pneumatic blondes. Jordan leered up at her. 'Getting better by the minute,' he said. 'You're new, aren't you?'

'I'm twenty-two,' she said. She shook her platinum-blonde hair, which reached almost to her waist. A small gold stud pierced her belly button.

'I meant . . .' Jordan started, but then he grinned. 'Forget it,' he said. 'Go on, then, darling, do your stuff.'

The other blonde who'd been dancing on the podium walked over, swinging her hips and flashing Donovan a beaming smile. 'I'm Angie,' she said. She slipped her arm around the other girl's waist. 'She's Kris.'

'With a K,' said Kris.

Fullerton leaned over the table. 'I know you, don't I?' he asked Kris.

Kris put her head on one side and pouted as she looked at him. 'Don't think so.'

'How long have you worked here?'

Kris frowned as if he'd asked her to solve a difficult mathematical equation. 'A week. I was at one of Terry's other clubs. He asked me to move here for a bit.'

'Which club?'

'Angels. Marble Arch.'

'Didn't know Angels was Terry's.'

'Yeah, it was his first club,' said Donovan. 'I used to drink there all the time.'

'I've seen you somewhere, I know I have,' said Fullerton.

'Leave the girl alone, Jamie,' said Donovan. He held out his hand. 'Come and give me a dance, Kris.'

'Give?' she said, tossing her long blonde hair. 'Nothing here's for free, you know.'

'I saw her first,' said Jordan.

'Let her choose,' said Donovan. He grinned up at Kris. 'Lady's choice.'

She looked at him, then at Jordan, then back at Donovan. Her smile widened and Donovan knew that he'd won. He grinned at Jordan. 'Never mind, mate.'

'Yeah, she probably goes for older men,' said Jordan.

'I do actually,' said Kris, taking off her bikini top and releasing her impressive breasts.

'Bloody hell,' said Fullerton, then he yelped as Mimi prodded him in the ribs. 'Hey, I was only looking,' he said.

Mimi had climbed down off the podium without him noticing. She sat down next to him and put her hand on his thigh. 'Are you going to buy me a drink or do I have to go back to the sad bastards over there?' she asked, pointing at the suited businessmen sitting around the podium.

'You drink what you like, lover. I am yours to command.'

Angie took off her top and straddled Jordan. His hands went up to her breasts. 'No touching,' she said. 'Club rules.'

Jordan took out his wallet and slipped the girl two fifty-pound notes. 'I can touch what the hell I want,' he said. 'Ricky's rules.'

Angie slid the notes into the top of her white stockings and thrust her breasts into Jordan's face. He sighed and slid down the sofa.

Kris laughed. She held out her hand to Donovan. 'Kris,' she said.

'Yeah, you said.'

'And you are?'

Donovan grinned. 'The guy you'll be dancing for.' He settled back on the sofa. Kris started to dance, a slow sinuous grind, her green eyes fixed on his. She had full lips and white, even teeth and she smelled of fresh flowers.

She put her lips close to his ear. 'Really, what's your name?' she whispered.

'Mr Mysterious,' said Donovan.

Kris wrinkled her nose. 'I know who you are, anyway.' She pushed her breasts together with her upper arms, emphasising her cleavage.

'Yeah?'

'Yeah. You're Den Donovan.'

Donovan frowned. 'How do you know that?'

'One of the girls told me. You're a friend of Terry's, aren't you?'

'Which girl?' asked Donovan suspiciously.

'Elizabeth.' She jerked a thumb towards the podium. 'The black girl. She's been here for years. Knows everyone. Remembers you. Said you were a big tipper and that you liked blondes.'

Donovan relaxed. 'That sounds about right.'

Kris was an accomplished dancer, totally at ease with her body. Donovan looked across at Fullerton, who had a glazed look on his face as Mimi ground herself against his hips, her mouth open and inviting.

Kris leaned forward, pouting and pushing her breasts together and giving him a close-up of her cleavage. Donovan felt himself grow hard and shook his head, annoyed at himself for reacting so physically to her charms. She saw the effect she was having on him and grinned.

Jordan was having simulated sex with Angie. She was sitting astride him and kissing him full on the mouth as she pounded against him.

The track came to an end and Donovan reached for his wallet. Kris shook her head. 'First one's on me, Den.'

'What?'

'It's not always about money. Specially for a friend of Terry's.'

Den took a fifty-pound note from his wallet and handed it to her. 'You're working,' he said, 'and I'm a punter. Take it.'

Kris looked like she would argue, but then she smiled and took the money. 'Thanks.'

'Pleasure was all mine.'

'Another?'

'Later, yeah?'

Kris kissed him on the cheek and sashayed back to the podium. She waved without looking back, knowing that he was still watching her, and he smiled to himself.

Jordan patted Donovan's leg. 'Good here, innit?'

Fullerton had opened his eyes again. He leaned over to Jordan and winked conspiratorially. 'Hey, Ricky. Fancy a line?'

'Dead right,' said Jordan.

'Den?' said Fullerton, and he tapped the side of his nose.

Donovan glared at Fullerton. 'For God's sake, Jamie. Are you still carrying?'

'Just a bit. Couple of lines.'

'Didn't you hear what I said to you before? I don't go near gear.'

'Leave him be, Den,' said Jordan.

'Yeah, well, you can say that when we're all behind bars.'

'We're among friends here,' said Jordan. 'Ain't that right, Jamie?'

Fullerton gave Jordan a thumbs-up.

'You're as bad as each other,' sighed Donovan.

A waitress was waving at Kris and miming that she had a phone call. Kris climbed down off the podium and hurried towards the bar area where a barman was holding the phone up.

'Come on, Den,' said Jordan. 'Lighten up.'

Donovan shrugged. Maybe he was being over-cautious. Jordan was right, Lapland was safe territory. An undercover cop wouldn't get within half a mile of the place, and those cops who did drink in the club were as bent as Dicko Underwood.

Jordan and Fullerton stood up and headed for the bathrooms. Donovan followed them, shaking his head. He liked Fullerton, but he seemed to be thinking with his nose.

Jordan pushed open the door to the gents' and checked that the cubicles were empty. As Donovan stood at the urinal, Fullerton used a platinum American Express card to shape six lines of cocaine on the marble surround of one of the sinks. They were long, thick lines. Fullerton was either a very heavy user or he was trying to impress.

Jordan rolled up a twenty-pound note and sniffed up two of the lines and then handed the rolled-up note to Fullerton. 'Oh, that's good,' said Jordan. 'I'll take five kilos of that.'

'Personal use?' asked Fullerton.

Fullerton attacked his two lines, then laughed as he licked his finger and ran it along the marble to get the last of the powder, which he then rubbed along his gums.

'You missed a bit,' joked Donovan, as he zipped up his flies.

'Oh, wow,' said Jordan. 'Can you feel that?'

'Are you sure you don't want some, Den?' asked Fullerton.

Donovan shook his head. 'Never touch it,' he said.

'All done?' Fullerton asked Jordan.

'Oh yes,' said Jordan. He grabbed Fullerton by the back of the neck. 'You're all right, Jamie. You're a bit mouthy, but you're all right.'

Fullerton had a lop-sided grin on his face and he was blinking rapidly. 'You're all right too, Ricky.'

'Bloody hell, are you two going to get married, or what?' said Donovan. He pulled open the door. 'Out you go or I'm throwing a bucket of water over you.'

The two men left and Donovan followed them. Jordan put his arm around Fullerton's shoulders and then tried to trip him up. Donovan sighed. They were behaving like a couple of schoolkids.

Kris was still on the phone and she was pacing up and down as she talked. Donovan went over to her.

'You should call the police,' she said into the phone. She flashed Donovan a tight smile and pointed at the receiver. 'Friend of mine's got a problem,' she mouthed.

'You can't let him get away with shit like that, Louise,' said Kris into the phone. 'Next time he might have a knife.'

'Anything I can do?' whispered Donovan.

'No, it's okay, Den,' said Kris, then she held up her hand to silence him as she listened to whoever it was she was talking to. Kris sighed. 'Den Donovan, he's an old pal of Terry's.'

'Not that old, thanks,' said Donovan.

Kris shook her head and turned her back on him. Then she looked at her watch. 'Okay, I'll come. Of course I will.' She listened again, and then she turned around to look at Donovan. 'Yeah, I'll ask him.' Kris nodded. 'I know, I'll see what he says.' She handed the phone back to the barman. 'Louise is a friend of mine; we worked together at another of Terry's clubs, Angels. A customer has just followed her home and tried to rape her. He's not there now but she's scared stiff that he might come back. I don't suppose you'd . . .'

'Of course,' said Donovan without hesitation. 'Knight in shining armour, me.'

'Really? I don't want to spoil your evening.'

'Come on. What's the choice? Drinking champagne with a couple of coke-heads or rescuing a damsel in distress?'

Kris grinned. 'Thanks. She sounded really desperate. Thing is, we're not allowed to leave with customers. You know the car park around the back?'

Donovan nodded. That was where Fullerton had parked his Porsche.

'Give me five minutes and I'll meet you there. Blue MGB.' She hurried off.

Fullerton was ordering a fresh bottle of champagne when Donovan got back to the table. Mimi was draped on his arm and caressing his thigh. Angie was giving Jordan a personal dance and had stopped complaining about him pawing her. Donovan sat down and sipped his champagne. After five minutes he put down his glass and patted Fullerton on the shoulder. 'I'm off,' he said.

'I'll come with you,' said Fullerton. He tried to stand up but Donovan pushed him back down.

'You enjoy yourself,' he said. 'I'll get a black cab. Catch you later. And thanks again for the paintings. You saved my life.'

Before Fullerton could say anything, Mimi leaned over and clamped her mouth over his. Donovan waved at Jordan, gave him a thumbs-up and headed for the door. The doormen all said goodbye to him and used his name, so they'd obviously been briefed that he was a friend of the owner.

Kris already had the engine running. She had changed into tight blue jeans and a light blue long-sleeved woollen top that showed off her washboard-flat midriff. 'Quick, get in,' she hissed. As soon as Donovan had closed the door she pushed down on the accelerator and shot out of the car park. She turned away from the club. 'God, I'm in so much trouble if anyone saw you,' she said.

'It's okay. Nobody did,' said Donovan.

Kris stamped down on the accelerator and shot through a traffic light that was just turning red. She screeched around a corner and whipped the MGB in front of a double-decker bus. Donovan squinted into Kris's driving mirror. Any car that might have been following would have been trapped behind the bus. She went through another set of lights at amber.

Donovan reached over and put a hand on her leg. 'Take it easy, it's not gonna help her if you get pulled over.'

Kris nodded and eased back on the accelerator. 'If he's hurt her, I'll kill him.'

'Does it happen a lot? Punters giving you grief?'

'Not to me, but to some of the girls, yeah. You can't let them get too close, you know. They've got to know it's just business.'

'What about you? Is it always business to you?'

She flashed him another sidelong glance. 'You mean, why are you sitting in the car with me?'

'Well, you haven't known me for long, have you?'

'I know of you, Den Donovan. Your reputation precedes you. Besides, I'm using you as weight, not inviting you into my bed.'

Donovan looked over his shoulder. The road behind was clear. 'Is that right?' he asked.

She grinned. 'We'll see.'

'And that's how you see me? Weight?'

'Again, your reputation precedes you.'

She swung the MGB over to the kerb and stopped inches from the rear of a black cab, stamping on the brake pedal so savagely that Donovan was jerked back by the seatbelt. She was out of the car before Donovan even had the belt off. He hurried after her.

Kris pressed one of six doorbells to the left of the front door. 'Come on, come on,' she said, jabbing at the button with her thumb.

The intercom crackled.

'Louise, it's me. Come on, let us in.'

The door buzzed and Kris pushed it open. Donovan followed her inside. The hallway was shabby with a threadbare carpet and fading wallpaper. Kris rushed up a flight of steep stairs.

Louise's flat was on the first floor and she had the door open with a security chain on. She unclipped the chain and opened the door wide for Kris. Kris hugged her. From the stairway Donovan could see a girl in her early twenties with a tear-stained face. She had black hair, cut in a bob that was slightly longer at the front than the back.

'This is Den,' said Kris, nodding at Donovan. 'Come on, let's sit down.'

Kris shepherded Louise into the flat. Donovan followed them and closed the door. Every light and lamp had been switched on. Kris took Louise over to a large leather sofa and sat down next to her. She pointed at a kitchenette and mouthed 'tea' to Donovan.

Donovan walked into the kitchenette. It was bright and spotless as if Louise rarely used it. He switched on a gleaming chrome kettle and went through cupboards until he found teabags.

By the time he carried a tray with three steaming mugs back into the sitting room, Kris was sitting with her arm around Louise's shoulder and Louise was dabbing at her eyes with a large handkerchief. Donovan put the tray down on the coffee table in front of the girls. 'Are you okay?' he asked Louise.

'I'm sorry,' she sniffed.

'You don't have to be sorry about anything,' said Donovan. 'What happened?'

'He pushed his way in and threatened to kill her, that's what happened,' said Kris.

'It was my fault,' said Louise. 'I thought if I talked to him, I could . . . you know . . .' She shook her head. 'He wouldn't have it. Said I had to be his girlfriend. Said if he couldn't have me no one could.'

Den went over and gently moved the handkerchief away from her face. Her left cheek was red and there were angry marks on her throat. 'He hit you?'

'He slapped me. Then he grabbed my throat and pushed me against the wall.' She smiled. 'I kneed him in the nuts and managed to lock myself in the bathroom with my mobile. Told him I was calling the cops.'

'You didn't, did you?' asked Donovan.

Louise shook her head. 'Fat lot of use they'd be,' she said. She patted Kris's leg. 'I called Kris.' Louise smiled at Kris. 'Thanks for coming.'

'Don't be stupid.'

Louise wiped her eyes with the handkerchief, then held out her hand to Donovan. 'Nice to meet you, anyway.'

'Pleasure,' said Donovan, shaking her hand. 'Who is he, this guy who hit you?'

'A punter. Seemed okay when I first met him. Good tipper. Fun to talk to.'

'How did he find out where you lived?' asked Donovan.

'I didn't give him my address, if that's what you mean,' she said defensively.

'No, I didn't mean that,' said Donovan quickly. 'How did he find you?'

'He must have followed me back from the club. He used to send me flowers here. Letters. Teddy bears. Tonight was the first time he turned up on my doorstep.'

'Do you know where he lives?'

Louise nodded. 'He wrote his address on the letters.' She sniffed. 'Kept saying he wanted me to live with him.'

Kris sighed and shook her head. 'What is it with twats like that? They think they can walk into a lap-dancing club and meet the woman of their dreams. What do they think we're doing there? Biding time until we meet our prince? Fuck that. Frogs is all we get.' The two girls laughed and hugged each other. Louise pointed at Donovan, still laughing. Kris realised what she meant. 'Present company excepted, of course,' she added. That set them off again, giggling and hugging each other.

Donovan sat with an amused smile on his face until the girls stopped laughing. They were both pretty and he could imagine them making a good living from the clubs. Louise was wearing a Gap sweatshirt and baggy jeans but her figure was clearly as impressive as Kris's – full breasts, long legs and a trim waist. Both girls had bright red nail varnish on their fingernails, but whereas Kris had full make-up, Louise had no lipstick or mascara. She looked as if she'd just got out of bed; totally natural, and even with the tearful eyes, thought Donovan, drop-dead gorgeous.

'Can I see the letters?' Donovan asked Louise.

She frowned at him, lowering her chin so that she was looking at him through her dark fringe, like a shy schoolgirl. 'Why?'

'Just want to see what sort of nutter you're dealing with,' said Donovan. 'Thing is, if he's not told the error of his ways, he might come back. And next time you might not get the chance to lock yourself in the bathroom.'

'I don't know . . .' said Louise hesitantly.

'Let him help,' said Kris.

Louise stood up and went over to a sideboard. She took out a sheaf of papers and handed them to Donovan. He flicked through them as Louise sat down next to Kris and sipped her tea. The letters were handwritten, a neat copperplate on good quality paper. A fountain pen rather than a ballpoint. 'How old is he, this guy?'

'Mid-forties, I guess.'

Donovan nodded. The content of the letters was at odds with the presentation. They sounded like the adolescent ramblings of a lovesick teenager rather than the thoughts of a middle-aged man: he wanted to take care of her, he hated the job she did, the life she had. He wanted to take care of her. Protect her. And he wanted her love and devotion. At the top of each letter was the man's address. A house in Notting Hill.

He'd signed the letters 'Nick'. With three kisses after it, the way a schoolgirl might sign a letter to a boy she had a crush on.

'What's his name?' asked Donovan.

'Nick Parker,' she replied.

'What does he do?' he asked.

'Stockbroker or something. A banker, maybe. To be honest, Den, I hardly listened to him. He was a punter. I danced for him, he tipped me and bought me drinks. I didn't lead him on.' She nodded at the letters. 'Not that way, anyway. I never led him to believe it was anything other than dancing. You know?'

Donovan handed the letters back to her. 'Yeah, I know.' Donovan gestured at some pieces of broken pottery under a bookcase by the window. 'Did he do that?'

Louise nodded. 'Broke a few things. I cleared up some.'

Donovan looked across at Kris. 'You've met this freak, yeah?'

'Yeah. Like Louise says, he seemed okay at first. Then he got a bit clingy. Glaring at anyone she talked to, bitching if she so much as looked at another punter while he was in the club.'

'Okay.' He finished his tea, then stood up. 'Do you want to give me a lift?' he asked Kris.

'Where to?'

Donovan gave her a tight smile. She knew where he wanted to go.

'Okay,' she said.

Nick Parker's house was a two-storey cottage in one of the prettier roads in Notting Hill. Expensive, thought Donovan, as he climbed out of Kris's MGB. Not as expensive as Donovan's own home in Kensington, but easily worth a million pounds.

Kris got out of the car and stood next to Donovan as he looked up at bedroom windows. 'What are you going to do, Den?' she asked.

'I'm going to teach him a lesson,' he said.

'And I'm here because . . . ?'

'Because I wouldn't want to teach the wrong guy a lesson,' said Donovan.

'I'm not sure about this,' she said hesitantly.

Donovan turned to look at her. 'Take it from me, if you let him get away with slapping a girl once, he'll keep on doing it.'

Kris frowned. 'That sounds like the voice of experience,' she said.

'My stepdad used to hit my mum. Way back when. I was too young to do anything at the time. I was only ten. By the time I was old enough to punch his lights out she was dead and I was in care.'

'God, he killed her?'

Donovan shook his head. 'Nah. Cancer. But even when she was sick, it didn't stop him pushing her around.' He looked back at the house. 'You've got to stand up to bullies,

Kris.' He walked towards the front door. It was painted a rich dark green with a brass knocker in the shape of a lion's head with a ring in its mouth. There was a doorbell to the left of the door but Donovan rapped with the knocker. Kris joined him on the doorstep. Donovan rapped again, three times.

The door opened wide. Nick Parker was middle aged and slightly overweight with a paunch held in by pinstripe trousers that seemed to be a size too small for him. 'Yes?' he said. His hair was thinning on top and he'd tried to conceal his bald spot with a comb-over.

'Is this him?' Donovan asked Kris. Kris nodded.

'What do you want?' Parker asked.

Donovan pushed him in the chest. Parker staggered back and Donovan rushed after him down the hallway. Kris followed him inside and closed the door. Framed pictures of hunting dogs lined the wall to his left and there was a huge gilt-framed mirror to the right. Donovan grabbed Parker's collar and flung him against the mirror. The glass cracked and pieces tinkled to the floor. Parker tried to speak but no words came out, just incoherent mumbling.

Donovan kept a grip on Parker's shirt collar and dragged him along the hallway. Parker scrambled along on all fours, choking. Donovan pulled him into the sitting room, then kicked him in the side. Parker fell on his back, gasping for breath.

Donovan looked around the room. The windows overlooked the street, but there were net curtains so no one could see in. Two overstuffed sofas in a beige fabric sat on either side of a large Victorian black metal fireplace. The room was quite feminine with porcelain figurines in a glass cabinet and crystal vases full of flowers on side tables. 'Is he married?' asked Donovan.

'Divorced,' said Kris, who was standing in the doorway, staring down at Parker. 'Wife left him a year or two back.'

Parker rolled over on to his stomach and tried to get to his feet. Donovan leaned down, grabbed him by the collar and yanked him up on his knees, then dragged him across the carpet and slammed his head into the fireplace. Parker's nose crunched against the metal and blood streamed down his face. 'Please . . . no . . . no . . .' he stuttered.

Donovan kicked him in the ribs and felt a satisfying crack. Parker rolled up in a foetal ball.

'Den . . .' said Kris.

Donovan turned around and pointed a finger at her. 'Don't say anything,' he said. 'Stay in the hall if you want, but this has to be done.'

Kris put a hand over her mouth but stayed where she was. Donovan smiled at the look of horror on her face. It was a look he'd seen many times before on people unused to violence. Real violence. Not the sort they were used to on television or in the movies, but the real thing with treacly red blood and splintered cartilage and broken bones.

Donovan turned back to Parker, who was coughing and spluttering.

'Who are you?' Parker gasped.

Donovan stepped over him and pulled a brass poker off its stand at the edge of the fireplace. He hefted it in his hand. It was a solid, heavy piece of metal.

'My wallet's in the bedroom,' said Parker. 'Take what you want.' He tried to get up but all the strength had gone from his legs and he fell back on to the carpet.

'I don't want your money,' said Donovan. 'This isn't about money.' He walked over to Parker and stood over him. 'You know Louise, yeah? From Angels?'

Parker put his hand up to his face. 'You've broken my nose,' he said, his voice faltering.

'I'm going to break more than that,' said Donovan. 'You know Louise, yeah?'

'Who are you? Her boyfriend?'

Donovan leaned down and grabbed a handful of Parker's thinning hair. He put his face close up to Parker's. 'No, I'm not her boyfriend. She doesn't want a boyfriend. She wants to be left alone. Do you understand that?'

'I love her,' said Parker. Tears began to trickle down his face, mingling with the blood from his nose and mouth. Donovan felt a wave of revulsion for the man.

'You don't love her,' said Donovan. 'You're obsessed with her. You've built some sad little fantasy around her, that's all. She doesn't love you. She doesn't even like you. She's scared of you.'

'If I could just talk to her . . .' said Parker.

Donovan shook his head. 'No, you're never going to talk to her again. You're not going anywhere near her, ever again.'

'She loves me . . .' wailed Parker.

Donovan twisted Parker's hair savagely and raised the poker above his head.

'Den, no!' shouted Kris.

'Go into the hall, Kris,' said Donovan, without looking at her.

'Den . . .' she protested.

'Do it, Kris.'

Parker tried to grab the poker but Donovan knelt down beside him and banged his head against the carpeted floor.

'Listen to me, and listen good!' Donovan hissed. 'You go near her again, and I'll kill you. Do you hear me?'

Parker nodded.

'I want to hear you say it,' said Donovan.

'I hear you,' said Parker, his voice trembling. He tried to clear his throat but began to choke on his own phlegm.

'Do you understand?' hissed Donovan.

Parker nodded.

'I can't hear you,' said Donovan.

Parker spat bloody phlegm on to the carpet. 'I understand.'

'I hope you believe me, Nick, because I can and will do it. And this is just a taste of what it'll be like.' Donovan brought the poker smashing down on to Parker's right knee. The kneecap cracked like a pistol shot and Parker screamed. Donovan clamped a hand over the man's mouth. 'Hush,' said Donovan.

Parker's whole body was trembling. Bloody froth pulsed between Donovan's fingers but he kept his hand over Parker's mouth until he'd stopped screaming. Donovan hit him again, whacking the left knee dead centre. Parker's eyes rolled upwards and he passed out.

Donovan stood up. He pulled out Parker's shirt-tail and used it to wipe the handle of the poker.

Kris was standing by the front door, hugging herself. She looked at him, then quickly looked away. Donovan gently held her chin between his thumb and first finger and turned her face towards him. She looked into his eyes, frowning as if she were trying to work out what he was thinking. Donovan smiled. 'He asked for it, Kris,' he said.

'I know,' she said quietly.

'You saw the marks on Louise's face. He hit her.'

'I know,' she said, with more certainty this time.

'This way he won't do it again.'

Kris put her hands on his shoulders. She kissed him on

the cheek. 'You don't have to explain, Den. I was just . . . shocked. Surprised. That's all.'

Donovan nodded. 'A week or two in hospital. He'll be fine.' That was a lie, Donovan knew. Parker would be in bed for a month, and wouldn't be walking for at least six. So far as Donovan was concerned, it served Parker right, but he didn't think Kris would want to hear that. 'Do you want to run me home?' he asked.

'I don't know,' she said in mock seriousness. 'What'll you do to me if I say no? Punch me in the face?'

Donovan laughed and licked the blood off his knuckles.

Kris pulled the MGB over at the kerb but kept the engine running. She looked out of the window at Donovan's house.

'Nice,' she said.

'Yeah. Do you wanna buy it?' said Donovan, deadpan.

'Oh yeah, like I can afford a place like that. How much is it worth?'

'I dunno. Prices have gone crazy over the last year or so. Three mill, maybe.'

Kris whistled softly. 'You live there alone?'

Donovan shook his head. 'No. Not really.'

'That sounds a bit vague, Den.'

'Yeah, well, I'm sort of in a transition stage at the moment. My wife has left me.'

Kris grinned. 'The number of times I've heard that. My wife doesn't understand me. We've grown apart. She hasn't touched me since the children were born. Blah, blah, blah.'

'My son found her in bed with another man.'

Kris's mouth fell open. 'You're serious?'

'Deadly.'

She nodded at the house. 'So is your boy in there now?'

Donovan shook his head. 'Nah, he's staying with my sister until I get things sorted.'

'Sorted?'

'I don't know if I'm cut out to be a single parent,' said Donovan.

'You're his dad. That's all that matters.'

'I guess,' said Donovan.

Kris looked at her watch. 'I'd better be getting back to Louise. Check that she's okay. I said I'd stay the night with her.'

'She's a nice kid.'

'You interested? I could put in a good word for you. She's young, free and single.'

Donovan grinned. 'I think my life's probably complicated enough as it is, but thanks for the offer.'

'Not your type?'

'Where are we, the playground?'

'Word is you like blondes.'

'My wife was a blonde. But I've never let hair colour get in the way of a good shag. She's a stunner, okay. Happy now?'

'I'll tell her,' said Kris. 'Seriously, Den. Thanks for tonight.'

'Happy to have been a help,' said Donovan. 'It's been years since I was in a fistfight. Brought back memories.'

'Not sure it was a fight, more of a beating up,' said Kris. Donovan climbed out of the sports car laughing and waved as she drove away.

'You got the registration number?' said Shuker as he clicked away with the SLR camera.

'No sweat,' said Jenner. 'Bit of all right, wasn't she?'

Jenner was sitting at a dressing table and writing in the log. A pair of high-powered binoculars lay on the table next to a Thermos flask and two plastic cups.

'Yeah, he's got a thing about blondes.' Shuker continued to take photographs until Donovan closed the front door. 'Wonder why she didn't go inside?'

Shuker and Jenner were Customs officers, and both were experienced surveillance operatives. Shuker was the elder of the two at thirty-six, but Jenner had been with HM Customs longer as he'd joined straight from school. They were in a flat diagonally opposite Donovan's that was owned by an Inland Revenue tax inspector. The bedroom was normally occupied by the inspector's ten-year-old daughter, but she'd been moved in with her sister and the whole family had been sworn to secrecy. The nature of the target hadn't been divulged to the family, just that it was a neighbour who was under surveillance. Shuker and Jenner were in the room for twelve hours a day, from midnight until noon, with two other Customs officers taking the alternate shift. Both men had plans for all the overtime they'd earn keeping an eye on Den Donovan. Shuker was saving for a Honda Gold Wing motorbike and Jenner had promised his wife and kids two weeks in Florida.

Donovan opened the fridge and sighed when he saw that there was no soda water. He opened the freezer section and cursed. No ice cubes, either. He sipped his Jack Daniels neat and went through to the sitting room. He sat down on a sofa and swung his legs up on to the coffee table. It was littered with glossy magazines. *Vogue*. *Elle*. *Marie Claire*. They were all Vicky's. He kicked them away. He should have put them into the black rubbish bags with the rest of her stuff. He wanted nothing of hers in the house.

He rested his head on the back of the sofa and stared up at the ceiling. 'What the hell am I going to do?' he asked out loud. Julia Lau had been unequivocal. There was no way he could take Robbie out of the country while Vicky's injunction was in force. And if he left the country without Robbie, he'd have a tough time convincing a judge that he was a fit parent. He had no choice. He had to stay. He had to make a home for Robbie, at least until he could get the injunction overturned. Or find out where Vicky was. He sipped his drink. The remote control was by his side, so he switched on the TV and flicked through the channels until he found Sky Sport. Liverpool against Chelsea. Donovan didn't support either team. He didn't really support any team. At school he'd been a United fan, but then the whole world had started to support the Reds and Donovan had lost interest. He'd hated running with the crowd, even as a kid. He half-watched the game. What was it they were paid these days? Millions. Millions of pounds for playing a game. The world had gone crazy.

Maybe he'd take Robbie to a soccer match. Might be fun. In fact, taking care of Robbie wouldn't be too difficult, he decided. All he had to do was to take him to and from school, feed him and clothe him. How tough could that be? Besides, it'd be good to spend some time with him. Quality time. Father and son time.

The cops and Customs would have him under the microscope, but so long as he didn't break the law there was nothing they could do. He took another sip of his Jack Daniel's, then remembered the Spaniard and cursed. Rojas would want paying for the Marty Clare job, and soon. Plus there was the work he was doing tracking down Vicky.

Donovan stood up, muted the television, and went through to his study. He took a notepad and pen from his desk drawer and started jotting down how much money he had. There was the cash he'd brought with him from Anguilla. The money he'd collected from the safe deposit box in Dublin. And the cash left over from the sale of the paintings. In all, about four hundred grand. Donovan nodded. Enough to pay Rojas and to keep himself going for a few months. Paying his legal fees might be a problem, but Laurence Patterson would probably give him some breathing space. He put down his pen. So long as nothing untoward happened, everything was going to work out just fine. And as soon as Rojas tracked down Vicky and Sharkey, he'd get his sixty million dollars back. Donovan smiled. He was looking forward to seeing Sharkey again.

Tina Leigh sat down in front of the computer and sipped her cappuccino. Her hands were trembling and coffee spilled over the lip of her cup, so she moved it away from the keyboard. She was at an internet café in Selfridges in Oxford Street. There were places closer to her flat that she could have used, but she liked to vary her schedule and she hadn't been to Selfridges in a long time. She'd walked from her flat: it was almost a mile but she'd wanted the time to get her thoughts in order.

She'd met him. She'd met Den Donovan. Tango One. After three years of waiting, three years of working in seedy lap-dancing bars, of being pawed and ogled and propositioned, she'd finally met him. And he liked her, she could tell that. Maybe Gregg Hathaway had been right, maybe she was Donovan's type. Her heart began to race and she fumbled for a cigarette. She lit one and inhaled deeply, then took a sip of her coffee. She smiled to herself. Nicotine and caffeine. Hardly conducive to slowing down her heart-rate, but just at that moment she needed both.

She wondered how Hathaway would react when he got her e-mail. She'd given him a wealth of intelligence over the years, and at least a dozen criminals were behind bars as a direct result of information she'd picked up in the clubs. She had long ago stopped being surprised at how willing hardened criminals, who could withstand hours of police interrogation without revealing anything other than their name, address and date of birth, would open up like shucked oysters as soon as they'd had a couple of bottles of champagne and a look at her tits.

So far Hathaway had done a good job of protecting her as a source. Any police action came long after she'd filed her reports, and cases were always backed up with official surveillance reports and forensics. She had never been so much as mentioned in a police report. The invisible woman. But Den Donovan was different. Den Donovan was Tango One. Tina wondered if Hathaway would still protect her as a source if it meant putting Donovan away. And if he did blow her cover, would that be the end of her career as an undercover agent? Or worse? Would it be the end of her police career period?

All those years ago, when she'd sat in the high-rise office with Assistant Commissioner Peter Latham, it had been made clear to her that she could never be a regular police officer. Her past precluded that. The one question she'd never asked was what would become of her when she was no longer useful undercover. A pension? Would they find her another job where her employer wouldn't be quite so concerned about the time she spent on the streets, trawling for punters and giving blow jobs in cars? Or would she be discarded once they had no more use for her?

Tina put her cigarette down on to an ashtray and sat with her fingers poised over the keyboard. She knew exactly what she was going to write. She'd had plenty of time to get her thoughts in order during the walk to the department store. What she didn't know was how Hathaway would react. Or what he'd ask her to do next. She'd met Den Donovan. She'd spoken to him. Spent time with him. She knew that that wasn't enough, however: Hathaway would want more. He'd want her to get up close and personal. The question was – how close and how personal? She began to type.

Donovan woke up at eight with a raging thirst and a hangover. He drank from the bathroom tap, then shaved and showered. He padded downstairs in his towelling robe and went into the kitchen. He desperately wanted a glass of milk or orange juice but the fridge was empty. There was a corner shop a couple of hundred yards down the road but Donovan couldn't face the walk. He made himself a black coffee and carried it through to the sitting room.

He unplugged the four mobiles that had been on charge overnight and connected another four. He sat down on the sofa, sipped his coffee, then called up Robbie's mobile, using the same phone he'd used last time he'd called his son. Robbie answered almost immediately.

'Dad!'

'Hiya, kid. You okay?'

'Where are you?'

'I'm at home,' said Donovan.

'Which home?'

'Our home. What are you doing?'

'Nothing much.'

'Change of plan. As of today, it's school. Okay?'

'Dad . . .' moaned Robbie.

'Don't "Dad" me. School. Has your mum called?'

'No. I don't want to speak to her anyway.'

'Okay. If she does call, give her this number. Tell her to call me. If she asks to see you, say no, okay?'

'I don't want to see her. Ever.'

'I know, kid. Don't talk to her, don't let her near you. And be careful of strangers, yeah?'

'Dad, I'm nine years old. I'm not a kid.'

'She might want to take you with her.'

'Sod that!'

Donovan smiled at his son's vehement reply. 'I'm just saying, she might send someone to the school, to take you away. Don't go with anyone other than me or Aunty Laura. Okay?'

'Wouldn't it be better if I just stayed at home?'

'Didn't you hear what I said? School. I have to act like a proper father and that means sending you to school every day.'

'So we're staying? In London?'

'For a bit, yeah.'

'Yes!' cheered Robbie.

'Happy now?'

'Yeah. Thanks, Dad.'

'So school. Today. Let me talk to Aunty Laura, will you?'

Robbie called out his aunt's name and a few seconds later she was on the line. 'What have you said to him? He's grinning like the cat that got the cream.'

'I'm staying for a while. We're going to move back into the house.'

'Good decision, brother-of-mine.'

'Yeah, well, we'll see,' said Donovan. 'I don't have

much choice at the moment. My lawyer says I can't take him out of the country, and if I'm going to get custody I'm going to have to play at happy families for a while.'

'Den!'

Donovan grinned. 'You know what I mean. I want to be with him, of course I do, but not here. Not in London. He's to go to school from now on. I've had a word with the headmistress. I'll pick him up tonight and we'll be at the house from now on. Thanks for everything. For letting him stay.'

'Not a problem, Den. You know that.'

Donovan thanked her again and cut the connection. The keys to Vicky's Range Rover were hanging on a hook in the kitchen. Donovan's first thought had been to sell the car right away as it was yet another reminder of his soon-to-be ex-wife, but common sense prevailed. He needed wheels, and if he didn't use the Range Rover he'd have to rent a car.

He took the keys and went out to the vehicle. He emptied the glove compartment of all her personal stuff – gloves, sunglasses, a half-empty pack of Tic tacs, cigarettes, suntan lotion – and threw it into the rubbish bin, then went back to the car and sat in the driving seat. He could still smell her perfume. 'You bitch!' he shouted, slapping the steering wheel hard. 'Bitch, bitch, bitch!'

He stormed back into the kitchen and pulled open cupboard doors until he found an aerosol of air freshener. He sprayed it liberally around the interior of the car. Lavender. He coughed in the sickeningly sweet perfumed mist, but at least it masked the annoying smell of her perfume.

Donovan edged the Range Rover out into the street. He didn't bother checking for surveillance. This was one trip he was quite happy for any watchers to know about. He drove to the King's Road in Chelsea and prowled around the back streets until he found a parking space, then he walked to the offices of Alex Knight Security. Knight's entrance was a simple black door between an antiques shop and a hairdresser's. Donovan pressed the bell button and a woman's voice asked who he was over the intercom.

'Den Donovan for Alex,' said Donovan. The door buzzed and Donovan pushed it open. He went up a narrow flight of stairs, at the top of which a striking brunette had a second black door already open for him.

'Mr Donovan, good to see you again,' she said.

'Sarah, you're looking good,' said Donovan. 'How's the boy looking after you?'

'Boy? I'm twenty-bloody-eight,' said Alex Knight, striding out of his office. He was tall and gangly with black square-framed spectacles perched high up on his nose. He was wearing a dark blue blazer and when he stuck his hand out to shake he showed several inches of bony wrist.

The two men shook hands. 'Yeah, well, you don't look a day over sixteen,' said Donovan. 'Whatever you're taking, I want some of it.'

'Clean living and early to bed,' said Knight. 'You should try it some time. Come on through.'

Knight's office was about twenty feet square but looked much smaller because every inch of wall space had been lined with metal shelving filled with electrical equipment and technical manuals. His desk was a huge metal table that was also piled high with technical gear. 'Coffee?' asked Knight.

Donovan declined and Sarah closed the door on them. On the back of the door was a blueprint of an electronic device that Donovan could make no sense of.

'So, you old reprobate, what can I do for you?' Knight pushed back his chair and put his feet up on the table. There was a hole in one of his suede loafers.

'I'm going to be back in the UK for a while, and I'm going to be under the microscope,' said Donovan. 'Cops, Customs, spooks. I need to be able to sweep my house and car, and to check if anyone who comes near me is wired.'

'Do you want me to do the sweeping?'

Donovan shook his head. 'No offence, Alex, but I want to do it myself.'

'No sweat,' said Knight, reaching for a notebook and pen, 'but I'd advise you to let me go over the house once. Show you the ropes, yeah?'

Donovan nodded.

Knight rested the notebook on his lap as he scribbled. 'What about your landline? I've got a gizmo that'll tell you if it's tapped.'

'Waste of time. I can pretty much guarantee that it will be,' said Donovan. 'I won't be using it for anything other than ordering pizzas. I'm more concerned about the house.'

Knight tapped his pen against his cheek. 'Yeah, but you're gonna need a hookswitch bypass detector, especially if the spooks are on your case. They can turn any land line into a room monitor and pick up anything that's said. Even when the phone's on the hook. I can fix one to each phone. Five hundred each. Worth the money, Den. No point in sweeping for bugs if your phone is a direct line to MI5.'

Donovan nodded. 'Okay. You're the expert.'

Knight scribbled on his pad. 'So far as sweeping goes, I've got a state-of-the-art scanner that'll do the job. Brand new RF detector from Taiwan. Pick up anything. Just run it around all suspect surfaces. You can use it on the car, too. I'll show you how to use it, a child can operate it.'

'Okay. And I'm going to need a personal unit.'

'Just what I was going to suggest. I've got a new model in from the States. Bit bigger than a pack of fags, you wear it on your belt like a bleeper. Vibrates when it picks up micro radio frequencies. You know they're wired, but they don't know that you know. Cool thing about this model is that it also picks up most makes of tape recorder. You wear a flat antenna under your watch band with the cable running up your sleeve. It's not one hundred per cent reliable, but close. It'll certainly pick up the shit that the Brits use. They're usually about five years behind the Yanks.'

Donovan grinned. Knight knew his stuff, which is why he'd been using him for the past four years, ever since Knight had picked up his second PhD and decided to leave academia for the commercial world. He wasn't cheap, but Knight's equipment had saved Donovan's skin on several occasions.

Knight tapped the notepad. 'Going back to the house. How about I fix up an acoustic noise generator for you? You're going to be able to sweep for RF bugs and I can give you a metal detector to pick up wired microphones in the walls, but it's easy to miss transmitters in AC outlets. Plus everyone's using laser or microwave reflectors these days, picking up vibrations from windows. Bloody hard to detect. But switch on the noise generator and they'll just pick up static.'

'Excellent,' said Donovan.

'Cash on delivery?'

'As always.' Donovan stood up and held out his hand. Knight swung his legs off the table and shook hands. 'Pleasure doing business with you, Alex.'

'Pleasure's all mine, Den. How's the wife?'

'Don't ask,' said Donovan. 'Just don't ask.'

Stewart Sharkey scrolled through the spreadsheet, a slight smile on his face. Sixty million dollars. He had sixty million dollars. He wondered how much space sixty million dollars would take up. A million was maybe two suitcases full. Sixty million would be one hundred and twenty suitcases. Sharkey tried to picture a hundred and twenty suitcases. He grinned. It was one hell of a lot of money. Invested in bog-standard shares and high-interest offshore accounts, it would earn four or five million dollars a year. More than enough to live on. To live well on. Sharkey had other plans for the money, however. Big plans. And if his plans worked out, he'd turn that sixty million into hundreds of millions. He'd do it legitimately, too. Property development. Central Europe, probably. Get in on the ground floor before they joined the EU bandwagon. There were fortunes to be made in the countries of the former Soviet Union, and Sharkey was the man to do it, now that he had the resources.

The mobile phone on the table next to the computer bleeped and Sharkey grabbed for the receiver.

'Stewart? It's David.'

David Hoyle. A lawyer based in Shepherd's Bush in west London. Sharkey had known him for years, but this was the first time he'd used him professionally.

'Hiya, David. I trust you're using a call box?'

'I am, Stewart, but is this really necessary?'

'You don't know Vicky's husband, David.' That was one of the reasons that Sharkey was using him. Hoyle had never done any work for Den Donovan, or anyone like him. He was a family lawyer who specialised in divorce work and had never been within a mile of a criminal court.

'Even so, Stewart, I feel a bit silly walking out of my office every time I talk to you.'

'A necessary precaution, David. I'm sorry.'

'Where are you?' Hoyle asked. The number that Sharkey had given him was a GSM roaming mobile. It was a UK number but Sharkey could use it anywhere in Europe.

'Not too far away,' said Sharkey. 'Best you don't know the specifics.'

'Oh please, Stewart. That would be covered by client confidentiality.'

Sharkey smiled. He knew that Den Donovan wouldn't be worried about a little thing like client confidentiality. 'How can I help you, David?'

'We've heard back from his lawyers. The husband is applying for sole custody. And of course he will be trying to have the injunction lifted.'

Sharkey grunted. They had expected that Donovan would want sole custody of Robbie. And that he'd want to take him out of the country. So far as Sharkey was concerned, he would be quite happy for Donovan to get what he wanted, but he had to keep Vicky happy, for a while at least, and that meant going through the motions.

'I assume that Victoria still wishes to apply for custody?' asked Hoyle.

'Absolutely,' said Sharkey.

'I would expect the hearing to be within the next two weeks,' said Hoyle. 'You do realise that Victoria will have to appear in person?'

'That's definite, is it?'

'I'm afraid so.'

'Then that's the way it'll have to be.'

'I'll get the papers drawn up, Stewart. I'll be in touch.'

Sharkey cut the connection and put the mobile phone

back on the table. There was no way he could allow Vicky to go back to London. The moment she set foot back in the UK, Donovan would get to her. And from her he'd get to Sharkey. It would all be over. Sharkey shuddered.

He stood up and walked over to a drinks cabinet and poured himself a brandy. 'Was that the phone?' asked Vicky, walking in from the terrace.

'The lawyer. He's on the case.'

'He served the injunction?'

Sharkey nodded. 'And Den's fighting it, like we knew he would.'

'Bastard. He showed no interest while he was away – now he wants to play the father.'

'It's going to be okay, Vicky. The injunction's in force, Den can't take him out of the country. He does that and he'll go straight to prison.'

'What about custody?'

'The lawyer's doing the paperwork now.'

'How long?'

'He didn't say. You know lawyers.' He raised the glass. 'Do you want one?'

'No, thanks. I thought I'd go out for a walk. Go to the beach maybe. Do you want to come?'

Sharkey sat down opposite his laptop. 'Not right now. Don't forget . . .'

'I know,' she said. 'Dark glasses. Sunhat. Don't talk to anyone.'

'Just in case,' said Sharkey. 'You never know who you might bump into.'

'How long's it going to be like this, Stewart?'

'Not much longer.'

Vicky walked in to the bedroom to change, and Sharkey sipped his brandy. He was already bored with Vicky. Bored with her dark moods, her insecurities, her constant whining. In a perfect world he'd just leave her, but it wasn't a perfect world so long as Den Donovan was in it. Hopefully the Colombians would soon catch up with Donovan, and when that happened then Sharkey's world truly would be perfect. With Donovan out of the way, he could walk out on Vicky without worrying about the repercussions. He'd be free and clear and in sole possession of sixty million dollars.

'You know I love you?' he called after her.

'I know,' she replied. 'I love you, too.'

Sharkey smiled to himself. It was all so easy.

One of the wheels on Donovan's supermarket trolley was sticking and the damn thing wouldn't go where he wanted it to. It had been a long time since Donovan had done the weekly shopping. In Anguilla his Puerto Rican cook did the shopping every day, and in London Vicky had handled all the household chores. He'd been putting it off long enough, but he was fed up with drinking black coffee and he had to prepare for Robbie's return. The freezer was practically empty, and what frozen food was still in there wasn't the sort of stuff that Donovan knew how to cook. He scanned the shelves looking for teabags, but all he could see was coffee. A hundred types of coffee, but no tea. He looked down at the contents of his trolley. A pack of apples, a double pack of Andrex toilet tissue and a sliced loaf. Hovis. He scratched his ear and tried to remember what was in the fridge. Or rather, what wasn't in the fridge. He needed milk. And Coca-Cola. Beer. Orange juice. Did Robbie drink orange juice? He tried to remember when they'd last had breakfast together. Probably in Anguilla, and there was always a big pitcher of freshly squeezed orange juice on the table at breakfast.

He finally reached the tea section and dropped two boxes of PG Tips teabags into his trolley. He looked around for the milk. Where the hell was it? Wouldn't it have been sensible to put the milk with the tea and the coffee?

Breakfast cereal. He'd need breakfast cereal. He looked around, but the only sign he could see told him that he was in the aisle for tea, coffee and soft drinks.

He reached the end of the aisle and came across lines of frozen food cabinets. He scooped up packs of fish fingers, beef burgers and TV dinners and stacked them in his trolley. Then he found the alcohol section and picked up two bottles of Jack Daniels and two packs of lager. He smiled to himself. At least he was getting the basics.

He finally found the milk section and put two large cartons into the trolley. He spent another twenty minutes wandering aimlessly around the aisles and promising himself that next time he'd make a list, before he headed for the checkout.

On the way home he stopped at a call box and phoned Underwood. 'Dicko, call me back, yeah?' He gave the detective the number of the call box and then replaced the receiver. Underwood phoned back fifteen minutes later.

'Now what?' asked the detective.

'I'm fine thanks, Dicko. Yourself?'

'As if you care. I presume this isn't social.'

'I need you to check someone out for me. Have you got a pen?'

'Bloody hell, Den. You can't keep using the Police National Computer as your own personal database.'

'What crawled up your arse and died?'

'Checks leave traces.'

'I just want to know who he is, Dicko. He doesn't seem wrong, but I just want to be sure.'

'Okay, but let's not make a habit of this. It's the small things that trip people up. A sergeant over at Elephant and Castle got sacked last week for doing a vehicle registration check for a journalist. Lost his job and his pension for a fifty-quid backhander.'

Donovan was going to point out that he paid Underwood a hell of a lot more than fifty pounds, but he bit his tongue, not wanting to antagonise the detective. He gave Underwood Fullerton's name and the registration number of his Porsche, and arranged to call him the following day.

Hathaway read through Christina Leigh's report for the third time. Putting her in as a lap-dancer had always been a long shot, and he still couldn't quite believe that it had worked. There was no mistake, however: not only had she met the man, but it had quickly become personal. If Christina played it right, she could build on the connection, get in under his defences. All she had to do was to take it slowly. She was Donovan's type, so hopefully he'd do the chasing.

He sent her a congratulatory e-mail and told her to play it safe, that she mustn't do anything to scare him off. Donovan had always been a pursuer of women, he loved the thrill of the chase, so if anything she'd have to play hard to get.

As he sent the e-mail to Christina, he received notification that he had a new e-mail waiting. He clicked on the envelope icon and opened an e-mail from Jamie Fullerton. Hathaway scrolled through Fullerton's report with a growing sense of elation. It was working. It was finally all coming together. Not only had Christina made contact, but Donovan was letting Fullerton get close, close enough to do real damage. On Hathaway's desk next to his VDU was a series of black and white surveillance photographs that had been taken outside the lap-dancing club. Fullerton had e-mailed Hathaway to tell him where he was going, so the surveillance was in place long before the black Porsche arrived. There were pictures of Donovan and Fullerton arriving, and photographs of Donovan leaving in the blue MGB. Two cars had been in place to follow Donovan from the club, but they'd lost the sports car at a set of lights. Not that that mattered. Christina's report had detailed in full what had happened later that evening.

Hathaway now had a connection between Donovan, Carlos Rodriguez and Ricky Jordan, a major distributor of hard drugs in Scotland. And whatever they were bringing in had something to do with VW Beetles. Fullerton had relayed the conversation virtually verbatim, but it was still light on specifics.

After a few minutes on the internet, Hathaway discovered that there was only one place where VW Beetles were still manufactured. Mexico. And Carlos Rodriguez ran most of his drugs through Mexico. Hathaway smiled to himself. Beetles packed with heroin or cocaine. And with Rodriguez involved, it had to be a huge shipment.

It took Hathaway less than an hour to ascertain that a shipment of sixty brand new VW Beetles was on its way to Felixstowe. He gnawed at a fingernail as he read through the details on his VDU. Then he reread Fullerton's report. Whatever was going down, it seemed that Donovan was now taking a back seat. Jordan was dealing directly with the Rodriguez cartel, though Fullerton had the impression that it was Donovan who'd set up the deal. Plus there was the two million pounds of Donovan's money that Fullerton had paid to Jesus Rodriguez.

The jumbled pieces of the mystery started to come together in Hathaway's mind. He forced himself to relax, letting his subconscious do the work, and then suddenly the solution to the conundrum popped into his head like a huge bubble of air rising to the top of a black lagoon. Donovan had fucked up, somehow. Maybe he'd failed to come up with the money for the consignment. Rodriguez had taken the two million pounds as a penalty payment, and taken over the deal with Ricky Jordan. Another bubble popped to the surface. Donovan was short of money, that's why he had had to sell the paintings. His money had gone. All of it. Stewart Sharkey had screwed Donovan's wife and he'd cleared out the bank accounts. Hathaway grinned. This was getting better and better. Donovan would move heaven and earth to get his money back, and while he was focused on that, he'd be less likely to realise what was going on around him.

It was time to increase the stakes. Hathaway didn't want to run the operation through Customs or the police. They'd both be tempted to let the drugs run to see where they went in an attempt to blow apart the entire network. That was the last thing Hathaway wanted. There was only one option. It was time to call in the Increment.

The traffic was backed up for almost half a mile to Robbie's school, mainly mothers in four-wheel drives. Donovan sat in the Range Rover playing an Oasis tape at full volume. Noel and Liam, two other Manchester boys who'd done well. Donovan wondered how much money the lads had made from rock and roll. Millions, for sure. Maybe ten million. But had they made as much as Donovan had? Sixty million dollars? Donovan tapped his fingers on the steering wheel. One thing was for sure: they hadn't had their accountant rip off every last dollar.

Robbie was waiting at the entrance to the school and he waved when he saw Donovan. He came running along the pavement. 'I thought you weren't coming,' he gasped as he climbed into the passenger seat.

'I said I would, didn't I?' The woman in the Honda CRV in front of them was refusing to move, so Donovan pounded on the horn. 'Come on, you stupid bitch, we've got lives here.'

'Dad! That's Mrs Cooper. Alison's mum.'

'Well, Alison's mother should learn to drive before she goes out on the road. And that car's way too big for her. She should be in a Mini.'

Robbie slid down his seat, his hands over his face.

Donovan pounded on the horn again, then grinned across at Robbie's obvious discomfort. 'Shall I ram her?'

'Dad . . . please . . .'

'Oh, come on, I was only joking.'

'I have to sit next to her.'

'Alison's mother? You sit next to Alison's mother?'

Robbie laughed. 'No, not Alison's mother. Alison. You know what I meant.'

Donovan eased off the accelerator. 'What do you want to eat tonight? I've got fish fingers. Roast chicken dinner. Roast beef dinner. Roast turkey dinner.'

'You're going to cook?'

'They're TV dinners. Birds Eye.'

Robbie waved goodbye to two of his friends. 'Can we have Burger King?'

'You're a growing boy. You're supposed to have vegetables and stuff.'

'I could have onion rings. And French fries.'

Donovan laughed. 'Yeah, why not. Do you know where the nearest one is?'

'Sure. Hang a left.'

Donovan grinned and followed Robbie's directions. Ten minutes later they were outside a Burger King. There were no parking spaces, so Donovan thrust a banknote into his son's hands and told him to hurry.

'Dad, this is a fifty-pound note!' complained Robbie.

'They'll have change. Hurry up.'

Robbie nipped inside and appeared a few minutes later with two large bags. Donovan held out his hand for the change before driving off.

Half an hour later they were eating their burgers in the kitchen, washing them down with Cokes. 'This was a good idea,' said Donovan. 'Saves on the washing up, too.'

Robbie wiped his ketchup-smeared lips with a serviette. 'I'm glad you're home, Dad,' he said.

Donovan reached over and ruffled his hair. 'You know you can always rely on me, right?'

Robbie nodded.

'You okay for pocket money?'

'I could always use more,' said Robbie. Donovan took out his wallet and gave Robbie a fifty-pound note. 'Dad, you can't give me fifty quid.'

'How much did your mum give you?'

'A tenner. But usually five twice a week. Monday and Friday.'

'Okay, well, how about we give you a raise? You're nearly ten, so I figure we can boost it to twenty a week. Okay?'

Robbie grinned. 'Okay.'

Donovan took back the fifty-pound note and gave his son a twenty. Robbie put the note in his pocket.

'What do you want to do tonight?' asked Donovan. 'Do you want to go and see a movie?'

'It's a school night,' said Robbie. 'And I've got homework.'

'Homework? They give nine-year-olds homework?'

'I've been given homework since I started at that school, Dad.'

'Yeah, exams are important. I wish I'd stayed on at school longer.'

'No you don't. Not really.'

Donovan frowned. 'What do you mean?'

'You've got no qualifications, have you?'

'Just the university of life and the school of hard knocks.'

'See, that's what you always say.' Robbie picked up the burger wrappers and paper cups and dropped them into the rubbish bin. 'You're rich, though.'

'Who says so?'

Robbie waved his arms around the kitchen. 'Dad, look at this place. Look at the Rolex on your wrist. Look at how much it costs to send me to that school. You're rich and you know you are.'

'Not as rich as Bill Gates.'

'I didn't say mega rich. I didn't even say rich rich. I said rich.'

Donovan smiled at his son's intensity. 'So what's your point?'

'There is no point, but you don't have to say that you wish you'd stayed in school when you know that's not true. You want me to stay in school because you want me to do something boring like be a doctor or an executive.'

'I do, do I?'

'Yeah. That's what Mom wanted, anyway. She was always going on at me to read science books and stuff. Kept saying she didn't want me turning out like you.'

'Maybe you don't want to turn out like me. Maybe you'd rather be a doctor hanging around with sick people and working yourself to an early grave.'

'No fear,' said Robbie scornfully.

Donovan stood up. He rushed forward and grabbed his son around the waist, laughing. He swung Robbie over his shoulder and started to spin around. 'Are you sure?' he shouted.

'Yes! I'm sure. Stop it. I'll be sick!'

Donovan continued to spin.

'Dad! Stop!'

'Do you give in?'

'Yes!'

Donovan put Robbie down carefully. His own head was spinning and he put his hand on a chair to steady himself.

Robbie was giggling and shaking his head. 'You're mad.'

Donovan took a step towards him, his hands reaching for his head. 'You want some more?'

'No!' laughed Robbie. He turned and ran out into the hall and up the stairs. He stopped halfway to check that Donovan wasn't chasing him.

'Come down when you've finished your homework,' Donovan shouted after him. 'I'll make cocoa.'

There were two of them, dressed in dark clothing and wearing black leather gloves. One picked the lock while the other kept watch, though at two o'clock in the morning they were the only two people in the office block. They'd come in through a skylight. It had been alarmed, but the man who was picking the lock had worked for more than twenty years for one of London's top security companies, and there wasn't an alarm system built that he couldn't bypass. Now he worked freelance for ten times what he used to earn as a technician. Men like Juan Rojas were happy to pay a premium for his skills, and for his silence.

He made short work of the lock, pushed open the door and headed for the beeping alarm box. He already knew the make of the alarm, and had memorised the manufacturer's four-digit access code. The alarm stopped beeping. He nodded at his partner and pointed at a door with 'David Hoyle' on it in gold capital letters at eye level. His partner went into Hoyle's office and started going through a mahogany veneer filing cabinet.

The man who'd disabled the alarm went through the filing cabinets in the general office. He was looking for any file with the name 'Stewart Sharkey' or 'Victoria Donovan'. Once he was satisfied that there were no such files in the cabinets, he accessed the office computer system, checking word processing files and e-mail address books. From Hoyle's office he heard the muffled tapping of gloved fingers on a keyboard as his partner accessed the solicitor's private terminal. After twenty minutes he was satisfied that there was no mention of the two names in the system.

The man went through all the desks in the office, checking address books, but found nothing. His partner came out of Hoyle's office, shaking his head. The two men left the same way they'd come.

The alarm buzzed and Donovan rolled over, trying to blot out the noise. It carried on buzzing. Donovan groped for the button on top of the alarm and hit it with the flat of his hand. He squinted at the digital read-out. Seven-thirty. Donovan groaned. He wasn't an early riser at the best of times.

He padded across the bedroom, put on his robe and opened the bedroom door. 'Robbie, are you up?' There was no answer so he walked along the landing and banged on Robbie's door. There was still no reply.

Robbie was curled around his pillow, snoring softly. Donovan shook him. 'Come on, it's time to get up.'

'Five more minutes,' said Robbie sleepily.

'You don't have five minutes,' said Donovan. He pulled back the quilt. 'Come on, rise and shine.'

Donovan opened the curtains wide and went downstairs. He switched the kettle on and made toast, but when he opened the fridge he realised that he'd forgotten to buy butter. Or marmalade. He filled bowls with Sugar Puffs and poured milk over them, then made a pot of tea. Then he poured two glasses of orange juice. Upstairs he heard the shower in Robbie's bathroom burst into life.

The doorbell rang and Donovan went to answer it. It was Alex Knight carrying a leather briefcase and a moulded black plastic suitcase. He seemed to be wearing the same dark blue blazer and black slacks that he'd had on the previous day. He smiled cheerfully at Donovan. 'Didn't get you up, did I, Den?'

'Bloody hell, Alex, what time do you call this?'

'The early worm catches the bird,' said Knight, carrying the cases in to the hallway. 'I'll start in the study, yeah?'

Donovan showed him through. Knight swung the suitcase up on to Donovan's desk and unlocked the lid. It was packed full of electrical equipment. Knight took out a small black box the size of a paperback book and showed it to

Donovan. There were two lights on the front, one green, one red, and an LCD readout. 'Hookswitch bypass detector,' explained Knight. 'It'll also tell you if the line's tapped. Two for the price of one.'

Donovan nodded. He'd seen similar devices before, but not that particular model.

'Green light means it's safe to talk. Red light means they're listening in. The LCD tells you if the phone's active. If it is, your best bet is simply to pull it out of the wall.' He winked at Donovan. 'Or make sure that anything you say, you want them to hear. I'll put one on every phone, then I'll sweep the walls.'

'You want a coffee?'

'Black with four sugars,' said Knight. He grinned. 'What can I say? Sweet tooth.'

'I'm surprised you've got any teeth left at all.'

Donovan went back into the kitchen and made coffee for Knight. As he was carrying it through to the study, Robbie came rushing downstairs. 'There's cereal on the table. Sugar Puffs.'

Robbie frowned at Donovan's robe. 'You're not driving me to school in that, are you?'

'What do you mean?'

'Why aren't you dressed?'

Donovan gestured with his thumb at Knight, who was taking apart the telephone on the desk. 'I'm sort of busy here, Robbie.'

'Typical,' sneered Robbie. He turned his back on Donovan and went into the kitchen.

'I'll call you a minicab,' said Donovan.

'I'm not going to school in a grotty minicab.'

'So walk.'

'Mum always ran me to school,' said Robbie.

'Yeah, well, she had fuck all else to do except spend my money and shag my accountant.'

Robbie took a step back as if Donovan had pushed him in the chest. Tears pricked his eyes.

Donovan realised he'd gone too far. 'Oh God, Robbie,' he said quickly. 'I'm sorry.'

Robbie picked up his backpack. 'I'll walk.'

Donovan put a hand on his son's shoulder but Robbie shrugged him off. 'Look, I'll call a cab. I know a firm, they've got Mercs. How about that, you can go in a Merc?'

Robbie ran down the hall and slammed the front door behind him. Donovan cursed and took Knight's coffee into the study.

Knight was still pretending to examine the phone on Donovan's desk.

'You got kids, Alex?' asked Donovan.

'I haven't been blessed yet,' said Knight with a straight face. He pushed his black-framed spectacles further up his nose.

'Probably best,' said Donovan. He looked at his watch. 'I've got to make a call.'

'Land line here's okay,' said Knight.

Donovan picked up one of his mobiles. 'Nah, I'll use this.'

Knight nodded at the mobile. 'You know they can key into those, even the GSM digitals?'

'Yeah, but only if they know the number. I'm going through Sim cards like there's no tomorrow.'

Donovan took the phone into the back garden, padding over the grass in his bare feet. He called Underwood at the number where the detective had said he'd be. It was a public phone box about half a mile from Underwood's flat in Shepherd's Bush. Underwood answered immediately. 'I'm late for work,' the detective complained.

'What did you find out?' asked Donovan.

'He's an art dealer, known to us. Thought to be receiving, but never been proved. Just whispers. To be honest, it's a resources thing. Take too much time and effort to target him. There are bigger receivers around. He's got a legitimate business that makes money, I think he just dabbles with stolen stuff. There's a couple of drugs busts, but both were small amounts of cannabis and he was warned both times. String of motoring offences but he's still got his licence. Just.'

'No chance that he's one of yours?'

'He's not a registered informer, and they're all registered these days. No registration, no case, you know that.'

'Cheers, Dicko.'

'What's the story on this guy?' asked the detective.

'He's sold some paintings for me, that's all. I had him around the house and I just wanted to be sure he was clean.'

Donovan thanked the detective and replaced the receiver. Donovan hadn't expected any revelations from Underwood. He had a sixth sense where undercover agents and grasses were concerned, and Jamie Fullerton hadn't set off any alarm bells. He was a bit too keen, but that was no bad thing. He'd certainly done a great job selling Donovan's paintings and delivering the bank drafts to Rodriguez. Fullerton's drug-taking was a potential problem, however. The last thing Donovan needed was to be caught anywhere near a Class A drug.

Donovan gulped his tea in the kitchen, then took the back off the mobile phone and took out the Sim card. Donovan took the card upstairs and flushed it down the toilet before shaving and showering. When he went back downstairs he was wearing black jeans and a Ralph Lauren blue denim shirt, the sleeves rolled up to his elbows.

Knight was in the sitting room working on the phone there. 'Soon be done downstairs, Den.'

'All clear?'

'So far. You sure they're looking at you?'

'No doubt.' Donovan nodded at the black box that Knight was attaching to the phone. 'They're foolproof, yeah?'

'For the standard surveillance stuff, yeah. Money-back guarantee. And the hookswitch gizmo is infallible. Your worry would be if it were spooks and they were watching you through satellite or microwave relay. Cops or Customs couldn't do that, but Six and Five could. That wouldn't show up this end.'

Donovan pulled a face. Since MI6 and MI5 had been allowed to switch their attentions to drug running and money laundering in addition to their standard national security remit, there was every chance that the spooks would be on his case. Not that it mattered. He always regarded all landlines as suspect, with the exception of randomly chosen public call boxes.

'Do you want me to show you the portable MRF detector?'

'Sure.'

Knight went over to his suitcase and took out a blue and white box. He opened it and slid out a white polystyrene moulding inside which was a grey plastic box the size of a bleeper, with a belt clip on one side. There were three jack points on one end and a digital display on the other. Knight removed a rechargeable battery from the polystyrene and tossed it to Donovan. 'Charge it up overnight. Charger's in the box. They say it'll last five hundred hours, but that's when it's on stand-by. Figure on forty-eight hours, so that's six days at eight hours a day.'

'I should call you when Robbie needs help with his maths homework.'

Knight took a second battery out of his jacket pocket and inserted it into the back of the detector. He went over to Donovan and clipped it on to his belt, then took a length of cable with a jack plug on one end and a thin Velcro strap on the other. He gave the strap to Donovan and told him to thread it through his shirt sleeve and to run the strap under the band of his Rolex. While Donovan ran the wire up his sleeve, Knight slotted the jack plug into the detector and switched it on.

When he'd finished hiding the strap under his watch band, Donovan rolled down his sleeve. The wire couldn't be seen and the strap was pretty much hidden. 'Clever,' said Donovan 'but does it work?'

Knight went over to his suitcase and took out a small tape recorder and switched it on. He motioned for Donovan to come closer.

'Do I have to keep my arm out or anything?' he asked.

'Nah, just walk normally. It should pick it up within six feet or so.'

Donovan took another step forward. Then another. When he was two paces away from Knight, the box on his belt began to vibrate. 'Yeah, there it goes.' He took a step back. The vibration stopped. He moved forward and it started again. 'Excellent.'

'It's even more sensitive to listening devices,' said Knight. He clicked the tape-recorder off and put it back in the suitcase. He took out a much larger black box, this one the size of a telephone directory, and two small speakers. 'Now this you'll like,' he said. He placed the box and speakers on the coffee table and ran a power lead to the nearest socket. 'Acoustic noise generator. White noise, all frequencies. It'll absolutely render every type of listening device useless, providing that you're closer to the speakers than you are to the bug. Switch it on and sit close to it, keep your voice down and the white noise will swamp what you're saying.'

'Downside is, they'll know that I'm trying to keep something from them,' said Donovan.

'Not necessarily,' said Knight, flicking a small red switch. A red light glowed and the room was filled with a static-like noise. Knight turned a white plastic knob and the volume increased. 'They're more likely to think they've got a technical problem. Vary it. Turn it down when your conversation's innocuous, turn it up when you're secret squirrel. It'll drive them crazy.' Knight stood up. 'Right, why don't I sweep the downstairs, show you the weak points, then I'll fix the phones upstairs.'

He took a portable RF detector from the suitcase. It looked like a small metal detector with a circular antenna on one end that was the size of a table tennis bat. He showed Donovan how to switch it on and how to read the LCD, then ran it along the skirting board. Donovan was already familiar with the procedure: he'd often swept the villa in Anguilla himself.

The phone rang. Donovan walked over to the sideboard and picked up the receiver, automatically checking the lights on the monitor. The green light was on. Safe to talk. It was Robbie. Donovan expected him to apologise for running out of the house, but Robbie had something else on his mind – he'd left his sports kit behind and he was supposed to be playing soccer that afternoon. Donovan said he'd take the kit to school for him and arranged to meet Robbie outside the gates at half past twelve.

They called it the Almighty. Major Allan Gannon wasn't sure who had named the secure satellite phone system, or when, but now it was never referred to by any other name. The briefcase containing the Almighty sat on a table adjacent to Gannon's desk when he was in his office at the Duke of York Barracks in London, a short walk from the upmarket boutiques of Sloane Square, and went everywhere with him.

Gannon was standing by the window, peering through the bombproof blinds at the empty parade ground, when the Almighty bleeped. It was an authoritative, urgent sound, none of the twee melodies so beloved of mobile phone users. The Almighty's ring broached no argument. Answer me now, it said. This is urgent. Not that Gannon needed to be told the urgency of calls that came through the Almighty. The only people who had access to the Almighty were the Prime Minister, the Cabinet Office, and the chiefs of MI5 and MI6.

Gannon strode over to the satellite phone and picked up the receiver. 'Increment,' he said curtly. 'Major Gannon speaking.'

The head of MI6 identified herself, and then began relaying instructions to Gannon. Gannon made notes on a pad attached to a metal clipboard which was pre-stamped with 'Eyes Only – Top Secret. Not For Distribution'.

The call was short, less than two minutes in duration. Gannon repeated the information he'd been given, and then replaced the receiver. The major's SAS staff sergeant looked up from his copy of the *Evening Standard.*

'Game on,' said Gannon. 'Freighter heading for Felixstowe. Interception as soon as it's in our waters. Possible drugs consignment.'

'Customs?' asked the sergeant, a fifteen-year veteran of the SAS.

'Spooks,' said Gannon. 'Specific instructions not to liaise with Customs at this point.'

'They do like their little games, don't they?' said the sergeant.

'Force of habit,' said Gannon. 'Since the Iron Curtain went down, they've got bugger all else to do. Still, ours not to reason why. Eight bricks should do it.' The Special Air Service and Special Boat Squadron units that the Increment had access to were split into groups of four, known as bricks. Each brick had a vehicle specialist, a medical specialist, a demolition specialist and one other with an extra skill, such as languages, sniping or diving. 'We'll go in with inflatables, no need for choppers.'

'Fifty–fifty split?'

'I think so,' said Gannon. 'Wouldn't want our lads to think they were being left out of it. No choppers, though, we'll be using inflatables. Get the SBS to pull out a subskimmer. No reason to expect any firepower at their end, but we go in fully equipped.' The major looked at his watch. 'Full briefing at eighteen hundred hours.'

Donovan found Robbie's sports bag by his bed. He put it on the passenger seat of the Range Rover, and was about to get into the car when he had a sudden thought. He went back into the house and got the portable RF detector and ran it over the outside and underneath of the Range Rover, then climbed into the back and swept the antenna over the inner surfaces.

A car pulled up in the road outside. Donovan looked up,

feeling vulnerable. He relaxed when he saw it was Louise, at the wheel of an Audi roadster. She waved and climbed out of the sports car. Donovan wondered what it was about girls who worked in the lap-dancing bars. They all seemed to want to drive powerful cars.

He got out of the Range Rover and waved back.

'I hope you don't mind me popping in on you like this,' she said. She was wearing a sheepskin flying jacket and blue jeans that seemed to have been sprayed on to her, and impenetrable black sunglasses. 'Kris told me where you lived.'

'No problem,' said Donovan. He looked at his watch. 'But I'm just on my way out.'

Louise's face fell. 'Oh. Okay. I just wanted to say thanks. Buy you a coffee, maybe.' She kept looking at the RF detector in Donovan's right hand while she was talking. Donovan put it in the back of the Range Rover.

'Tell you what, why don't you give me a lift to my boy's school? I've got to drop off his soccer kit. Then you can take me for coffee.'

Louise smiled. It was, thought Donovan, a very pretty smile. He'd only seen tears and a trembling lower lip when he'd been around at her flat. She turned and went back to the roadster and Donovan found himself unable to tear his eyes from her backside as she walked. He could see why she was able to afford a car like that. She looked over her shoulder and caught him watching her.

Donovan quickly looked away. He took Robbie's sports kit out and locked up the Range Rover. She was gunning the engine as he got into the passenger seat. 'Nice motor,' he said.

'My toy,' she said. 'You can navigate, yeah?'

* * *

'Does all right, doesn't he?' said Shuker, swinging the SLR camera around to photograph the departing Audi. 'First the blonde, now the brunette. Both lookers. See the body on that one?'

Jenner put down his binoculars and wrote down the registration number of the roadster. The blonde had turned out to be a lap-dancer, and Jenner was prepared to bet money that the brunette was in the same line of business. 'If you had the millions he had, you'd probably have totty like that, too.'

'Hey, I do all right,' said Shuker, offended.

'Of course you do. Tell them you work for HM Customs and they go all misty eyed, don't they?'

'It's the bike. Birds love bikes.'

'Nah, birds say they like bikes until they get married. Then they want you to sell the bike and buy a car.'

'Not the sort I go out with. But Donovan, he's got the lifestyle, hasn't he? What do you think the house is worth?'

'Two and half. Maybe three.'

'Can't they sequester his assets?'

'He's the Teflon man. House is in his wife's name, I think. Or a trust. Untouchable, anyway. Even if anything was proved against him.' Jenner yawned. The two Customs officers were working a treble shift and would be in the room for a full thirty-six hours. They took it in turns to sleep on the single bed whenever Donovan left the house, and it was Jenner's turn for a nap.

'What do you think about tagging his car?' asked Shuker, rewinding his film.

'You saw him checking it. No point if he's going to be doing that every day. We'd just be showing our hand. That's what I'm recommending, anyway.'

'He knows we're watching him. Operator like Donovan,

he knows surveillance as well as we do. And that guy this morning. The nerd. He's got to be counter-surveillance, right?'

'We'll know when the registration check comes back, but yeah, he looked technical. If he is, there's no point in us wiring up the house. Not unless we just want to annoy him.'

'I'm up for it,' said Shuker.

'It's not our call,' said Jenner, 'but I'm going to be suggesting laser mikes. See if they'll run to it. I think we'll be wasting our time, though: Donovan's not going to say a dickie bird in his house or on the phone.'

Donovan gave Louise directions to Robbie's school. She handled the car confidently and was a far better driver than Kris. She was quick, but whereas with Kris his heart had been in his mouth at her sudden changes of speed and direction, he was able to relax with Louise at the wheel.

'Kris told me what you did,' she said. 'Thanks.'

'It was nothing.'

She flashed him a sideways look and he saw his reflection in the black lenses. 'It was one hell of a thing, Den. You took a risk doing that.'

'Nah, he was out of condition. A middle-class wanker.'

'That's not what I meant. You weren't scared of . . . repercussions. You went right ahead and did what you did. For me.'

'Repercussions? Like him wanting to get his own back? Don't worry about that. His type are cowards. That's why they hit women in the first place, to make themselves feel big.'

The traffic lights ahead of them turned amber and Louise brought the car to a smooth stop. She reached over and switched on her cassette. Oasis. Donovan smiled at the coincidence. It was the same tape he'd been playing in the Range Rover.

'I meant the police. The cops could have been called, but you weren't worried. You just went right on in.'

'Like a bull in a china shop, you mean?'

Something vibrated on Donovan's hip. He wondered if it was the car, and he shifted position, but the vibration continued.

'You weren't hot headed. You were cold. Calculating.'

Donovan reached into his pocket, figuring that it must be one of his mobile phones that was vibrating. Then he remembered that device that Knight had given him and he stiffened.

'What's wrong?' asked Louise, looking at him sideways.

'Cramp,' lied Donovan. It was the RF detector. The car was bugged. He was talking about beating a man to within an inch of his life and the car was bloody well bugged. She was setting him up. Louise was leading him on, getting him to talk about it, getting him to confess. He made a play of rubbing his side. What the hell was he going to say? What had he said already? Had he given them enough evidence already?

The Oasis track ended. The lights changed to green and Louise pulled away, but she kept looking across at him. 'Are you all right? Do you want me to pull over?'

Donovan shook his head. The next track started. Suddenly realisation dawned. He reached out and switched the tape off. The detector stopped vibrating immediately.

'Not an Oasis fan, huh? Thought you would be, both being from Manchester.'

'How do you know that?' asked Donovan. He hadn't told Kris where he was from.

'Oh, give me a break, Den,' she laughed. 'That's hardly an Oxbridge accent you've got there.'

Donovan pressed the start button again. The tape restarted. So did the vibration. He switched it off. The vibration stopped.

'Make your mind up,' she said.

Donovan smiled and relaxed back in the bucket seat. 'Sorry,' he said. 'I'm jumping at shadows at the moment.'

They arrived at Robbie's school. Robbie was waiting outside the gates, peering down the road. He didn't notice Donovan sitting in the passenger seat of the Audi. 'Won't be long,' said Donovan, climbing out of the sports car with Robbie's bag.

Robbie frowned as he saw Donovan getting out of the Audi. 'Who's that?' he said, looking through the windscreen.

'A friend,' said Donovan, holding out the sports bag.

'A girlfriend?'

'She's a friend and she's a girl, so that would make her a girlfriend, right? Now do you want this, or not?'

Robbie took the bag.

'A thankyou would be nice,' said Donovan.

'Who is she?'

'She's just a friend. Okay? I helped her and she came around to the house to say thank you. Then she said she'd give me a lift to drop your gear off. You know I hate driving in the city.'

'You're a terrible driver,' Robbie mumbled.

'I'm a great driver,' Donovan protested.

'You lose your temper too easily. You keep hitting the horn. And you don't use the mirrors enough.'

Donovan stood up. 'I'll pick you up tonight, yeah? In the Range Rover.'

Robbie nodded. 'Okay.' He held up the bag. 'Thanks for bringing this.'

'You give them hell. Score lots of goals.'

'I'm a defender, Dad.'

'Defenders can score. Don't let them put you in a box. You see an opportunity to go for the goal, you take it, right?'

'It's a team game, Dad,' laughed Robbie, and he ran off.

Donovan went back to the car. He grunted as he climbed back into the passenger seat. He felt too old to be getting in and out of low-slung sports cars.

'Everything okay?' asked Louise.

'He thinks you're my new girlfriend.'

'As opposed to an old one?'

'As opposed to his mother.'

'Ah,' said Louise, putting the Audi into gear. 'Starbucks okay?'

'My favourite coffee.' He stared silently out of the window.

'Penny for them?' asked Louise, stopping to allow a pensioner to drive her Toyota out of a side road.

'Robbie says I'm a crap driver.'

'And are you?'

'I don't think so, but what guy does, right?'

'Quickest way to end a relationship,' laughed Louise. 'Tell a guy he's lousy in bed or that he's crap behind the wheel of a car.'

'You in a relationship right now?' asked Donovan. Immediately the words left his mouth he regretted them. It was a soppy question.

Louise didn't seem bothered by his probing. She shrugged. 'Difficult to have any regular sort of relationship, doing what I do,' she said.

'Great way to meet guys, though,' said Donovan.

Louise raised her eyebrows and sighed. 'Yeah, right. I'd really want to go out with the sort of guy who thinks shoving twenty-pound notes down a girl's G-string is a sensible way to spend an evening.'

'Beats sitting in front of the TV,' said Donovan with a smile.

'And would I want to go out with a guy who knows what I do for a living? What does that say about him?'

'You mean, if a guy really cared for you, he wouldn't want you to do what you do?'

'Exactly.'

'Maybe he'd think it better you have a career. My soon-to-be ex-wife never did a day's work in her life. She went from her father's house to mine. From one provider to another.'

'Soon-to-be ex-wife? You're getting divorced?'

'Something more permanent, hopefully,' said Donovan. Then he shook his head. 'Joke.'

'Didn't sound like a joke,' said Louise.

'I'm still a bit raw,' said Donovan.

'You'll heal. Here we are.' She parked the car at a meter and jumped out before Donovan could continue the conversation. She fed the meter and locked the car, then went into the coffee shop with Donovan. He reached for his wallet but she slapped his hand away. 'No way. My treat, remember? Cappuccino okay?'

Donovan got a table by the window while Louise fetched their coffees.

She sat down opposite him and slid a foaming mug over to him. She clinked her mug against his. 'Thanks. For what you did.'

'It was a pleasure.'

Louise sipped her cappuccino and then wiped her upper lip with a serviette. 'I don't want you thinking I'm a victim, Den. A damsel in distress, maybe, but I'm not a victim. I fought back.' She took off her sunglasses. Her left eye was still puffy and the redness had given way to dark blue bruising.

Donovan smiled. 'You should see the other guy,' he said softly.

'I kneed him in the nuts and he probably wouldn't have done this if he hadn't caught me by surprise. Doing what I do, I know how to handle men.'

'I'm sure you do,' said Den, straight faced.

She grinned and put her sunglasses back on. 'You know what I mean. There's a psychology to it. A way of maintaining control.'

'I'm sure there is.'

'He caught me unawares. It won't happen again. I am really grateful, Den. You barely know me, but you were there when I needed someone. Friends, yeah?'

Donovan nodded enthusiastically. He picked up his mug and clinked it against hers again. 'Definitely,' he said.

'You've been a bad boy, haven't you?' said the woman. She was in her late twenties with shoulder-length red hair. She was wearing a black leather miniskirt, thigh-length black shiny plastic boots with four-inch stiletto heels and a black mask, the type that Catwoman used to wear in the old Batman TV show. She had a riding crop in her hands and she flexed it as she paced up and down across the blood-red carpet.

'Yes, mistress,' said David Hoyle. Hoyle was naked and tied at his wrists and ankles to two planks of wood that had been nailed together to form an X-shaped cross that stood in the middle of the room. On his head was a black leather hood with holes for his eyes and a zipper across his mouth.

'And what happens to bad boys?' asked the woman, slowly running the crop from his left knee up to his groin.

Hoyle's scrotum contracted in a reflex action that was part fear and part sexual excitement. It was the mixture of emotions that he craved, that kept him returning to the basement flat in Earl's Court. The fear and the excitement, followed by a relief that was far more intense than he'd ever had with his wife in almost twenty years of marriage. 'They have to be punished,' he said, his voice a hoarse whisper, muffled by the mask.

She slowly unzipped the mouth hole. 'That's right,' she said, walking around behind him and dragging the crop along his skin. 'How do you think you should be punished?' she asked.

Hoyle swallowed. His mind was in a whirl. It wasn't often that his mistress allowed him to choose the method of punishment, and he had to choose carefully. The crop was too easy. The paddle barely hurt. The burning candle wax was painful, but it meant lying down and he had grown to enjoy being punished standing up. Or bending over. At the thought of bending over he felt himself grow hard and he knew what he wanted her to do to him.

The door to the chamber was thrown open with a bang and Hoyle's erection died on the spot. Two men stood there. Men with hard faces and crew-cuts, big shoulders and tight smiles on their faces. One of them pointed a finger at the woman. 'Out,' he said.

She nodded meekly. She put her crop on its hook on the wall, then walked out of the chamber, her hips swinging as if deliberately trying to tease Hoyle. The two men stood behind the lawyer. He tried to twist around to see what they were doing, but his mistress had done too good a job with his bonds. He started to breathe heavily and he could feel sweat beading all over his body. His insides went liquid and he knew that he was close to soiling himself. All the excitement had evaporated. All he felt now was fear.

A third man appeared in the doorway. He wasn't quite as big as the two men who stood somewhere behind Hoyle, but he was over six feet tall. He was wearing a long grey overcoat and had his hands thrust deep into the pockets. There was something familiar about him, but Hoyle was sure he hadn't met him before – he had a great memory for faces. Then it hit him. He looked like a younger version of Sacha Distel. When the man spoke, however, his accent was Spanish, not French. 'Mr Hoyle, I presume,' he said.

'Who are you?' asked Hoyle.

'That doesn't really matter,' said the man, 'considering the predicament you're in. What is more important to you is what do I want. And what I will do to you if you don't co-operate.'

The man walked into the chamber and closed the door. The only illumination came from a dozen candles around the room, and their flickering cast eerie shadows on the walls. He turned and looked at a shelf laden with dildos and vibrators of various shapes and sizes. He took his gloved right hand out of his pocket and picked up a huge black dildo. He looked at it with an amused smile on his lips, and then turned to Hoyle. He held up the dildo. 'She puts this up your arse, does she?'

Hoyle shook his head, a sick feeling in the pit of his stomach.

'Bit big for you, is it?' said the man. 'Working your way up to it? How would you like one of my guys to push this up you?'

Hoyle shook his head, more emphatically this time.

The man grinned and put the dildo back on the shelf. He looked around as if trying to find something to wipe his hand on. There was a pink towel on a radiator and he picked it up, wiped his gloves, and then tossed it on to a black leather-covered vaulting horse. The man gestured at the horse. 'She ties you to that?' he asked.

Hoyle nodded.

'I've never seen the attraction in this,' said the man. 'Domination. I don't think I'm the least bit submissive. The idea of a woman hitting me . . .' The man faked a shudder. 'There are so many better things a woman can do.' He grinned. 'I guess that's why they call it the English vice, isn't it?'

He walked over to Hoyle and stood in front of him. Hoyle flinched as the man reached up and held the zipper over his mouth. He ran the zipper back and forth several times, an amused smile on his face, then zipped it closed.

'You get given a get-out word, don't you? A word you can use when the pain gets too much. When you really want it to stop, right?'

Hoyle nodded.

'Just so you know, Mr Hoyle, I won't be giving you such a word. The only way you're going to stop me is by doing what I want. Do you understand?'

Hoyle nodded again. His penis had shrunk to nothing and sweat was dripping down his back.

'Good,' said the man. He stepped back and pointed up at a brass light fitting in the ceiling, below which was suspended an etched-glass bowl. 'Did you know there was a camera up there? She records everything. For insurance. In case a client should die down here, she could prove that it was all consensual. She keeps the tapes. I've got all your sessions. I'm about halfway through them.' The man grinned. 'You're a naughty, naughty boy.'

Hoyle screamed as something hit him hard on the left thigh. Hoyle's eyes watered. One of the men was brandishing a cane.

'Now, on the plus side, if you do what I want, I'll make sure that nobody else ever sees those tapes. Your wife. Or your partners. Or the tabloids. Or your mother.' The man unzipped the mouth slot. 'Say thank you, David.'

'Thank you,' said Hoyle hoarsely.

The man nodded and zipped the slot closed. 'On the negative side, if you don't agree to do what I ask, my men will keep hurting you until you change your mind. They're experts at inflicting pain. Not the pretend sort that hookers like her dole out. Real pain. Crippling pain. Permanent pain.'

The cane slashed into Hoyle's other thigh and he cried out again, his screams muffled by the leather hood.

'Where is Victoria Donovan?'

Hoyle shook his head. The cane whipped through the air and pain seared across his stomach. He screamed. Tears streamed down his face and soaked into the leather.

'Where is Victoria Donovan?' asked the man again.

'I can't tell you,' said Hoyle.

The man frowned and unzipped the mouth slot. 'You're mumbling, David,' he said.

'I can't tell you,' said Hoyle, 'because I don't know. He won't tell me where he is.'

'He?'

'Stewart. Stewart Sharkey. The man she's with.'

The cane swished again, and smacked into his stomach, a fraction of an inch lower than the previous time. Hoyle screamed and his whole body went into spasm for several seconds. Hoyle's mistress knew how to use the cane so that it didn't leave a mark, but Hoyle knew that the welts he was getting now would be on his body for weeks.

'Before you get any ideas about that hooker calling the police, I've paid her to take a week's vacation,' said the man. 'And I've promised her that we'll have cleaned up by the time she gets back. Seems we've got mutual friends. Now, how do you get in touch with him?'

'Phone.'

'There's no number in your office.'

'Stewart told me not to write it down.'

'UK number?'

'A mobile.'

The man took out a mobile phone. 'Right, here's what we're going to do, David.'

Stewart Sharkey's mobile phone trilled. 'Who is it?' asked Vicky, standing at the entrance to the terrace, a glass of champagne in her hand.

Sharkey forced himself to smile. He wanted to snap at her, to ask her how he was expected to know. He wasn't psychic, for God's sake. He picked up the phone and pressed the green button.

'Stewart, it's me, David.'

'Yes, David.' Hoyle sounded stressed. 'Is there a problem?'

'No, no problem,' said Hoyle. 'Everything's going ahead as planned. I've some forms for Victoria to sign, that's all. For the custody application.'

'Can't you sign them on her behalf?'

Vicky frowned and mouthed, 'Who is it?'

'No can do, Stewart. Sorry. It has to be her.'

Sharkey put his hand over the bottom of the phone. 'It's

the lawyer. You've got to sign some papers.' Vicky visibly relaxed and Sharkey realised that she thought the call might have been from her husband.

'Stewart? Are you there?'

'Relax, David. It's okay. What about faxed copies? Would that do?'

'Has to be originals, I'm afraid. Is there any possibility of you both coming to the office in the next few days?'

'Absolutely none,' said Sharkey. He winked at Vicky and she took a quick sip of her champagne. 'You'll have to have them couriered out here,' he said.

There was a pause as if Hoyle had taken the phone away from his mouth, then he coughed. 'That's fine,' he said. 'Where shall I send them to?'

'Have you got a pen?' asked Sharkey.

Juan Rojas put away his mobile phone. 'See, that wasn't so hard, was it?' he asked Hoyle.

Hoyle had sagged against the wooden cross. The strength had gone from his legs and all his weight was on his wrists. 'Please don't kill me,' he sobbed.

'Wouldn't that be the ultimate thrill for you?' asked Rojas. 'Bit like Christ, dying on the cross.'

'I don't want to die,' Hoyle moaned. Urine splattered on to the carpet and Rojas wrinkled his nose in disgust.

'No one wants to die,' said Rojas. 'No one's ever begged me to kill them.' A thoughtful look crossed his face. 'Actually, that's not true. There was a man once, in Milan. After what we'd done to him, he really did want to die. Begged and begged.' Rojas smiled. 'I've no wish to kill you, David. None at all. I'm going to leave you here for a couple of days. One of my men will come in to give you water.' He nodded at the sodden carpet. 'Might even put a bucket under you. After forty-eight hours we'll let you loose. We'll still have the videos, so I'd expect you to hold your tongue about what's happened.' Rojas walked up close to Hoyle, taking care not to stand in the damp patch of carpet. 'Say thank you, David.'

'Thank you,' said Hoyle weakly.

Rojas grinned and slowly zipped up the mouth slot on the black leather mask.

Donovan took the portable RF detector off before driving the Range Rover to Robbie's school. The traffic moved at a snail's pace, and yet again most of the vehicles on the road seemed to be mothers on the school run.

Donovan switched his cassette player on. Oasis. He smiled as he remembered the coincidence that he and Louise had the same tape. They'd chatted for the best part of an hour in Starbucks. She was a smart girl and seemed to be making a good living as a dancer. Like Kris, she kept insisting that she didn't go with customers, but Donovan couldn't help wondering how else she could afford the Audi roadster. Still, he figured it wasn't any of his business. She'd given him her mobile number when she'd dropped him off at home and asked him to call her some time. She'd also made a point of telling him the address of the club where she danced. Twice.

Robbie wasn't at the gates when Donovan arrived at the school. A young mother with four schoolgirls in the back of a Mercedes four-wheel drive pulled out in front of him and he whipped the Range Rover into the space.

He tapped his fingers on his steering wheel as he waited. Being a single parent wasn't so bad, he thought. It was a bit of a nuisance having to drive Robbie to and from school, and the early mornings were a pain, but Robbie was clearly low maintenance. Once Donovan had his money back, maybe he'd stay in London. He had enough to live comfortably for the rest of his life. Very comfortably. When Vicky had been in the picture, Donovan had been driven to keep putting deals together, partly because of the desire to keep increasing his fortune, but also because he enjoyed it. He got a buzz out of outwitting the various agencies that were tasked with defeating the drugs barons. There was nothing like putting together a successful multi-million-pound drugs deal, arranging the finance and the shipping, moving people and money around the world like pieces on some gigantic chessboard, followed by the elation of carrying it off successfully. Some of the best parties he'd been to had been in the wake of successful drug deals. Donovan smiled to himself. Could he turn his back on that? Would he be satisfied doing the school run until Robbie was old enough to drive? Years of shopping at Tesco and ferrying sports kit and helping with homework?

Robbie ran out of the school gates, waving at Donovan. Donovan grinned and waved back. Yeah, he thought, maybe he would at that.

'How did the match go?' Donovan asked as Robbie climbed into the passenger seat and tossed his sports bag into the back.

'Won 3–1,' said Robbie. 'My pass gave us the second goal.'

'Good for you,' said Donovan and gave his son a high-five. 'How are you at grocery shopping?' he asked as he started the car and edged out into the line of four-wheel drives.

'Mum always does . . .' Robbie corrected himself quickly. 'Did the shopping. During the day. She said it was quieter.'

'Yeah, well, I didn't do too good a job when I went on my own. Thought you might have a better idea of what we need. Okay?'

'Okay,' said Robbie.

When they got to the supermarket, Donovan pushed a trolley while Robbie ran from shelf to shelf, grabbing at tins, bottles and packets and tossing them in. He stocked up with essentials including washing-up liquid, and soap, things that Donovan would never have thought of until he'd run out.

'Can you do spaghetti?' Robbie asked.

'Sure,' said Donovan. 'You boil it and throw it against the wall. If it sticks, it's cooked.'

Robbie laughed and put two packs of spaghetti into the trolley, along with several jars of bolognaise sauce, then they walked together to the checkout.

'What are you going to do, Dad?'

'About what?' asked Donovan.

'About work. You can't just sit around the house all day.'

'Your mother seemed to manage quite nicely.'

Donovan paid for the groceries and he and Robbie took the carrier bags out to the Range Rover.

'What do you do, Dad? Your job?'

'You know what I do. I'm a businessman.'

'But what do you actually do?'

Donovan got into the front seat and opened the door for Robbie. Robbie got in and fastened his seatbelt. 'What's brought this on?'

'Nothing. It was my friends, that's all. We were talking about what our dads did, and I said you were back and they were asking what you did. I said you were a businessman, but they were asking what sort of business and I said you were out in the Caribbean and they were asking what you did out there. That's all. I think they thought it was strange that I didn't know. Like it was a secret.'

'It's no secret, Robbie,' said Donovan, starting the engine. 'It's boring, that's all. Import–export. I buy and sell things. Move them from country to country.'

'But what sort of things?'

'Anything. Whatever people want to buy and sell. You buy at one price and if you can sell at a higher price, you make a profit. Sell a lot of it and you make a lot of profit. Simple. You don't need a PhD to understand that.'

'Yeah, but I still don't know what it is you sell.'

'Commodities. Could be anything. Cement, say. I might buy cheap cement and sell it to a construction company in America. Or I might buy fertiliser in Argentina and sell it in China.'

'And that's why you had to be in Anguilla a lot?'

Donovan frowned. 'Your friends were asking why I was in Anguilla?'

'No, that was me. You never really said why you were away such a lot.'

'It was business, Robbie. Swear to God.'

Robbie nodded. 'I know,' he said, as Donovan started the car and drove home.

The Increment moved in just before midnight. Major Gannon and his staff sergeant sat in one of three high-speed inflatables, bobbing in the Atlantic just a few miles from where the ocean merged into the English Channel. The major was in radio contact with a subskimmer some ten miles away to the west.

The subskimmer, built by Defence Boats, had been designed for covert operations. It could be used as a high-speed surface craft capable of carrying ten troopers and all their equipment at speeds of up to thirty knots, or it could operate as a submersible with twin electric motors, going down to a depth of up to fifty metres.

'Affirmative,' said Gannon into his radio. He turned to the two men sitting behind him. They were both MI6 operatives and had identified themselves only by first names. James and Simon. Gannon doubted that these were their real names. Unlike the eight troopers who were also in the inflatable, the MI6 men weren't armed, but they wore SAS black fire-retardant suits, body armour, composite helmets and communications units inside their respirators. 'They're going into snorkel mode,' Gannon told them. 'They should be boarding within thirty minutes.'

The subskimmer was able to travel half-submerged, with only the divers' heads, the exhaust pipes and air inlet above the surface, making it almost impossible to be spotted, either by eye or by radar. On board the subskimmer were two four-man bricks of SBS troopers in full diving gear. They would clandestinely board the freighter prior to Major Gannon and his men making a more straightforward frontal approach.

As well as the eight SAS troopers in the inflatable with the major, a further eight SAS troopers from Boat Troop and eight SBS troopers were positioned in two more inflatables some fifty metres away to his right. Gannon wasn't expecting trouble, but he knew it was better to be over-prepared. Even though the freighter was owned by a respectable shipping company and operating on a scheduled route, there was always a chance that an over-enthusiastic crewman might grab a weapon of some sort.

Twenty minutes later and Gannon got word over his

radio that the SBS advance party was on board and concealed. Gannon radioed that the inflatables were to move in. The engines roared and the three boats surged forward through the waves.

The DHL courier walked into the hotel lobby and up to the reception desk. 'I have a delivery for Monsieur Stewart Sharkey,' he said in fluent French. The receptionist, a man in his forties with a spreading handlebar moustache, grunted and nodded at a man sitting at the far end of the reception area, sitting on a long low sofa and reading a copy of *Le Monde.*

The courier walked across the marble floor, under three huge crystal chandeliers. 'Monsieur Sharkey?'

The man lowered his paper. '*Oui?*'

'I have a package for you from London. Can you sign here please?' said the courier in accented English.

The man stood up and took the computerised clipboard. He scrawled a signature on the LCD screen and handed the clipboard back to the courier. The courier held out the package, an A4 manila envelope, then he frowned. He checked the serial number on the label stuck to the envelope against the readout on the clipboard and cursed.

'I am sorry, Mr Sharkey. I have the wrong envelope. I will have to get it from the van.'

'No problem,' said the man.

'Would you come with me? It would save time.'

'I'm not sure . . .' the man began, but the DHL courier had already walked away, so he followed him.

The DHL van was parked about fifty feet from the entrance to the hotel. The courier opened the rear door of the van and poked his head inside, mumbling something in French.

The man walked up behind him. 'Have you got it?' he asked.

The courier whirled around and pressed the twin prongs of a small black stun gun against the man's throat. He pressed a switch on the gun and the man jerked once and slumped forward, his mouth working soundlessly. The courier caught him and pushed him into the back of the van. Two pairs of hands grabbed the man's jacket and hauled him inside. The door slammed shut as the courier walked around to the driver's door.

The sound of the doorbell jarred Donovan out of a dreamless sleep. He rolled over and looked at his alarm clock. It was just before midday. He'd been asleep for almost three hours. He hadn't undressed when he'd got home from the morning school run, he'd just stretched out on the bed intending to nap for half an hour or so. Downstairs, the doorbell rang again, then someone knocked on the door, hard. Donovan sat up. He went downstairs. 'Okay, okay, I'm coming,' he muttered as the doorbell rang again. He opened the door, blinking his eyes. It was Ricky Jordan and Charlie Macfadyen and they both looked as mad as hell. Jordan was reaching inside his black Armani jacket.

Donovan knew something was wrong and he tried to close the door. He was too slow – Macfadyen put his shoulder against the door and barged through, Jordan following close behind.

'You bastard!' shouted Macfadyen, slamming Donovan against the wall.

Jordan kicked the door closed and pulled a gun from inside his jacket. He thrust the barrel under Donovan's chin. 'You got cut out of the deal, so you fucked it up for us,' he shouted.

Donovan glared at the gun. 'You brought a fucking gun into my house? How stupid are you, Ricky?'

Jordan snarled at Donovan and pushed the gun harder against Donovan's chin, forcing his head back against the wall. 'You are fucking dead meat, mate,' he spat.

'Yeah, right,' said Donovan. 'Of course I am. You're going to pop me and then walk out of here. Earth to Planet Jordan, you wouldn't get fifty feet.'

Jordan frowned. 'Why not?'

'Because I'm Tango fucking One, that's why,' said Donovan. 'Every man and his dog are watching me.'

'No one stopped us coming in, did they?' said Jordan.

'Well, you haven't shot me yet, have you?' said Donovan. 'Pull the trigger and see what happens.'

Jordan looked at Macfadyen, who shrugged.

Donovan smiled, trying to put them at ease. 'While you're deciding what to do, how about we have a beer?' he said. 'They're in the fridge, Charlie.'

'Beer?'

'If you want something stronger, all the booze is in the cabinet in the sitting room.'

'We didn't come here for fucking beer, Den,' said Macfadyen.

'Well, like I said, the sky's gonna fall in if you fire that thing in here, so why don't we have a beer and then you can shoot me somewhere else.'

'Are you taking the piss, Den?' asked Macfadyen.

'I'm just trying to be civilised,' said Donovan. 'Go on, Charlie, get the beers. Ricky and I'll carry on the conversation in the sitting room.' Donovan grinned at Jordan. 'If it makes you feel any happier, Ricky, you can keep on pointing it at me.'

Jordan looked across at Macfadyen, who nodded. 'Yeah, why not?'

Macfadyen went down the hall to the kitchen. Jordan slowly took the gun away from Donovan's neck. 'No tricks, yeah?' he said.

Donovan walked into the sitting room. He put his finger against his lips and then made a cut-throat gesture with his right hand. Jordan frowned and opened his mouth to speak. Donovan hissed and put his fingers against his lips again. He went over to the sideboard and picked up the acoustic noise generator that Alex had left. He put it on the coffee table, plugged it in and switched it on. The room was filled with static.

'What the fuck's that?' said Macfadyen, walking in with three cans of lager. He tossed one to Donovan and put one down on the coffee table for Jordan.

Donovan sat down on the sofa and motioned for Jordan to sit down next to him. 'It masks the sound of our voices. In case they're using laser microphones.'

Macfadyen looked around nervously.

'I swept the place this morning,' said Donovan, 'and I've got the phones monitored.' He nodded at the box of electronics. 'This is just to be on the safe side, but keep your voices down, yeah? Now what the fuck is going on?'

Macfadyen took a copy of the early edition of the *Evening Standard* from his jacket pocket and tossed it on to the coffee table. Donovan read the headline and cursed. 'SAS SWOOP ON £100 MILLION COCAINE HAUL.' The story was bylined by the paper's chief reporter, who had clearly been well briefed on the operation. The SAS had swooped on a freighter carrying VW Beetles from Mexico. Cocaine had been packed into the cars.

Cocaine with a street value of a hundred million pounds. That was an over-estimate, Donovan knew.

'That's bollocks, a hundred million,' he said, and Macfadyen nodded.

At street level the consignment would probably be worth sixty million pounds. Maybe seventy, depending on how prices held up. The authorities, be they cops, Customs or the Security Service, always over-estimated because it made them look good, and the bigger the haul, the more column inches they'd get. But whatever the value, the drugs had been intercepted and Jordan and Macfadyen were looking for someone to blame. Donovan's mind raced. If they really did believe that he had given up the deal, they wouldn't hesitate to kill him. If their roles were reversed, Donovan would do the same.

'I don't see any mention of Customs,' said Donovan. 'The reporter only mentions the SAS.'

'That's not the point, Den,' said Macfadyen. 'The point is, someone must have grassed.'

'And you think I'm a sore loser, is that it? A dog in the manger?'

'Dog in the manger, wind in the willows, chicken in the fucking basket, call it what you want, but you're the obvious candidate.'

'Right,' agreed Jordan, nodding furiously.

'And what exactly would I have to gain by grassing you up?' asked Donovan.

'Brownie points with HM Customs?' said Macfadyen.

'Yeah, well, like I said, I'm not sure that it was a Customs bust. When they do catch anyone, they're normally rushing to take the credit. But do you seriously think I'd risk pissing off a man like Rodriguez to get Brownie points with anyone?'

'You've got to admit, the timing does look bloody suspicious, Den,' said Macfadyen.

'It wasn't me, lads. Hand on heart.'

'Then who?' asked Jordan. 'If not you, who?'

'Who knows?' said Donovan. 'Maybe someone on your team. Maybe you've been under surveillance yourself. You can't wear Armani suits and drive around in flash cars and not get noticed.'

'It wasn't us,' said Jordan, defensively. He still had the gun pointing at Donovan's stomach and his finger was on the trigger.

'Fine. So it wasn't you. And it wasn't me. Which means it was either someone working for Rodriguez or someone on the outside. Someone on the ship got suspicious about the cargo. Maybe enough palms weren't greased in Mexico. Or it might even have been bad luck. We all know there's a million and one things can go wrong with every deal. Something else – why didn't they follow through? Why didn't they let it run?'

'Maybe they didn't want to lose the gear,' said Macfadyen.

'Bollocks. They'd have saturation surveillance: they'd tag the gear, the works. You've got to ask why they didn't do that.'

'Why do you think they didn't?' asked Jordan.

'Could be they already know,' said Macfadyen. 'Could be you already told them.'

'So why are you here giving me grief and not sitting in a cell drinking tea out of a paper cup? Don't you think if I were trying to stitch you up I'd have done it properly?'

'Maybe they screwed up,' said Jordan.

'Act your age, Ricky. The SAS boarded the ship in the middle of the night. Does that sound like a lack of planning?'

'That still doesn't answer the question – why didn't they let the consignment run?' said Macfadyen.

'I don't know, Charlie. Answer that and maybe we'll find out who grassed the deal.'

'Shit,' said Macfadyen.

'You can say that again,' said Donovan.

'We're down millions on this deal,' said Jordan. 'We're down millions with nothing to show for it.'

'That's the rules of the game and you both know it,' said Donovan. 'You budget for losing one in four consignments. You build it into your costs. You did that, right?'

'Sort of,' said Macfadyen.

'Sort of?'

'Not all the money was ours. We got three mill off a Yardie gang in Harlesden.'

Donovan raised his eyebrows. 'Smart move,' he said, his voice loaded with sarcasm. 'I thought you didn't do business with the Yardies.'

'This guy's cool.'

'Yeah, well, if he's cool, why are you worried?'

'Because it was the first deal he'd done with us. He's going to think we ripped him off.'

'So explain it to him. Anyway, that's your problem, not mine.'

'We've lost a lot of money, Den. A shedload.'

'Nothing compared to what I'm down,' said Donovan.

'What do you mean?' asked Macfadyen.

Donovan closed his eyes. 'Forget it,' he said. 'It doesn't matter.'

Jordan jabbed the gun into Donovan's ribs. 'It matters,' he said.

Donovan opened his eyes. 'My accountant ripped me

off for sixty million dollars. A big chunk of that was on its way to Rodriguez.'

Macfadyen pounced. 'Including our money, yeah?'

Donovan nodded.

'So that's why Rodriguez wanted to deal with us direct?'

Donovan nodded again.

'So our money never got to Rodriguez? You've still got it.'

Donovan sighed. 'I can see where you're going, Charlie, but you're wasting your time. I haven't got your money.'

'No, but neither has Rodriguez. So that wasn't our consignment.' He grinned. 'We haven't lost shit.'

'Your deal was with the Colombians. Not me.'

'You never gave them our money, so the buck stops with you.'

'You're not listening to me, Charlie. I haven't got a penny to my name.'

'You've got this house.'

'It's in a trust. For my boy. Can't be touched. I've fuck all, Charlie, until I can get my hands on Sharkey.'

'Sharkey?'

'My accountant. I've got people looking for him. You know Rodriguez is going to be asking the same question you are. He's going to want to know who grassed the deal.'

'I bet he is,' said Macfadyen.

'Yeah, well, bear in mind he might think it was you two.'

'What do you mean?'

'You're the new factors in the equation. If he's going to suspect anyone, he's going to suspect you. And that would explain why they went in while the ship was still at sea. To distance it from you.'

'That doesn't make sense,' said Macfadyen. 'Why would we bust our own deal?'

'I'm not saying you did,' said Donovan. 'I'm just saying that Rodriguez is going to want to talk to you.'

Macfadyen sat back in his chair. 'This is a fucking nightmare,' he sighed.

'Yeah, well, bursting in here and waving a gun around doesn't help,' said Donovan.

'What do we do?' asked Macfadyen. He gestured at Jordan's gun, which was still levelled at Donovan's midriff. 'Put it away, Ricky.'

Jordan looked as if he might argue, then he nodded and slipped the automatic inside his jacket.

'First, you two have got to keep a low profile. They'll trace the coke back to Rodriguez, and if they link you to him they're gonna be on your case. I'll talk to Rodriguez. Second, I can offer you a way of making your money back. If you're interested.'

'What?' asked Macfadyen.

'Heroin. From Afghanistan.'

'I'm not dealing with the fucking Turks, Den,' said Macfadyen. 'I've been burned before with them.'

'Yeah, they're mad bastards,' said Jordan. 'You can't trust them.'

'I'm not doing this through the Turks,' said Donovan. 'I might get them to come in as investors, but the deal's mine.'

'How much?'

'For you guys, ten grand a key.'

Macfadyen looked at Jordan and raised an eyebrow. Jordan nodded. Then Macfadyen's eyes narrowed. 'Yeah, but delivery where? It's no fucking good to me over in Amsterdam, even at that price.'

'In the UK, mate. South of London, but if you want I'll get someone to drive it up north to you.'

'You can get Afghan heroin into the UK for ten grand a key?' said Jordan in disbelief. 'Who the fuck do you think you are, Den, David bloody Copperfield?'

'It's not magic, Ricky. I've just got a way of getting it in direct, bypassing all the middle-men.'

'What, like Star Trek, you're gonna get Scotty to beam it down?' said Macfadyen.

'Actually, not far off that.'

Macfadyen and Jordan shared another look and Donovan could practically hear the wheels turning in their heads. Ten grand a kilo was a great price. On the street in Edinburgh prices were as high as a hundred and twenty grand a kilo once it had been cut, and Macfadyen and Jordan had their own chains of dealers. They'd be able to keep the bulk of the profits themselves.

'How do we know we won't be throwing good money after bad?' asked Macfadyen.

'Because this is my deal, Charlie. Me and a couple of guys who've come up with a sure fire way of getting the gear in under the noses of Customs. As much gear as you can buy. I've got everything riding on this one, so I'm gonna make damn sure it works out okay.'

'What do you think?' Macfadyen asked Jordan.

Jordan nodded slowly. 'It's easier to shift than coke. Give us a chance to put two fingers up to the Dutchmen, wouldn't it? They keep jacking their prices up. If we show them we've got an alternative supply it's gonna put pressure on them.' He nodded more enthusiastically. 'Yeah, I say go for it. Let's go in for five hundred keys.'

Macfadyen nodded. 'Yeah, okay. How about I bring O'Brien in on this? Dublin prices are up, he'd be in for five hundred keys.'

'Okay,' agreed Donovan, 'but get him to pay twelve a

key. And tell him we don't want Euros. It's pounds or dollars. No one wants Euros.'

'Is this going to be a regular, Den, or a one-off?' asked Jordan.

'Ricky, it's going to run and run,' said Donovan, smiling broadly.

'What about the Yardies?' asked Macfadyen.

'Fuck the Yardies. They're big boys.'

'The guy's a vicious bastard. He's going to want answers.'

'A minute ago you said he was cool.'

'Yeah, well, that was before we lost three million quid of his. You're going to have to talk to him.'

'Me? Why me?'

'Because he's not going to believe a word I tell him from now on. But you're Den Donovan. He knows about you.'

'Because you told him, right? For fuck's sake, Charlie, can't you ever keep your big mouth shut?'

Jordan winced. 'He already knew who you were,' said Macfadyen quickly. 'That was one of the reasons he was so keen to do the deal.'

'Charlie, you had no business telling anyone I was involved. How the hell have you managed to stay out of prison? Hasn't it occurred to you that maybe these Yardies are the ones who gave the deal away?'

'Give me some credit, will you, Den? All I said was that I was doing a coke deal and that you were involved. I didn't say from where, I didn't say how, I didn't say when. Hell, Den, you hardly told me anything. It was only when we met that Jesus guy that we heard about the Beetles. The Yardies don't even know about that.' He pointed at the *Evening Standard*. 'They won't even know that that's their coke. Though I guess they'll put two and two together pretty sharpish.'

'So you want me to tell him his three million's gone? And how do you think he'll react to that?'

'I dunno, Den. How do you think he'll react if I tell him that his three million never got to the Colombians?'

Macfadyen stared at Donovan, who met his gaze with unblinking eyes. The threat hung in the air between them like a storm cloud about to break. Jordan looked from one to the other, waiting to see who would speak first.

Eventually Donovan nodded slowly. 'Okay,' he said. 'What's his name?'

'PM,' said Macfadyen. 'His sidekick's the brains of the outfit, though. Doesn't say much but you can see the wheels are always turning. Watch out for him. His name's Bunny.'

Juan Rojas walked into the warehouse, rubbing his gloved hands together. 'Everything go to plan?' he asked.

A man was stripping off the uniform of a DHL courier. 'Like a lamb to the slaughter,' he said. All trace of a French accent had vanished.

Rojas slapped the man on the back. 'You ditched the van?'

'The guys are doing it now.'

'Excellent,' said Rojas.

He walked to the middle of the warehouse where a man sat on a straight-backed wooden chair. Thick strips of bright blue insulation tape bound his arms and legs to the chair and another strip had been plastered across his mouth.

Rojas cursed. 'This isn't Sharkey,' he said. Rojas ripped off the strip of insulation tape. The man gasped.

'I've a message from him,' said the man. 'He said Donovan can go fuck himself.' The man smiled.

Rojas's lips tightened. 'Where is he?'

'I don't know. He's not here in Paris, that's for sure. I only spoke to him on the phone.'

Rojas cursed.

'There's more.'

'Go on.'

'He said you're to phone him. You have his mobile number, right?'

Rojas nodded. 'Right. Did he tell you what I'd do to you, when I found out that you'd set me up?' He took a small automatic from his coat pocket.

The man smiled. 'He said you'd be a professional. He said you'd appreciate the irony. And he said he'd transfer a quarter of a million dollars to any account you nominate. I'm to give him the account number in person.'

Rojas looked at the man. A smile slowly spread across his face and he put the gun away. 'He is a good judge of character,' he said. 'Luckily for you.'

'Yeah, that's him,' said Shuker, peering through his binoculars. 'Charlie Macfadyen. Big wheel in Edinburgh. Brings in most of the city's coke and heroin. Don't know the other guy, though.'

'Wonder what it was all about?' said Jenner, as the motordrive on his SLR clicked and whirred. Down in the street, the two men walked away from Donovan's house towards a gleaming red Ferrari.

'Dunno. They went in looking like they were going to kill him, and half an hour later they're best of friends.'

The bedroom door opened and two men walked in – Shuker and Jenner's replacements. One of them was carrying a copy of the *Evening Standard*. 'You seen this?' he said, tossing the paper to Shuker.

Shuker looked at the headline, then held it up for Jenner to read. 'You thinking what I'm thinking?' asked Shuker.

Jenner nodded.

Donovan switched off the noise generator and put it back on the sideboard. His ears ached from the constant static sound. He paced up and down as he went through his options. Carlos Rodriguez had lost his cocaine and his money and would be looking for revenge. Donovan had managed to talk around Macfadyen and Jordan, but Rodriguez wouldn't be so easy. And if Rodriguez sent his nephew, Donovan doubted that he'd even be given a chance to explain.

Donovan could run, but wherever he went the Colombians would find him eventually. And running would mean leaving Robbie behind. The only way to mollify Rodriguez would be to reimburse him for the lost cocaine or to find out who had given up the deal to the authorities, and he wasn't in a position to pursue either option. Donovan cursed. He had no room to manoeuvre. None at all. He was virtually out of funds, stuck in the UK, and top of the most wanted list. Donovan couldn't see how it could get any worse.

He put on a brown leather jacket, picked up three fully charged mobile phones and slotted them into various pockets. He rolled up the *Evening Standard*, got the keys to the Range Rover, secured the house, and drove off. He didn't bother sweeping the car or looking for a tail. He drove to Marble Arch and parked in an underground car park, then walked to Marble Arch Tube station. He bought a one-day Travelcard allowing him unlimited use of the underground system, then caught a Central Line train to Oxford Circus station.

After twenty minutes of swapping trains and lines, he finally got off at Charing Cross. He spent ten minutes walking aimlessly around the station, checking reflections, doubling back, walking into dead ends. He was clean. He was sure he was clean.

He went over to a bank of public phones and shoved in his BT phone card. He called Directory Enquiries for the number of the Intercontinental and then called the hotel and asked for Rodriguez's room. The receptionist said he'd checked out two days earlier. Donovan replaced the receiver. With any luck, Rodriguez had gone back to Colombia. That at least gave Donovan some breathing space. Maybe.

He dialled the Spaniard's number, but the answer machine kicked in. Donovan didn't identify himself, just asked Rojas to call him on the mobile.

Next he called the Yardie whom Macfadyen had brought in on the Colombian coke deal. The man answered. 'Yo?'

'PM?'

'Who wants to know?'

'I'm a friend of Macfadyen's.'

'So?'

'So he wanted me to talk to you.'

'I'm listening.'

'Face to face.'

'Fuck that.'

'He thought I should explain why the deal he cut you in on has gone belly up.'

'Say what?'

'Can you read, PM?'

'What the fuck you mean?'

'Buy the *Standard*. Front-page story. When you've read

it, call me back on this number.' Donovan gave him the number of one of the mobiles he was carrying, then hung up.

He used another of his mobiles to phone Underwood. The detective wasn't pleased to hear from Donovan, but Donovan cut his protests short and told him to call him back as soon as possible.

Donovan's next call was to Jamie Fullerton. He arranged to meet him at his gallery later that afternoon. Finally he called Louise.

Donovan sat on a bench in Trafalgar Square, rereading the article on the cocaine bust. One of the mobiles rang. Donovan pressed the green button. It was PM.

'What the fuck's going on, man?' asked PM.

'Your phone clean?'

'Only had it two days, and after this the Sim card goes in the trash.'

'You don't know me, PM, but you know of me. I put Macfadyen on to the deal. He cut you in. He wants me to talk through what happened.'

'Where and when?'

'This evening. Say seven.'

'Where?'

'You choose. I don't want you jumpy.'

'You being funny?' bristled the Yardie.

'I was actually being considerate. Letting you choose the turf.'

PM gave him the address of a house in Harlesden, then cut the connection.

Donovan waited, then walked around the square, watching tourists photographing themselves next to the huge lions that stood guard around Nelson's Column.

Louise arrived at two o'clock, walking up the steps of the National Gallery and standing at its porticoed entrance. She was wearing sunglasses and a long dark blue woollen coat with the collar turned up. Donovan watched her from the square until he was sure that she hadn't been followed.

She waved as she saw him walking towards her. He hugged her and gave her a kiss on the cheek. 'Thanks for coming,' he said.

'It's all very mysterious,' she said.

'Yeah, sorry. Had to be. Come on in.'

'In here?'

'Sure. You never been inside an art gallery before?'

'Never.'

'You'll love it.'

Donovan ushered her inside and to the right, into the East Wing.

'God, it's huge,' whispered Louise.

Donovan grinned. 'You don't have to whisper, it's not a funeral.'

Louise stopped in front of a painting of sunflowers, the colours so vibrant that they seemed to jump off the canvas. Half a dozen Japanese tourists were clustered around the painting listening to a commentary on headphones, nodding enthusiastically. Louise was a head taller than all of them so she had an unobstructed view. She took off her sunglasses. 'It's beautiful,' she said. She read the details on the plaque to the left of the picture, then looked at Donovan, clearly surprised. 'It's a Van Gogh,' she said.

'That's right.'

'But they're worth millions.'

'Sure. And some.'

They were standing less than five feet away from the

canvas and there was nothing between them and it. No bars, no protective glass. 'We could grab it and run,' she said.

'We could,' said Donovan, 'but there are security staff all around and every square inch is covered by CCTV.'

Louise craned her neck but couldn't see any cameras.

'Don't worry, they're there,' said Donovan.

'So what is it with you and art galleries?' she asked.

Donovan shrugged. 'Ran into one to hide from the cops. I was fourteen and should have been at school. Two beat bobbies were heading my way so I nipped into the Whitworth gallery.'

'Where's that?'

'Manchester. Huge building, awesome art, but I didn't know that when I went in. I walked through a couple of the galleries, just to get away from the entrance, and then I got to a gallery where a volunteer guide was giving a talk about one of the paintings.

'She was talking about this painting. It was a huge canvas, the figures were pretty much life size. Two Cavaliers with feathered hats facing each other with a pretty girl watching them.' Donovan smiled at her. 'You know, I've forgotten who painted it, but I'll never forget the way she talked about it. It was as if she could see something that I couldn't.' He shook his head. 'No, that's not right. We could all see the painting, but she had a different way of seeing. She understood what the artist was trying to say. The story that he was trying to tell. The painting was about the two guys arguing over the girl, of course, but it was way more than that. There were political references in the paintings, there was historical stuff, things that you just wouldn't see unless someone drew your attention to it. I tell you, she talked about that one painting for almost thirty minutes. By the end I was sitting cross-legged on the floor with my mouth wide open.'

A multi-racial crocodile of inner-city primary-school children walking in pairs, holding hands and chattering excitedly, threaded its way past them, shepherded by four harassed young female teachers.

'I kept going back. Sometimes I'd join up with classes of kids about my age, sometimes I'd sit in on the volunteer lectures. Sometimes I used to sit on my own and try to read paintings myself.' He smiled apologetically. 'I'm being boring. Sorry.'

'You're not,' said Louise.

Donovan smiled. 'It opened my eyes. I know that's a cliché, but it did. You see, a painting isn't just a picture of an event like a photograph is. A photograph is totally real, it's what you'd see if you were there. But a painting is the artist's interpretation, which means that everything that's in the painting is in for a reason. Each one is like a mystery to be solved.'

Louise's smile widened and Donovan tutted. 'I'm being patronising, aren't I?'

Louise shook her head. 'I was smiling at your enthusiasm,' she said. 'You're like a kid talking about his comic book collection.'

They walked through the double doors to another gallery, this one full of Impressionist paintings. It wasn't Donovan's favourite room and he barely glanced at the canvases.

'Can I ask you something?' said Louise.

'Sure.'

She looked across at him apprehensively. 'Promise me you won't get upset.'

'Sure,' he said.

'Your wife left you, right?'

Donovan nodded.

'You must have known her better than you know anyone in the world, right?'

'I guess so.'

'And you didn't see it coming?'

'I suppose I was too busy doing other things. I was away a lot.'

'Do you miss her?'

'Do I miss her?' said Donovan, raising his voice. Heads swivelled in his direction, and one of the curators flashed him a warning look. Donovan let go of her hand and bent his head down to be closer to hers. 'Do I miss her?' he repeated. 'She screwed my accountant. In my bed.' His face was contorted with anger and she took a step away from him. He put his hands up. 'I'm sorry,' he said. 'Touchy subject.'

'I can see.'

Donovan looked around. An elderly couple were openly staring at him and he glared menacingly at them until they looked away. He took a deep breath. 'And you're right. I should have seen the signs. There probably were clues when the two of them were together. It must have been going on for a while.'

'And there weren't any signs?'

'Like I said, I was away a lot.'

'Which is a sign in itself,' she said.

Donovan looked at her with narrowed eyes and a growing respect for her intelligence. Louise was a bright girl.

'I mean, if everything was hunky dory, you'd have spent more time with her, right?'

'There were other considerations,' said Donovan.

'For instance?'

'This is getting to be like an interrogation,' he said.

'I just want to know who I'm getting involved with, that's all.'

'Is that what you're doing? Getting involved?'

She turned and walked away, then looked back at him over her shoulder. 'Maybe,' she said.

Donovan caught up with her and they walked together through the Sackler Room, where the gallery kept its paintings by Hogarth, Gainsborough and Stubbs. Donovan admired the way that Louise hadn't asked what it was he'd wanted. He'd kept the phone conversation as brief as possible, just saying that he needed a favour and that he wanted to meet her outside the National Gallery. Most people would have arrived bursting with questions, but Louise had seemed happy just to chat.

'I do appreciate you coming, Louise,' he said.

'I owe you, Den. Whatever it is you need, I'm here for you.'

Donovan nodded. 'How much do you know about what I do?' he asked.

'Enough, I guess. Kris said you had a reputation.'

'She's probably told you right. I've got a problem. Some guys think I've double-crossed them and they're going to be after my blood. I haven't, but in my business it's often perceptions rather than the reality of the situation that count. Thing is, I need someone to take care of Robbie until I get it sorted.'

Louise frowned. 'You want him to stay with me?'

'Is that a problem?'

She shook her head. 'No, it's just . . . well, he doesn't know me.'

'That's the point. I could put him with my sister, but that's the first place they'll look if he's not at home. Nobody knows that I know you.'

'Exactly,' said Louise. 'You've no idea who I am, yet you're putting me in charge of your son.'

'If it's too much trouble, forget I asked.'

'No, it's not that,' she said earnestly. 'I'm happy to help, believe me, but I'm looking at it from your point of view. With the best will in the world, Den, I'm a complete stranger to you.'

Donovan grinned. 'I know where you live and I know where you work. I know the registration number of your car, and I know that you work for Terry Greene and Terry's a mate from way back.'

Louise nodded slowly. 'Okay, but there's another thing you've got to bear in mind. I'm not a mum, Den. I've never taken care of a kid before.'

'He's nine. He doesn't need much looking after. Feed him, make sure he cleans his teeth and give him the TV remote. He'll be fine. And it'll only be for a few days. Just until I get things sorted.'

Louise folded her arms. 'I can't believe you trust me that much.'

'Are you saying I can't?'

She shook her head. 'No. I'm just . . . I don't know, surprised. Touched.'

'I'll pay you.' Donovan reached for his wallet.

'No!' said Louise quickly. 'I don't want your money, Den. I'm happy to do this for you.'

'I'll collect him from school and bring him straight round. It'll mean you not going to work.'

'That's okay. I was going to stay off until my eye healed anyway.'

Donovan hugged her. 'Thanks, Louise. I was starting to run out of people I can trust.'

Sharkey's mobile rang. He picked it up. Vicky came in from the bedroom, naked except for a towel, still wet from the shower.

'Stewart Sharkey?'

The accent was Spanish. Sharkey smiled. Den Donovan was so predictable sometimes. 'Ah, Juan Rojas. It would either be you or the Pole. And just between the two of us, I always thought you were the more professional.'

'You are making me blush, Mr Sharkey.'

'The guy you have knows nothing. Absolutely nothing.'

'I realise that,' said Rojas. 'I have already released him. I trust you will adhere to your end of the agreement?'

'You gave him the account number?'

'I did.'

'The money will be in your account within forty-eight hours. You do realise that it's Donovan's money?'

'While it is in your possession, it's your money to do with as you wish,' said Rojas.

'I doubt that Den will see it that way,' said Sharkey.

Vicky was watching Sharkey with a confused look on her face. Sharkey turned around so that he didn't have to look at her.

'What about Hoyle? I assume you have him.'

'Temporarily. I will make a phone call. I am not being paid to kill lawyers. Unfortunately.'

'Donovan has paid you to kill me, hasn't he?'

'Of course.'

'And there's no point in my offering to pay you more?'

Rojas chuckled.

'I thought not,' said Sharkey.

'Much as money is my driving force, there are ethics that have to be adhered to. You do understand?'

'Of course I understand,' said Sharkey.

'I will find you,' said Rojas quietly. 'Eventually.' There was no menace in the voice. It was for the Spaniard a simple statement of fact.

'I've enough money to hide for a long, long time,' said Sharkey.

'Yes, you do, but no one can hide for ever. Not from me.'

'We'll see.' Sharkey hesitated. He knew he should keep the call short, but there was something he wanted to know. 'How did you feel, when you knew that I set you up?' he asked.

'What do you mean?' asked Rojas.

'When you found out that the guy wasn't me. That I wasn't even in Paris.'

'You didn't fool me. Not for a second.'

'What?'

'I'm standing right behind you, Mr Sharkey.'

Sharkey whirled around, his mouth open, throwing up his free hand as if warding off a blow. Vicky took a step back, her eyes wide, a look of horror on her face. Sharkey's head jerked left and right, his heart pounding. There was no one there.

'What's wrong?' asked Vicky.

Rojas chuckled in Sharkey's ear. 'Made you look,' he said, and cut the connection.

One of the mobiles in Donovan's leather jacket burst into a tune. It was the theme from *The Simpsons*. Louise grinned. 'Fan of the show, are you?' she asked. They were walking across Trafalgar Square towards the Tube station.

'Robbie's been playing with them,' said Donovan. 'I've told him I'll tan his hide if he doesn't stop.'

'It's cute,' said Louise.

Donovan pressed the green button. It was Underwood. 'Hang on, Dicko. Give me a minute.' He put his hand over the receiver. 'Louise, I'm gonna have to talk to this guy. Sorry. Do you want to go on ahead? I'll bring Robbie around at about five thirty. Okay?'

If Louise was hurt by him wanting to take the call in private, she didn't show it. 'Sure,' she said. 'I'll get some shopping done. You take care, Den.' She kissed him softly on the cheek and walked away, putting on her dark glasses and pushing her hands deep into her pockets.

Donovan wanted to call her back and ask her to wait for him, but he steeled himself: there was no way he would jeopardise Underwood's position by talking to him in front of anyone else. He turned his back on her and put the phone to his ear. 'Dicko, sorry about that. Busy day.'

'While I'm lying on a beach with a piña colada?'

'Jeez, you are becoming a moaning old fart,' said Donovan.

'I'm a desk man these days, Den. It's not like it used to be when I was out and about. Then I could stop by and chew the fat. These days it's noticed if I go out. Questions get asked.'

'Yeah, well, speaking of questions, I've got one for you.'

The detective sighed mournfully but Donovan carried on talking.

'I need a check on two Yardies out Harlesden way. One's called Tony Blair, goes by the nickname PM. The other's Bunny. I don't know his real name.'

'At least I don't have to phone a friend on this one,' said the detective. 'The file's been across my desk several times.

They're big players in north-west London. Crack and heroin. Some legit businesses for cleaning the cash. Drinking dens in tough neighbourhoods that we do our best to steer clear of. What's your interest?'

'Need to know, Dicko. Sorry. If you know about them, how come they're still up and running?'

'How long have you been Tango One? Just because they're targeted doesn't mean they get put away.'

'Are you sure there's not more to it than that?'

'Spit it out, Den. I'm not psychic.'

'Do they have someone on the inside?'

'Well, gosh, Den. I'll just raise it at the next meeting of Bent Detectives Anonymous, shall I?'

'Don't get all sensitive on me,' said Donovan. He was starting to get annoyed at the detective's constant whining. 'Have there been rumours? Are they getting tipped off?'

'I don't think so. They're just smarter than the average black gang-banger, that's all. In particular, this Bunny character has his head screwed on all right. PM was just a small time teenage dealer until Bunny hooked up with him. Now he's a sort of . . . what's that thing that Robert Duvall did for Marlon Brando in *The Godfather*?'

'*Consigliere?*'

'What's that mean?'

'It's an advisor.'

'Yeah. That's what Bunny does for PM. Keeps him out of the shit. Word is that Bunny's gay, but PM doesn't hold it against him. That's the talk, anyway. You got info on them might put them away? Be a feather in my cap.'

'If I do, Dicko, you'll be the first cop I'll call.'

'One other thing,' said the policeman. 'There doesn't seem to have been any money paid into my account over the past couple of weeks.'

'Don't worry,' said Donovan. 'Cheque's in the post.'

Donovan spent an hour going in and out of several department stores in Oxford Street until he was satisfied that he wasn't being tailed, then he walked to Fullerton's gallery, checking reflections in windows and doubling back three or four times to make absolutely sure that no one was following him.

Fullerton's gallery was on the third floor of a building in Wardour Street. The entrance was a glass door between a coffee bar and a photographer's store. He pressed a button and was buzzed in. He walked slowly up the stairway looking at framed reproductions of Old Masters on the walls.

The gallery itself was bright and airy with white walls and skylights and a light oak floor. The paintings on the walls were an eclectic mix of old oils and modern acrylics, but it was all good-quality work.

Fullerton came striding over from a modern beech and chrome desk, his hand outstretched. There was no one else in the gallery.

'Den, good to see you,' said Jamie.

They shook hands. 'Business quiet?' asked Donovan.

'I had a couple of viewings arranged but I put them off, figured you'd want a word in private, yeah? Do you want a drink? I've got shampoo in the fridge.'

'Nah, I've got to pick up Robbie from school, and it wouldn't be a good idea to turn up smelling of drink.'

'Coffee, then? It's the real Italian stuff.'

'Yeah, coffee's fine. Thanks.' Donovan had his portable MRF detector on and he walked slowly around the gallery, passing the left hand close to any surfaces where a listening device could have been concealed. The bleeper on his belt remained stubbornly silent. The gallery was clean.

Donovan sat down on a low-slung leather sofa and studied the paintings on the wall opposite until Fullerton returned with two china cups on delicate saucers. He sat down next to Donovan. 'Everything okay?' he asked.

'Not really,' said Donovan. 'Did you read about that big cocaine bust? The one where the SAS went in?'

'Shit, that was yours?'

'Sort of,' said Donovan. 'I set it up but then it got taken over by that guy we met in the club. Ricky. It all turned to shit, so now they're looking for the leak. If there was a leak.'

'Anything I can do to help?'

Donovan sipped his coffee. 'Good coffee, mate.'

'Yeah, I've got one of those Italian jobbies. I can do the frothy stuff, too. I'm serious, Den. If you're in a jam, I'd be happy to help.'

'Maybe there is something you can do. It depends.'

'On what?'

'On how much you want to get involved. In what I do.'

'Den, so long as it's safe and I make a profit, I'm your man.'

Donovan nodded. 'Maury said you know people with money, guys with lots of cash, not necessarily legal.'

'Good old Maury.'

'Is he right?'

'Sure. The art business is a great place to hide cash. Moveable assets, saleable around the world. And when you sell you get an auction-house cheque.'

'Okay, here's the scoop. I have a very sweet deal that I'm setting up, and I'm looking for guys who can market heroin. Top-grade heroin from Afghanistan. I can get it way, way cheaper than any wholesaler can supply it in this country, or anywhere in Europe.'

'How cheap?' asked Fullerton.

‘Delivered to the UK, ten thousand pounds a kilo. That’s about one third of the regular dealer price. Almost a tenth of the street price.’

Fullerton nodded. ‘A wrap’s a couple of quid at the moment, works out at about seventy quid a gram. Seventy grand a kilo on the street.’

‘This is good gear, though, Jamie. Right from the source. Totally uncut. I reckon street value would be nearer a hundred grand a key in London.’

‘I’m sure I could get some interest, Den. How much are we talking about?’

‘As much as you want,’ said Donovan.

‘You can’t leave it as open-ended as that.’

Donovan sighed. ‘I’m going to be bringing in eight thousand keys.’

‘No fucking way!’

Donovan grinned. ‘Like I said, it’s a sweet deal. See what interest there is, but be bloody careful. I’m going to want money up front, and I’ll arrange for it to be delivered anywhere they want in the UK.’

‘They’re going to want to know how you’re getting it into the country.’

‘No can do, Jamie.’

‘But you can tell me, right?’

Donovan pulled a face. ‘Maybe later, but at the moment, all anyone needs to know is that the gear will be in the UK. And soon. Providing we get the down payment together.’

‘And how much is that?’

Donovan smiled. If Fullerton knew the cost of the consignment, he’d know how much Donovan was paying per kilo. And how much profit Donovan would be making on the deal. ‘Let me worry about that, yeah?’

* * *

DC Ashleigh Vincent checked her wristwatch. 'Log him back home at sixteen hundred hours on the dot, Connor. Arrived in a black cab.'

Vincent's partner grunted and reached for a metal clipboard hanging on the wall.

Vincent gave him the registration number of the taxi, and then took a swig from her bottle of mineral water.

The two Drugs Squad detectives were in the back of a van painted in British Telecom livery parked about a hundred yards away from Donovan's front door. Vincent was sitting on a small fishing stool on top of which she'd placed an inflatable cushion and she'd stripped down to a t-shirt and jogging shorts. Sweat was trickling down her back. The front windows of the van were open a couple of inches to allow in some air but there was nothing in the way of a breeze to cool them down. The one saving grace was that Vincent's partner hadn't been eating curry the night before. Vincent envied the Customs investigators who were holed up in an apartment in the terrace facing Donovan's house. That was the proper way to do surveillance, she thought. All the comforts of home: a shower when they needed one, a bed for a quick nap and a proper toilet instead of a plastic bucket.

Vincent put her binoculars back to her eyes. 'Hang on, he's coming out again. Heading for the Range Rover. Log him out at sixteen oh-four.'

Donovan climbed into the front seat of the Range Rover and started the engine.

Vincent wiped her brow with a small towel. It was such a waste of her time, she thought. At first she'd been excited at being part of the team on the trail of Tango One, but she'd soon realised that she was nothing more than a clerk, noting when he entered and left the house. Word had come down from up high that all surveillance on Donovan had to be non-obtrusive. There was to be no covert entry of his house, no following his car, no attempt to find out where he was going or whom he was seeing. Vincent knew that meant only one thing – the powers that be already knew what Donovan was up to. Which meant they had someone on the inside. Which meant that Vincent's input into the operation was close to zero.

She watched through the binoculars as Donovan drove to the end of the street and turned on to the main road. 'I hope they throw away the key,' she muttered.

Donovan beeped the horn of the Range Rover when he saw Robbie walking out of the school gates. Robbie waved and ran over.

'I wasn't sure if you'd be here,' said Robbie, climbing into the front passenger seat and throwing his backpack into the rear of the car.

'Said I would, didn't I? O ye of little faith.'

Donovan kept checking his mirror as he drove away from the school. They reached a roundabout and he drove around it twice before shooting towards an exit without indicating.

'Dad, what are you playing at?' asked Robbie.

'What?'

'You're driving like a nutter.'

'You can get out and walk if you want.'

'And this isn't the way home either.'

'Yeah, I wanted to talk to you about that,' said Donovan. 'There's been a change of plan.'

'What do you mean?'

'I need you to take a few days off school.'

Robbie sighed theatrically. 'I wish you'd make up your mind,' he said. 'You just told me I had to go.'

'I know, but something's happened. Until I get it sorted, I need you to stay with someone.'

'What are you talking about, Dad?'

Donovan checked his rear-view mirror. There was no one on his tail. 'I've got a bit of a problem about the house. We can't stay there for a while.'

'What sort of problem?'

'A gas leak. I had the gas people out and they said it's not safe.'

'So I'm going to stay at Aunty Laura's?'

'Not exactly. You remember that lady who gave me the lift to school with your soccer kit?'

'I'm not staying with her,' said Robbie, pouting. He folded his arms and put his chin on his chest. 'Why can't I stay with Aunty Laura?'

'Because I say you can't. You'll like Louise. She's okay.'

'I'm not staying with your girlfriend.'

'You'll do what I bloody well tell you to do. And she's not my girlfriend.'

'You can't make me.'

Donovan glared at his son. 'What do you mean, I can't make you? You're nine years old.'

'That doesn't mean you're in the right.'

Donovan drove in silence, fuming. Robbie sat glaring out of the window, kicking the footwell. Eventually Donovan couldn't stand the sound of the kicking any longer. 'Stop that!' he yelled.

'Stop what?' asked Robbie, innocently.

'You know what. That kicking.'

'I don't want to stay with that woman. If I can't stay in my own house, I want to stay with Aunty Laura.'

'You can't.'

'Why not? Has she got a gas leak, too?'

Donovan gritted his teeth. A car ahead of him slowed to turn right without indicating. Donovan pounded on the horn. 'Look at that moron,' he said. He swerved around the stationary car, mouthing obscenities at the driver.

They came to a red light and Donovan brought the car to a halt.

'Okay, look, I'll be honest with you,' he said. 'I've upset some people, Robbie. Over a business deal. These people aren't very nice and I'm a bit worried about them coming around to the house and doing something.'

'Like what?'

'I don't know, but I'd feel safer if you stayed somewhere else. And didn't go to school. Normally I'd say stay with Aunty Laura and Uncle Mark, but these people might know where they live, too. That's all.'

'So you were lying about the gas leak?'

Donovan nodded. 'I'm sorry.'

Robbie looked at him scornfully. 'That was the best you could come up with? Weren't you ever a kid, Dad?'

Donovan grinned. 'It was bad, wasn't it.'

'It was stupid. How long do I have to stay with her?'

'A few days. I'll be there most of the time.'

'Has she got Sky?'

Donovan shrugged. 'I think so.'

'Okay, then. I don't want to miss *The Simpsons*.'

Jamie Fullerton paced up and down his gallery, a glass of champagne in his hand. His computer was switched on and Fullerton stared at the monitor as he paced. Eight thousand kilos of heroin. Den Donovan was planning to bring eight thousand kilos of heroin from Afghanistan into the UK, and Fullerton had the inside track.

Ten thousand pounds a kilo was cheap. Very cheap. Especially for delivery in London. In Amsterdam the price was close to twenty thousand pounds a kilo, and then there was the added risk of getting it into the country. If Donovan was preparing to sell it at ten thousand a kilo, he must be buying it at a fraction of that price. Which meant he was getting it close to the source. Afghanistan, probably. Or Pakistan. Or Turkey. Any closer to Europe and the price would increase dramatically. But if Donovan was getting his heroin at or close to the source, how was he going to get it into the UK?

Fullerton knew that he should tell Hathaway what he'd found out. The whole purpose of Fullerton going undercover was to gather evidence against Tango One. By rights he should send Hathaway an e-mail immediately. Something was holding Fullerton back, though, and as he paced around his gallery, he tried to work out what it was. Was it that he liked Den Donovan? That he felt guilty about betraying a man who was close to becoming a friend? Or was it because Donovan was offering Fullerton a chance to make a lot of money? Easy money. In the three years since Hathaway had set Fullerton up with the Soho gallery, Fullerton had stashed away almost a million pounds dealing in works of art, legal and otherwise, and it was money he was pretty sure Hathaway was unaware of. Fullerton could put that cash into Donovan's deal and treble it. He'd be a player. It would mean crossing a line, but over the years that Fullerton had been undercover, that line had blurred to such an extent he was no longer sure where he stood, officially or morally. And as he paced up and down his gallery, sipping his champagne, he was becoming even less sure which side of the line he was on.

Donovan pressed the bell to Louise's flat and the front door lock clicked open. She had the door to her flat open as they got to the landing. She'd changed into a sweatshirt and jeans and clipped back her hair with two bright pink clips.

'You must be Robbie,' she said, holding out her hand.

'Yeah, if he's my dad then I must be,' said Robbie sourly. Then his face broke into a grin. 'You've got Sky, right?'

'Sure.'

Robbie shook hands with her. 'You are his girlfriend, aren't you?'

'Not really.'

'Do I have to sleep on a sofa?'

Louise shook her head. 'No, I've got a spare bedroom.'

'With a TV?'

Donovan pushed the back of Robbie's head with the flat of his hand. 'When did you get so picky?' he said. He held up a small suitcase. 'I've packed some of his things, and I'll bring more around tomorrow.'

'Are you going right away? I've got shepherd's pie in the oven.'

'No, I can stay,' said Donovan.

Louise showed Donovan and Robbie into the sitting room. She pointed down the hallway. 'Robbie, your bedroom's on the right. There's a bathroom opposite.'

Donovan handed the suitcase to his son. 'And keep it tidy, okay?'

'It's all right, I've got my own bathroom,' said Louise.

'You don't know this one. He never picks up after himself.'

'Oh, he's a guy, then, is he?' laughed Louise.

Robbie took his case to his room while Louise busied herself in the kitchenette.

'You really cooked?' asked Donovan.

'It's only shepherd's pie, Den. It's no biggie. Do you want coffee?'

'Sure. Thanks.' He went over to a sideboard and took his mobile phones out of his jacket pocket and lined them up. There were four of them.

'Expecting a call?' asked Louise.

'Different people have different numbers,' said Donovan. 'Helps me keep track of who's who.'

'Paranoia?'

'Maybe.'

'Which number do I have?'

Donovan picked up one of the Nokias and waggled it. 'Only you've got this number,' he said.

'I'm flattered.'

Robbie came back into the sitting room. 'Okay?' asked Donovan.

'Yeah, it's fine,' said Robbie. 'Are you staying here as well?'

Louise looked at Donovan and raised an expectant eyebrow.

'I'll be popping in and out,' he said.

'Because there's only two bedrooms, and the bed in mine is really small.'

'It's a single,' said Louise. 'Your dad can sleep on the sofa, if he decides to stay.'

'And how long have I got to stay here?'

'It's not a prison, Robbie,' said Donovan. 'Like I said, a few days.'

'Are you hungry?' asked Louise.

'Yeah,' said Robbie. 'Starving.'

One of the mobile phones lined up on the sideboard burst into life.

Donovan picked it up. It was the Spaniard.

'It's not good news, *amigo.*'

'I'm sorry to hear that,' said Donovan.

'He's not in Paris,' said Rojas. 'He had someone else pick up the papers.'

'Bastard!' hissed Donovan.

'Language,' chided Robbie.

Donovan glared at him.

'If I were to guess, I would say that he is somewhere in France,' continued Rojas. 'A big city. Nice or Marseilles perhaps. But we are not in a guessing game here, of course. He could well have moved on by now.'

'But you're still on the case?'

'Of course,' said Rojas. 'I have a number for him. Do you have a pen?'

Donovan clicked his fingers and waved for Robbie to get him a pen. He put his hand in his trouser pocket and pulled out a Tesco receipt. Robbie gave him a pen, scowling.

'Okay, Juan, go ahead.' Rojas gave him the number. 'That's a UK mobile, yeah?' asked Donovan.

'Yes. A roaming GSM.'

'Can we find him through the number?'

Rojas whistled through his teeth. 'If it was a land line, I have contacts in the phone company who could help us, but mobiles are a different matter. I can certainly find out which numbers he has called, but locating the handset would require a warrant and would have to be done at a senior police level or by one of the intelligence agencies. Even in Spain I think it unlikely I would be able to do it. In France . . .' He left the sentence unfinished.

'Okay, Juan. Thanks anyway. Onwards and upwards, yeah?'

'There is one other thing, *amigo*. Just so there is no misunderstanding down the line. Sharkey is paying me a quarter of a million dollars not to hurt his accomplice. The man we picked up in Paris.'

'I have no problem with that, Juan.'

'It is always a pleasure doing business with you, *amigo*.'

Donovan cut the connection.

'Who was it?' asked Robbie, flicking through the channels on the TV.

'None of your business,' said Donovan. 'And get your feet off Louise's coffee table. Haven't you got homework to do?'

'Tomorrow's Saturday,' said Robbie. 'I've got the whole weekend.'

After dinner, Robbie gathered up their plates and took them into the kitchenette.

'You've got him well trained,' said Louise.

'He's doing it to impress,' said Donovan.

'I'm not,' said Robbie.

'Do you want a coffee?' asked Louise. 'Or something stronger? I've got whisky. Or beer?'

Donovan looked at his watch. 'I've actually got to be somewhere. I'm sorry.'

'You're not going out?' Robbie called from the kitchenette.

'Business,' said Donovan.

'It's okay, Robbie, we can watch TV,' said Louise.

Donovan scooped up the mobiles off the sideboard and put them in the pockets of his jacket. 'You be good, yeah?' he said to Robbie.

'Do you want to borrow the car?' asked Louise.

Donovan shook his head. 'Nah, I'm going to be using taxis.'

'There's that paranoia again,' teased Louise.

'It's not that. It's just that where I'm going, it's likely to get broken into.'

Louise tossed him a door key. 'In case you get back late,' she said. 'Save you waking me up.'

Donovan thanked her and went outside in search of a black cab.

The address PM had given him was in a row of terraced houses in Harlesden. Donovan could feel the pounding beat of reggae music through the seat of the cab long before they reached the house. The driver twisted around in his seat. 'Are you sure about this?' asked the driver. 'It looks a bit ethnic out there.'

Donovan could see what the man meant. Half a dozen burly men in long black coats were standing guard at the open door to the house, four with shaved heads glistening in the amber streetlights, two with shoulder-length dreadlocks. A dozen young black men and women were waiting to be admitted, moving to the sound of the pounding beat inside. Several were openly smoking joints. It was the sort of street the police never patrolled. If they turned up at all it would be mob-handed with riot shields and mace. Parked both sides of the street were expensive BMWs and four-wheel drives, most of them brand new.

'Yeah, this is it,' said Donovan, handing the driver a twenty-pound note. 'Keep the change, yeah?'

'Thanks, guv,' said the driver. 'Good luck.'

Donovan got out of the cab and the driver drove off quickly without putting his 'For Hire' sign on.

Donovan walked to the head of the line of people

waiting to go in. He nodded at the biggest of the bouncers, who was wearing an earpiece and a small radio microphone that bobbed around close to his lips. 'I'm here to see PM,' said Donovan.

The man nodded, his face impassive. 'He expecting you. Third floor. Door with "Fuck off" on it.'

'That would be irony, would it?' asked Donovan.

'That would be the way it be,' said the man.

Donovan pushed his way through the crowded first floor and found the stairs. The air was thick with the smell of marijuana and sweat, and the music was so loud his teeth vibrated. Teenagers sitting on the stairs drinking beer from the bottle looked up at him curiously as he walked up to the second floor. The wooden stairs were stained and pockmarked with cigarette burns.

One of the second-floor bedrooms had been converted into a bar. There were tin baths filled with ice and loaded with bottled beer, and a table full of spirits and mixers. Two black guys with turtle-shell abdomens and red and white checked bandanas were passing out bottles and shoving banknotes into a metal box without handing back change. There were several white girls around, predominately thin and blonde and baring their midriffs, but no white males. Donovan was attracting a lot of attention, but there didn't seem to be any hostility, just curiosity.

One small man with waist-length dreadlocks and a vacant stare grinned at Donovan, showing a mouthful of gold teeth, and offered him a puff at his soggy-ended joint, but Donovan just shook his head.

He went up to the third floor of the building. At the top of the hallway two young blacks wearing headsets and almost identical Nike hooded tops, woollen hats, tracksuit bottoms and trainers, moved aside without speaking to

Donovan. The big man must have told them he was on his way up.

The 'Fuck Off' sign was written with black lettering on a gold background. Donovan knocked and the door opened partially. A pair of wraparound sunglasses reflected Donovan's image back at him in stereo.

'Den Donovan,' said Donovan.

The man opened the door without speaking. Donovan walked into the room. Half a dozen West Indians were sitting around the room on sofas, most of them smoking spliffs and drinking beer. Sitting behind a desk was a young black man with close-cropped hair wearing what looked like a Versace silk shirt. Around his neck hung a gold chain the thickness of a man's finger, and on his left wrist he wore a solid gold Rolex studded with diamonds.

'PM?'

The man at the desk nodded.

'Den Donovan.'

'I know who you are,' said PM. Standing behind PM was a black man well over six feet tall dressed in a black suit and grey T-shirt. He had shoulder-length dreadlocks and a goatee beard.

Donovan smiled amiably. 'Charlie and Ricky said I should swing by. Pay my respects.'

'What happened to my money, Den?'

'Your money paid for the coke, and the coke is sitting in one of The Queen's warehouses,' said Donovan. He walked over to a sofa and sat down. 'It's swings and roundabouts. A percentage of deals go wrong. You have to live with that. Build it into your price.'

'That don't answer my question.'

'If you want to know why the deal went wrong, you're asking the wrong person.'

'Someone grassed.'

'Probably.'

'And it was your deal.'

'I set it up, yes, but these things grow. More people get involved. The more people get involved, the greater the risk.'

PM slammed his hand down on to the desk. 'Fuck the risk. I want my money back.'

'We all lost on this deal, PM.'

PM reached into a drawer and pulled out a massive handgun, a black metal block with an inch-long barrel and an extra-long clip. Donovan recognised the weapon. It was a Mac-10 machine gun. Lethal at short range, but unpredictable. It was a spray-and-pray weapon. Spray the bullets around and pray you hit something. 'PM, you pull the trigger on that and there's gonna be bullets flying all around the room.'

'Yeah, but first one's gonna be in your gut.'

'You know they pull to the right, yeah? To the right and up.'

'So I'll aim left and low.'

The man with the dreadlocks took a step forward. He fixed Donovan with a cold stare. 'You got any suggestion as to how we can get our money back?' he asked. The fact that he was the only one other than PM to open his mouth meant he was probably the one called Bunny, PM's adviser.

'You have to write it off. You can put that thing against my head and threaten to blow my brains out all you want, but I don't have your money. We're all in the same boat: you, me, Ricky, Charlie, the Colombians who supplied the stuff.'

'When things go wrong, there's always someone at fault.'

'Agreed, but I didn't fuck up. Neither did Charlie and Ricky. The Colombians are experts. It was either bad luck or someone new to the equation.'

'You pointing the finger at us?' asked Bunny.

'There's no point in trying to apportion blame,' said Donovan. 'We have to move on.'

'And how do we do that?' asked Bunny.

PM seemed to relax a little. He put the gun back in the drawer, then leaned back and swung his feet up on the desk. He clicked his fingers at one of his men and the man fetched him a bottle of beer.

'I can cut you in on another deal. Heroin.'

'Price?'

'Ten thousand a key.'

PM drank his beer as Bunny rattled off quickfire questions.

'Source?'

'Afghan. Pure.'

'Delivered where?'

'UK. South of England.'

'Specifically.'

'An airfield.'

'You're flying it in?'

'That's the idea.'

Bunny leaned forward and whispered into PM's ear. PM nodded as he listened but kept his eyes fixed stonily on Donovan's face.

'How much?' asked PM, when Bunny had finished whispering.

'Up to you.'

'We'll go eight a key. And we'll take two hundred.'

'Eight? I said ten.'

'Yeah, but you owe us for the coke deal. And I figure if

you're letting us in at ten, you're getting it for three or four, right?'

Donovan didn't say anything. He was paying the Russians three thousand dollars a kilo, about two thousand pounds. Even letting the Yardies in at eight grand he was still making a profit of three hundred per cent.

'I'd be cutting my throat at eight, PM. Nine.'

'Eight five.'

Donovan hesitated, then nodded. 'Eight five it is. You're sure you can move two hundred?'

PM's eyes hardened. 'You think we're smalltime, huh?'

'Two hundred is a lot, that's all.'

'We can move it.'

'That's great. I'll get Charlie to arrange the money with you.' Donovan stood up.

'One thing,' said PM coldly. 'This gets fucked up, so do you. Bad luck twice in a row ain't no bad luck. I'll be pointing more than my finger. Clear?'

'Clear, PM.'

The man with wraparound sunglasses opened the door and the pounding music billowed into the room. 'You drive here?' asked Bunny.

'Cab,' said Donovan. 'Was worried about losing the CD player.'

Bunny laughed throatily. 'I'll walk you down, fix you up with a ride.'

Donovan nodded his thanks, and Bunny followed him down the stairs and out on to the street.

'Thanks for taking the heat off me,' Donovan said to Bunny.

'The safety was on,' said Bunny.

'Yeah, I saw that.'

'Figured you did.'

They walked slowly down the road, talking in quiet voices.

'Couldn't ask everything I wanted to know without cutting across the man, but this Afghan gear, where's it coming from?' asked Bunny.

'The easy answer to that is Afghanistan, but that's not what you mean, right?'

'Ain't no way you're flying it out of Afghanistan. There's opium there, but the processing is done outside. Pakistan. Or Turkey maybe.'

'My contacts are in Turkey.'

'And you're flying it direct?'

Donovan nodded.

'That's a long flight,' said Bunny.

'I've got a big plane.'

'Two thousand miles and some.'

'Like I said, I've got a big plane. Let me ask you something. Has PM got the weight to move two hundred keys?'

'We wholesale some already. He's got dealers all over north London and contacts south that'll buy up any surplus. He can move it.'

Donovan nodded. 'Then this could be the start of a beautiful friendship.'

Bunny smiled thinly. 'We'll see about that. It's a bit premature to start enumerating any KFC ready meals. When do you tell us where we collect?'

'Day of delivery.'

'Which will be when?' asked Bunny.

'Assuming all the money is in play, within the next twenty-four hours, probably three days.'

'That quick?'

'The Turkish end is all ready to go. Charlie'll get the details to you.'

Bunny shook his head. 'No, we deal with you on this one. No discussion.'

Donovan wanted to argue, but it was clear from Bunny's tone that there was nothing he could say that would get him to change his mind.

'Okay,' said Donovan. 'You call me direct when you've got the money. It's going to be electronic transfer through SWIFT. No used notes in suitcases.'

'Not a problem. We have money in the system.'

Donovan gave him the number of one of his mobiles. 'Call this from a landline. Don't identify yourself, just give me the number but transpose the last two digits. I'll call you back from a call box.'

There was a squeal of brakes from a car in the street. Donovan whirled around. A large Mercedes had pulled up opposite them. The front passenger window was open and something was thrust through the opening. Donovan cursed. It was a gun. A big gun. He'd been so involved in the conversation with Bunny that he hadn't been aware of the car driving down the street. The gun jerked and there was a loud series of muffled bangs. Bullets thwacked into the wall of the house behind Donovan. He felt an arm across the back of his neck, pulling him down. It was Bunny.

'Down, man, get down!' Bunny yelled.

Bullets were hitting the concrete pavement all around Donovan. Now there were two guns spewing out bullets. Bunny grabbed Donovan's jacket collar and hauled him behind a black Wrangler Jeep just as its windows shattered into a thousand glass cubes.

Donovan looked up at Bunny. The West Indian was crouched over him. 'Stay down, man!' Bunny yelled.

The Jeep crashed to one side as its tyres were ripped apart by the gunfire. Puffs of dust exploded on the brick walls of the terraced houses, and glass was shattering everywhere. Bullets whizzed all around them.

Donovan looked back at the house they'd just left. Two West Indians had pulled handguns from inside their coats and were blasting away at the Mercedes. The Mercedes leaped forward and then braked again. Now the gunmen had a clear shot at Bunny and Donovan around the side of the Jeep.

'Bunny, watch out!' Donovan yelled.

Bunny whirled around just as one of the machine guns burst into life. Bullets thwacked into the front of the Jeep, shattering its headlights. Two bullets slammed into Bunny's chest and he fell back on to Donovan.

More West Indians ran out of the house brandishing guns. One of the men had a Mac-10 like PM's and he fired a burst at the Mercedes, thudding holes into its boot. The Mercedes sped off.

Donovan crawled out from under Bunny, expecting to see his chest a bloody pulp. Instead Bunny was rubbing his chest and scowling. 'Bastards,' he said.

He sat up. 'You okay?' he asked Donovan.

'Am I okay? What the fuck do you mean, am I okay?'

Donovan got to his feet and helped Bunny up. Half a dozen of Bunny's crew came running up.

'Why aren't you . . .?' asked Donovan, his whole body shaking.

'Dead?' asked Bunny. He lifted up his shirt and showed Donovan a white Kevlar bullet-proof vest. 'Pretty much compulsory in Harlesden these days,' he said. 'You should get one.'

'I don't think you'll catch me around here again,' said

Donovan. He clapped Bunny on the shoulder. 'I owe you, mate. I'm like a fucking elephant, I won't forget this.'

'We're not home free yet,' said Bunny, looking around. In the distance they could hear sirens and there were shouts from the house. Doors were opening all along the street. 'The Operation Trident boys'll be on their way. They move fast on black-on-black shootings before any witnesses disappear into the woodwork. We've got to move. Come on.'

Bunny headed down the street, away from the house. Donovan followed him. Donovan knew that Bunny was wrong about it being a black-on-black attack. As the car had been driven away, Donovan had seen a face he recognised in the back seat. Jesus Rodriguez.

Louise shuffled the playing cards and laid them out on the coffee table. She'd been playing patience for more than two hours, half concentrating on the cards, half watching the television with the sound muted.

The door to the spare bedroom opened and Robbie appeared, rubbing his eyes. 'I can't sleep,' he said.

'Do you want a drink? Cocoa or something?'

Robbie nodded and sat down on the sofa. Louise went through to the kitchenette and put a pan of milk on to boil.

'That's patience,' said Robbie, pointing at the cards.

'That's right.'

'You know you can play it on computer. It comes with Windows.'

'I know. But I haven't got a computer here.'

'Everyone's got a home computer these days,' said Robbie.

'Not me. Besides, I like the feel of the cards. It's relaxing. That's why people play patience.'

'It's boring.'

'Yeah, you're right. But it gives you something to do with your hands.'

Louise stirred cocoa powder into the hot milk, then poured the cocoa into a mug.

She gave the mug to Robbie and sat down next to him. 'Thanks,' he said. He took a sip. 'How do you know my dad?' he asked.

Louise shrugged. 'He helped me when I needed help.'

'You didn't know him when my mum was around, did you?'

Louise shook her head. 'I only met him a few days ago. When he came back from the Caribbean.' She reached over and stroked his hair. 'Why, are you worried that I might have taken him away from your mum?'

'No way!' said Robbie vehemently. 'She was the one having the affair.'

'Because I didn't meet your dad until after your mum left. Cross my heart.'

'She didn't leave,' said Robbie. 'She ran away.'

'I'm sorry.'

'It doesn't matter.' He took another sip of cocoa.

'You know your dad loves you, don't you? That's why he brought you here. So that you'd be safe.'

'He said some people were after him. Do you know who they are?'

'No. He didn't tell me. He just said he needed somewhere for you to stay.'

'He never says anything about what he does. It's like it's all some big secret.'

Louise gathered up the cards and shuffled them slowly. 'You're lucky to have a dad,' she said.

'It's not luck. It's biology.'

'I mean to have a father who's around. My dad died when I was a kid. Younger than you.'

Robbie put his mug on to the coffee table and wiped his mouth. 'So your mum took care of you, did she?'

'Sort of. For a while. Then she married again.' Louise shuddered at the memory of her stepfather. 'That's why I left home.'

'Your stepfather didn't like you?'

'Oh, he liked me all right. He liked me too much. Couldn't keep his bloody hands off me.'

Robbie looked away, embarrassed.

Louise reached over and put a hand on his leg. 'I'm sorry, Robbie. Bad memories.' She forced a smile. 'Do you want to play cards? Until you feel sleepy?'

'Okay. What do you want to play?'

'Guest's choice.'

'Blackjack.'

Louise frowned. 'You're sure?'

'Yeah,' said Robbie eagerly. 'Can we play for money?'

Louise looked at him through narrowed eyes. 'Am I being hustled here?'

'Do you want a beer?' asked Bunny, opening the door to a small fridge.

'Yeah, cheers,' said Donovan.

The two men were in a room five minutes' walk away from the shooting, above a minicab office. They'd hurried through the office with Bunny nodding a greeting to two big Jamaicans who'd been sitting on a plastic sofa and a West Indian in a Rasta hat who was talking nineteen-to-the-dozen into a microphone. Bunny had taken Donovan up a flight of stairs and through a door on which had been tacked a sign saying 'Management Only'.

Bunny tossed Donovan a can of lager and sat down behind a cheap teak veneer desk. 'We'll hang out here for a while, till things quieten down. Just in case someone gives your description to Five-O.'

'I thought we all looked the same.'

Bunny flashed Donovan a tight smile and popped the tab on his can of beer.

Donovan looked around the room. There was worn lino on the floor and a bare minimum of furniture. The desk, two chairs, and a filing cabinet. Sheets of hardboard had been nailed over the window and the only light came from a single naked bulb in the centre of the ceiling. 'Nice place you've got here,' he said.

'It serves its purpose.'

'The taxi firm is yours?'

'None of it's mine, PM's the top man.'

'Yeah, right,' said Donovan. He took a long gulp of beer. 'You use the taxi business to clean your cash?'

'Some. But it makes money, too. Try getting a black cab in London any time after nine. Especially if you want to come out this way. We can pretty much charge what we want. We even pay tax.'

Bunny leaned back in his chair and unbuttoned his shirt. He examined his Kevlar vest.

'You were lucky,' said Donovan. 'The way they were spraying bullets, you could have got hit in the head.'

'Firing from a car, they'd be lucky to hit anything. They've been watching too many movies.'

Donovan took another drink from his can. 'How long have you been with PM?' he asked.

'Three years, thereabouts.'

'Not thought about setting up on your own? Or joining a bigger operation?'

'Why? You recruiting?'

'You've got your head screwed on, seems you'd make more working for yourself than helping PM up the slippery pole.'

Bunny shrugged. 'I do okay.'

'You're holding his hand,' said Donovan.

'Don't let him hear you say that, he's young but he's hard.'

Donovan raised his can in salute. 'No offence, Bunny,' he said. 'I was just making an observation.'

'I'm happy with the way things are, Den. But if you were to make me an offer . . .' Bunny left the sentence hanging.

'You'd be an asset, that's for sure. I've not met many who throw themselves in front of a bullet for me.'

'That's not the way it went down, and you know it,' laughed Bunny. 'I practically fell on top of you.'

'Whatever,' said Donovan. 'The simple fact is that if it wasn't for you and that vest, I'd be lying on the street in a pool of blood. Seriously, Bunny, if I was going to be in this for the long haul I'd make you an offer, but after this Turkish deal, I'm out of the game.'

'For good?'

Donovan grinned. 'For as long as the money holds out. And that'll be for a long, long time. I've got a boy needs looking after. Robbie. Nine years old.'

'Your son?'

Donovan nodded. 'His mum's done a runner so I'm going to be a single parent. For a while at least. You got kids, Bunny?'

Bunny shook his head.

'Married?'

Another shake of the head. Donovan kicked himself

mentally. Underwood had said that Bunny was gay. He'd clean forgotten but Bunny was a big man, well muscled and hard faced, and there wasn't the slightest thing about him that was in the least bit effeminate. 'Yeah, well considering how unlucky I've been in the marital stakes, you're probably well out of it,' said Donovan. He sipped his beer. 'What about the drugs game, Bunny? You see a future in it for you?'

'Long term, the only future's prison, right? You've got to quit while you're ahead. Make your stash, get it in legit businesses, then leave the dirty stuff behind. It's always been that way. Half the land in this country is owned by the descendants of robber barons of the Middle Ages. In a hundred years' time, drugs money will have become old money and no one will remember where it came from. Take your son. Nine, you said? You'll put him in a good school, a top university, then you'll have enough money to set him up in whatever he wants to do. His children will be another step removed, and eventually it'll all be clean and no one will care.'

'So long as we don't get caught.'

Bunny grinned and raised his can of beer. 'Here's to not getting caught!'

Donovan grinned. He leaned over and clinked his can against Bunny's.

Donovan stayed in the office with Bunny for the best part of an hour, then Bunny arranged for a minicab to run Donovan home. Donovan decided to go to his house in Kensington rather than disturbing Louise. He had the cab drop him half a mile from the house and he went in through the communal gardens and the back door.

He showered and had a whisky, and then put his

mobiles on charge on the bedside table before diving under the quilt. He was asleep within minutes.

When Donovan woke up it was light and a pop song was playing. He rolled over and groped for whichever mobile was ringing, cursing his son. He'd told Robbie several times not to mess with the phones. They were too important to be played with.

As he picked up the phone that was ringing, he realised that it was his son's. Robbie must have put his phone on the sideboard in Louise's flat next to Donovan's and he'd picked it up by mistake. Whoever was calling had blocked their ID. Donovan pressed the green button and held the phone to his ear.

For several seconds there was silence, then a voice. 'Robbie?' It was Vicky. 'Robbie?' She sounded close to tears. 'Robbie, talk to me.'

Donovan wanted to cut the connection, but he couldn't bring himself to press the red button. He sat up in bed and looked at the clock on the bedside table. It was seven o'clock in the morning.

Vicky sobbed. 'Oh Robbie, I'm so sorry.'

'He's asleep,' said Donovan.

'Den. Oh God.'

'What do you want, Vicky?'

'I want to talk to Robbie.'

'Like I said, he's in bed.' Donovan didn't want to tell her that Robbie wasn't sleeping at the house. And he certainly didn't want to tell her about Louise.

There was a long silence, broken only by Vicky's sniffling. 'I'm sorry, Den,' she said eventually.

'Not sorry enough,' he said. 'Not yet.'

'Please don't be like that, Den.'

‘After what you did? I think I’ve earned the right to be any way I want.’

‘I didn’t mean it to be this way, Den. I was lonely. You left me on my own too long.’

‘I was making a living. I was paying for your bloody house, your car, your holidays, your shopping trips. You never had to work a day in your life, Vicky. Not one fucking day. And I paid for that.’

‘So you own me, is that it? You paid for the clothes on my back, so I have to be the quiet little wifey sitting at home, grateful for your odd appearance?’

‘We talked about it. You knew my situation. I was Tango One. Most wanted.’

‘Well, at least you were number one at something, because you were a lousy husband and a lousy father.’

‘Fuck you,’ said Donovan. He pressed the red button but instantly regretted it. He stared at the phone’s readout, hoping that she’d call back, but she didn’t.

He began idly to flick through the phone’s menu. He flicked through the message section. Robbie had a stack of saved messages. Donovan grinned as he read them. Probably girlfriends. Idle chit-chat. Childish jibes at teachers. Stupid jokes. Then Donovan froze. ‘I’M BACK. COME HOME NOW – DAD.’ The message had been sent when Donovan had been on the beach in St Kitts, talking to Carlos Rodriguez. That was why Robbie had gone rushing home from school and found Vicky in bed with Sharkey.

The message had been sent from a UK mobile. Donovan didn’t recognise the number, but there was something familiar about it. He tapped out the number and put the receiver to his ear. The phone was switched off and there was no answering service.

Donovan looked at the digits on the phone's readout, deep creases across his brow. Where had he seen that number before? He rolled out of bed and pulled his wallet out of his trouser pocket. He flipped it open. The Tesco receipt was sticking out of one of the credit card slots. He slowly slid it out and looked at the telephone number he'd written on it. The number that the Spaniard had given him. The numbers matched. Donovan cursed. It had been Stewart Sharkey who'd sent the text message to Robbie. He'd wanted to be caught in bed with Vicky. It had all been planned.

Another phone rang. The landline. Donovan went over and looked at the eavesdropping detector. The green light was on. No one was listening in on the line. Maybe it was Vicky, calling back on the house phone. He picked up the receiver.

'We have to meet,' said a voice. A man. English.

'Who is this?' asked Donovan.

'I know what you're doing and I need to talk to you,' said the voice.

'Yeah, right. How old do you think I am? Twelve?'

'It's about Stewart Sharkey.'

'What about him?'

'What do you think? Do you want your money back, or not?'

Donovan hesitated for a few seconds, then sighed. 'Where?'

'Camden Market. In four hours.'

'You've got to be joking.' Camden Market on a Saturday morning had to be one of the most crowded places on the planet.

'Safety in numbers,' said the man. 'You know you are being watched? A bedroom across the street. And a British

Telecom van. I wouldn't want you bringing any strangers to the party.'

'I'll make sure I'm clean,' said Donovan. 'How will I find you?'

'I'll find you,' said the man. The line went dead.

Donovan caught a black cab to Oxford Street and spent fifteen minutes in the Virgin Megastore looking for tails. The record store's clientele was mainly young and scruffy, so police and Customs agents would find it harder to blend. He spotted two definites and a possible.

He left the store, dived into another black cab and had it drive him to Maida Vale and drop him on the south side of the Regent's Canal opposite the Paddington Stop, the place where he'd watched for the arrival of Macfadyen and Jordan. He paid off the driver and dashed across the footbridge and ran along Blomfield Road to Jason's, a restaurant with a sideline running narrowboat trips along the canal. The route terminated at Camden Market. Donovan had timed it so that he arrived just as a boat was preparing to leave.

He bought a ticket and climbed aboard. There were almost twenty passengers on the boat, mainly tourists. It was a pretty trip, cruising by the vast mansions of Little Venice and through Regent's Park, but Donovan was barely aware of the passing scenery. His mind was racing, trying to work out who had called him. It wasn't the Colombians, that was certain. They wouldn't want him in a crowded place like Camden Market. Ideally they'd want him alone and tied to a chair. Why the market? Safety in numbers, the man had said. But safety for whom? For Donovan? Or for the caller? He adjusted the Velcro collar under his wristwatch. The personal RF detector was already switched on.

They arrived at Camden and the grey-haired boatman jumped out and secured the narrowboat, then announced that they'd be returning in forty-five minutes and that passengers should be back by then if they intended returning to Little Venice.

Donovan walked through the market. It was packed with tourists and teenagers in shabby clothing. There were shops and stalls everywhere selling New Age rubbish, handmade pottery, secondhand clothes, incense, posters, CDs, T-shirts with smart-arse slogans. Donovan couldn't see a single thing he'd ever want to buy, but figured that Robbie would probably have had a great time. Donovan scanned the faces around him. It would be impossible to spot a tail. There were just too many people milling around, and at times he was shoulder to shoulder with shoppers. It was crazy, thought Donovan. It was the last place in the world he'd choose for a meeting.

Suddenly there was a man standing in front of him. A face that Donovan recognised. A short man with thinning, sandy hair and a cocksure smile on his face. 'Long time, no see, Donovan,' said the man.

'Gregg Hathaway,' said Donovan, shaking his head. 'Can't say this is a pleasant surprise.'

The two men stood with their feet shoulder-width apart, like boxers eyeing each other up at the weigh-in. People were having to flow around them like a river parting around rocks.

Donovan moved his left hand forward, closer to Hathaway, but the detector on his belt stayed resolutely quiet. Hathaway's own left hand also moved and Donovan glanced down. He saw a thin strip of Velcro under the man's watchband and smiled.

'State of the art,' said Hathaway, smiling too. 'The difference is, the taxpayer paid for mine.'

'Still with Customs, then?' asked Donovan. He edged a little closer to Hathaway and moved his hand again. No reaction from the bleeper. If Hathaway hadn't come wired, then what did he want? A chat about old times? They really were old times, because it had been more than ten years since Donovan had seen him.

Hathaway patted his right knee. 'Not much of a future for me in Customs and Excise after you put a bullet in my leg.'

'Sorry to hear that,' said Donovan. He looked around. Was he about to be arrested, was that it? Had Hathaway brought him to Camden Market so that he could be grabbed in the crowd? There was certainly no way that Donovan could run, there were just too many people.

'I'm here on my own, Donovan,' said Hathaway. He was wearing a dark blue duffel coat with the hood up, brown trousers and brown, scuffed Timberland boots. He looked like a trainspotter, thought Donovan, and he blended perfectly into the crowds around him.

'What's this about?'

'Let's walk.'

Hathaway turned to his right and started walking towards the canal. Donovan went with him, trying to keep close to the man's side, but it was difficult with there being so many people. Donovan's detector vibrated and he jerked. He looked around. Hathaway was also looking left and right, a frown on his face. They both saw the man at the same time. Long hair, sallow complexion, tattered jeans and a camouflage combat jacket covered in badges. Donovan smiled and so did Hathaway as the same thought went through their minds. An undercover drugs officer. As easy to spot as a nun in a brothel. As the man walked away from them, their bleepers stopped vibrating.

Hathaway led Donovan through a shop-lined courtyard to a small coffee shop with several outside tables. Two American tourists were just leaving and Donovan and Hathaway grabbed their table. Hathaway ordered two coffees from a young waitress who had half her head shaved.

All the other tables were occupied, so when Hathaway spoke it was in little more than a whisper. 'You've done well over the years,' he said.

Donovan shrugged. He knew Hathaway wasn't bugged, but that didn't mean he was going to say anything that was even remotely incriminating. Donovan was there to listen, to find out what Hathaway wanted. He continued to scan the crowds for familiar body shapes and clothing, but he knew that it would be impossible to spot any watchers. There were just too many people.

'Relax, I came alone, Donovan,' said Hathaway. 'I've as much to lose being seen talking with you as you have.'

'I'm just soaking up the atmosphere, Gregg,' said Donovan. 'Who are you with, then, if it's not Customs?'

'A different bunch,' said Hathaway. 'People who don't mind so much that I can't run the hundred metres in twelve seconds any more.'

'What do you want, an apology? You should be grateful, mate. I've done a lot worse.'

'Oh, I know you have, Donovan. In some ways I got off lightly. I mean sure, I lost my job and my wife, but at least you didn't tie me to a chair and cut me to bits while you videotaped it.'

Their coffees arrived and the two men sat in silence until the waitress moved away again.

'You've never cared about the rights and wrongs of drugs, have you?' asked Hathaway, keeping his voice low.

'You said you had information about Sharkey. Or was that just to get me here?'

Hathaway sipped his coffee. He grimaced. 'This taste like real coffee to you? Tastes instant to me.'

'Coffee's coffee,' said Donovan.

'I'm interested in your thought processes, that's all. It's not that you don't have a sense of right and wrong, is it? You know the difference. You just don't care. Am I right?'

Donovan leaned across the table towards Hathaway. 'Does anyone really care?' he whispered. 'I mean, really care. And at the end of the day, does it really matter?'

Hathaway met Donovan's stare and shrugged. 'I don't know. I think that's the question I'm asking myself.'

'My mum was a good person,' said Donovan. 'Really good. Do anything for anybody. My father walked out on her when I was six. Just didn't come back from work one day. He was last seen at the bus station and that was it. Did she deserve it? Did she fuck. Few years later she met up with man number two, a right piece of work. Friday night recreation for him was getting pissed in the pub and then knocking her around. She never fought back, never shouted, just suffered in silence. You'd think he'd have mellowed, but it just made him worse. So did what goes around come around? Of course it didn't. She got cancer and died a horrible death. I still remember her screaming. He pissed off, and me and my sister were put in care. Do I know what's right and what's wrong? Damn right I do. Do I care?' Donovan smiled thinly and shook his head. 'So what do you want, Gregg?'

'The morality of selling drugs isn't a problem for you, is it? That's rhetorical. No need for you to answer.'

'I know what rhetorical means, you patronising cripple.'

Hathaway looked genuinely hurt. 'There's no need to be offensive, Donovan,' he said. 'I didn't mean to be patronising.'

'Fine, then I didn't mean to be offensive. Can we get on with whatever it is you want?'

'I guess my point is that the whole moral status of what we both do is a very grey area. Always has been. Tobacco and alcohol kill millions more than drugs, but they're controlled by public companies so they're okay. Legitimate. You take the cocoa plant and make chocolate. That's legal. Extract cocaine and it's illegal. You take a naturally growing plant, dry the leaves, wrap them up in paper and sell them to millions. Legal. Take another plant, extract the sap, process it into something you can smoke, heroin, and that's illegal. No morality, just the powers that be making decisions about what people can and cannot do. But you understand that better than me, don't you?'

'About drugs?'

'About morality. You know none of it really matters, right? It's just a game. Someone else sets the rules, we choose which side we want to be on, and we play the game. I chase you. You try to get away. Cops and robbers. Cowboys and Indians. And at the end of the day there's never going to be a winner. The game just goes on, right?'

Donovan shrugged. 'Maybe,' he said. He couldn't see where the conversation was going. He wanted to scream at Hathaway, to grab the man by the throat and shake him until he told him what it was he wanted.

'See, it doesn't really matter which side you're on, does it? You choose your side then you play the game. It's like when we were kids. Didn't really matter if you were a cop or a robber. A cowboy or an Indian.'

'I'm going,' said Donovan. He started to get to his feet, but Hathaway held up his hand. 'I'm almost done,' he said.

Donovan sat down again.

'I want you to understand what it is you taught me when you put that bullet in my leg all those years ago. You taught me that it doesn't matter which side you're on, all that matters is how you play the game. And for that, I want to shake your hand.'

Hathaway reached out his right hand. Donovan looked down at it, frowning. The fingernails were bitten to the quick. He slowly put out his own hand and shook. As their hands made contact he felt something hard in Hathaway's palm. Donovan realised it was a folded piece of paper. He tried to pull his hand away but Hathaway tightened his grip like a vice.

'You're trying to set me up,' hissed Donovan. That's what this had all been about. Hathaway was planting drugs on him. Donovan looked around frantically, expecting to see police closing in on him.

'Don't be stupid, Donovan,' soothed Hathaway. 'Why would I plant a two-quid wrap on you? You deal in thousands of kilos. It's going to be all or nothing.' He slowly shook Donovan's hand, then eased his grip. Donovan felt the paper pressing against his own palm. 'Take it,' said Hathaway.

Donovan pulled his hand away. He opened the piece of paper. There was a typewritten address on it in capital letters. An address in the South of France.

'Sharkey's there,' said Hathaway softly.

'How do you know that?'

'Tracked his phone. Easy peasy when you work for the good guys. I know you have your ways, but our ways are more efficient. Unlimited resources, so long as you have access. And I've got access.'

'And what do you want? A drink?'

Hathaway looked scornfully at Donovan. 'How much would you give me? A few grand. This isn't about a few grand. Besides, you seem to have forgotten that you're pretty much broke at the moment.'

'If it's not about a bung, then what is it about?' asked Donovan.

Hathaway grinned and tapped the side of his nose. 'Need to know, Donovan. All in good time. At the moment, just don't look this gift horse in the mouth. You go and get your money, then we'll talk again.'

Donovan looked at the address again. 'Is she still with him?' he asked.

'I gather so.' Hathaway stood up, grunting as he put his weight on his right leg.

'Bitch.'

'You've got to learn to live and let live,' said Hathaway, rubbing his right knee.

Donovan slipped the piece of paper into his pocket.

'Maybe next time we should meet at the National,' said Hathaway.

Donovan stiffened. He knew about his meeting with Louise?

Hathaway smiled at his discomfort. 'Word to the wise,' he said. 'You might be able to shake off the cops by whizzing around the Underground, but all we do is sit and watch you via a link to the Transport Police's CCTV control room. We don't need to put people down after you. We just watch you on TV and wait for you to surface.' He threw Donovan a sloppy salute. 'Catch you later, yeah?' Hathaway turned and walked away, dragging his right leg slightly. He edged into the shopping crowds and within seconds Donovan had lost sight of him.

Stewart Sharkey pulled the wide brim of his hat low over his eyes and waved at the waiter. He ordered an omelette and a café latte and a bottle of good wine in fluent French, then settled back and scanned the front page of *Le Monde*. He'd have preferred to have read one of the British tabloids, but it was important to maintain his cover. So far as anyone knew, he was French, a Parisian businessman taking a well-earned break from the heat of the capital. When he and Vicky were out, she had to keep her mouth shut, because even if she tried to speak French it was glaringly obvious that she was English. Meals outside the apartment were taken in silence unless there was no one within earshot, and even then conversation was limited to snatched whisperings. Frankly, Sharkey preferred to dine alone.

There was little in the newspaper about what was happening back in the UK. Like the English, the French were extremely parochial about their news. He turned to the sports pages. At least the French appreciated English soccer.

Sharkey heard chair legs scrape against the flagstones and he lowered his paper. A man in his thirties grunted and lowered himself into a chair at the table next to Sharkey's. The man ordered a coffee and lit a small cigar. Sharkey went back to reading the paper.

'Checking the currency rates?' said a voice. Sharkey lowered his paper again. The man at the next table tapped ash into a glass ashtray and nodded at the paper. 'Seeing how many francs you get to the pound.' The man spoke English, but with an accent, and not French.

Sharkey formed his face into a pained frown, trying to make it clear that he wasn't looking for a conversation. 'I'm sorry, I don't speak English,' he said in his perfect French.

'The pound. Is it better to hold the pound, do you think, or dollars?'

'I'm sorry, I have no interest in the currency markets,' said Sharkey in French, raising the paper and flicking it to make a cracking sound.

The man leaned forward and blew smoke over the top of the newspaper. 'Are you sure about that, Mr Sharkey? I would have thought that with sixty million stolen dollars, you'd be very interested.'

There was another scraping sound behind Sharkey and he looked over his shoulder. Two men sat down at the table behind him. Big men with dark brown skins and thick moustaches, black sunglasses and flashy gold rings on their fingers. The black lenses of their sunglasses stared back at him impassively.

'Yes, they are with me, Mr Sharkey.'

Sharkey put down his paper. 'Who are you?' He glanced left and right, praying silently that there would be a gendarme close by. Officially, he had done nothing wrong and he had nothing to fear from the authorities.

'You don't know me, Mr Sharkey. And please don't bother looking around for help.' He reached into his pocket and brought out a small Taser stun gun. 'You know what this is, Mr Sharkey?'

Sharkey nodded. It generated a high-voltage pulse that could disable a man in seconds, producing the equivalent of a massive heart attack or epileptic fit.

'There are two ways we can handle this,' the man continued, an amiable smile on his face. 'I can press this against your neck and give you twenty thousand volts. You go down, I announce that I am a doctor and my two friends behind you offer to transport you to hospital in their very roomy Mercedes Benz. You wake up in about ten minutes with a very bad headache.'

Sharkey sighed. 'And the alternative?'

'I pay your bill and mine. We smile and walk to the car together.' The man caressed the stun gun with his thumb. 'Which is it to be, Mr Sharkey?'

'Whatever he is paying you, I will pay you ten times as much.'

The man shook his head. 'Please do not embarrass yourself, Mr Sharkey. We are all professionals here.'

Sharkey closed his eyes. He could feel tears welling up and he blinked them away. He had come so close, so damn close. He pushed back his chair and stood up. He felt almost light headed and he knew that it was the endorphins kicking in, the body's protective mechanism swamping his system with chemicals. It was all over. Den Donovan had won and he had lost.

He forced himself to smile. 'Okay,' he said. 'Let's go.'

Vicky turned around in the shower, letting the water play over her face. She twisted the temperature control and gasped as the water turned icy cold. She ran her hands over her face, pulling back her hair. Sharkey kept telling her she'd have to dye it, but she didn't want to, she enjoyed being blonde. She'd agreed to cut her hair shorter and to wear a hat and dark glasses whenever she stepped outside, but that was as far as she was prepared to go.

As she turned off the shower she heard the door to the apartment open and close. 'Stewart? Is that you?' she called, then shook her head in annoyance. Of course it was him. Who else would be letting themselves in with a key? She wrapped a towel around herself and checked her reflection in the mirror. There were dark patches under her eyes and her skin was dry and flaking. She needed a morning in a spa, being worked on by experts. A massage, a long soak, then a facial and a skin-toning session. A seaweed wrap, maybe. She needed pampering, but Sharkey was practically keeping her a prisoner in the apartment. Damn him. Damn him and damn Den Donovan. They were as bad as each other. They chased, they wooed, they pursued, then when Vicky finally opened up her heart to them, they walked all over her. Treated her like a possession, something to be owned and put on show. Vicky smiled sadly at her reflection. Except that Sharkey wasn't even able to put her on show. She was like a bird in a cage, available for him and him alone. A secret possession.

She heard him walking into the bedroom. 'Did you forget something?' she called.

She opened the bathroom door, then jumped as she saw the man standing there, his arm outstretched to grab hold of the handle. Her mouth fell open and she took a deep breath, ready to scream, but before a sound left her throat a second man stepped from the side of the door and clamped a cloth over her mouth. Her nostrils were filled with a sickly-sweet odour and then the room started to swim. She felt the strength drain from her legs and everything went black.

Louise cooked lasagne and opened a bottle of red wine. Donovan sat down at the dining table as she heaped the pasta on to three plates. 'Robbie, there's salad in the fridge. Can you get it for me?'

'Sure,' said Robbie, dashing off to the kitchen.

'He's a good kid,' said Louise.

'He likes you,' said Donovan, pouring wine into their glasses.

'It's mutual.' Louise sat down next to him. She picked up her glass and clinked it against his. 'It's nice having you both here.'

Robbie returned with a glass bowl filled with salad and put it on the table.

One of Donovan's phones started ringing. He pressed the green button. It was the Spaniard. 'Hang on, Juan, let me get some privacy,' said Donovan, standing up. 'It's a madhouse here.'

'Well, thank you very much,' said Louise.

Donovan grinned. 'I need to speak to this guy, sorry. I'll go outside.'

Donovan left the apartment and hurried downstairs and out of the front door. He spoke to the Spaniard again as he walked along the side of the house to the garden. 'Yeah, sorry about that, Juan. How did it go?'

'Your money is back in your account,' said the Spaniard.

Donovan pumped the air with his fist. 'Juan, you are a fucking star!'

'Yes, I know.'

'You took your fee out first, right?'

'Of course I did, *amigo*. And my expenses.'

'Whatever it cost, you are worth it, you dago bastard.'

'I couldn't have done it without knowing where he was,' said the Spaniard.

'A little bird told me,' said Donovan. 'I can't say any more than that.'

'Your little bird is very well informed,' said the Spaniard. 'I myself could do with a little bird like that.'

'How was Sharkey?'

'Co-operative. Eventually. It took several toes and three of his fingers, but he told us everything.'

'Still alive?'

'Just.'

'Make sure he's never found, Juan.'

'Thy will be done. And your wife, *amigo*, what about your wife?'

Donovan walked to the far end of the garden. A couple of sparrows were squabbling over a bread crust that had been placed on a wooden bird table.

'*Amigo*? Your wife?'

Donovan closed his eyes. 'Have you hurt her?'

'Not yet. We have her restrained, but we haven't harmed her. I wanted to talk to you first. She is very afraid, *amigo*. If you wanted her to learn a lesson, I feel she has learned it.'

'Did she see what you did to Sharkey?'

'No, but she was in the other room. She heard everything.'

'Let me speak to her.'

The phone went quiet. Donovan heard rustlings and muffled voices, then Vicky was on the line. 'Den . . .' she said. 'Den, I'm sorry. Really.'

'I'm sure you are,' said Donovan coldly.

'I didn't know how much he'd taken. I swear to God, I didn't. He told me he was just taking some of it, so you'd have to talk to us. I swear.'

'He cleaned me out, Vicky. And a big chunk of the money didn't belong to me. It was promised to some Colombian guys. You've no idea what a spot you put me in.'

'I didn't mean to, Den. Honest.' She began crying again.

Donovan turned around. He looked up at the house. Robbie was at one of the windows, looking down. Robbie waved and Donovan waved back.

'Sharkey wanted me dead, Vicky. Do you understand that? He knew that I owed that money to the Colombians, and he knew what they'd do to me when they didn't get it.'

Vicky didn't say anything, she just kept sobbing into the phone.

'There's something else you don't know,' continued Donovan. 'Sharkey wanted Robbie to find you in bed with him.'

'No . . .' sobbed Vicky.

'It's true, Vicky. He sent him a text message. Pretended it was from me. He wanted to be caught. He wanted you to have to run away with him. He used you, Vicky. From day one.'

'No . . .'

Robbie was still looking out of the window at Donovan. Donovan turned so that his back was to the house. 'From day one. He didn't love you, he didn't want you. He just wanted my money. And once he had that and I was out of the way, he was going to dump you.'

'What are you going to do, Den? What are you going to do to me?'

'What do you think I should do, Vicky? After what you did to me, what do you think I should do?'

'I don't know,' she sobbed. 'I'm sorry, Den. I swear to God, I'm so sorry. Please don't tell Robbie.'

'Robbie already knows, remember?'

'About the money. I meant, about the money. And about this. Just tell him I went away.'

'Vicky . . .'

'I'm sorry . . .' she said, then all Donovan could hear were sobs.

'Look, Vicky, don't cry. Okay? Just stop crying.'

'I do love you. And I love Robbie.'

'Vicky, stop. Please. Nothing's going to happen to you. I promise.'

Vicky sniffed. 'What do you mean?'

'The men there. They won't hurt you. I promise.'

'You're going to let me go?'

Donovan hesitated, wondering if he were doing the right thing. 'Yes,' he said eventually.

'Oh, thank you, Den. Thank you, thank you, thank you. I'll never hurt you again, I promise. I'll never let you down again.'

Donovan took a deep breath. 'You're not going to get the chance, Vicky. You're not to come near me again. Not within twenty miles. I'm not going to stop you coming back to England, because that's where your family are, but you don't come near me. Or Robbie.'

'Den . . . please.'

'I mean it, Vicky.'

'But Robbie's my son. You're my family.'

'The time for thinking about that was before you let him catch you in bed with Sharkey. We're not your family any more. Robbie and I are family. You walked out on us.'

'Den, this isn't fair.'

'Don't go there, Vicky. You're well behind in the fairness stakes. But I will let you see Robbie. On his birthday. On your birthday. Christmas. I'll even throw in Mother's Day. When he's twelve he can decide how much time he spends with you. Do you understand?'

'Okay,' she said, and sniffed again. 'Okay. If that's how it has to be.'

'One other thing. You drop the injunction. Talk to your lawyer. I think he's going to be quite happy to lose you as a client after what he's been through. You give up all rights to Robbie. Go back on that and the men there will come looking for you again. They can bury you next to Sharkey. Are we clear on that?'

'Yes. I'll do what you say. And Den . . .'

'Yeah?'

'I really am sorry.'

'Put the Spaniard back on.'

There were more muffled voices and then Rojas was on the line. 'Are you okay, *amigo*?'

'I'm fine, Juan.' He took a deep breath. 'Let her go, yeah? Hold her until you've disposed of Sharkey, then let her go.'

'That's a good decision, *amigo*.'

'I hope so.'

Donovan cut the connection and put the phone back in his pocket and went back into the house.

Louise and Robbie looked up as he walked back into the flat.

'Is something wrong, Dad?' asked Robbie.

'Nah, everything's fine,' said Donovan, 'but I'm going to have to go out for a while.' He nodded at Louise. 'Can I borrow your car?'

'Sure,' said Louise. She stood up and picked up the keys from the sideboard. 'Can I help?'

'I've just got to do something.'

'Be careful, yeah?'

Donovan laughed. 'Honest, it's nothing. I have to do something online, that's all.'

Louise kissed him on the cheek. Donovan winked at Robbie over her shoulder. 'Look after her, okay?'

'Are you coming home tonight?' asked Robbie.

'I hope so.'

Donovan went downstairs and climbed into Louise's Audi. He used one of the mobiles to call Fullerton. 'Jamie? I need a favour. You've got a computer, yeah?'

'Sure, Den. Come around. We need to talk anyway.'

Fullerton gave Donovan the address of his flat. Donovan drove to Docklands and parked the Audi on a meter.

Fullerton met him at the lift. 'Thought you had a computer at your place,' said Fullerton.

'I'm under surveillance, there's a chance they've tapped the phone line. Plus they've got gear these days that can read what's on a screen from outside the house.'

'Bollocks,' said Fullerton.

'Nah, it's true. My security guy was telling me about it.' Fullerton led Donovan to his computer. It was already switched on and connected to the internet.

'It's based on the technology that the TV detector vans use to see what channel your TV is watching. It's just been developed so that it can read whatever information is on screen. Customs have had it for at least three years.'

Donovan wasn't worried about using Fullerton's computer. Underwood had told him that the art dealer wasn't under surveillance and as always he was going to carry out all transactions via proxy servers that would leave no trail. Donovan tapped away on the keyboard. He logged on to the site of the Swiss bank into which Rojas had put the money he'd taken from Sharkey. Donovan grinned as he saw that there was just under fifty-five million dollars in the account. 'Yes!' he said.

'Good news?' asked Fullerton.

'I'm back in the black,' he said.

'Glad to hear it.'

'To the tune of fifty-five million dollars. If you've got any of that shampoo around, now might be a good time to crack open a bottle.'

Fullerton went off to the kitchen.

Donovan transferred ten million dollars to Carlos Rodriguez's account. Legally and morally he figured he didn't owe the Colombian a penny, but after the attempted hit last night, it was clear that legality and morality currently didn't form part of Rodriguez's vocabulary. When he'd finished, he defragmented the disk and then sat down on one of the sofas.

Fullerton came back with an opened bottle of Krug champagne and two glasses. He poured champagne for the two of them and they clinked glasses. 'To crime,' said Fullerton.

Donovan laughed and sipped his champagne. 'How much have you got so far, Jamie?' he asked.

'Five million, definite. Three from dealers, two from guys in the City who'll want the gear selling on.'

'That's not a problem. You've got the cash in your account, yeah?'

Fullerton nodded. 'Offshore. It's well clean.'

Donovan picked up a pen and started writing numbers down on a notepad. Five million pounds from Fullerton. O'Brien in Dublin was in for five hundred kilos at twelve grand a kilo. He'd already sent six million pounds through to Donovan's account. Five million pounds had already come from Macfadyen and Jordan, and PM had sent through the one million seven hundred thousand pounds for his two hundred kilos. That made a total of just under eighteen million pounds. Almost twenty-six million dollars. More than enough.

'We're home and dry, Jamie,' he said. 'We're over

budget. Even without what I've got in my account. It's a done deal.'

They clinked glasses again.

'How much have we got?'

'Twenty-six million US. Bit less maybe. Depends on the exchange rate.'

'And for that we get how much?'

Donovan tapped his nose. 'That's for me to know.'

'Oh come on, Den. If you can't trust me by now . . .'

'It's a lot, Jamie.'

Fullerton dropped down on to a sofa and put his feet up on a coffee table. 'Bastard!' he said, only half joking.

Donovan took a long drink of champagne, then put his glass down by the keyboard. 'Okay, don't fucking sulk,' he said. 'My guys are bringing in eight thousand kilos. For the money we've taken in, we've got to hand over about two thousand. That means profit for me is . . .'

'Six thousand kilos of high-grade Afghan heroin. Street value six hundred million pounds!'

'Nah, it's not as simple as that, Jamie. I'm not gonna be standing on street corners selling wraps. That's the only way you get a hundred grand a kilo. I'll have to sell it wholesale, and even if I could get top whack I wouldn't get more than twenty grand a kilo.'

'That's still a hundred and twenty million pounds, Den. Fuck me.'

Donovan smiled at Fullerton's enthusiasm. 'If I were bringing in a few hundred kilos I could get twenty, but this consignment is just too big. I can hardly keep it in my loft and sell it bit by bit. I'm gonna have to sell it off to someone with a distribution network, and in the UK that means the Turks. The Turks buy their raw material at about the price I'm paying. Their expenses are that much higher than mine because they bring it overland, but that still works out at about eight thousand pounds a kilo by the time they get it into the UK. They're not going to pay me more than that. Probably a fair bit less. If I'm lucky I'll get six grand a kilo.'

'Six grand a kilo, six thousand kilos, that's still thirty-six million quid.' Fullerton raised his glass to Donovan. 'I salute you, Den.'

Donovan picked up his own glass and toasted Fullerton. 'Back at you, Jamie. And a chunk of that money is for you. Couldn't have done it without you.'

'Nah,' said Fullerton. 'You could have funded it yourself.'

'Wasn't sure I'd be getting that money back, Jamie. That's an added bonus.'

'Fifty-five million dollars is one hell of a bonus, Den.'

The two men sipped their champagne.

'These guys who are bringing the gear in. You've used them before?'

Donovan shook his head. 'No, this is the first run. They're good guys, though. Russians.' Fullerton got up and refilled Donovan's glass. 'They were flying for the army in Afghanistan,' Donovan continued. 'Huge transporter planes, almost as big as jumbos. Ilyushins, they're called. The Russians used them to fly troops and cargo, up to forty thousand kilograms. Jamie, these things can carry battle tanks.'

'So you're using the Russian army to fly drugs halfway around the world?'

'Nah, they left the army a few years back. They were working in Afghanistan when the Soviet empire fell apart. The Russians stopped paying their soldiers, and after six months with no salary they just took the planes. Flew two of them out of Afghanistan to Luxembourg. Reregistered them and set up their own air freight company, subcontracting out to charities and relief agencies. If a charity wants to fly food or medicine into Africa or wherever, they call these guys. They're working out in Turkey at the moment, flying stuff out to the earthquake survivors.'

'And Turkey is where they turn Afghanistan opium into heroin.'

'Got it in one, Jamie. And it's mainly Russian chemists doing it. My mates have got contacts. We do in one hop what it takes the Turks weeks to do. They bring their gear overland, through God knows how many countries, and at every border there are palms to be greased.'

Donovan put his glass down again. 'Right, let's get that money transferred into my pal's account, then we're off and running.'

After he left Fullerton's flat, Donovan used an international calling card to phone Carlos Rodriguez in Colombia.

'I heard you were no longer with us, my friend.'

'Not for the want of Jesus trying,' said Donovan. 'If it makes you feel any better, I did soil a perfectly good pair of boxer shorts.'

Rodriguez chuckled. 'What is it you want, Den?'

'I want you to call Jesus off,' said Donovan. 'I've just transferred ten million dollars into your account.'

'And you got that money from where, my friend?'

'My accountant. I found him.'

'Congratulations. Ten million, you say?'

'Check for yourself, Carlos.'

'I will, my friend. And if what you say is true, I will talk to my nephew.'

'Thank you, Carlos.'

'I am sorry for any unpleasantness.'

'I understand, Carlos. If the positions had been reversed, I'd have been the one spraying you with bullets.'

Donovan hung up. His next call was to a Turkish businessman who lived in a twelve-bedroom mansion overlooking Wimbledon Common. A while later he caught a black cab to Wimbledon and spent the best part of three hours with the man.

Donovan got back to Louise's flat just after midnight. He let himself in and smiled as he saw that she was asleep on the sofa, curled up around a cushion. A half-finished game of patience was laid out on the coffee table.

He went over to her and brushed her cheek. She murmured but didn't wake up. He leaned over her and blew gently in her ear. 'Wake up, sleepyhead.'

She opened her eyes and squinted up at him. 'Oh, hi Den. Sorry. I was waiting up for you.'

'You didn't have to. But thanks.'

Louise sat up and rubbed her eyes sleepily.

'How's Robbie?' Donovan asked.

'He went to bed at ten,' she said. 'Made me promise to get you to go and say goodnight when you get back. What time is it?'

'Late. Go on, you go off to bed and I'll make up the sofa.'

She stood up, then lost her balance and fell against him. He caught her, his hands instinctively slipping around her waist. She looked up at him, her mouth only inches from his, and before he knew what he was doing Donovan was kissing her. His tongue probed inside her mouth and she responded, grinding her hips against his, then just as quickly she pushed him away, gasping for breath.

'I'm sorry,' said Donovan.

'It's okay,' she said, brushing the hair from her eyes.

'No, that was stupid.' He realised that he was still holding her around the waist and he released his grip, but she made no move to back away from him. 'After what you went through with that guy, the last thing you want is some man mauling you.'

'It's not that, Den. Honest. And you're not just some man.' She kissed him on the cheek, close to the mouth, then slid her hand around his neck and kissed him again, softly on the lips. When she broke away this time, it was slowly and with a soft caress along his cheek. 'It's just that with Robbie next door, and everything else. Now's just not the time.' She gestured around the flat. 'And this isn't really the place. It wouldn't feel right. Do you understand?'

Donovan smiled. 'Sure. He's already caught one parent in the act.'

'You know what I mean, though?'

'I know exactly what you mean. Now off to bed, I'm knackered.'

'Everything's okay?'

Donovan nodded. 'Everything's just fine. Couldn't be better.'

The shower was running when Tina got up so she made toast and coffee and had the table set by the time that Donovan came into the room. 'Robbie up yet?' he asked.

Tina shook her head. Donovan knocked on his son's bedroom door and shouted for him to get out of bed. He sat down at the table and bit into a piece of dry toast.

'Do you want to do something today?' he asked.

'Like what?'

'I don't know. Shopping. The zoo.'

'The zoo?' laughed Tina.

'You know what I mean. Get Robbie out of the house.'

'I'm going to have to go out for a while,' said Tina. 'But in the afternoon, sure.'

'Anything I can help you with?'

Tina shook her head. 'Shopping. Woman's stuff. I won't be long. How did it go yesterday?'

'Better than I'd hoped,' said Donovan. He drank his coffee. 'I got the money back. The money my wife cleared out of my bank accounts.'

'Den, that's great news. That's brilliant.'

'It's better than a kick in the head. I've paid off the guys who were after me, so I'm almost free and clear.'

'Almost?'

'Just one more deal.'

Tina sat down at the table. 'Can't you stop now? You've got your money back.'

'I've got to see this one thing through, Louise. Too many people will lose money if I pull out now.'

Tina reached across the table and held his hand. 'Den . . .' she said.

The bedroom door opened and Tina pulled back her hand. Robbie walked out, dressed in a Simpsons T-shirt and jeans. 'Hey, just because it's Sunday doesn't mean you don't shower,' said Donovan.

'Can't I have breakfast first?'

Donovan waved at him to sit at the table.

'Do you want me to cook?' asked Tina. 'I've got bacon and sausages.'

'I'll do it,' said Donovan. 'You go get your stuff.'

Tina picked up her bag and left. She walked to the main road and caught a black cab to an Internet café. She kept glancing over her shoulder but knew that there was no reason for anyone to be following her. Donovan trusted her completely. Trusted her with his only son.

She paid the taxi driver and went inside the café. It was one she'd used several times before to file reports to Hathaway.

Tina sat at the computer terminal and lit a cigarette. Two schoolgirls at the next terminal were giggling to each other as they sent messages to a chat room, while a teenage boy at a machine in the corner kept looking around guiltily and turning his VDU so that no one else could see what he was looking at.

A waitress brought over a cappuccino and put it down next to Tina. 'Are you okay there?' she asked in a New Zealand accent. 'You know what you're doing?'

Tina forced a smile. 'Technically,' she said.

'I'm sorry, but it is no-smoking here.'

'Okay. Sorry.' Tina took a long drag and prepared to stub it out.

'No worries,' said the waitress. 'If no one complains, I don't care. I'm a twenty-a-day girl myself. But if you see a sour-faced guy with acne, that's my boss, so get rid of it quick, yeah?'

'Thanks,' said Tina gratefully. She waited until the waitress had gone before logging on to Hathaway's website. Over the past few days she'd heard enough one-sided telephone conversations to get a rough idea of what was going on. She'd heard Donovan talking to someone called Charlie, and they'd discussed Turks and a plane. He'd spoken to someone called PM about money being transferred, and she kept hearing him talking about 'gear' and 'heroin'.

Donovan was putting together a major deal and it was going to happen the following day. Tina wasn't sure where, though she'd heard Donovan say 'airfield' several times, so she'd assumed it was coming in by plane. As he'd said 'airfield' not 'airport', Tina thought that must be significant. It wasn't coming into Heathrow or Gatwick.

Tina began to type, then she hesitated. For the first time in three years of being undercover she felt guilty about what she was doing. She took no pleasure in betraying Den Donovan.

Donovan and Robbie were watching television when Louise arrived home. 'Get everything you wanted?' asked Donovan.

Louise held up a Safeway carrier bag. 'Do you still want to go out?' she asked.

'Dad said we could go to the Trocadero and play video games if it's okay with you,' said Robbie excitedly.

'Fine by me,' said Louise. 'Let me put this stuff away and we're out of here.'

They drove to central London in the Audi and spent the best part of two hours in the Trocadero, with Robbie rushing from machine to machine.

Several times Donovan caught Louise watching Robbie with a wistful look on her face.

'You never wanted children, Louise?' he asked.

'I'm not sure,' she said.

'I thought all women had maternal instincts.'

'Yeah, well you never met my mother,' said Louise. 'My family situation isn't something I'd wish on any kid.'

'Just because you had a rough time doesn't mean your kids will. Sometimes we learn from the mistakes our parents make.'

'Yeah, and sometimes we repeat them. I'm not sure if it's worth the risk.'

They watched as Robbie went over to a racing video game and sat in its bucket seat, expertly guiding a computer-generated car through a series of sharp turns.

'I wouldn't mind kissing you again,' said Donovan. 'Sometime.'

Louise turned and looked at him, her eyebrows raised. 'Where did that come from?' she asked.

Donovan shrugged. 'I just wanted you to know, that's all. Things are a bit crazy just now, but in a few days everything will be sorted. Maybe then . . .'

'Maybe then what?'

'Bloody hell, Louise. Don't make me beg. I'm only asking for a date.'

Louise laughed. 'We'll see.'

'I'm serious.'

'So am I,' said Louise. She looked at him in silence, and then shook her head.

'What?' asked Donovan.

'I don't know. I just wish we'd met under different circumstances. That I wasn't a dancer. That you weren't doing what you're doing. That we'd just met in a normal way. In a supermarket or in a pub.'

'We met, and that's all that matters.'

Louise looked as if she wanted to say something else but then she turned away and went over to stand behind Robbie. Donovan could see that something was troubling her, but he didn't want to press her. She'd tell him eventually.

After Robbie had tired of playing video games they ate Chinese food in Chinatown and went home to spend the evening watching TV. Louise and Donovan drank a bottle of wine together. Donovan slept on the sofa, and this time there was no goodnight kiss from Louise.

* * *

Donovan walked into Tina's sitting room, his hair still wet from the shower. Tina was in the kitchenette, frying sausages. 'Good morning,' she said. 'You want breakfast?'

'Just coffee,' said Donovan.

Robbie was on the sofa in his pyjamas, watching cartoons.

'Hey, just because you're not going to school doesn't mean you can lie around half naked all day.'

'I'm not half naked,' said Robbie.

'Get dressed. Now.'

Robbie scowled and went off to the bedroom.

Tina handed Donovan a mug of coffee. 'Are you okay?' she asked.

'Sure. Why?'

'You keep frowning.'

'Yeah? Sorry.' He drank his coffee. 'I've got a busy day, that's all.'

The landline rang and Tina answered it. She listened and frowned, then handed the phone to Donovan. 'It's for you,' she said.

'No one knows I'm here,' said Donovan.

'It's a man. He asked for you.'

Donovan took the phone. 'Who is it?' he snapped.

'That's no way to talk to an old friend,' said a voice.

'Who are you?'

'It's Hathaway, Donovan.'

'How did you get this number?'

Hathaway chuckled. 'That's for me to know, Donovan. We need to meet.'

'I'm busy.'

'I know you're busy, Donovan. That's what we need to talk about. You've got the money back from Sharkey, right? Now I've got more information for you. Information that you're going to want.'

Donovan looked at his watch. It was nine o'clock. He had to be at the airfield at four o'clock in the afternoon, and it was a two-hour drive from London. He had time. 'You know Blomfield Road? Little Venice?'

'I know it, but since when have you been setting the venues?'

'I'm not going to Camden again. Little Venice is quiet, there are plenty of ways in and out, not too many people.'

'Donovan, if I wanted to take you down, I'd have people outside your door right now. I just want to talk. The information I gave you last time was solid gold. What I have for you today is even better.'

'There's a bridge over the canal, opposite a pub called the Paddington Stop. I'll see you there in four hours. One o'clock. I can't get there any earlier, I've got things to do.'

'One o'clock is fine.'

The line went dead.

Donovan finished his coffee and went into the kitchenette. 'I'm going to have to go out.'

'When will you be back?' asked Tina.

'I'm not sure. Late.'

'How late?' pressed Tina.

'God, I don't know. Have I got a curfew now?'

'Don't go, Den. Please.'

Donovan smiled. 'I have to.'

She put the frying pan by the sink. 'You're up to something, aren't you? You're working. I know you are.'

Donovan reached up and brushed a stray lock of hair from her face. 'Best you don't know,' he said.

'Is that how you treated Vicky? Kept her at a distance? Pushed her away?'

Donovan frowned. 'What's brought this on?'

Tina hugged him and put her head against his chest. 'Just stay here. Let someone else take the risk, Den. Let's take Robbie out. Go somewhere. Have a day out.'

Donovan put his hands on her shoulders and looked into her eyes. 'What do you think's going on, Louise?' he asked.

She shrugged his hands away. 'I've heard you on the bloody phones, Den. I know what you're doing. You're bringing gear in and today's the bloody day.'

'Have you been spying on me?'

'Don't be stupid, Den. This is a small flat and your phones have been ringing red hot for the last twenty-four hours.'

'I have to go.'

Tina shook her head. 'No you don't. You don't have to go. You can walk away. Walk away from it all.'

'We'll talk about it later,' he said.

Tears welled up in Tina's eyes.

'Louise, I'm sorry, I have to go.'

'Damn you, Donovan!'

Donovan took a step back from her, genuinely surprised at the intensity of her reaction. 'I don't have time for this now, Louise. We'll talk about it later.'

'And what if there isn't a later, Den?'

Donovan pressed a finger against her lips, then he leaned over, kissed her on the forehead, and hurried from the flat. Tina rushed after him but he closed the door without looking back.

She leaned against the door, her eyes filled with tears. She'd wanted to say more, but she couldn't. She couldn't tell him, because the truth was that she was betraying him. She was helping to set him up.

She wiped her eyes and sniffed. And who was the man who'd phoned? Donovan always made and received calls on his mobiles, he never used her phone. There had been something vaguely familiar about the man's voice, but for the life of her Tina couldn't place it. Whoever it was, he'd unnerved Donovan.

Robbie came out of the bedroom. He stopped in the hallway when he saw Tina was crying. 'What's wrong?'

Tina shook her head. 'Nothing.'

'He'll come back,' he said. 'Don't worry.'

Tina nodded and wiped her eyes again. 'I'm sorry,' she said.

'It's not your fault,' said Robbie. 'That's just the way he is.'

'I know,' she said.

She held out her arms and Robbie rushed towards her and hugged her. 'It'll be okay,' he said soothingly.

Tina patted Robbie's head. She knew that it wasn't going to be okay. It was going to be far from okay.

Donovan waited on the bridge, whistling softly to himself. He adjusted the Velcro band under his watchstrap and then put a hand on the detector unit on his belt. Everything was going according to plan. Jordan and Macfadyen had already left for the airfield. Donovan had called PM and told him where the plane was landing and what time to get there. And he'd arranged to meet Fullerton at Hyde Park Corner so that they could drive to the airfield together. The only fly in the ointment was Gregg Hathaway.

A narrowboat chugged underneath the bridge. A grey-haired woman in her seventies had her hand on the tiller and she gave Donovan a cheery wave as the boat went by. Donovan waved back.

He straightened up and saw Hathaway walking down Formosa Street, a laptop computer case hanging from one shoulder.

Hathaway was grinning as he walked to the middle of the bridge. 'Lovely day for it,' he said cheerily.

'What is it you want?' asked Donovan.

'I want to be rich, happy, to be with somebody who loves me. Children would be nice. Pretty much what every man wants.'

The detector on Donovan's belt remained still. Hathaway wasn't wearing a recording device or transmitter. 'You know what I mean,' said Donovan.

Further down the canal a middle-aged angler threw a handful of ground bait into the water.

'I want to talk,' said Hathaway.

'Try the Samaritans,' said Donovan.

'I'll miss your sense of humour, Donovan.' He looked at his wristwatch.

'Got somewhere to go?' asked Donovan.

'No, but you have, haven't you?'

'I'm tired of playing games, Hathaway. What do you want?'

Hathaway smiled without warmth. 'You didn't think twice before putting that bullet in my leg, did you?'

'I thought about killing you.'

'I bet you did. Have you any idea how that bullet changed my life?'

'Got you a better job, didn't it?'

'I loved being in Customs, Den. Loved working undercover. I was bloody good at it.'

Donovan flashed Hathaway a sarcastic smile. 'Clearly you weren't. If you'd been any good, I wouldn't have made you.'

'Someone grassed me. One of your informers.'

Donovan shook his head. 'You gave yourself away. I forget now what it was, but it was down to you. Some story you told. Some anecdote. You told it wrong. Told it like you'd memorised it. Like it was a script.'

'Bullshit!'

'Why would I lie? To hurt you?' Donovan chuckled. 'We're beyond that, aren't we?'

'It was the job I'd always wanted. I was one of the good guys, fast track. Then you shot me and I'm in hospital for three months. And three months after that I'm sitting at a desk in human resources being told that there is no place for me in the leaner, meaner Customs and Excise. Thank you for your loyal service and good night.'

'You got a pension, right? Disability?'

'Peanuts. Wife didn't like the idea of my being thrown on the scrapheap at twenty-four, so she went off in search of pastures new.'

'Women, huh?' said Donovan sarcastically. 'What can you do with them?'

'You changed my life, Den. You didn't give me a choice, didn't consider the ramifications, you just went ahead and did it. Now I'm going to do the same to you.'

'You're going to try to put me behind bars, is that it? You want me in prison?'

'I want your money.'

Donovan's jaw dropped.

'All of it,' added Hathaway.

'What do you mean, all of it?'

'All the money that you got back from Sharkey. I want it. And I want it now.'

'You're out of your mind.'

'I know everything, Donovan. I know about the plane, I

know about the heroin. I know about Macfadyen and Jordan. I know about the airfield. To use the vernacular, you are fucked. You have one way out. Only one. You give me the money. Do that and I'll let you go ahead with the Turkish deal.'

Donovan shook his head in confusion.

'I know, bit of a shock to the system.' Hathaway looked at his watch again. 'I reckon they'll still be loading the plane, don't you? Another hour before it gets into the air. There's probably no way you could reach them now. Even if you wanted to.'

Donovan cursed. He turned to walk away, then stopped. He opened his mouth to speak but he was too confused to say anything. He closed his mouth and stared at Hathaway. He wanted to lash out, to kick the man to the ground and to keep kicking until he was unconscious. Or worse.

Hathaway smiled as if he could read Donovan's mind. 'Face it, Donovan, I've got you by the short and curlies. But look on the bright side: whatever you make from the Turkish deal you get to keep, so it's not as if I'm leaving you penniless.'

Donovan shook his head. 'Why would I give you the money?'

'Because if you don't, you're going to prison. Possibly for the rest of your life. Eight thousand kilos of heroin, Donovan. Conspiracy to import. They'll throw away the key. Plus there's the Mexican deal. The Beetles. Mexico is next door to the States, and Rodriguez has been shoving cocaine over the border like there's no tomorrow. I link you to Rodriguez and the DEA will want a piece of you.'

'You've got fuck all. You've got fuck all and you know it.'

'Excuse me, but I know where the plane is going to land. I know what's on the plane. I know where the plane is coming from. And I know who's paying for the consignment. Does it seem like I'm missing anything there?'

'Knowing is one thing, proving is another.'

'I have proof,' said Hathaway confidently.

Donovan paced up and down the bridge, shaking his head. 'Fine, you've got proof, but you've overplayed your hand. All I have to do is to walk away. I walk away from the deal and you've got nothing.'

Hathaway smiled. 'Conspiracy doesn't depend on you taking delivery, Donovan. You put the deal together. That I can prove.'

'Bollocks.'

'I have people undercover. Close to you.'

'Now I know you're lying.'

'Your infallible sense of smell? You can always spot an undercover cop or Cussie? You always took pride in that particular skill, didn't you? Well, I got people in under your radar, Donovan. Up close and personal.'

Donovan stopped pacing and stared at Hathaway. Could he be telling the truth? Is that how he knew about the plane? But who? Who was the traitor? Who had betrayed him? Jordan and Macfadyen? Had they been turned when the Mexican deal went belly up? It had always struck Donovan as suspicious that Customs hadn't let the consignment run. Now he knew why. Jordan and Macfadyen had done a deal. Their freedom in exchange for Donovan's. They'd helped set him up.

'I know who it is,' he said confidently.

Hathaway shook his head. 'No you don't,' he said. 'I guarantee you don't.'

'We'll see.'

'The thing is, Donovan, you can't afford to be wrong, can you? You're wrong on this and you lose everything. You lose your money and you lose your freedom.'

'I'll risk it.' He turned to go.

'It isn't Ricky Jordan. And it isn't Charlie Macfadyen,' said Hathaway quietly.

Donovan stopped. 'If it was them, you'd hardly tell me, would you?'

'Agreed, but I'm telling you it's not them. You have my word.'

Donovan laughed out loud. 'Your word? Your fucking word? Now it's coming down to you crossing your heart like a bloody Cub Scout. Why should I believe a word you tell me?'

Hathaway patted the laptop computer case. 'Because I have proof.'

Donovan stared at the computer case. 'What sort of proof?'

Hathaway looked at his watch again. 'We're going to have to start the ball rolling, Donovan. That plane is getting closer.'

'What do you want?'

'I told you what I wanted. You got sixty million dollars from Sharkey. I want it.'

'I don't have sixty million. I owed ten million.'

'To Rodriguez?'

Donovan nodded.

'Fifty million, then.'

'I had to pay for the recovery of the money, plus there was the cash that Sharkey spent.'

'Why don't you just tell me how much is left? And don't bother lying, because I can find out.'

'Forty-five mill,' said Donovan.

'That's what I want, then. Forty-five million dollars. That's the price of your freedom. The price of your life.'

'So I give you forty-five million and you tell me who the undercover agent is?'

'Agents. Plural.'

'And how do I give you the money? Used notes?'

'Sarcasm doesn't become you, Donovan.' Hathaway tapped the case again. 'We do it online. Same way Sharkey took the money off you. Same way you got it back off Sharkey.'

Donovan shook his head. 'Do I look like I was born yesterday? I transfer forty-five million to you, then you show me sheets of blank paper. Where does that leave me?'

'That's not how we'll do it. You transfer five million. I show you proof. You transfer more money. I show you more proof. At any point you can stop. But believe me, Donovan, you won't want to stop. The proof I'm offering is unequivocal.'

'And what then? You give me the names, you give me the proof. What then?'

'I walk away.'

'And the agents?'

Hathaway took a deep breath as if steadying himself for what he was to say next. 'You do what you have to do, Donovan.'

'You know what that will be,' said Donovan coldly. It wasn't a question.

'It's a game, Donovan. That's what you taught me. It's a game and there are winners and there are losers. I'm doing what I have to do to be a winner.'

'You're a callous bastard, Hathaway.'

'Well, gosh, Donovan. Sticks and stones. Are we going to do this or are you going to prison for twenty years?'

Donovan stared at Hathaway for several seconds, then he nodded slowly. 'Okay,' he said quietly. 'Let's see what you have.'

Gregov took his hands off the controls as the autopilot kicked in. He opened his flight case. 'What do you feel like?' he asked Peter.

Peter shrugged. 'Aerosmith?'

Gregov nodded appreciatively. 'Good choice.' He took out a cassette and slotted it into the player and turned the volume all the way up. The cockpit was soon filled with pounding rock music. The two Russians jerked their heads in time with the beat.

Behind them, in the massive cargo bay, eight thousand kilos of heroin were loaded on to five wooden pallets. The heroin had begun life as opium harvested in the poppy fields of the eastern Afghanistan province of Nangarhar. The opium had been carried by camel over the border into Turkey where it had been processed into morphine and then into heroin by Russian chemists. Gregov had paid a thousand dollars a kilo for the heroin, a total of eight million dollars for the load, which meant that the one flight alone was going to generate a profit of sixteen million dollars.

'What are you going to do with your share?' shouted Gregov.

Peter shrugged. 'I don't know. What are you going to do?'

Gregov laughed sharply. 'I don't know. I'll think of something. One thing's for sure, I'm going to get laid a lot!'

Peter picked up a bottle of Johnnie Walker Black Label and took a swig. 'You get laid a lot anyway,' he said, tossing the bottle over to Gregov.

Gregov drank from the bottle, then wiped his mouth with the back of his hand. 'Yeah, but at least I won't have to screw the ugly ones any more.'

The laptop screen flickered into life. Hathaway nodded at the bench. 'Take a pew, Donovan.' Hathaway had set the computer up on one of the trestle tables on the terrace outside the Paddington Stop. 'I tell you what, get us a couple of beers, yeah? We should celebrate.'

'I've nothing to celebrate yet,' said Donovan. He went into the pub, bought two pints of lager and carried them back outside. Hathaway had placed his mobile phone next to the laptop and was connecting to the internet through the computer's infrared link. Donovan put the glasses on the table and sat down next to Hathaway.

'You haven't got a cigarette, have you?' asked Hathaway.

'I don't smoke,' said Donovan.

'I gave up, but I could do with a smoke right now.' He turned the laptop towards Donovan, then handed him a piece of paper on which was written the details of a numbered Swiss account. 'Five million,' said Hathaway.

Donovan put his hands on the keyboard, then he paused. What if he was being conned? What if Hathaway was setting him up for something? He closed his eyes, his mind spinning. He was being rushed, pushed and shoved into doing something he wasn't comfortable with, but what choice did he have? If Hathaway did have undercover agents in play, then he was facing life behind bars.

'Five million,' repeated Hathaway. 'We don't have all day.'

Donovan made the transfer. Hathaway watched the screen intently. When he was satisfied that the money had been transferred, he opened a Velcroed document pocket on the side of the laptop case and took out an envelope. He handed it to Donovan. 'Cheap at half the price,' he said.

Donovan opened the envelope. Inside was an application form to join the Metropolitan Police. It had been filled out in neat capital letters. Clifford Warren. Twenty-nine years old. An address in Harlesden. Donovan frowned. Clifford Warren? He didn't know anyone called Clifford Warren. There was something else in the envelope. A photograph and another sheet of paper, folded in half. Donovan slid them out. The photograph was a six-by-four head and shoulders shot of an unsmiling black man. Short hair. A square chin. A slightly flattened nose. Bunny. Donovan cursed.

He unfolded the sheet of paper. It was a print-out of an e-mail message. An e-mail to Hathaway detailing the flight from Turkey and when and where the plane was due to arrive in the UK.

'Like I said,' murmured Hathaway, as if he were speaking in church, 'unequivocal proof.' He patted the computer case. 'For the next one, I'm going to need another fifteen million.'

Donovan hesitated, but his fingers stayed on the keyboard.

'Getting rid of one is no good,' whispered Hathaway. 'It's all or nothing, Donovan.'

Donovan bit down on his lower lip, knowing that Hathaway was right and hating himself for it. He input the instructions to transfer the fifteen million dollars as Hathaway watched. Hathaway rubbed his chin. He was breathing heavily and Donovan could feel the man's warm breath on his cheek with each exhalation.

When Donovan had finished, Hathaway handed him a second envelope. It contained another Metropolitan Police application form and a photograph. James Robert Fullerton.

'No fucking way,' said Donovan under his breath.

'I'm afraid so,' said Hathaway.

'I've seen him take drugs. He handles stolen gear.'

'Deep cover,' said Hathaway. 'Deep, deep cover.'

There was another sheet of paper inside the envelope. Donovan opened it out. It was a print-out of an e-mail that Fullerton had sent to Hathaway, packed with details about the shipment of VW Beetles from Mexico.

'Funnily enough, I didn't hear a peep from him about the Turkish flight,' said Hathaway. 'He's either playing his cards very close to his chest or he's going over to your side.'

'Bastard,' said Donovan. Donovan stared at the head and shoulders photograph of Jamie Fullerton. 'I trusted him,' he said quietly.

'Of course you did,' said Hathaway. 'Wouldn't be much point in him being undercover and you not trusting him, would there?'

Donovan tore up the photograph and threw the pieces on the floor.

'And last but not least . . . twenty-five million dollars,' said Hathaway. 'Twenty-five million dollars and you get the third and final name.'

'How do I know you're not bluffing? How do I know there aren't just two?'

'You have my word,' said Hathaway. 'Have I told you anything yet that isn't true?'

Donovan glared at the man. 'You bastard,' he hissed.

Hathaway grinned. 'Maybe, but I'm the bastard who's got the key to you staying out of prison. I've already got twenty million, Donovan. I could walk away now a happy man. Do you want me to do that?' Hathaway started to get up.

'No,' said Donovan, quickly. He knew that Hathaway was right. He needed all three names. Two out of three wouldn't keep him out of prison.

Donovan made the transfer and Hathaway slid a third envelope across the table. 'And with that, I'll say goodbye,' said Hathaway. He held out his hand. 'Thanks for everything,' he said.

Donovan ignored Hathaway's outstretched hand. 'What are you going to do now?'

'I'm going to retire. Do all those things I've always wanted to do. I already have several identities fixed up and ready to go. That's the beauty of working for the good guys. I've got real passports. Real paperwork. All I have to do is to slot myself into a new life. A life where I have forty-five million dollars.' He nodded at the envelope. 'Aren't you going to open it?'

Donovan shook his head. He didn't want Hathaway to see his reaction to the contents of the envelope. He had a horrible feeling that Hathaway had saved the best until last.

Hathaway stood up. 'In that case, I'll bid you *adieu*,' he said. He closed up the laptop and put it back in its case.

'I hope you get cancer,' said Donovan quietly.

'Don't get all bitter and twisted,' said Hathaway, zipping the case closed. 'I've given you your freedom. I've given you the names of the bastards who were setting you up for a fall. There's no way we're going to be best friends, but I think a little appreciation is called for.'

Donovan stared impassively at Hathaway but said nothing.

Hathaway shrugged. 'I guess I'll just have to settle for

the money,' he said, then turned and walked away towards Warwick Avenue Tube station.

Donovan waited until Hathaway had turned the corner before opening the envelope. He slid out the by-now familiar application to join the Metropolitan Police. Christina Louise Leigh. The photograph was upside down and he slowly turned it over. The girl in the picture had long blonde hair instead of a short brunette bob, but there was no doubt who she was. Donovan stared at the photograph in disbelief.

He stood up, still staring at the photograph. Louise? He'd trusted Louise with his only child. He'd let her into his life, shared his innermost thoughts with her. He'd let her in through his defences and all the time it had been a lie. She was a cop. A fucking cop. Which meant that everything, every single thing, that she had told him had been a lie.

Bunny, Jamie and Louise. All of them traitors. All of them police officers. All of them working to put him away. And he'd trusted all three of them. How could he have been so stupid? Hathaway had been right: Donovan had prided himself on being able to spot undercover agents, on being able to read people and to see them for what they really were. How had he been so wrong with these three?

He walked back across the bridge and along the towpath. He almost felt as if his mind had separated from his body and he was watching himself walking by the side of the canal. His head was down and in his right hand he held the envelopes that Hathaway had given him.

A narrowboat, painted in garish scarlet and green, was moored opposite the Paddington Stop. On its roof was a line of flowerboxes filled with pansies of a dozen different hues and several brightly polished brass coalscuttles.

Donovan climbed on board the rear of the boat and tapped twice on the wooden door. It was opened by a woman in her late forties holding a clipboard and a stopwatch. She smiled and moved to the side to allow Donovan in.

Alex Knight was sitting in front of a bank of CCTV monitors. He took off a large pair of headphones and grinned at Donovan.

'Did you get it?' asked Donovan.

Knight had half a dozen long-range directional microphones and as many video cameras targeting the area. He had placed two men posing as anglers on the canal side, a man and woman inside the pub, two men in a flat overlooking the canal, and two teams on tower blocks close by. There was also a camera and a directional microphone in a British Telecom van parked on Blomfield Road and two small radio-controlled cameras mounted on streetlights close to the bridge.

'Every word,' said Alex. 'Sound and vision. I'll get it edited and boost the sound where necessary. Should have it done by this evening.'

'Tomorrow morning should be okay,' said Donovan. 'First thing.'

Knight nodded at the envelopes in Donovan's hand. 'Bad news, huh?'

'I've had better,' admitted Donovan.

'I couldn't help overhearing – that being what you were paying for and all – but he didn't take all your money, did he?'

'Most of it,' said Donovan, 'but don't worry, I've enough put by to settle your account.'

'Thought didn't even cross my mind, Den,' said Knight with a grin.

* * *

Raymond Mackie threw open the door and waddled into the room. A dozen expectant faces looked up from around a polished oak table. The Head of Drugs Operations had called the meeting on the third floor of Custom House in Lower Thames Street at short notice. Very short notice. Heads of department had been given just twenty minutes to assemble and had been told that there were to be no excuses.

Mackie threw a manila file on to the table and lowered himself into the high-backed leather chair at the head of the table. 'No time for niceties, gentlemen,' he said. 'And lady,' he added, nodding at the one female member of the team. 'The wonder boys at Vauxhall Bridge have finally decided that they want to start sharing intelligence and have dropped a very hot potato into our laps. I got the call just half an hour ago, so I've no presentation materials and no written notes to hand out. Please listen carefully.'

He paused for a couple of seconds to make sure that he had their undivided attention.

'A planeload of Afghanistan heroin is currently being airlifted from Turkey, en route to the UK. Eight thousand kilos.'

Mackie let the amount sink in before repeating it.

'Eight thousand kilos. London street value, in the region of eight hundred million pounds. *Guinness Book of Records* time. The plane is a Russian-made Ilyushin Il-76, not much smaller than a jumbo jet.' Mackie looked at his watch. 'According to the wonder boys, it will be landing at an airfield in South-east England in about four hours. We're going to need SAS back-up on this rather than armed police, but I want as many of our senior people there as possible. I want this to be seen as a Customs operation, not a special forces job. Drugs has been and always will be a Customs priority and this is our chance to show what we can do.'

A hand went up at the far end of the table.

Mackie smiled. 'If I can read your mind, the answer to your question is Den Donovan. Tango One.'

'Is that it?' asked Fullerton, his head on one side. Off in the distance was a faint throbbing sound.

'Maybe,' said Donovan. 'Take it easy, Jamie. Relax. It'll be here when it's here.'

Bunny and PM stood some distance away, deep in conversation.

'What do you think they're talking about?' asked Fullerton.

'Probably discussing when they should pull out their guns and blow us all away so that they can keep all the gear for themselves,' said Donovan.

Fullerton's eyes widened and Donovan slapped him on the back. 'Joke, Jamie. Joke. Jordan and Macfadyen have given everybody a going-over with a metal detector: there's nobody here carrying so much as a pocket knife.'

It was just after seven o'clock in the evening and dusk was settling in. The airfield was a former RAF base that had been declared surplus to requirements during a round of defence cutbacks in the early 'nineties. Until a more permanent use could be found for the facility, the Government had leased the property to a loose-knit group of European Union charities to use as their UK base. Its single runway was almost two thousand metres long. Along one side of the runway ran a line of metal storage sheds in which several charities and emergency aid groups stored equipment and supplies. Various logos were painted on the sliding doors of the sheds, including the insignia of the charity that was chartering the Russian plane. Beyond the sheds stood four large hangars which used to house RAF bombers.

Donovan and Fullerton were standing in front of the charity's shed next to half a dozen rented Transit vans, each with its own driver. Jordan and Macfadyen had supplied the drivers, all men whom they had used before and trusted.

Bunny and PM had brought five of their own men and two large trucks with the name of a laundry company on the sides. The backs of the trucks were already open in anticipation of the plane's arrival.

A Russian came up and nodded at Donovan. He'd introduced himself to Donovan when he'd opened the gates for the vans to drive on to the airfield, but the name seemed to contain four or five syllables and Donovan hadn't been able to remember it.

'Hiya, mate, how's it going?' asked Donovan.

'Plane is coming,' said the Russian. 'I switch on lights.'

'Great. Thanks.'

The Russian walked off towards the tower building, most of which had been converted to offices.

Donovan turned to Fullerton. 'What is his name?'

Fullerton shook his head. He didn't know either. 'What about the Turks? Where are they?'

'We'll meet up with them later.'

'Not like Turks to be so trusting,' said Fullerton.

'Bit of a racist statement, Jamie.'

'You know what I mean. Consignment this size, you'd think they'd want to be here.'

'It's all in hand, Jamie. Don't worry.' Donovan slapped Fullerton on the back. 'Come on, cheer up. You're in the big time, now. That's what you wanted, isn't it?'

'Sure,' said Fullerton. He smiled, but there was a worried look in his eyes. 'Of course it is. The big time.'

Donovan glanced over at PM and Bunny. The two black men looked back at him impassively. Donovan grinned and gave them an exaggerated thumbs-up. PM's face broke into a smile but Bunny continued to stare at Donovan, stony faced.

The landing lights came on, two bright white stripes down either side of the runway.

Jordan and Macfadyen strolled over. They were wearing heavy jackets with designer labels. 'Are we on?' asked Jordan.

'Looks like it,' said Donovan.

Fullerton scanned the skies. 'Which way is east?' he asked.

Donovan pointed off to their right. 'Over there.' He narrowed his eyes. 'I think I see it.'

'God, my heart's pounding,' said Fullerton. 'Like I've run ten k.'

One of Donovan's phones buzzed, and he pulled it out of his pocket. He'd been sent a text message. 'Adrenalin,' said Donovan. 'Nothing like it.'

'Yeah, you're right. Better than a coke rush.'

'Better than anything, because this rush comes with tens of millions of pounds of readies attached,' said Donovan. He grinned. 'That's it. See it?' Donovan looked down at his mobile phone and scrolled through the text message. 'DEN – IT'S A TRAP. RUN. LOUISE.' He smiled to himself and deleted it.

Fullerton nodded. 'Yeah. Bloody hell, it's happening, it's actually happening.'

Donovan put the phone back in his pocket. He shouted over to PM and Bunny and gestured at the sky. 'Here we go,' he yelled at them. 'That's us.'

Everybody was now staring up at the sky and pointing. The plane was at about five thousand feet, flying below an impenetrable layer of grey cloud. The engine noise was louder now, and the plane seemed to be descending quickly, as if in a hurry to get on the ground. The undercarriage and nose-heel dropped down and the flaps lowered. The plane was coming in straight to land. It had a large T-shaped tail unit with a high-set swept back wing on which were mounted four turbofan engines.

'Can you imagine if it crashed and burned?' said Fullerton. 'The whole of the south of England would be on a heroin buzz for weeks.'

Donovan didn't reply. He just watched the approaching plane with a half smile on his lips. 'Come on,' Donovan whispered to himself. 'Come to Daddy.'

The flaps were lowered and the plane visibly slowed, then the nose came up and the wheels hit the concrete with a squeal and puffs of black smoke and then the plane was rolling by them. Donovan caught a glimpse of a grinning pilot through the windshield as the plane went by, but he couldn't tell if it was Gregov or Peter.

Fullerton began to jump up and down. 'We did it. We fucking did it!' He punched the air, then turned and hugged Donovan. 'Fucking hell, Den, we did it.'

Donovan patted Fullerton on the shoulder. 'Yeah,' he said quietly. 'We did, didn't we?'

The giant transport plane turned off on to a taxiway and then turned again so that it rolled back towards them. Bunny and PM walked over, their hoods up on their black Puffa jackets.

'Okay, guys?' asked Donovan.

'Will be once I see the stuff,' said PM.

'You okay, Bunny?' asked Donovan. 'Don't see you smiling.'

'Like the man said, all we see now is a plane.'

The plane slowed and then stopped, about a hundred yards away from where they were standing. The engines shut down one by one.

'Right, let's get the vans over there,' said Donovan.

The engines of the Transit vans burst into life and Bunny motioned for his drivers to get into the laundry trucks. That was when all hell broke loose.

Three helicopters came in low from the west, swooping over the wire perimeter face and then breaking away from each other to land at different parts of the field. One hovered close to the tower building, and six men clothed in black, holding automatic weapons, jumped out. A second helicopter disgorged more armed men on the far side of the plane and they ran to surround it. The third helicopter landed at the end of the line of storage sheds. Another six armed men piled out and started running towards Donovan and his crew, guns at the ready, their boots pounding against the concrete.

'What the fuck's this?' hissed Fullerton.

Donovan said nothing. He didn't try to run and he didn't show any emotion other than a slight smile as he slowly raised his hands in the air.

An armoured Land Rover crashed through the gate in the perimeter fence and then turned sharply to the left, allowing a dozen faster vehicles to speed by. Half were police cars, blue lights flashing but sirens off, and half were dark saloons filled with big men in black jackets.

Two of the Transit vans roared off, but a burst of automatic fire ripped out the tyres of one, and the other was rammed against the wall of one of the sheds by a police car. Police officers surrounded the van and dragged out the stunned driver. Jordan and Macfadyen made a run for it, but both were rugby-tackled to the ground by police officers.

PM was about to run, but Bunny dropped a hand on his shoulder. 'Don't bother, bro. These are heavy people. Don't give them no excuse to get heavier.'

PM nodded grimly, then slowly followed Donovan's example and raised his arms above his head. Bunny did the same.

The armed men in black surrounded Donovan and his men, swinging their weapons from side to side, their faces hidden behind respirators. They wore heavy black body armour over black uniforms.

'Fuck me, it's the SAS,' whispered Fullerton.

'Just stay calm, Jamie,' said Donovan. 'Hands in the air.'

Men in black jackets with 'CUSTOMS' written on the back in bright yellow piled out of the saloon cars and walked towards the plane.

SAS troopers were waving at the pilots to open the door at the front of the fuselage. To make sure they got the message, they fired a quick burst of gunfire over the top of the plane.

The door opened and one of the SAS troopers shouted clipped instructions to the pilots.

Hands started patting down Donovan. He looked to his left. It was a burly, unsmiling police sergeant.

'It's okay, I'm not armed,' said Donovan. 'None of us is.'

'Pity,' said one of the SAS troopers, his voice muffled by the respirator.

'Fuck you,' said PM. 'You wanna try something without

all that hi-tech crap? Huh, probably isn't even a man inside that RoboCop suit.'

'Easy, PM,' said Bunny.

The ramp at the back of the plane began to open. 'Open Sesame,' whispered Donovan.

The sergeant finished searching Donovan and moved on to Fullerton. Donovan slowly lowered his hands. No one stopped him.

The end of the ramp scraped against the concrete. The sergeant nodded at two young constables. 'Take him over there, lads,' said the sergeant. 'Someone wants a word with him.' The two police officers escorted Donovan to the back of the ramp, where an obese man wearing a black Customs jacket a size too small was waiting for him.

'Den Donovan,' said the man, barely able to contain his glee. 'You've no idea what a pleasure it is finally to meet you. Raymond Mackie, Head of Drugs Operations, Customs and Excise.'

'Yeah, I know who you are,' said Donovan. 'They call you the Doughboy, don't they? Why is that? Can't just be because you're a fat bastard, can it?'

Mackie's eyes hardened. 'Up until today you were designated Tango One, Donovan, but as of this evening you're no longer a target, you're a prisoner. Come on, I can't wait to see what eight thousand kilos of heroin looks like.'

Mackie strode up the ramp, breathing heavily, flanked by four young Customs officers wearing similar black nylon jackets. One of the police officers pushed Donovan in the small of the back.

'Okay, okay,' said Donovan, glaring at the man. The officer was barely half Donovan's age. 'Be nice, yeah?'

Donovan followed Mackie and the Customs officers up

the ramp into the cavernous interior of the plane. Two men in their twenties wearing stained khaki jumpsuits were sitting on two seats fixed to the fuselage. Other than the two men, the plane was empty.

One of the men waved at Mackie. 'We want claim political asylum. Okay?'

Mackie's jaw dropped. 'What?'

The other man punched his colleague on the shoulder. 'He make joke,' he said to Mackie. 'My friend has big mouth. Make big joke.'

Mackie looked around the vast space, five times the height of a man, his mouth still open in astonishment. The other Customs officers were equally surprised. 'What the hell's going on?' spluttered Mackie.

A door opened at the far end of the cargo area and Gregov stepped out carrying a white plastic carrier bag in one hand. He walked through the hold. Two SAS troopers, their weapons hanging from slings, followed him.

Gregov opened the carrier bag and took out two cartons of Marlboro cigarettes. He held them out to Mackie. 'I was going to declare them,' he said. 'Honest I was.' He winked at Donovan. 'Hiya, Den. Good to see you again.'

Jamie Fullerton took a swig of his beer and plonked it down on the desk next to his computer. He stared at the screen and for the one hundredth time checked to see if he had e-mail. There were no new messages for him. Fullerton had sent a full report to Hathaway on what had happened at the airfield and had expected an immediate reply.

Hathaway must have known about the abortive raid at the airfield and must have realised by now that Fullerton had been there. Fullerton had said in his e-mail that Donovan had only told him about the flight at the last minute and that there hadn't been time to get a message to Hathaway.

Fullerton had been held in a cell for an hour, interrogated by two plainclothes detectives whose hearts clearly weren't in it, and then released. No laws had been broken, not the least because of Donovan's insistence that nobody carried a gun. They were all guests of the Russian aviation company, and the Ilyushin had filed a valid flight plan. It was suspicious, there was no getting away from that, two dozen men and a convoy of vans all waiting for an empty plane, but there was nothing illegal about it.

Fullerton had tried calling Donovan's mobile several times but it was switched off.

He took another drink of beer, then decided he needed something stronger. Something with a real buzz to it. He headed for the bathroom where he kept his coke. The door intercom buzzed as he walked down the hallway and he stopped to look at the CCTV monitor. It was Charlie Macfadyen.

Fullerton picked up the receiver. 'Charlie? What do you want?'

'We want a word about yesterday's fiasco,' said Macfadyen, running a hand over his shaved head.

Fullerton buzzed him up. He went back to his computer and checked one final time but there were still no new messages. He shook his head, switched off the computer and picked up his beer bottle.

He had the door open for Macfadyen by the time the elevator reached his floor. Macfadyen wasn't alone. There were two men with him. Fullerton didn't know their names but he recognised them from the airfield – they had been driving two of the rental vans.

'What's up, Charlie?' asked Fullerton, though he could

see that Macfadyen was in no mood for polite conversation. Macfadyen's mouth was a tight line and his eyes were as cold and dispassionate as a reptile's.

'Not much,' said Macfadyen, walking into Fullerton's flat.

'You said you wanted a word?' said Fullerton. He still had the door open, but Macfadyen's companions made no move to walk inside.

'Yeah,' said Macfadyen. He reached behind his back and pulled a large automatic from a holster clipped to his belt. He thrust the gun against Fullerton's chest. 'And the word is grass.'

Bunny paced up and down his sitting room. He punched PM's number into his mobile phone, but for the hundredth time he went straight through to his message service. Where the hell was PM? And what the hell had gone wrong?

Had Donovan been tipped off? And if he had, why had he gone to the airfield? If he'd known that police and Customs were going to turn up with SAS back-up, why hadn't he just got on the first plane back to the Caribbean?

Bunny had been watching Donovan when the helicopters swooped over the perimeter fence. There'd been no panic in the man's eyes, no attempt to run, he just stood and watched the helicopters with an amused smile on his face.

The police had roughly searched Bunny and PM, practically kicked them to the ground before going through their clothing, and the next time he'd been able to catch a glimpse of Donovan he was being taken to the rear of the transport plane. Just before Bunny had been thrown into the back of a police van, he had seen Donovan being escorted up the ramp into the bowels of the giant plane. There had been no sign of tension on Donovan's face. Just a quiet, almost self-satisfied, smile. It was as if he knew what was coming. As if it had all been planned.

They'd all been split up at the police station. Bunny had been asked if he wanted a lawyer but he'd just shaken his head. He'd given them his name and address and his date of birth, but other than that he'd remained resolutely silent. Without the drugs, there was no case. Even conspiracy to import wouldn't stand up, not with the plane arriving empty.

Two detectives had questioned him and then he'd been left in a cell for six hours. He hadn't seen PM again. As soon as he'd been released, Bunny had caught a cab home. He wanted to get on the internet and get a message to Hathaway, though there was no doubt in Bunny's mind that Hathaway already knew what had happened. He figured that he should stay put until PM got in touch, though. Two drug deals had turned to shit and PM would want to know why.

The doorbell rang and Bunny jerked as if he'd been stung. He hurried over to open the door, but not before making sure that the security chain was on.

It was Jordan. With three other men Bunny had last seen at the airfield.

'How's your luck, Bunny?' asked Jordan.

'I've had better days,' said Bunny, wondering why Jordan had turned up on his doorstep. 'You here for a reason, or is this social?'

Jordan leaned forward so that his face filled the gap between the door and the frame. 'We think we know who the rotten apple is,' whispered Jordan. 'You'll never guess.'

Bunny unhitched the security chain and opened the door.

'Who is it?' he asked.

Jordan pushed Bunny in the chest with the flat of his hand, and he staggered back, his hands flailing out for balance. Jordan kept moving forward, pushing him again, harder this time. Bunny fell backwards over a coffee table and crashed to the floor. Jordan reached his right hand inside his jacket and pulled out a gun.

'It's you, scumbag!' roared Jordan, pointing the gun down at Bunny's surprised face.

Robbie walked out of the spare bedroom, rubbing his eyes sleepily. Tina was lying on the sofa, wrapped up in a bathrobe. 'Why aren't you in bed?' he asked.

'I was waiting for your dad,' she said, sitting up and running a hand through her hair.

'He always stays out late,' said Robbie, sitting on the sofa next to her. 'Sometimes all night. It used to drive Mum crazy.'

'What about you? Didn't you worry?'

Robbie shrugged. 'He always comes back eventually. I guess.'

'Suppose he didn't?' said Tina. 'Suppose one day he didn't come back? What would you do?'

'What do you mean?'

'You know. Suppose he went out and didn't come back? Stayed away for a long time?'

'You mean if he died?'

Tina pushed him and he pretended to fall off the sofa. 'No, I didn't mean if he died. Just if he couldn't come back. What would you do?'

Robbie sat up and leaned back against the sofa. 'Could I stay with you?'

'Maybe,' said Tina quietly. 'Would you like that?'

'I don't want to go back to her. My mum. Not after what she did. I suppose I could stay with Aunty Laura and Uncle Mark, but I'd rather stay with you.' He looked up at her. 'Is something wrong?'

Tina shook her head. 'No, everything's fine.' She picked up her mobile and called Donovan's number again. It just rang out. No answer. No message service. She had no way of knowing if the phone was even working, or if he'd received the text message she'd sent.

'He always has it switched off,' said Robbie. 'Don't worry.'

They both heard the knock at the door and jumped. Robbie stood up and ran over to the door. 'Robbie, check first,' shouted Tina. 'And use the chain.'

There was the sound of a key being inserted in the lock and Tina opened her mouth to scream, but then Donovan opened the door.

'Den! It's you!' said Tina.

Donovan grinned and closed the door. He picked up Robbie and swung him around. 'How many keys have you given out, then?'

'But you knocked.'

'I didn't want to walk in on anything, now did I?' said Donovan. He put Robbie down and pushed him towards the spare room. 'Get ready for school.'

'What?'

'You heard. School.'

'But you said—'

'I've changed my mind,' interrupted Donovan. 'Get ready.' He grinned at Tina. 'Get your glad rags on, kid, let's go out and celebrate.'

'Celebrate?'

'We did it, Louise. Wasn't as smooth as I'd hoped, but we did it.' He took her in his arms and hugged her. 'Go on, get ready. We'll drop Robbie off at school and then there's some people I want you to meet.'

'Den . . .'

Donovan put a finger against her lips. 'Later,' he said. 'We can talk later.'

He pushed her towards the bedroom. She wrapped the robe around herself and closed the door then leaned against it, her heart pounding. He knew. She was sure that he knew. Something had gone wrong, something had gone very wrong, and now he was going to make her pay.

Her mobile phone was on its charger on the dressing table and she fumbled for it. With trembling fingers she tapped out the number that Gregg Hathaway had given her three years earlier. Her lifeline.

She pressed the phone to her ear and listened as it rang out. It rang. And rang. No one answered it. No answering service kicked in. It just rang. Tina took the phone away from her ear and stared at it in disbelief. How could that be? Hathaway had assured her that the phone would be manned seven days a week, twenty-four hours a day. Something must have gone wrong, but what? She called up directory enquiries and in a whispered voice asked for the main switchboard for the Metropolitan Police.

The number was answered by a brisk female voice.

'I want to speak to Assistant Commissioner Peter Latham,' Tina said, cupping her hand over her mouth so that her voice wouldn't carry.

'I'm sorry, could you speak up, please,' said the woman.

Tina went into her bathroom and turned on the cold tap. 'Assistant Commissioner Peter Latham, please,' said Tina.

'He's no longer with the Metropolitan Police,' said the woman. 'Can anyone else help?'

Tina felt suddenly dizzy and she held on to the sink for support. 'No, it has to be him,' she said. 'How can I get hold of him?'

'Assistant Commissioner Latham retired two years ago on grounds of ill-health,' said the woman.

'Right, but where is he now? This is very urgent. Life and death.'

'I'm afraid he passed away six months after he retired,' said the woman. 'Can I put you through to his successor's office?'

There was a knock at the bedroom door. Three quick taps. 'Louise?' asked Donovan. 'You okay in there?'

Tina switched off the phone. 'Yes, just going into the shower,' she said, trying desperately to stop her voice from shaking.

She showered and dried herself, then tried Hathaway's number again. There was still no answer.

She threw on a dress, put on lipstick and mascara, then gave her hair a quick brush. She stared at her reflection. She looked as guilty as hell. She tried to smile, but it was the smile of a terrified dog. 'It's okay,' she whispered to herself. 'It's going to be okay.' She took a deep breath. 'It's okay,' she said more confidently. 'You can deal with this.' Another deep breath, then she nodded to herself. 'I've been through worse than this and I've coped.'

'Are you okay?' Donovan shouted again. 'I'll huff and I'll puff and blow the door down.'

'All right, big bad wolf,' replied Tina brightly. 'Here I come, ready or not.'

She opened the bedroom door. Donovan nodded appreciatively. 'Looking good,' he said.

'Why thank you, kind sir.'

Robbie was putting his books into his backpack. He'd changed into his school uniform. 'I don't see why I have to go to school,' he moaned.

'To get an education,' said Donovan, ruffling his hair.

Robbie shook him away. 'First I'm not to go, then you say I'm to go, then you pull me out, now you tell me I've got to go back. That's hardly consistent.'

'It's an inconsistent world,' said Donovan. 'Isn't it, Louise?'

Tina nodded.

They drove to Robbie's school in the Audi roadster, Tina at the wheel and Robbie in the back. Several of Robbie's friends saw him getting out of the car, and that seemed to cheer him up. Donovan figured that there was probably more kudos arriving in a sports car than a Range Rover. 'I'll pick you up tonight,' said Donovan.

'Yeah, I'll believe that when I see it,' said Robbie ruefully, but he returned Donovan's wave before heading into school.

'Now what?' asked Tina.

'Now we go celebrate,' said Donovan. He looked at his watch. 'Party time.'

'It's half past eight in the morning.'

'Now don't be a party-pooper, Louise,' said Donovan. 'It's not every day I fly eight thousand kilos of gear around the world.'

He gave Tina directions and settled back in his seat. She drove across London to St John's Wood. Donovan told her where to park and climbed out of the car.

Tina locked the Audi, looking around. 'Here?' she said.

'Nah, here's where we lose our tail,' said Donovan.

'I didn't see anyone following us,' said Tina.

'Yeah, well, you wouldn't, not if they were any good,' said Donovan. 'Come on. Home stretch.'

'Tango One is out of the vehicle,' said the detective into his handset. 'On foot. Repeat on foot.'

'Go after him, Alpha Seven,' crackled the speaker. 'Softly, softly, yeah?'

The detective nodded at the driver. 'Let's go.'

The two plainclothes policemen got out of the saloon and walked quickly in the direction they'd seen Donovan and the girl heading.

'I've got a bad feeling about this,' said the detective.

'He didn't know we were on his tail,' said the driver. 'He didn't look around and she hardly checked her mirror.'

'He knows,' said the detective. 'He can smell us.'

The driver grinned. 'You maybe, but I showered in the station.'

Ahead of them they saw the girl's back disappearing down an alley. 'Who is she, anyway?'

'Lap dancer. She's been taking care of his kid.'

'Nice tits.'

'I'm sure she'll be chuffed at the compliment, coming from a connoisseur such as yourself. What the hell are they up to?'

'Going for a quickie in the open air?'

'At nine o'clock in the morning? I doubt it. Oh shit, I know what he's doing.' The detective put his transceiver to his mouth. 'Alpha Seven, he's going to cross the canal on foot. We need cover on the south side of the canal. We're going to lose him.'

The transceiver crackled. 'Affirmative, Alpha Seven.'

The two men hurried down the alley. It branched left

and right. 'This way,' said the detective. The driver rushed after him.

The alley led to the canal towpath. A metal footbridge ran across the canal, barely twenty feet above the surface of the water. Donovan and the girl were already dashing down the steps on the far side. A car was waiting at the side of the road, its engine running.

The detective grabbed the driver's arm and pulled them back. There was nothing they could do on foot and there was no point in showing themselves. 'Tango One is getting into a blue saloon. Possibly a Vauxhall. Registration number unknown. We've lost him. Repeat, we have lost Tango One.'

'What do you mean "we", Alpha Seven?' crackled the transceiver.

'What's going on, Den?' asked Tina as the blue saloon accelerated away from the kerb.

Donovan flashed her a smile. 'Gatecrashers,' said Donovan. 'Can't be too careful.' He leaned forward and patted Kim Fletcher on the shoulder. 'Nice one, Kim,' he said. 'Did you get the other thing?'

Fletcher popped open the glove compartment and handed Donovan a video cassette. 'He said something about the early worm catching the bird.'

Donovan stroked the matt black video cassette.

'What is it?' asked Tina.

'The entertainment,' said Donovan. He patted her on the leg. 'Come on, Louise, cheer up. You're behaving like a right wet blanket.'

Tina forced herself to smile.

'That's better,' said Donovan.

He and Tina sat in silence as Fletcher drove through the

morning traffic. He kept checking his mirrors and twice did a series of left turns to make sure that he wasn't being followed, then he drove east towards Docklands.

Tina stared out of the window with unseeing eyes, wondering where Donovan was taking her. And why. Did he know who she was? Or did he just suspect and wanted to interrogate her, to find out for sure? And if he was just suspicious, could she lie her way out of it? Or was she better just to confess all, tell him that she was a police officer? No one murdered a police officer in cold blood, not even Tango One.

Now that Fletcher had shaken off any tail, Tina knew that she was on her own. There would be no last-minute rescue, no cavalry charge over the hill. No one knew where she was or the trouble she was in. Why had no one answered the phone? Where was Hathaway? He'd promised her that there would always be someone at the end of the line. It was her get-out-of-jail-free card. Her lifeline. And the one time she'd needed it, it had failed her.

Fletcher indicated he was turning right. He used a small remote control unit to open a set of metal gates and then the car bobbed down into an underground car park. They parked close to an elevator. A balding man with a curved scar above his left ear and a black leather jacket was waiting by the elevator door.

Donovan hugged the man. 'Everything okay, Charlie?'

The man nodded. Donovan introduced him to Tina. 'Charlie Macfadyen,' he said. 'One of the best.'

'Pleased to meet you,' said Tina.

'Everybody here?' Donovan asked Macfadyen.

'Just waiting for the guest of honour,' said Macfadyen. He punched the elevator button and the door rattled open. The three men stepped to the side to allow Tina to walk in first. She felt her legs trembling but she kept her head up and her lips pressed tightly together. She walked into the lift and then turned to face them, feeling like a condemned prisoner about to be taken before the firing squad.

Macfadyen pressed the button for the top floor. The penthouse. The door rattled shut. Donovan hummed to himself as the lift rode upwards.

Macfadyen winked at Tina. 'All right, love?' he asked. 'Not scared of heights, are you?'

Tina shook her head. No, it wasn't heights that she was scared of.

The lift doors opened into a large airy hallway. At one end of the hallway was a window with a panoramic view of the Thames. Another man was waiting outside the door to the penthouse suite. He pushed the door open and grinned at Donovan. 'Okay, Den?'

'Perfect, Ricky,' said Donovan. 'I don't think you've met my date, have you? Louise, this is Ricky. Ricky Jordan.'

Jordan stuck out his hand and Tina shook. Jordan grinned at her with amused eyes. They were toying with her, Tina knew. They were all toying with her like cats torturing an injured mouse.

'In you go, Louise,' said Macfadyen.

Tina walked into the apartment. It was a large loft-style space with exposed brickwork and girders, and floor-to-ceiling windows that looked out on to the river. Three men were standing by the window, looking out and talking in hushed voices. They turned to look at her, their faces hard and unsmiling.

Tina looked to her right. Two men were tied to chairs, strips of insulation tape across their mouths. One of the men was black, the other white. Next to the two men was a third chair. Donovan gestured at it. 'Take a seat, Louise.'

'I'm okay, thanks,' she said.

Donovan's eyes hardened and he pointed at the chair.

'What's this about, Den?' she asked.

'You know what this is about,' he said. 'Now sit down or I'll have the boys tie you down.'

Fletcher closed the door and stood with his back to it, his arms folded across his barrel-like chest.

Tina sat down. She looked across at the two bound and gagged men. The black man was staring straight ahead, his back rigid, his jaw tight. The white man was looking around as if trying to find a way out. His face was bathed in sweat and the tape across his mouth moved in and out in time with his breathing.

Donovan stood in front of the white man. He held out a sheet of paper. Tina looked across but couldn't see what it was. 'James Robert Fullerton,' said Donovan. He dropped the sheet of paper on to Fullerton's lap, then stepped across to stand in front of the black man. 'Clifford Warren.' Donovan held the sheet of paper a few inches in front of Warren's face. Tina could make out a crest on top of the sheet. The crest of the Metropolitan Police. Donovan placed the sheet of paper on Warren's lap.

He held out a third sheet in front of Tina. Her heart sank as she recognised it. It was her application to join the Met.

'Den . . .' she said, but Donovan put a finger against her lips.

'Don't speak,' he said. 'Don't spoil the moment. If you say anything, I'll have them gag you, okay?'

Tina nodded.

'Good girl,' he said. 'Christina Louise Leigh.' He held out the sheet. Tina took it but didn't look at it.

Donovan took a few steps back, then slowly began to clap. He clapped for several seconds, a sarcastic smile on his face. 'I want to applaud the three of you,' he said. 'You fooled me. You absolutely fooled me. I wouldn't have made any one of you as a narc, but then you're like no other narcs, are you? You're not in any undercover unit with the Met or NCIS and your handler was a spook.'

He smiled at the look of confusion on their faces.

'Didn't you know, Gregg Hathaway's a spook? MI6. You were being run by the Secret Intelligence Service.'

'No, that's not right,' protested Tina, but Donovan silenced her with a cold look.

'I've been trying to work out over the last twelve hours why you fooled me. Why I didn't spot you. I guess it's because you're none of you playing a part, are you? You are what you are. Even down to using your real names.' He turned to look at Ricky Jordan. 'I mean, what undercover agent uses their own name, right?' Ricky nodded at Donovan. Donovan looked at Macfadyen, who also nodded in agreement. 'See,' said Donovan, 'it's not how it's normally done. Undercover cops and Cussies adopt a persona. They put on an act. But you, Jamie, you really are a drug-taking womaniser who deals in stolen art. Bunny, you're running with the guys you grew up with. You couldn't do that if you weren't one of them. They'd spot a fake a mile off. And Louise, you really are a lap dancer. And I think if we'd gone a bit further down the line, you'd have slept with me. I mean, is that above and beyond, or what?'

Donovan took the video cassette out of his jacket pocket and walked over to a wide-screen TV. He slotted the cassette into the video recorder.

'You were all playing yourselves, that's why I was

fooled. You were real. But you were being used, every one of you. Whatever you thought you were doing, whatever noble cause you thought you were serving, Hathaway had his own agenda.'

Donovan picked up a remote control unit and pressed 'play'. Alex Knight had done a great job with the sound, and he'd used close-ups wherever possible. There was no doubt who the two men on the bridge were, or what they were saying.

Jordan and Macfadyen watched the video with confused looks on their faces. All Donovan had told them was that Fullerton, Warren and Louise were undercover cops – they didn't know who Hathaway was. As the video showed Hathaway and Donovan walking along the bridge to the pub, the sound quality went down and Knight had put subtitles along the bottom of the screen so that they could follow the conversation, but the sound improved once the two men were sitting at the trestle table and working on the laptop computer.

Louise looked over at Donovan, but he kept his eyes on the television screen.

When the tape came to an end, Donovan switched off the TV. Fullerton's eyes were wide and staring and his nostrils flared from the effort of breathing. His face had gone a deep crimson. Donovan walked over and ripped the insulation tape off his mouth. Fullerton gasped.

Warren had slumped in his chair. Donovan pulled the tape off his lips. It came away with a tearing sound.

'Bit of a surprise that, hey, Bunny?' asked Donovan. He stood in front of the TV. 'Just in case anyone didn't quite follow what was going on there, Gregg Hathaway stung me for forty-five million dollars. In return, I got you. He sold you out. And as you saw on the tape, he was quite happy for me to kill all three of you.' He grinned savagely. 'Any thoughts?'

Fullerton, Warren and Louise were all too stunned to say anything.

'You gave him the money?' asked Jordan in disbelief. 'You gave him forty-five million dollars?'

'What choice did I have, Ricky? I needed to know who the rotten apples were. Suppose it had been the Russians? Suppose there was no gear on the plane? Suppose it had been one of the Turks? I had to know who was bad so that I could see what was salvageable.'

'The heroin,' said Fullerton. 'What happened to the heroin?'

'It's exactly where it's supposed to be,' said Donovan. 'Three thousand kilos is in Germany with our Turkish friends. Five hundred kilos is being driven up to Scotland to keep the smackheads in Edinburgh and Glasgow happy for the next six months or so. Another thousand kilos should be on the Holyhead ferry heading for Dublin. PM's got his, the Turks have got theirs, the price of a wrap in London is probably going to fall twenty per cent, but if the dealers are smart they'll hold back the bulk of it, ease it on to the market.'

'But the plane was empty,' said Warren.

'Of course it was,' said Donovan. 'The Russians, their job is to get supplies into out-of-the-way places, places where there aren't mile-long runways. How do you think they do that, Bunny? You can't just land a fifty-metre four-engined jet plane on the side of a hill.'

'Parachutes,' whispered Fullerton. 'They dropped the gear.'

'Precision-guided offset aerial parachute delivery, is what they call it,' said Donovan. 'They can drop almost two thousand kilos from thirty thousand feet and land it to within three hundred feet of their target. The parachute has an airborne guidance unit and it homes in on a transmitter on the ground. They dropped two chutes over Germany and three about fifty miles east of the airfield.'

'You bastard,' said Fullerton. 'You set us all up. The business at the airfield, you knew the plane was coming in empty.'

'I wanted to see what Hathaway would do,' said Donovan. 'The deal was that he gave me you and let me bring the gear in. Seems like he thought he could have it both ways: get to keep my money and put me behind bars for twenty years. Oh yes, and have you three killed into the bargain. He'd be free and clear.'

Jordan walked over. 'Are we going to do it, Den? Are we going to off them?'

'I'm thinking about it, Ricky.'

'You can't kill us,' said Fullerton. 'We're cops.'

'That's the thing, Jamie. Are you? Are you really cops? Or are you grasses? There's a difference.'

'We work for the Met.'

Warren nodded. 'We're cops.'

'You're cops if Hathaway stuck to whatever bargain it is that he offered you, but he doesn't seem to be a man of his word, does he?' He gestured at the video recorder. 'Do you want me to play it again for you?'

'We're on the Met's payroll,' said Fullerton. 'We get a salary. Promotions. Shit, we even get overtime.'

'I'm not saying you haven't been paid your thirty pieces of silver, Jamie. I'm just questioning whether or not Hathaway actually put you on their payroll. And if he did, maybe he's covered his tracks. Wouldn't take much to delete all reference to you from the computers.'

'Let's off 'em,' said Jordan in his Liverpudlian whine. 'They fucked over the Mexico deal, didn't they?'

'Jamie did, yeah. Hathaway showed me an e-mail he sent. Bunny didn't know about it and nor did Louise.' Donovan nodded at Tina. 'Or is it Tina? Which do you prefer?'

'Either,' said Tina. 'My mother called me Louise.'

'Tina, Louise, who gives a fuck?' said Jordan. 'They're grasses. Let's do 'em.'

'A couple of weeks ago and I'd have agreed with you, Ricky, but now I'm not so sure. We've got the gear, we're in the clear, and maybe they've seen the light.'

'What do you mean?' said Macfadyen.

'They can't give evidence against us. They're all compromised. Any case based on their evidence is going to be laughed out of court. And after what Hathaway's done to them, I don't think they're going to be looking to continue their careers as undercover cops, or whatever it is they are. They're no threat to us.'

'They cost us a bundle on that Mexican deal.'

'Agreed, but they all played their part in putting together the Turkish thing. Couldn't have put the financing together so quickly without Jamie's help, and Bunny saved my life, for God's sake. And Louise, well, that's personal. But all three of them made a difference. Maybe not the difference that they were planning to make, but all's well that ends well, yeah?'

'I don't know about this, Den,' said Macfadyen.

'Killing them doesn't do anything for us,' said Donovan.

'It'd make me feel better,' said Jordan.

'Yeah, well, that's something you're going to have to deal with, Ricky. You don't take someone's life just to make yourself feel good. You do it because it serves a purpose, and I don't think that killing these three is going to make a blind bit of difference to our lives. Letting them live might, though.'

Macfadyen and Jordan frowned. They exchanged a look, and Jordan shrugged. 'What are you talking about?' he asked. 'You're not making any sense.'

Donovan nodded at Fullerton. 'Jamie here didn't grass up the Turkish deal. Why not, Jamie?'

Fullerton shook his head. 'I don't know.'

'Yes, you do.'

'I was confused. That's all. I wasn't sure.'

'You wanted the deal to succeed, didn't you? You didn't want Hathaway to know about it because you wanted it to go ahead.'

Fullerton nodded.

'Because of the money?'

Fullerton shook his head. 'It wasn't just the money. I don't know what it was.'

'I do. For the kick. You wanted to see if you could do it. And you did, Jamie. You played the game and you won. We won. We made them look stupid and we made millions. How did that feel?'

'Yeah, it felt good. When that plane landed, it was like, better than a coke rush. And when the SAS piled in I was so freaked. I thought I'd lost everything. I thought Hathaway would hang me out to dry.' Fullerton stopped talking. He looked guiltily across at Warren and Louise, and fell silent.

'See what I mean?' Donovan said to Macfadyen and Jordan. 'You should use him. He's got a taste for it.' Donovan grinned at Fullerton. 'What about it, Jamie? They stitched you up, why not show them what you can do on the other side of the fence? You're a natural.'

Fullerton nodded slowly. 'Work with you, you mean?'

'Nah, I'm retiring, Jamie. For a few years at least. I've got things to do.' He jerked a thumb at Macfadyen and Jordan. 'But Charlie and Ricky could do with your help. With me out of the game they'll need someone to hold their hands.'

Donovan walked over to Warren. Warren stared up at him defiantly.

'And you, Bunny, what the hell were you thinking of? You know how cops hate blacks. Always have and always will. All that crap about institutional racism is just that. It's not the institution that's racist, it's the people. And you're not going to change the people with seminars and handbooks and codes of practice.'

Warren shrugged.

'They were using you, that's all,' said Donovan.

'They said I could make a difference. And I wanted to.'

'A difference to what? To the drugs business? You think that putting me away would have stopped drugs getting into the country? All the cops and Customs do is regulate the price, Bunny. Supply and demand. They increase the percentage of interceptions and the price goes up, that's all. The price goes up, we make more money, and the addicts on the street go out and rob a few more cars and houses to pay the extra.'

Warren looked down, unwilling to meet Donovan's stare.

'Fuck it, Bunny, being an undercover cop isn't going to get drugs off the street. You want to do that, go be a social worker and make people's lives better so that they don't want drugs. Go be a businessman and create jobs so that people have got a reason to get up in the mornings. But don't kid yourself that playing cops and robbers is going to make a blind bit of difference to the drugs trade. It's here to stay, and everyone from the Government down knows that. The cops and Cussies know that. Do you have any idea how many of them are on the take, Bunny? From me personally? Hasn't the way Hathaway behaved shown you how corrupt the whole business is, their side and mine?'

Warren looked up defiantly. 'What is it you want me to say, Den? That I've been fucked over? Well, I have. I can see that.'

'I want to know what you're going to do about it, Bunny.'

'That's an impossible question to answer. I'm dead on the streets now. PM'll be after my blood.'

Donovan nodded. 'Maybe he doesn't know. No reason for Hathaway to have told him.'

'Too many people know. Everyone in this room, for a start. It's not gonna stay a secret. I lied to him, man. Big time. He's never gonna forgive that.'

Donovan shrugged. 'You might be surprised what people will forgive, Bunny. Besides, PM got his gear at a rock bottom price. It's pushed him a lot higher up the food chain and he's gonna need you to keep him on the straight and narrow.'

Warren shook his head. 'Nah, not PM. I've made him look stupid and he ain't gonna stand for that. He's gonna want to show that he's on top of it. I'm gonna have to go.'

'Go where?'

'Fuck you, man. I ain't telling you anything.' He shook his head. 'I'll tell you one thing for free, though.' He nodded with his chin at Fullerton. 'I ain't like him. I don't get no buzz from what I did. Drugs kill people. Kill people, kill communities, kill whole fucking countries. And it ain't no good just saying if it wasn't you it'd be someone else. It's got to stop somewhere. It might as well be you.'

'So you've got what you wanted, Bunny. As of today, I'm out of it. But you know what? It won't make a shred of difference.'

'You're really quitting?' asked Macfadyen.

'I've got all the money I need, Charlie,' said Donovan. 'Even with what Hathaway took. It's all offshore, I'll get it well laundered and put into something legit. I've been telling my boy I sell cement. Might even do that.' He grinned. 'Swap one powder for another.'

'And what about me, Den?' asked Tina.

Donovan folded his arms. 'What about you, Louise? Are you going to apologise, say sorry for lying to me? You weren't the first woman to lie to me and I don't expect you'll be the last, but it would be nice to hear an apology.'

'I'm sorry, Den.'

'Yeah, I've been hearing that a lot lately.'

'There's nothing I can say, is there?'

Donovan shook his head, his lips forming a tight line.

Tina crossed her legs and arms and stared at the floor.

'I saw the look on your face this morning. When you opened the door and I was there. You were relieved, weren't you?' said Donovan quietly. 'You thought I'd been pulled, and when you saw I hadn't been you were pleased.'

Tina nodded but still didn't look up.

'And last night, when I was leaving, you tried to stop me going.'

Tina nodded again. 'I wanted to tell you. I did, Den. But I couldn't.'

'Because you're a cop?'

Tina sighed. 'Yes.'

'Being a cop didn't stop you sending me that text message, did it?'

Macfadyen frowned. 'What text message?'

'It doesn't matter, Charlie.'

'I didn't think you'd got it,' said Tina.

'I got it,' said Donovan.

'I didn't want you to go to prison,' said Tina. 'I didn't want Robbie to be without his dad, I didn't want . . .'

'What?' asked Donovan.

Tina wiped her eyes with the back of her hand. 'Nothing.'

Donovan stepped forward and put a hand on her shoulder. She rubbed the side of her head against his hand like a dog wanting its ear tickled.

'They used you, Tina. They treated you like a whore. They were worse than pimps because they pretended you were doing it for some greater good.'

'I know,' she said softly.

'Get yourself sorted out, Louise. You shouldn't let anyone use you like that. Least of all someone whose only aim was to sell you out.'

She wiped her eyes again. 'I will.'

'Then give me a call.'

Tina looked up in surprise. 'What?'

Donovan mimed putting a phone to his ear. 'Phone me. Robbie'd like to see you.'

Tina smiled gratefully.

'So that's it?' said Jordan. 'We're just going to let them go?'

Macfadyen sighed. 'Ricky, if you don't shut up, I'll shoot you myself.'

'I'm just saying . . .'

'Don't say,' said Macfadyen. 'It's Den's call. Good on you, Den. Where are you going?'

'Home,' said Donovan. 'I've got some soccer kit needs washing. And beds to make. Shopping to do.' He grinned. 'A woman's work is never done, hey, lads?'

Three Months Later

The rooster kicked out and the metal spur attached to its left claw ripped through the stomach of its adversary. Blood spattered across the sawdust and the crowd cheered and yelled. Fistfuls of pesos were waved in the air, but Hathaway doubted that anyone would be prepared to bet on the underdog. There were few comebacks in cockfighting. It wasn't like with humans: bouts couldn't be fixed to hype up the entertainment value. The cocks went in, they fought, the better fighter won. Victory might come by virtue of being faster, or stronger or having more heart, but once one of the cocks was on top, death came quickly.

Hathaway had been to cockfights in Thailand, but he found them a lot less satisfactory because the Thais didn't fit spurs to the birds, so the bouts were longer and scrappier. Maybe it was because the Thais were Buddhists and didn't want to inflict unnecessary pain, but Hathaway thought the Roman Catholic Filipino way was actually kinder. Kills were generally quicker and cleaner.

Hathaway wasn't a great fan of the Philippines, but it was the perfect place to hide, for a while at least. It was a country where pretty much anything could be had for a price, where security and privacy could easily be acquired, and where there were enough Westerners with shady pasts for yet another one to blend in with few questions asked.

The money was all stashed away offshore where it could never be found. Hathaway had become an expert at tracing hidden money and he had put his skills to good effect. He had bought an isolated villa on the outskirts of Manila, made friends with the local police chief, and hired a dozen of the chief's men as his personal bodyguards. He never went anywhere without at least four of them in attendance, and as he stood at the edge of the cockfighting pit all four were within fifty feet, enjoying the cockfight but keeping a watchful eye out for potential threats.

So far as Hathaway was concerned, there was only one potential threat – Den Donovan. Hathaway had no illusions: at some point Donovan would be looking to get his money back. Donovan was still Tango One, however, and the powers that be would be doing everything they could to put him behind bars. It was just a matter of time.

The fact that the drugs hadn't been on the plane when it had landed had meant that Donovan had escaped prison that time, but his luck couldn't hold out for ever. The abortive drugs bust had actually helped Hathaway, in that it gave him a good reason for resigning. His direct superior had spent an hour trying to convince him to stay, and the head of Human Resources had offered to find him a non-operational role within the organisation, but Hathaway had continued to insist that he should take the blame for the débâcle and had walked out. He hadn't even bothered to fill in his pension forms or empty his desk.

Of course, Hathaway would much have preferred for the drugs to have been on the plane and for Donovan to have been put away for twenty years, but sometimes not everything went to plan. Sometimes you had to go with the flow. Tango One would get sent down eventually, and if he didn't, Hathaway had more than enough money to have Donovan taken out of the equation by other methods. More permanent methods.

In the pit, the winning bird lashed out again and the weaker bird went down, blood streaming from its neck. Grim-faced men in straw hats were screaming for the stricken bird to get up and fight, but Hathaway knew that they were wasting their breath. It had been a mortal blow.

Hathaway didn't want to have to take out a contract on Donovan unless it was absolutely necessary. It wasn't that he had moral reservations about ordering the death of another man, especially a man like Donovan, but paying for an assassination left a trail that could be followed. There were plenty of professionals around who could do the job, but if anything went wrong even the most professional of killers would give up the name of his employer in exchange for a reduced sentence. It wasn't a risk that Hathaway was prepared to take, not yet.

The owner of the winning bird stepped forward and picked it up, holding it high above his head to a series of rousing cheers from the men who'd won money on the fight, and boos and catcalls from those who'd lost.

A small boy ran out with a bucket and threw fresh sawdust down over the bloodstained parts of the ring, while one of the winning owner's assistants picked up the dead bird and carried it away. It was traditional for the winning owner to eat the losing bird.

Hathaway looked over his shoulder. There were more than five hundred men crammed into the warehouse around the ring. No women. Almost all the spectators were locals: Western sensibilities were often offended by the sight of two cocks doing what came naturally.

Hathaway stiffened as he noticed that one of the few Westerners around the arena was looking in his direction. He was a man in his thirties wearing a beige safari suit. There was something familiar about the man – a vague tickle somewhere in Hathaway's memory suggested that they'd met some time in the past. Hathaway frowned. As a rule he had an almost infallible memory for faces. The man raised an eyebrow and nodded at Hathaway. Hathaway smiled instinctively, and nodded at the man. Was it a greeting from someone who recognised Hathaway, or just a nod of recognition between two outsiders?

Hathaway racked his memory. Male, mid-thirties, good looking, well built, two-day growth of beard. Ray-Ban sunglasses. Good teeth. Hathaway's mental filing system drew a blank. Then Hathaway realised why the man seemed familiar and he smiled slowly. He was the spitting image of the French crooner. What was his name? Distel, that was it. Sacha Distel. He was looking at a much younger version of Sacha Distel. Hathaway relaxed. The guy was probably mistakenly recognised all the time. Hathaway gave him a small wave, then turned to watch the next cocks being prepared for battle. The man in charge of Hathaway's security had seen the unspoken exchange and he looked across at Hathaway for guidance. Hathaway nodded at him and mouthed, 'It's okay.'

In the pit, a pot-bellied man with a battered straw hat was attaching shiny metal spurs to a bird with jet-black feathers. Hathaway looked over at the black bird's opponent. It was a totally white bird with a scarlet crop. Hathaway smiled. He liked white birds. It always made the bloodletting look that much more dramatic. He waved a handful of pesos at one of the bookmakers and placed a bet on the black bird. Hathaway was feeling lucky.